# THE QUALITY OF LACEY'S MERCY IS NOT STRAINED . . .

Lacey relaxed. He smiled like a shark feeding. "This far away, there's maybe a ten-second delay," he said, and dropped flat on the floor beside the safe.

"What—" Allen began. He groped for the power-gun in his belt. The shock wave from the explosion reached him before he could draw. The wave front drove the mahogany bar at an angle before it, pulping all of Allen's body between his neck and his diaphragm.

Lacey did not really expect to live through the blast. It drove down the hundreds of kilometers of tunnels like a multi-crowned piston, shattering whatever stood in its way. The Boxcars and everything in it were gone, driven meters or kilometers down the tunnel in a tangle of plastic and splinters and blood; everything but Lacey and the safe that shielded him.

The air was choking, but with dust and not K2— yet. The rebounding shock waves of the blast would suck the stockpiled gas into every cranny of the tunnel system soon, but at least the lethal cargo had not ridden the initial wave front. Lacey rose slowly, sucking air through the hard fabric of his sleeve. Once the ground beside him came into focus, he saw a dropped powergun. He picked it up and began to stagger toward an unblocked staircase.

Those who knew Jed Lacey best thought he was merciless. They were wrong. He used his weapon repeatedly before he climbed to the street. That was the only mercy available to the hideously mangled forms who mewled at him in agony.

—from "Underground"

# BAEN BOOKS by DAVID DRAKE

**The RCN Series**
*With the Lightnings*
*Lt. Leary, Commanding*
*The Far Side of the Stars*
*The Way to Glory*
*Some Golden Harbor*
*(forthcoming)*

**Hammer's Slammers**
*The Tank Lords*
*Caught in the Crossfire*
*The Butcher's Bill*
*The Sharp End*
*Paying the Piper*

**The General Series
(with S.M. Stirling)**
*Warlord*
*Conqueror*
*The Forge*
*The Chosen*
*The Reformer*
*The Tyrant*

**The Belisarius Series
(with Eric Flint)**
*An Oblique Approach*
*In the Heart of Darkness*
*Destiny's Shield*
*Fortune's Stroke*
*The Tide of Victory*
*The Dance of Time*

**Edited by David Drake**
*Armageddon*
(with Billie Sue Mosiman)
*The World Turned Upside
Down*
(with Jim Baen & Eric Flint)

**Independent Novels &
Collections**
*All the Way to the Gallows*
*Birds of Prey*
*Cross the Stars*
*The Dragon Lord*
*Foreign Legions*, edited by
David Drake
*Grimmer Than Hell*
*Northworld Trilogy*
*Ranks of Bronze*
*The Reaches Trilogy*
*Redliners*
*Seas of Venus*
*Starliner*
*The Undesired Princess and
The Enchanted Bunny*
(with L. Sprague de Camp)
*Lest Darkness Fall and To
Bring the Light*
(with L. Sprague de Camp)
*Killer*
(with Karl Edward Wagner)

# GRIMMER
# THAN HELL

# DAVID DRAKE

BAEN

# GRIMMER THAN HELL

This is a work of fiction. All characters and events portrayed in this book are fictional, and any resemblance to real people or incidents is purely coincidental.

A Baen Books Original

Baen Publishing Enterprises
P.O. Box 1403
Riverdale, NY 10471
www.baen.com

ISBN: 0-7434-8830-X
ISBN 13: 9-780-7434-8830-3

Cover art by Stephen Hickman

First paperback printing, July, 2003
Third paperback printing, May, 2006

Library of Congress Catalog Number 2002034194

Distributed by Simon & Schuster
1230 Avenue of the Americas
New York, NY 10020

Production by Windhaven® Press, Auburn, NH
Printed in the United States of America.

# CONTENTS

Introduction: Coming Home by the Long Way.......................1

Rescue Mission ........................................................5

When the Devil Drives ............................................32

Team Effort ............................................................77

The End .................................................................110

Smash and Grab ....................................................131

Mission Accomplished ...........................................165

Facing the Enemy...................................................188

Failure Mode .........................................................216

The Tradesmen ......................................................245

Coming Up Against It ............................................264

With the Sword He Must Be Slain .........................286

Nation Without Walls..............................................312

The Predators ........................................................348

Underground ..........................................................383

For Edmund D. Livingston, Sr.

Ed was proud to have served as a Marine rifleman on Okinawa and been part of the unit which landed in Yokosuka—without ammunition—two days before the Japanese surrender.

I'm equally proud to have been his friend in later years.

# INTRODUCTION
## Coming Home by the Long Way

A few years ago I collected my humorous stories in *All the Way to the Gallows*. In my introduction I admitted that I wasn't best known for writing humor.

This is what I'm best known for writing.

The impetus for this book was a fan suggestion that with surveillance cameras becoming increasingly prevalent all over the world, it would be a good time to get the Lacey stories back in print. I thought about the notion.

I only did three stories in the series, in the late '70s. Lacey is a man with all the ordinary human feelings—which he suppresses ruthlessly, as he suppresses everything else that might prevent him from accomplishing his task. He has no goals, no dreams, no friends; but he's very, very good at his job.

A friend once suggested that the Lacey stories were even clearer descriptions of how I felt about Viet Nam and what I'd become there than the Hammer stories

1

I was writing at the same time. She may have been right.

I don't want to get back into that mindset, but neither did I want to turn the setting into a shared universe. Lacey is, if you'll forgive me, a more personal Hell than that.

The original collection, *Lacey and His Friends* (with an absolutely wonderful Steve Hickman cover, by the way), bound in a couple novellas which showed the kinder, gentler, David Drake. There *is* a kinder, gentler David Drake; but I'm not as defensive as I used to be about the other parts of me, and they're real too.

The remaining pieces in the present collection are close in tone to the Lacey stories. They're military SF of one sort or another, though "or another" covers a pretty wide range.

Three are odd-balls. Billie Sue Mosiman and I edited an original anthology titled (and about) *Armageddon*. I wrote "With the Sword He Must Be Slain" for that volume.

Steve Stirling's Draka series is set in an alternate universe in which Evil wins. Steve turned the setting into a shared universe with the volume *Drakas!* and asked me to contribute.

Evil doesn't win in my books (well, I'll admit it's sometimes hard to pick the good guys) and I was a little uncomfortable with the assignment, but Steve's a friend and has written stories for me. If I'd known he wasn't going to do a story for his own collection, I might have begged off; but I didn't, and "The Tradesmen" resulted. It has a very dense structure, so much so that my outline amounted to 60% of the wordage of the finished story. As a piece of craftsmanship, I'm proud of it.

"Coming Up Against It" had a very strange genesis. Bill Fawcett got a deal for the two of us to consult on backgrounds for a computer game, for which we'd be paid an absurdly large amount of money. Part of the deal was that I would write a story in the game universe for binding in with the game. I wrote the story.

We did commentary on the initial background and sent it in. The new version came back to us, not a refinement but a totally new scenario. We did more commentary. The response was yet again a totally new scenario. I don't recall how many iterations we went through on this, but I do remember that I was getting steamed. (I later heard the rumor that somebody in the company was keeping the meter running as a favor to the outside contractor doing the scenarios, a buddy who'd fallen on hard times.)

My story, "Coming Up Against It," was based on a situation that was edited out of the game early in the process. I didn't even think I had a copy of the story (I'd tried to put the whole business out of my head; I was *really* angry about being dicked around), but it showed up while I was searching for other things. It appears here for the first time.

And by the way, this is a prime example of a deal that was too good to be true turning out to be too good to be true.

Bill Fawcett sold the Battlestation shared universe with me as co-editor. I'd been doing a lot of work in shared universes by that time, and I decided that the two volumes of the original contract would be my last for a while. I wrote my two stories, "Facing the Enemy" and "Failure Mode," so that they'd give closure to the series. You don't ordinarily get that with life, but it's something I strive for in fiction.

And that brings me very directly to the six stories which open this volume. They come from a slightly earlier shared universe that Bill developed and I co-edited: The Fleet. They follow a special operations company in a future war against aliens. (Parenthetically, most of my Military SF doesn't involve aliens; possibly because I don't recall ever being shot at by an alien when I was in Viet Nam or Cambodia.) Each story is self-standing but they have a cumulative effect and are, I believe, some of the best Military SF I've written.

What the Fleet stories *don't* have is closure; that too, I think, has something to do with me and Southeast Asia. The series ended and I thought I'd walked away from it, just as I thought I'd walked away from a lot of other things back in 1971.

Then, years later, I wrote *Redliners*, a novel about a special operations company fighting aliens until things went badly wrong . . . except that in *Redliners* they got a second chance. They *and their society* got a second chance. They got closure, and in a funny way so did I. Since *Redliners* I've been able to write adventure fiction that's a little less cynical, a little less bleak, than what I'd invariably done in the past when I wrote action stories.

I don't think I'd have been able to write *Redliners* if I hadn't previously written the Fleet stories. I'm awfully glad I did write them.

Dave Drake
david-drake.com

# RESCUE MISSION
## A Story of The Fleet

"Is it true," demanded one of the First Platoon corporals in a voice that filled the echoing bay of the landing craft, "that this whole operation is so we can rescue Admiral Mayne's nephew from the Khalians?"

Captain Kowacs looked at the man. The corporal stared back at the company commander with a jaunty arrogance that said, *Whatcha gonna do? Put me on point?*

Which of course was the corporal's normal patrol position.

Kowacs took a deep breath, but you learned real fast in a Marine Reaction Company that you couldn't scare your troops with rear-echelon discipline. Trying to do that would guarantee you were the first casualty of the next firefight.

"No, Corporal Dodd," said Kowacs. "Admiral Mayne is planning coordinator for this mission, but neither he

nor any nephews of his have anything behind-the-
scenes to do with it."

He glared at his assembled company.

The behind-the-scenes order had come from Grand
Admiral Forberry; and it was Forberry's son, not a
nephew, who'd been snatched—no body recovered, at
any rate—when the Khalians raided the Pleasure Dome
on Iknaton five years before.

Nobody else spoke up; even Dodd looked abashed.

Kowacs gazed at the hundred and three pairs of
waiting eyes—wondered how many of them would have
any life behind them in twenty-four hours—

Sighed and thumbed the handset controlling the holo
projector.

The image that formed above Kowacs' head was
fuzzy. The unit was intended for use in a shielded
environment, while the bay of the landing ship *Bonnie
Parker* was alive with circuits and charged metal.

No matter: this was the 121$^{st}$ Marine Reaction Company, not an architectural congress. The projector would
do for the job.

"Fleet Intelligence believes this site to be the
Khalians' major holding facility for human prisoners on
Target," Kowacs said, referencing the hologram with
a nod. "Their slave pen. Reconnaissance indicates that
slave ships land at a pad three kilometers distant—"

A second hologram bloomed briefly, the scale of distance merging it with one wall of the big room.

"—and their cargoes are carried to the holding
facility by air trucks which touch down on the roof of
the Administration Building," Kowacs continued as the
image of the outlying spaceport disappeared. The
building in the center of the main hologram brightened and began to rotate in three dimensions while
the Marines squinted.

"Based on analysis of captured Khalian structures,"

Kowacs said, "Intelligence believes the building is an integral polyborate casting, probably of two above-ground levels—"

"That high and the weasels only got two floors?" demanded a sergeant from the Heavy Weapons platoon. She was concerned, not gibing like Dodd earlier. "Them little bastards, they *like* low ceilings."

"Good point, Sergeant Rozelle," Kowacs said, as if he liked to be interrupted . . . but soldiers who were too dumb to think for themselves were too dumb to trust with your life in a reaction company. "Intelligence believes the building is scaled to the needs of human—slave—intake. But there aren't any windows, and there may well be a third level inside."

Kowacs cleared his throat. Before any of the half dozen Marines poised with further questions could interrupt again, he continued, "The walls and roof are rigid enough to withstand considerable stress, but they're apt to shatter once their integrity is breached. Intelligence believes that strip charges will hole them and that plasma bolts should crumble sections large enough for easy entry."

Almost the entire complement of the 121st was veteran. Even the scattering of newbies were aware that Fleet Intelligence believed a lot of things—but all Fleet Intelligence knew for sure was that no analyst's butt was going to be on the line if his belief were false.

"The admin building is separated from the camp proper by double fences with fifteen meters between them," Kowacs continued as the hologram of the building froze and that of the fenced area brightened in turn. "The intermediate separation is believed to be mined and is swept by automatic weapons sited on the building's roof coping. The fence may be electrified."

Marines nodded, easy in the knowledge that barriers

impassible to a bunch of unarmed civilians were going to be a piece of cake to *them*.

The forty-eight buildings splayed like a double row of spokes around the hub of the admin building, twelve and thirty-six, brightened as the hologram fence dimmed.

"Beyond that are the slave pens and workshops themselves," Kowacs said.

Just for a moment he paused, his mouth half open— prepared speech interrupted by memories of Khalians and slaves. . . . Memories of his father and mother, dead on Gravely, and his sister's body left behind two weeks later on LaFarge when the same raider landed to replenish its stock.

Its larder.

"Intelligence doesn't even guess at the structure within the compound," Kowacs forced his tongue to continue, though it was several moments more before his eyes were focusing again on the Marines. They were draped over folded bunks and the equipment crated to deploy with them. Some of them looked back at their captain with vacant expressions that Kowacs knew must mirror his of a moment before.

"There may be guards in the barracks, there may not," he continued thickly, damning the emotion that clogged his throat and made him less able to do his job—

Of erasing every living weasel from the universe.

"If there are guards, they probably don't have weapons; but most of you know an unarmed Khalian can still be a dangerous opponent."

"It's still a fucking pelt, too," growled someone from a corner of the bay.

"Yeah, it's that too," Kowacs said in a voice with an edge. "And any Marine taking trophies while there's still a job to do, I'll take his ears myself. Do you understand?"

The newbies thought that was a threat. The veterans knew it was a promise.

Kowacs took a deep breath and, fully in control of himself and the situation again, continued as the hologram changed, "The outer perimeter is a double fence again, but with guard towers on the exterior."

The tower images glowed like strung jewels.

"Most of them are automatic weapons," Kowacs said without expression, "but there are rapid-firing plasma guns—"

Six of the jewels stood out from the rest.

"—for anti-vehicle defense; and there are a pair of missile batteries. Ship-killers."

"Fuckin' A," said Dodd. He wasn't interrupting, just vocalizing what all the Marines in the bay were thinking right now.

Kowacs included.

"Sir?" asked Sergeant Atwater of Third Platoon, a black Terran who was in line for a slot in the Officer Training Unit. "What forces are being committed to this assault?"

"Right," said Kowacs. "The *Carol Ann Fugate* and the *Ladybird Johnson* will land as close to the perimeter as they can. The One-Twenty-second is responsible for the west half—"

That portion of the hologram brightened.

"—and the One-Twenty-third handles the rest. Kamens and Eckland think their companies are nearly as good as mine—"

The back of Kowacs' mind wore a smile at the scene in Admiral Mayne's office, when he and his fellow company commanders had been told their assignments.

"—so I guess they'll be able to take care of the job."

"Ah, sir?" said Atwater, his eyes narrowed on the completely-highlighted perimeter of the slave compound. "Ah—where will *we* be?"

"The *Bonnie Parker* sets down on the roof of the admin building," Kowacs said quietly.

He didn't bother to change the hologram; everyone else in the bay was staring at the face of their commander, including the platoon leaders who'd already been briefed on the plan. "You're the best there is in the Fleet, Marines. Anybody doubts you, tell him suck on *that*."

Nobody said anything at all.

"Yeah, well," Kowacs continued after a moment. "Your platoon leaders will give you your individual assignments in a moment. Ah—"

He looked out over his company. "Ah, I have been ordered to, ah, emphasize to you that the high command considers Khalian prisoners to be a first priority of all the Target landings, this one included."

He cleared his throat. "Any questions before I turn you over to your platoon leaders?"

"You mean you want us to bring in weasels *alive*, Cap'n?" Dodd blurted in amazement.

Beside Dodd sat Sergeant Bradley, who acted as Kowacs' field first—company headquarters, headed by the Table of Organization 'First Sergeant,' was back on Port Tau Ceti, forwarding supplies, mail, and replacements to the company. Bradley was a man of middle height; his flesh was drawn so tightly over his bones that the pink keloid, replacing his hair since a too-near plasma burst, did not appear unusual.

Now he turned to Dodd, lifted the junior non-com's chin between his thumb and forefinger, and said very distinctly, "Did he *say* that, dickhead?"

"No, Sergeant," Dodd whispered.

Bradley faced front with the disdain of a fisherman releasing an undersized catch.

"Any other—"

"Sir?" said Atwater crisply. His arm was lifted but

only the index finger was raised, a compromise between courtesy and honor. "Will there be some feints to draw off Khalian forces in the area before we go in?"

Kowacs nodded, but that was a comment on the cogency of the question, not a response to it.

"There's concern," he said carefully, "that when the Khalians realize that we've landed on their homeworld, their first reaction will be to execute their slaves. Therefore—"

He paused, too clearly aware of the Marines he was leading. This would be a suicide mission if the general invasion timing were off by an hour, maybe even by a few minutes.

"Therefore," Kowacs continued, "a ground-attack ship will go in ahead of us to prep the defenses. We—the assault component—will follow at a three-second interval. No other Alliance forces will be committed to Target until we're on the ground."

"Fuckin' A," somebody repeated in a whisper that echoed throughout the bay.

Commodore Herennis stood as stiff as if a weasel were buggering him in Kowacs' tiny office—a cubicle separated from the landing bay by walls of film which blurred light and sound into a semblance of privacy. Anger wasn't the only emotion holding Grand Admiral Forberry's military secretary rigid—but it was one of the emotions.

"I told you," said Kowacs from the room's only chair—Herennis had refused it, and there wasn't floor space for both men to stand—"that while I didn't care to leave my men just now, I would of course obey a direct order to report to you on the flagship."

He was holding his combat knife toward the striplight in the ceiling; its wire edge was too fine for his eyes to focus on it, no matter how hard he squinted.

"You *knew* I couldn't formally give an order like that!" Herennis snapped.

Kowacs looked up at the smartly-uniformed staff officer—his social, military, and (no doubt) intellectual superior.

"Yes, Commodore," said the Marine captain softly. "I suppose I did. Now, if you care to state your business, I'll take care of it the best way I can."

"Yes, I . . . ," Herennis said. His body quivered as embarrassment replaced anger as his ruling emotion. "Here is the, the chip that was discussed."

The hologram would take up only a corner of the data capacity in the Marines' helmets, nestled among the sensors and recorders that let the high command look over each man's shoulder after the action.

From a safe distance.

Kowacs set his knife on the fold-down desk that doubled as a keypad when he chose to power up his computer terminal. He took the holochip from the commodore and inserted it into the bulkhead projector. The unit was balky; he had to jiggle the handset several times before there was a hum and a face appeared in the air near the filmy opposite wall.

"That's the boy?" Kowacs said. "Well, I'll have it downloaded into the men's helmets before we go in."

The Honorable Thomas Forberry wasn't a boy, not really. His image looked to be mid-forties, and that was at least five years back. Blue eyes, a ruddy complexion—dark blond hair with curls as perfect as an angel's tits.

For all its pampering, the face was hard and competent. Young Thomas hadn't followed his father into the Fleet, but he ran the family's business concerns, and the Forberrys would have been rich even without the opportunities a grand admiral has of profitably anticipating economic changes.

Used to run the family business.

"Ah, five years could. . . ." Kowacs began, letting his voice trail off because he didn't choose to emphasize the changes five years as a weasel slave could make in a man—even if he survived.

"Yes, he's aware—" Herennis said, then caught himself. "Ah, I'm aware of that. I'm, ah, not expecting. . . . I know you must think—"

Kowacs waved his hand to cut off the staff officer's words, his embarrassment.

"Look, Commodore," he said gently. "Nobody in my outfit's got a problem about releasing Khalian prisoners. If it takes something, whatever, *personal* to give the high command the balls to cut the orders—okay, that's what it takes. Tell your friend not to worry about it."

"Thank you, Captain," Herennis said, sounding as if he meant it. He wasn't done speaking, but he met the Marine's eyes before he went on with, "The unofficial reward, ah, I've promised you is considerable in money terms. But I want you to realize that neither I nor—anyone else—believes that money can recompense the risk you and your men are running."

"Commodore . . . ," Kowacs said. His hand was reaching for the leather-wrapped hilt of his knife, but he restrained the motion because Herennis might have misunderstood. "I lost my family in the Gravely Incident."

"I'm sor—" but the Marine's hand moved very sharply to chop off the interruption.

"About half my team could tell you their own version of the same story."

Kowacs saw the doubt in his visitor's eyes and smiled. "Yeah, that high a percentage. Not in the Marines in general, and sure as *hell* not in the whole

Fleet. But you check the stats on the reaction companies, not just mine, and see what you find."

Herennis nodded and touched his tongue to his lips.

"Besides that," Kowacs went on with the same tight,
worn smile—a smile like the hilt of the knife his hand
was, after all, caressing, "we're the ones that hit dirt
first after the raids. We've seen everything the weasels can do to human beings. Do you understand?"

Herennis nodded again. He was staring at Kowacs
as if the Marine were a cobra on the other side of a
pane of glass.

Kowacs shut off the holo projector. "You're right,
Commodore," he said. "None of my team does this for
the money, yours or the regular five-percent danger
allowance.

"But you couldn't pay us *not* to take this mission,
either."

The *Bonnie Parker*'s thunderous vibration was bad
enough on any insertion, but this time they were going
down in daylight. The bay was brightly illuminated, so
you could look at the faces of the Marines beside you—
blank with fear that was physical and instinctive.

Or you could watch the landing vessel's wiring and
structural panels quiver centimeters under the
stress—far beyond their designed limits—and wonder whether this time the old girl was going to
come apart with no help from the weasel defense
batteries at all.

A shock lifted all the Marines squatting on the deck.

Kowacs, gripping a stanchion with one hand and his
rifle with the other, swore; but the word caught in his
throat and it wasn't a missile, just the shock wave of
the ground-attack ship that had plunged down ahead
of them in a shallow dive that would carry it clear of
the landing zone—

If its ordnance had taken out the missile batteries as planned.

Kowacs wanted to piss. He did what he had learned to do in the moments before hitting hot LZs in the past.

Pissed down his trouser leg.

Three plasma bolts hit the *Bonnie Parker* with the soggy impact of medicine balls against the hull. The ship rocked. The magnetic screens spread the bursts of charged particles, but the bay lights went off momentarily and the center bank stayed dark even after the rest had flickered into life again.

"About *now*—" said Corporal Sienkiewicz, two meters tall and beside Kowacs in the bay because so far as the Table of Organization was concerned, she was his clerk.

Kowacs and Bradley could file their own data. There was no one in the company they thought could do a better job of covering their asses in a firefight.

Sienkiewicz' timing was flawless, as usual. The *Bonnie Parker*'s five-g braking drove the squatting Marines hard against the deck plates.

Automatic weapons, unaffected by the screens, played against the hull like sleet. The landing vessel's own suppression clusters deployed with a *whoompwhoompwhoompwhoomp* noticeable over the general stress and racket only by those who knew it was coming.

The *Bonnie Parker* was small for a starship but impressive by comparison with most other engines of human transportation. She slowed to a halt, then lurched upward minusculely before her artificial intelligence pilot caught her and brought her to hover. The landing bay doors began to lift on both sides of the hull while the last bomblets of the suppression clusters were still exploding with the snarl and glare of a titanic arclight.

"Get 'em!" Kowacs roared needlessly over his helmet's clear channel as he and the rest of the company leaped under the rising doors in two lines, one to either side of the landing vessel.

Thrust vectored from the *Bonnie Parker's* lift engines punched their legs, spilling some of the Marines on the roof's smooth surface. Normally the vessel would have grounded, but the weight of a starship was almost certain to collapse a pad intended for surface-effect trucks. The old girl's power supply would allow her to hover all day.

Unless the weasels managed to shoot her down, in which case she'd crumple the building on top of the Marines she'd just delivered.

Well, nobody in the One-Twenty-first was likely to die of ulcers from worry.

There were half a dozen dead Khalians sprawled on the part of the roof Kowacs could see. Their teeth were bared, and all of them clutched the weapons they'd been firing at the landing vessel when the suppression clusters had flayed everything living into bloody ruin.

There was a sharp *bang* and a scream. Halfway down the line on Kowacs' side of the vessel, Corporal Dodd up-ended. One of his feet was high and the other was missing, blown off by the bomblet unexploded until he'd managed to step on it.

"Watch the—" one of the platoon leaders called on the command channel.

At least one plasma gun on the perimeter had survived the ground attack ship. The weasel crew turned their weapon inward and ripped a three-round burst into the *Bonnie Parker* and the deploying Marines.

One bolt hit the waist-high roof coping—Intelligence was right; the polyborate shattered like a bomb, gouging a two-meter scallop from the building. Kowacs was pushed backwards by the blast, and half a dozen of the Marines near him went down.

The other bolts skimmed the coping and diffused against the landing vessel's screen with whip-lash cracks and a coruscance that threw hard shadows across the roof. Kowacs' faceshield saved his eyes, but ozone burned the back of his throat and he wasn't sure that anyone could hear him order, "Delta Six, get that f—"

Before anyone in Heavy Weapons, Delta Platoon, could respond to the order with their tripod-mounted guns, Corporal Sienkiewicz leaned over the coping and triggered her own shoulder-carried plasma weapon.

The weapon was a meter-long tube holding a three-round magazine of miniature thermonuclear devices. The deuterium pellets were set off and directed by a laser array, part of the ammunition and consumed by the blast it contained.

The crack of the out-going plasma jet was sharp and loud even to ears stunned by the bolts that had struck nearby. Downrange, all the ready munitions in the guard tower blew up simultaneously. The blast across the dull beige roofs of the slave barracks was earth-shaking.

"Assigned positions," Kowacs ordered, looking around desperately to make sure that his troops weren't bunching, huddling. Because of the *Bonnie Parker*, he had only half a field of view. Maybe all the Marines who'd jumped from the port side were dead and—

"Move it, Marines! Move it!" he shouted, finding the stairhead that was the only normal entrance on the building's roof.

"Fire in the hole!" warned the First Platoon demo team that had laid a rectangle of strip charges near one end of the flat expanse. The nearest Marines—except the assault squad in full battle suits—hunched away. Everyone else at least turned their faces.

"Fire in the hole!" echoed Third Platoon at the opposite side of the roof—so much for everybody being dead, not that—

The entry charges detonated with snaps that were more jarring to the optic nerves than to the ears. Each was a strip of adhesive containing a filament of PDM explosive—which propagated at a measurable fraction of light speed. The filament charges were too minute to have significant effect even a meter or two from the strip, but the shattering force they imparted on contact was immense.

A door-sized rectangle of the roof dropped into the building interior. Marines in battle suits, their armor protecting them against the glassy needles of polyborate shrieking and spinning from the blast, criss-crossed the opened room with fire from their automatic rifles. Their helmet sensors gave them targets—or their nervousness squeezed the triggers without targets, and either way it gave the weasels more to think about.

Similar bursts crackled from the other end of the roof, hidden by the *Bonnie Parker* and attenuated by the howl of her lift engines.

"Alpha ready!" on the command channel, First Platoon reporting. Kowacs could see the Marines poised to enter the hole they'd just blown in the roof.

"Beta ready!" The two squads of Second Platoon under their lieutenant, detailed to rappel down the sides of the windowless building and secure the exits so that the weasels couldn't get out among the helpless slaves in a last orgy of destruction.

"Kappa ready!" Third Platoon, whose strip charges had blown them an entrance like the one Kowacs could see First clustered around.

"Delta ready!" Heavy Weapons, now with a tripod-mounted plasma gun on each side of the roof. One of

the weapons was crashing out bolts to support the units
securing the perimeter.

"Gamma ready!" said Sergeant Bradley with a skull-
faced grin at Kowacs from the stairhead where he
waited with Sienkiewicz and the two remaining squads
of Second Platoon.

"All units, go!" Kowacs ordered as he jogged toward
the stairhead and Bradley blew its door with the strip
charges placed but not detonated until this moment.

Three of Second's assault squad hosed the opening.
Return fire or a ricochet blasted sparks from the center
Marine's ceramic armor. He staggered but didn't go
down, and his two fellows lurched in sequence down
the stairs their bulky gear filled.

"Ditch that!" Kowacs snarled to Sienkiewicz as she
slung the plasma gun and cocked her automatic rifle.

"It's my back," she said with a nonchalance that was
no way to refuse a direct order—

But which would do for now, because Kowacs was
already hunching through the doorway, and she was
right behind him. The air was bitter with residues of
the explosive, but that was only spice for the stench
of musk and human filth within.

You could make a case for the company commander
staying on the roof instead of ducking into a building
where he'd lose contact with supporting units and the
high command in orbit.

Rank hath its privileges. For twelve years, the only
privilege Kowacs had asked for was the chance to be
where he had the most opportunity to kill weasels.

The stairs were almost ladder-steep and the treads
were set for the Khalians' short legs. One of the clum-
sily armored Marines ahead of Kowacs sprawled onto
all fours in the corridor, but there were no living
weasels in sight to take advantage of the situation.

Half a dozen of them were dead, ripped by the rifle

fire that caught them with no cover and no hope. One
furry body still squirmed. Reflex or intent caused the
creature to clash its teeth vainly against the boot of
the leading Marine as he crushed its skull in passing.

The area at the bottom of the short staircase was
broken into a corridor with a wire-mesh cage to either
side. The cage material was nothing fancier than hog-
fencing—these were very short-term facilities. The one
on the left was empty.

The cage on the right had room for forty humans
and held maybe half a dozen, all of them squeezed into
a puling mass in one corner from fear of gunfire and
the immediate future.

The prisoners were naked except for a coating of
filth so thick that their sexes were uncertain even after
they crawled apart to greet the Marines. There was a
drain in one corner of the cage, but many of the human
slaves received here in past years had been too terrified to use it. The weasels didn't care.

Neither did Kowacs just now.

"Find the stairs down—" he was shouting when
something plucked his arm and he spun, his rifle-stock
lifting to smash the weasel away before worrying about
how he'd kill it, they were death if you let 'em touch
you—

And it wasn't a Khalian but a woman with auburn
hair. She'd reached through the fencing that saved her
life when it absorbed the reflexive buttstroke that would
have crushed her sternum and flung her backwards.

"Bitch!" Kowacs snarled, more jarred by his mistake
than by the shock through his weapon that made his
hands tingle.

"Please," the woman insisted with a throaty determination that over-rode all the levels of fear that she
must be feeling. "My brother, Alton Dinneen—don't
trust him. On your *lives*, don't trust him!"

"Weasel bunkroom!" called one of the armored Marines who'd clumped down the corridor to the doorways beyond the cages. "Empty, though."

"Watch for—" Kowacs said as he jogged toward them. Bradley and Sienkiewicz were to either side and a half step behind him.

The Khalian that leaped from the 'empty' room was exactly what he'd meant to watch for.

A marine screamed instinctively. There were four of them, all members of the assault squad burdened by their armor. The weasel had no gun, just a pair of knives in his forepaws. Their edges sparkled against the ceramic armor—and bit through the joints.

Two of the Marines were down in seconds that blurred into eternity before Sergeant Bradley settled matters with a blast from his shotgun. The Marines' armor glittered like starlit snow under the impact of Bradley's airfoil charge. The Khalian, his knives lifted to scissor through a third victim, collapsed instead as a rug of blood-matted fur.

Cursing because it was his fault, he shouldn't have let Marines manacled by twenty kilos of armor lead after the initial entry, Kowacs ran to the room in which the weasel had hidden.

It was a typical Khalian nest. There was a false ceiling to lower the dimensions to weasel comfort and a heap of bedding which his sensors, like those of the first Marine, indicated were still warm with the body heat of the Khalians who'd rushed into the corridor to be cut down in the first exchange of fire.

Except that one of the cunning little bastards had hidden *under* the bedding and waited. . . .

You couldn't trust your sensors, and you couldn't trust your eyes—but you could usually trust a long burst of fire like the one with which Sienkiewicz now hosed the bedding. Fluff and wood chips fountained away from the bullets.

"Hey!" cried one of the assault squad who was still standing. Kowacs spun.

An elevator door was opening across the hall.

The startled figure in the elevator car was bare chested but wore a red sleeve that covered his right arm wrist to shoulder. The Khalian machine-pistol he pointed might not penetrate assault-squad armor, but it would have stitched through Kowacs' chest with lethal certainty if the captain hadn't fired first. Kowacs' bullets flung his target backward into the bloody elevator.

"Sir!" cried the Marine who hadn't fired. "That was a friendly! A man!"

"Nobody's friendly when they point a gun at you!" Kowacs said. "Demo team! Blow me a hole in this fucking floor!"

Two Marines sprinted over, holding out the partial spools of strip-charge that remained after they blew down the door.

"How big—" one started to ask, but Kowacs was already anticipating the question with, "One by two— no, *two* by two!"

Kowacs needed a hole that wasn't a suicidally-small choke point when he and his troops jumped through it—but the floor here had been cast in the same operation as the roof and exterior walls. He was uneasily aware that the battering which gunfire and explosives were giving the structure would eventually disturb its integrity to the point that the whole thing collapsed.

Still, he needed a hole in the floor, because the only way down from here seemed to be the elevator which—

"Should I take the elevator, sir?" asked an armored

Marine, anonymous behind his airfoil-scarred face
shield.

"No, dammit!" Kowacs said, half inclined to let the
damn fool get killed making a diversion for the rest
of them. But the kid was *his* damn fool, and—

"Only young once," muttered Sergeant Bradley in
a mixture of wonder and disdain.

"Fire in the hole!" cried one of the Demolition
Team.

Kowacs squeezed back from the doorway to give the
demo team room to jump clear, but the pair were too
blasé about their duties to bother. They twisted around
and knelt with their hands over their ears before the
strips blew and four square meters of flooring shuddered, tilted down—

And stuck. The area below was divided into rooms
off-set from those of the upper floor. The thick slab
of polyborate caught at a skewed angle, half in place
and half in the room beneath.

An automatic weapon in that room fired two short
bursts. A bullet richocheted harmlessly up between the
slab and the floor from which it had been blasted.

"Watch it!" said Sienkiewicz, unlimbering the
plasma gun again. She aimed toward the narrow
wedge that was all the opening there was into the
lower room.

It was damned dangerous. If she missed, the bolt
would liberate all its energy in the nest room, and the
interior walls might not be refractory enough to protect Gamma.

But Sienkiewicz was good; and among other things,
this would be a real fast way to silence the guns
beneath before the Marines followed the plasma bolt.

The demo team sprinted into the corridor; Kowacs
flattened himself against the wall he hoped would hold
for the next microsecond; and the big weapon crashed

a dazzling line through the hole and into the building's lower story.

Air fluoresced at the point of impact and lifted the slab before dropping it as a load of rubble. Kowacs and Bradley shouldered one another in their mutual haste to be first through the opening. Sienkiewicz used their collision to lead them both by a half step, the plasma gun for the moment cradled in her capable arms.

It wasn't the weapon for a point-blank firefight; but nothing close to where the bolt struck was going to be alive, much less dangerous.

Kowacs dropped through the haze and hit in a crouch on something that squashed under this boots. The atmosphere was so foul in the bolt's aftermath that the helmet filters slapped across his mouth and nose in a hard wedge.

The Marines were in a good-sized—human-scale—room with a cavity in the floor. There was nothing beneath the cavity except earth glazed by the plasma bolt that had excavated it.

This was a briefing room or something of the sort; but it was a recreation room as well, for the chairs had been stacked along the walls before the blast disarrayed them, and two humans were being tortured on a vertical grid. The victims had been naked before the gush of sun-hot ions scoured the room, flensing to heat-cracked bones the side of their bodies turned toward the blast.

But the plasma gun hadn't killed them. The victims' skulls had been shattered by bullets, the bursts the Marines had heard the moment before Sienkiewicz blew them entry.

Several of the chairs were burning. They were wooden, hand-made, and intended for humans. On the wall behind the grid was a name list on polished wood, protected from the plasma flux by the torture victims and a cover sheet of now-bubbled glassine. The list was headed DUTY ROSTER.

In English, not the tooth-mark wedges of Khalian script.

Each of the six other bodies the blast had caught wore a red right sleeve—or traces of red fabric where it had been shielded from the plasma. They had all been humans, including the female Kowacs was standing on. She still held the Khalian machine-pistol she had used to silence the torture victims.

"*Renegades,*" Sergeant Bradley snarled. He would have spat on a body, but his filters were in place.

"Trustees," Kowacs said in something approaching calm. "The weasels don't run the interior of the compound. They pick slaves of the right sort to do it. Let's—"

He was looking at the door and about to point to it. More Marines were tumbling through the hole in the ceiling, searching for targets. The air had cleared enough now that Kowacs noticed details of the body flung into the doorway by the blast. Its arms and legs had been charred to stumps, and its neck was seared through to the point that its head flopped loose.

But the face was unmarked, and the features were recognizable in their family relationship to those of the woman caged upstairs.

Nobody had to worry about treachery by Alton Dinneen any more.

"—*go*, Marines!" Kowacs completed. Because he'd hesitated momentarily, Bradley and Sienkiewicz were already ahead of him.

They were in a long hallway whose opposite wall was broken with doorways at short intervals. Somebody ducked out of one, saw the Marines, and ducked back in.

Bradley and Sienkiewicz flanked the panel in a practiced maneuver while Kowacs aimed down the corridor in case another target appeared. He hoped their backs were being covered by the Second Platoon Marines who'd been able to follow him. The survivors of the assault squad couldn't jump through the ceiling unless they stripped off their battle suits first.

"Go!"

Sienkiewicz fired her rifle through the doorpanel and kicked the latch plate. As the door bounced open, Bradley tossed in a grenade with his left hand.

The man inside jumped out screaming an instant before the grenade exploded; Bradley's shotgun disembowelled him.

They'd all seen the flash of a red sleeve when the target first appeared.

The trustee's room had space for a chair, a desk, and a bed whose mattress had ignited into smoldering fire when the explosion lifted it.

He'd also had a collection of sorts hanging from cords above the bed. Human skin is hard to flay neatly, especially when it's already been stretched by the weight of mammary glands, so the grenade fragments had only finished what ineptitude had begun.

Short bursts of rifle fire and the thump of grenades echoed up the corridor from where it kinked toward Third Platoon's end of the building. Nobody'd had to draw those Marines a picture either.

First and Third would work in from the ends, but Kowacs didn't have enough men under his direct command to clear many of the small individual rooms. He'd expected weasel nests. . . .

But there were only two more doors, spaced wide apart, beside the briefing room in the visible portion of the hall.

"Cover us!" Kowacs ordered the squad leader from Second Platoon. "Both ways, and *don't* shoot any Marines."

In another setting, he'd have said 'friendlies'. Here it might have been misconstrued.

His non-coms had already figured this one, flattening themselves to either side of the next door down from the briefing room. Kowacs' fire and Sienkiewicz' criss-crossed, stitching bright yellow splinters from the soft wood of the panel. Bradley kicked, and all three of them tossed grenades as the door swung.

There was no latch. The panel's sprung hinges let the explosions bounce it open into the corridor with its inner face scarred by the shrapnel.

Kowacs and his team fanned through the door, looking for targets. Nothing was moving except smoke and platters jouncing to the floor from the pegs on which they'd been hanging. In the center of the floor was a range. There were ovens and cold-lockers along three of the walls.

Well, there'd had to be a kitchen, now that Kowacs thought about it.

The man hidden there picked the right time to wave his hand from behind the range that sheltered him— a moment after the Marines swung in, ready to blast anything that moved, but before a quick search found him and made him a certain enemy.

"Up!" Kowacs ordered. *"Now!"*

He was plump and terrified and hairless except for a wispy white brush of a moustache that he stroked with both hands despite obvious attempts to control the gesture.

"The rest of 'em, damn you!" roared Bradley, aiming his shotgun at the corner of the range from which he expected fresh targets to creep.

"It's only me!" the bald man blubbered through his hands. "I swear to God, only me, only Charlie the Cook."

Sienkiewicz stepped—she didn't have to jump—to

the range top. Her rifle was pointed down and the
plasma gun, its barrel still quivering with heat, jounced
against her belt gear.

"Clear!" she reported crisply. Charlie relaxed visibly,
until he saw that Kowacs was reaching for the handle
of the nearest cold-locker.

"Not me!" the civilian cried. "Charlie only does what
he's told, I swear to God, not—"

Sienkiewicz saw what was in the locker and saved
Charlie's life by kicking him in the teeth an instant
before Bradley's shotgun would have dealt with the
matter in a more permanent way.

Heads, arms, and lower legs had been removed in
the course of butchering, but there was no doubt that
the hanging carcasses were human.

Kowacs stepped over to the sprawling prisoner and
cradled his rifle muzzle at the base of the man's throat.
"Tell me you cooked for the weasels," he said quietly.
"Just say the fucking words."

"No-no-no," Charlie said, crying and trying to spit
up fragments of his broken mouth before he choked
on them. "Not the Masters, never the Masters—*they*
don't need cooks. And never for me, never for Charlie,
Charlie just—"

"Cap'n?" Bradley said with the hint of a frown
now that he'd had time to think through his impulse
of a moment before. Shooting a clearly unarmed
captive. . . . "The, ah—"

He tapped the side of his helmet, where the
recorder was taking down everything he said or did for
after-action review by the brass.

Kowacs grabbed the prisoner by the throat and
lifted him to his feet. Charlie was gagging, but the
Marine's blunt fingers weren't stranglingly tight.
Kowacs shoved the man hard, back into the open
locker.

"We'll be back for you!" he said as he slammed the door.

Some day, maybe.

Kowacs was shuddering as he ejected the partially-fired magazine from his rifle and slammed in a fresh one. "Told a guy yesterday I'd seen everything the weasels could do to human beings," he muttered to his companions. "Guess I was wrong."

Though he didn't suppose he ought to blame this on the Khalians. They just happened to have been around as role models.

"One *more!*" Sienkiewicz said with false brightness as her boots crashed to the floor and she followed Bradley into the hallway again.

The squad from Second Platoon had been busy enough to leave a sharp fog of propellant and explosive residues as they shot their way into the sleeping rooms on the opposite side of the corridor. They hadn't turned up any additional kills, but they were covering Kowacs' back as he'd ordered, so he didn't have any complaints.

He and his non-coms poised at the third door in this section. It jerked open from the inside while he and Sienkiewicz took up the slack on their triggers.

Neither of the rifles fired. Bradley, startled, blasted a round from his shotgun into the opening and the edge of the door.

"*Don't shoot!*" screamed a voice from behind the doorframe, safe from the accidental shot. "I'm unarmed! I'm a prisoner!"

Kowacs kicked the door hard as he went in, slamming it back against the man speaking and throwing off his aim if he were lying about being unarmed. The room was an office, almost as large as the kitchen, with wooden filing cabinets and a desk—

Which Sienkiewicz sprayed with half a magazine,

because nobody'd spoken from *there*, and anybody in concealment was fair game. Splinters flew away from the shots like startled birds, but there was no cry of pain.

Starships or no, the Khalians weren't high tech by human standards. In a human installation, even back in the sticks, there'd have been a computer data bank.

Here, data meant marks on paper; and the paper was burning in several of the open file drawers. The air was chokingly hot and smoky, but it takes a long time to destroy files when they're in hard copy.

The man half-hidden by the door stepped aside, his hands covering his face where Kowacs had smashed him with the panel.

He didn't wear a red sleeve, but there was a tag of fabric smoldering on one of the burning drawers.

What had the bastard thought he was going to gain by destroying the records?

Kowacs was reaching toward the prisoner when the man said, "You idiots! Do you know who I am?"

He lowered his hands and they did know, all three of them, without replaying the hologram loaded into their helmet memories. Except for the freshly cut lip and bloody nose, the Honorable Thomas Forberry hadn't changed much after all.

"Out," Kowacs said.

Forberry thought the Marine meant him as well as the non-coms. Kowacs jabbed the civilian in the chest with his rifle when he started to follow them.

"Sir?" said the sergeant doubtfully.

Kowacs slammed the door behind him. The latch was firm, though smoke drifted out of the gouge next to the jamb.

"They'll wipe the chips," Kowacs said.

"Sir, we *can't* wipe the recorders," Bradley begged. "Sir, it's been tried!"

"We won't have to," Kowacs said. He nodded to Sienkiewicz, lifting the plasma weapon with its one remaining charge. "We'll leave it for the brass to cover this one up."

And they all flattened against the wall as Sienkiewicz set the muzzle of the big weapon against the hole in the door of the camp administrator's office.

# WHEN THE DEVIL DRIVES
## A Story of The Fleet

"Captain Miklos Kowacs?" asked whoever was sticking his hand through the canvas curtain to tap Kowacs on the shoulder as he showered with his men. "Could I have a quick minute with you?"

"*Whoo!* I dropped the soap, sweetie," called one of Kowacs' Marines in a falsetto. "I'll just bend over and pick it up!"

Kowacs lifted his face to the spray of his shower for an excuse not to look at the guy interrupting. The horseplay of his unit, the 121st Marine Reaction Company—the Headhunters—was as relaxing to him as the steamy hammering of the water. He didn't want to think about anything else just now, and he didn't see any reason why he should.

"If I *was* Nick Kowacs," he said, "I'd have just spent six hours in my hard suit, picking through what used to be the main spaceport on this mudball. Bug off, huh?"

He turned his head slightly. Some of the water recoiling from him spurted through the gap in the canvas to soak the intruder in its rainbow spray.

"Yeah, that's what I wanted to check," the voice continued flatly. "I'm English—I've got the Ninety-Second—and we—"

"Hell and damnation!" Kowacs muttered in embarrassment as he slipped out through the canvas himself. The decontamination showers were floored with plastic sheeting, but the ground outside the facility had been bulldozed bare and turned to mud by overflow and the rain. It squelched greasily between his toes.

"Sorry, Captain," he explained. "I thought you were some rear echelon mother wanting to know why I hadn't inventoried the week's laundry."

"S'okay," English said. "The *Haig*'s about to lift with us, and I needed to check one thing with you about the port."

The Ninety-Second's commander didn't carry Kowacs' weight; but he was a hand's breadth taller, with curly hair and the sort of easy good looks that made him seem gentle to somebody who didn't know English's reputation.

Kowacs knew the reputation. Besides, he'd seen eyes like English's before, pupils that never focused very long on anything because of the things they'd seen already.

Kowacs had eyes like that himself.

Sergeant Bradley, the Headhunters' field first, slipped out of the shower behind his commanding officer. "Anything I can do to help, sir?" he asked.

Stripped, the noncom looked as thin as a flayed weasel. He was missing one toe, a plasma burst a decade before had left half his scalp hairless and pink, and much of the body between those two points bore one or another form of scarring.

"No problem," Kowacs said—and there wasn't, but it was nice to know that there was always going to be somebody to watch his back. It kept you alive in this line of work; and more important, it kept you as sane as you could be. "Captain English heads up the Ninety-Second. This—" shifting his gaze to the taller officer— "is First Sergeant Bradley."

"Toby," said English, shaking with Bradley—both of them with hands wet from the shower. "Not 'captain' yet anyway, though maybe after this last one . . ."

"Hey!" said Bradley with enough enthusiasm to ignore the fact that English was obviously distracted. "You guys did a *hell* of a job on the port! Nothin' left but rubble and cinders. Say, they got you looking for that weasel commando that shot up Post Bessemer two nights ago?"

"Ah," said English. "No, we're about to lift. As a matter of fact—"

Bradley didn't need the glance Kowacs gave him. "Sorry, sir," he said as he ducked back into the shower facility. "*Damn* good to meet you!"

English spent a moment marshaling his thoughts after Bradley had left the two officers alone again— if alone was the right word for men standing beside one of the main roads crisscrossing the huge base.

Base Thomas Forberry—named to commemorate symbolically the hundreds of thousands of civilians whom the Khalia had murdered—had been woodland and farms gone to brush when the Fleet landed to retake Bethesda less than a month before. Now it had a hundred kilometers of perimeter fence with bunkers and guard towers; a nearby spaceport and naval dockyard ten times bigger than the port that had served the planet before the Khalian invasion; buildings to house more people than there were indigenous humans in the portion of the planet now under the

Fourth District Military Government installed here at Base Forberry—

And seven thousand five hundred hectares of mud—the inescapable result of any military construction project save those undertaken in deserts, ice caps, or vacuum.

"Ah," said Kowacs—he'd have helped English say what he needed to if he'd had the faintest notion of what it was. "Bradley was right. I don't think—" he paused; but it was true, so he said it, "anybody could've done a better job on the port than you guys did. You'll get your second star for sure."

"Had a lotta help from the indigs," English said, letting his eyes slant away toward the horizon. "They got us through the perimeter, you know?"

"No shit?" said Kowacs. He hadn't heard anything about that.

He was vaguely aware that he was standing stark naked beside the road. Some of the admin types who'd landed when the shooting pretty much stopped might take that badly, but modesty wasn't a useful virtue among troops who spent most of their time either in the field or packed into the strait confines of a landing vessel.

"I guess . . ." said Toby English with a diffidence that must have been as unusual to him as it would have been in the man to whom he was speaking. "That what your sergeant said was the straight goods? Nothing left at the port?"

"Oh, look, man, I'm sorry," said Kowacs who finally thought he knew what was bothering the other officer. "Look, we recovered two of your people. But the third one, the suit transponder still worked but there was half the tail of a destroyer melted across him. Nothing we could do, but we tried."

"Thanks," said English with a smile that was genuine

but too brief for that to have been the real problem. "Dead's dead. Don't mean nothin'."

"Yeah," said Kowacs, agreeing with the meaning rather than the words. "We've all sent home eighty kilos of sand with a warning to the family not to open the coffin."

"Ah," English continued, looking away again. "I guess you'd've checked if there was any bunkers under the Terminal Building? I thought there might've been."

"No bunkers," Kowacs said, keeping the frown off his forehead but not quite out of his voice.

"That was downwind of one of the destroyers that cooked off," he continued carefully. "The fission triggers of her torpedo warheads, they burned instead of blowing. But it was hot enough that our suits are still in there—" he pointed toward the plastic dome of the decontamination building, "and they thought we ought to shower off pretty good ourselves."

English smiled falsely. "Yeah," he said. "Look, liftoff was twenty minutes ago, and—"

Kowacs put a hand on the other Marine's arm to stop him. As gently as he could, he said, "There were a lot of bodies inside, but only indigs and weasels. No Marine equipment. What happened out there?"

English shrugged and said, "Don't matter a lot. I told you, the indigs got us through the perimeter. I think most of 'em got out again before things started to pop, but—the On-the-Spot agent running the unit, Milius . . . She was keeping the weasels occupied inside the Terminal Building."

He met Kowacs' gaze with clear, pale eyes of his own. "She had balls, that one."

"Trouble with sticking your neck out . . ." said Kowacs softly, looking toward a distance much farther in time than the horizon on which his eyes were fixed. "Is sooner or later, somebody chops it off."

"Don't I know it," English agreed bitterly. His voice and expression changed, became milder. "Don't we all. Look, I gotta run."

He paused, then added, "Hey. If it can't be the Ninety-Second gets those weasel hold-outs, I hope it's you guys."

"I hope it's us lifts-off tomorrow," Kowacs called to the taller officer's back; but English was already busy talking to a truck driver, bumming a ride to the spaceport and a no-doubt-pissed naval officer.

The Ninety-Second was one of the half-companies shoe-horned into Fleet combat units instead of being carried in a purpose-built landing craft the way the Headhunters were. People whose proper business was starships generally didn't have much use for the ground-specialty Marines . . . but at least the destroyer *Haig* hadn't lifted off while the Ninety-Second's commander did his personal business.

Most of Kowacs' marines were done showering and had filed back into the changing room. They'd have to don the same sweaty uniforms they'd worn for six hours under their hard suits while searching the shattered port, but the shower had raised their spirits.

Bradley was still waiting behind the canvas. So was Sienkiewicz, who looked as tough when naked as she did with her clothes on—and who was just as tough as she looked.

The twenty nozzles down either side of the canvas enclosure were still roaring happily, spewing out water that had been brought twenty kilometers through huge plastic aqueducts. The drains that were supposed to carry it away were less satisfactory. At least half the water spilled out of the enclosure and found its own way slowly toward the lowest point in Base Forberry.

In an unusual twist of justice, that point was the parade ground surrounded by base headquarters and the offices of the military government, located in a valley where they couldn't be sniped at by the few Khalia still alive on Bethesda.

"Everything copacetic, sir?" Bradley asked with a smile to suggest that he hadn't been listening through the canvas while the officers talked.

"No problem," Kowacs grunted. And there wasn't, not one you could do anything about. Couldn't help the dead, like English had said. "Let's get back to barracks and find fresh uniforms."

"Ah—we were wondering about that, sir," the field first sergeant said. "The trucks are still pretty hot, even after we hosed 'em off."

Kowacs shrugged as he strode toward the changing room. "It's that or walk," he said. "I'll get 'em into a drydock over at the naval base as soon as I can, but Marine ground equipment is pretty low priority over there.

"And this place—" he waved toward the closed chamber in which robot arms were scrubbing the hard suits, "isn't big enough to hold trucks."

Sienkiewicz laughed in a throaty, pleasant— feminine—voice. "What's the matter, sarge?" she asked Bradley. "You expect a little low-level radiation to kill *us*?"

All three of them laughed, but there was no humor in the sound.

The summons set off the bell and red flasher at either end of the barracks: it was a Priority One call. Marines threw down their mid-afternoon tasks and jumped to arms even before they heard the specifics of the message.

There was only one thing on Bethesda now that could justify a Priority One call to the Headhunters. A single Khalian unit, an infiltration commando, hadn't

died in heroically useless defense with the hundreds
of thousands of other Khalia. The hit-and-run attacks
of that surviving handful of weasels had been making
things damned hot for the invasion forces.

The problem was beyond the equipment and experience of the Alliance troops that made up the bulk
of the ground elements involved in Bethesda's recovery.

But it was made to order for the 121$^{st}$ Marine
Reaction Company.

Kowacs slid on his helmet. "Go ahead," he said as
his hands fumbled with the shirt he'd hung over the
back of the chair he was sitting on. The information
would be dumped into the unit's data bank, but he
liked to get his orders directly as well. It made him
feel that he was involved in a human process, not just
an electronic game.

Of course it would be the computer which decided
whether they made the strike by truck or loaded onto
the *Bonnie Parker* to drop straight onto the weasels,
trading longer preparation time for faster transit to the
target area. Computers were great for that sort of
computation, but humans—

"Captain Kowacs," said the synthesized voice of an
artificial intelligence. "You are directed to report to
District Governor, Admiral the Honorable Saburo
Takami, immediately."

"Huh?"

"A vehicle has been dispatched for you. It will arrive
in one-point-five minutes. That is all."

"Aye, aye," Kowacs said dazedly, not that the electronic secretary would have given a damn even if it
hadn't broken the connection already. Priority fucking
One.

He'd set it up so that all Priority One calls were
slaved through the barracks loudspeakers. Everybody

was staring at Kowacs as he stomped toward the door, sealing his shirt front while his hands were full of the equipment belt which he hadn't had time to sling on properly yet.

"Daniello," he called to his senior lieutenant, "hold the men in readiness."

Nobody bothered to ask *what* they were to be ready for.

Corporal Sienkiewicz was already waiting outside with bandoliers of ammunition and two unloaded assault rifles. She handed a set to her commanding officer.

Because of the weasel raids, the military government was still treating the Fourth District as a combat zone. Personnel leaving Controlled Areas—bases and defense points—were ordered to carry weapons at all times, though the weapons were to be unloaded except on approved combat operations.

And Sienkiewicz was right: there was no telling what Kowacs was going to hear from Admiral Takami, or how fast the District Governor would expect him to respond.

It was just that Kowacs didn't like to have a gun around when he talked to administrative types. It turned his thoughts in the wrong directions.

The jeep was strack and expensive, running on vectored thrust instead of the air cushion that would have been perfectly satisfactory on the plastic roadways of the base. The vehicle arrived within seconds of the time the AI had given Kowacs; and the driver—an enlisted man—had a voice almost as superciliously toneless as that of the machine when he said, "My orders are to transport one only to District Headquarters."

"Then your orders were wrong," said Kowacs as he and Sienkiewicz got into the jeep. He hadn't intended her to come, and he didn't need a bodyguard at

District Headquarters—the sort of guarding that the big corporal *could* do, at any rate.

But neither was some flunky going to tell him he couldn't bring an aide along if he wanted to.

The jeep sagged under the weight of a big man and a very big woman. Cursing under his breath, the driver lowered the surface-effect skirts and pulled back into traffic on the air cushion's greater support.

Base Thomas Forberry was loud with vehicles, construction work, and the frequent roar of starships landing or lifting off from the nearby port. During lulls in the other racket, Kowacs could hear the thumping of plasma cannon from the perimeter. Some officers of the units on guard duty were "clearing their front of areas of potential concealment."

Blasting clumps of trees a kilometer away wouldn't prevent the infiltration attacks the surviving Khalia were making; but it did a little to help the boredom of guard duty in a quiet sector.

The civilian detention facility lay along one side of the road. Scores of wan indigs stared out at the traffic, careful not to come too close to the electrified razor ribbon that encircled the prison camp. The military government had already started rounding up Bethesdans who were reported to have collaborated with the Khalia. They'd be held here until they'd been cleared—or they were handed over to the civilian authorities for trial.

When the Fleet got around to setting up a civilian administration.

"Poor bastards," Kowacs muttered, looking away from the bleak hopelessness of the internees as the jeep crawled past at the speed of the trucks choking the base's main north-south boulevard.

Sienkiewicz shrugged. "They live in the same barracks as us," she said. "They eat the same rations. They sit on their butts all the time without a goddam thing to do, just like we do."

Kowacs met her eyes.

"So tell me where their problem is?" she concluded.

"Same place ours is," Kowacs agreed without much caring whether the driver could hear him also. "And we're going there now."

The parade square in the center of Base Forberry had been covered with plastic sheeting as soon as the three-story Base HQ and the District Government building were finished—and before crews had completed the structures on the other two sides of the square. Tracked machinery had chewed up half the sheeting and covered the remainder with mud of a biliously purple color.

It was the same color as the silt which had seeped into Admiral Takami's office when storm winds flexed the seams of the pre-fab building.

Kowacs saluted as carefully as he could, but he'd never been much of a hand at Mickey Mouse nonsense. The District Governor frowned—then scowled like a thunder-cloud when he noticed the Marine was eyeing the purple stain along the edge of the outer wall.

The other naval officer in the room, a commander with good looks and only a hint of paunch, smiled at Kowacs indulgently.

"Well, Kowacs," Admiral Takami said, "Sitterson here tells me we need you in this district. I'm not going to argue with my security chief. What's a government for if not security, eh?"

"Ah?" Kowacs said. He couldn't understand what the governor meant.

He *prayed* that he didn't understand what the governor meant.

"What the governor means," said Commander Sitterson in a voice as smoothly attractive as his physical appearance, "is that the ground contingents are all well and good for large-scale operations, but we need a real strike force. The governor has had the 121$^{st}$ transferred from Naval command to the Fourth District government."

Well, Kowacs had never believed God listened to a marine's prayers.

"Well, I'll leave you men to get on with it," Takami said dismissively. "I have a great deal of work myself."

As Kowacs followed the security chief out of the office, he heard the governor snarling into the microphone embedded in his desk. He was demanding a work crew with mops and scrub brushes.

"I thought you'd rather hear about your reassignment from the governor rather than from me directly," Sitterson said in the anteroom. "Not a bad old bird, Takami. Won't get in the way of our carrying out our job. Did you keep the car?"

"No sir," Kowacs said. He was trying to grasp what had just happened to him and his unit. He couldn't.

"No matter," Sitterson said, though his frown belied his words. "We'll walk. It's just across the square."

He frowned again as he noticed that Sienkiewicz, carrying both rifles, followed them out of the building.

"My clerk," Kowacs said flatly.

"Yes, that reminds me," Sitterson replied. "I'll want one of your men on duty at all times in my outer office. I have living quarters in the building, you know. I can't be too careful."

Kowacs' skin burned as anger drove blood to its surface. "Ah, sir," he said. "We're a Marine *Reaction* Company."

"Well, I *want* men who can react, don't I?" Sitterson retorted.

Kowacs said nothing further.

Security Headquarters was kitty-corner from the government building, a hundred meters away; but Kowacs had never thought Sitterson needed the vehicle for any reason but status. It was a windowless single-story structure, three times as long as it was wide—a module rather than a pre-fab. The door was at one end; Sitterson buzzed for admittance instead of touching the latch himself.

The door opened to reveal an aisle running half the building's length. There were four closed doors to the left and eight barred cells on the right. The individual civilians in five of the cells leaned with their arms against their sides and their foreheads resting against the back wall.

It was an extremely painful position. The petty officer who'd opened the door had a long shock rod with which to prod any of the prisoners who sagged or touched the wall with a hand.

"Interrogation rooms," Sitterson said, gesturing toward the closed doors. He chuckled and added with a nod toward the cells, "I like my visitors to see that we mean business, here. This is the only entrance to the building."

"What have they done?" Kowacs asked in a neutral voice.

"That's what we're here to find out, aren't we?" Sitterson replied with a broad grin.

One of the women in the holding cells was sobbing, on the verge of collapse. Kowacs lengthened his stride, drawing the security chief a little more quickly with him to the door at the far end of the aisle.

They weren't quite quick enough into the office beyond. As Sienkiewicz shut the door behind them, Kowacs heard the reptilian giggle of the shock rod loosing its fluctuating current. The woman screamed despairingly.

The senior petty officer behind the huge desk threw Sitterson a sharp salute without getting up. He didn't have room enough to stand because of the data storage modules in the ceiling, feeding the desk's computer.

Sitterson tried to project a sense of his own power—but the quarters assigned his operation were a far cry from even the jerry-built luxury of the District Government Building.

Fleet officers assigned to admin duty on the ground weren't usually the best and the brightest of their ranks. That was something Kowacs had to remember—though he wasn't sure how it would help him.

"Colonel Hesik has reported, sir," said the petty officer, nodding toward the tall, intense man who had leaped to attention from the narrow couch opposite the desk.

"Wait here, Hesik," Sitterson said as he strode between desk and couch to the room's inner door.

Kowacs eyed—and was eyed by—the tall man as they passed at close quarters.

Hesik's uniform was of unfamiliar cut. It was handmade, with yellow cloth simulating gold braid on the pockets, epaulets, and collar tabs. The slug-throwing pistol he wore in a shoulder holster was a Fleet-issue weapon and well worn.

Hesik's glare was brittle. Kowacs wouldn't have had the man in his own unit in a million years.

Sitterson's personal office had almost as much floorspace as the governor's did, though the ceiling was low and the furnishings were extruded rather than wood.

On the credit side, the floor didn't seep mud.

"Have a seat, Captain," Sitterson said with an expansive gesture toward one of the armchairs. Another door, presumably leading to living quarters as cramped as the reception area, was partly screened by holo projections from the interrogation rooms they had walked past. In the holograms, seated petty officers confronted civilians standing at attention, nude, with their clothes stacked on the floor beside them.

"We'll be working closely together, Captain," the security was saying. "I don't mind telling you that I regard this assignment as an opportunity to get some notice. It's a job we can sink our teeth into. If we handle the situation correctly, there'll be promotions all around."

The bearded civilian in the projection nearest Kowacs was babbling in a voice raised by fear and the clipped sound reproduction, "Only eggs, I swear it. And maybe butter, if they asked for butter, maybe butter. But they'd have taken my daughter if I hadn't given them the supplies."

"Ah, Commander," said the Marine, wondering how he'd complete the sentence. "I'm not clear why my unit rather than . . ."

Rather than anybody else in the universe.

"Your daughter was involved in this?" asked the holo-grammic interrogator. "Where is she now?"

"*She's only eight!* For god's sake—"

Sitterson made a petulant gesture; the AI in his desk cut the sound though not the visuals from the three interrogations.

The security chief leaned over his desk and smiled meaningfully at Kowacs. "I know how to handle collaborators, Captain," he said. "And so do you—I've heard what went on on Target. *That's* why I asked for the 121st."

For a moment, Kowacs couldn't feel the chair beneath him. His body trembled; his mind was full of images of his drop into the Khalian slave pens on Target—and the human trustees there, with their tor-ture equipment and the abattoir with which they aped the dietary preferences of their Khalian masters.

Every trustee in his sight-picture memory wore the features of Commander Sitterson.

Kowacs didn't trust himself to speak—but he *couldn't* remain silent, so he said, "Sir, on Target the prisoners were turning out electronics, stuff the weasels can't make for themself."

He lurched out of his chair because he needed to move and by pacing toward the wall he could innocently break eye contact with the security chief. "That stuff, giving the weasels produce so they don't put you on the table instead—that's not collaboration, sir, that's flat-ass survival. It's not the same as—"

But the words brought back the memories, and the memories choked Kowacs and chilled his palms with sweat.

"Well, Captain," Sitterson said as he straightened slightly in his chair. "If I didn't have responsibility for the safety of the hundred and forty thousand Fleet and allied personnel, stationed in this district, I might be able to be as generous as you are."

The commander's stern expression melted back into a smile. "Still," he went on, "I think your real problem is that you're afraid you won't see any action working with me. I'll show you how wrong you are.

"Send in Colonel Hesik," he told his desk. The door opened almost on the final syllable to pass the tall man.

Kowacs started to rise but Sitterson did not, gesturing the newcomer to a chair.

"Hesik here," the commander said, "was head of the resistance forces in the district before our landing. He's been working closely with me, and—" he winked conspiratorially toward the Bethesdan, "I don't mind telling you, Captain, that he's in line for very high office when we come to set up a civilian government."

Hesik grinned in response. The scar on his right cheek was concealed by his neatly groomed beard, but it gave his face a falsely sardonic quirk when he tried to smile.

"Tell Captain Kowacs what happened to your unit three months ago, Hesik," Sitterson ordered.

"Yes sir," said the indig—who had better sense than to try to make something of his shadow "rank," which if real would have made him the senior officer in the room. He was willing to act as Sitterson's pet—for the reward he expected when the Fleet pulled out again.

"We were organized by Lieutenant Bundy," Hesik said. He kept his eyes trained on a corner of the room, and there was a rote quality to his delivery.

"Technical specialists were landed six months ago to stiffen local resistance," Sitterson added in explanation. "Bundy was a top man. I knew him personally."

"We were hitting the weasels, hurting them badly," Hesik resumed. His voice had bright quivers which Kowacs recognized, the tremors of a man reliving the past fears which he now cloaked in innocent words. "There were other guerrilla units in the district too—none of them as effective as we were, but good fellows, brave . . . Except for one."

The Bethesdan swallowed. As if the bobbing of his Adam's apple were a switch being thrown, his head jerked down and he glared challengingly at Kowacs. "This *other* unit," he said, "kept in close touch with us—but they never seemed to attack the Khalia. Avoiding reprisals on innocent civilians, they explained."

One of the hologram civilians had collapsed on the floor. Her interrogator stood splay-legged, gesturing with a shock rod which did not quite touch the civilian.

"And perhaps so," Hesik continued. "But we heard very disquieting reports about members of that unit frequenting the spaceport, where the Khalia had their headquarters. We tried to warn Lieutenant Bundy, but

he wouldn't believe humans would act as traitors to
their race."

"Kowacs here could tell you about that," Sitterson
interjected. "Couldn't you, Captain?"

Kowacs spread his hand to indicate he had heard
the security chief. His eyes remained fixed on Hesik.

"They called us to a meeting," the Bethesdan said.
"We begged the lieutenant not to go, but he laughed
at our fears."

Hesik leaned toward Kowacs. "We walked into an
ambush," he said. "The only reason any of us got
out alive was that Lieutenant Bundy sacrificed his
life to warn the rest of us."

"Doesn't sound like selling butter to the Khalians,
does it, Captain?" Sitterson commented in satisfaction.

"Them?" Kowacs asked, thumbing toward the hologram interrogations.

"Not yet," said the security chief.

"But," Hesik said in a voice bright with emotion, "my
men have located the traitors, where they're hiding."

"Up for some real action, Captain?" Sitterson asked.
"You said you were a reaction company. Let's see how
fast you *can* react."

"Download the coordinates," Kowacs said, too
focused to care that he was giving a brusque order to
his superior. He'd taken off his helmet when he entered
the building. Now he slipped it on again and added,
"How about transport?"

Sitterson was muttering directions to his AI. "You
have trucks assigned already, don't you?" he said, looking up in surprise.

"You bet," Kowacs agreed flatly. "Priority One," he
said to his helmet. "This is a scramble, Headhunters."

His helmet projected onto the air in front of him
the target's location, then the route their computer had
chosen for them. That decision was based on

topographical data, ground cover, and traffic flows along the paved portion of the route.

"How many bandits?" Kowacs demanded, pointing a blunt finger at Hesik to make his subject clear.

"Sir," said Daniello's voice in the helmet, "we still don't have the hard suits back from decontamination."

"Twenty perhaps," said Hesik with a shrug. "Perhaps not so many."

"Fuck the hard suits," Kowacs said to his First Platoon leader. "We got twenty human holdouts only. Pick me and Sienkiewicz up in front of the security building when you come through the parade ground."

"On the way," said Daniello.

"We're going too," said Commander Sitterson, jumping up from behind his desk as he saw to his amazement that the Marine was already headed for the door.

"Please yourself," Kowacs said in genuine disinterest.

It occurred to him that the weasel commando in the area might have human support. And a group of turncoats like these could tell him something about that— if they were asked in the right way.

Satellite imagery reported seventeen huts in the target zone, which made Kowacs think Hesik had underestimated the opposition. By the time the four trucks were in position, each in the woods half a kilometer out from the village and at the cardinal points around it, Kowacs had better data from long-term scanning for ion emissions and in the infrared band.

The Bethesdan was right. There couldn't be as many humans at the site as there were dwellings.

For the last five kilometers to their individual drop sites, the trucks overflew the woods at treetop level on vectored thrust. It was fast; and it was risky only if the target unit had more outposts than seemed probable, given their low numbers.

"Probable" could get you dead if one guy happened to be waiting in a tree with an air-defense cluster, but that was the chance you took.

"Hang on," warned the driver—Bickleman from Third Platoon. Kowacs didn't trust somebody assigned from the motor pool to know what he was doing—or be willing to do it in the face of enemy fire, when people's lives depended on their transport bulling in anyway.

The truck bellied down through the canopy with a hell of a racket, branches springing back to slap the men facing outward on the benches paralleling both sides. A limb with a mace of cones at its tip walloped Kowacs, but his face shield was down and the scrape across his chest was nothing new. He held the seat rail with one hand and his rifle with the other, jumping with the rest of his unit as soon as they felt the spongy sensation of the vehicle's underside settling into loam.

The bustle of Third Platoon taking cover briefly, then fanning out in the direction of the village, was only background to Kowacs for the moment. He had the whole company to control.

Bradley and Sienkiewicz covered their commander while he focused on the reports from the other three platoons—"Position Green," the drop completed without incident—and the hologram display a meter in front of him which was more important than the trees he could see beyond the patterns of light.

"Advance to Amber," Kowacs said. A blue bead glowed briefly in the holographic heads-up display projected by his helmet and all the others in the unit, indicating that the order had been on the command channel.

They moved fast through the forest. The Headhunters were used to woods—as well as jungles, deserts, or any other goddam terrain weasels might pick to stage a raid—and here speed was more important than the threat of running into an ambush.

Kowacs couldn't see much more of Third Platoon than he could of the rest of the company. The undergrowth wasn't exceptionally heavy, but there were at least two meters between each marine and those to either side in the line abreast.

"Gamma, Amber," reported the Third Platoon leader, somewhere off to the left. Kowacs knelt with the rest of the unit around him, rifle advanced, waiting for the remaining platoons to reach the jump-off point.

"Beta Amber"/"Alpha Amber," reported Second, and First Platoons in near simultaneity. There was a further wait before Delta called in, but they were the Heavy Weapons Platoon and had to manhandle tripod-mounted plasma guns through the undergrowth.

Anyway, Delta had reported within a minute of the others, not half a lifetime later the way it seemed to Kowacs as his fingers squeezed the stock of his rifle and his eyes watched green beads crawl across the ghostly hologram of a relief map.

The only difference between Position Amber and any other block of woodland was that it put each platoon within a hundred meters of the village. The huts were still out of sight, though Second and Heavy Weapons would have clear fields of fire when they wriggled a few meters closer.

"Alpha, charge set," reported Daniello whose platoon had the job of driving a small bursting charge a meter down into the soil.

"Beta, sensors ready," answered his Second Platoon counterpart who had set the echo-sounding probes on the other side of the village.

"Fire the charge," Kowacs said.

As he spoke, there was a barely audible thump off to the right and somebody shook his arm to get attention.

"What's going—" demanded Commander Sitterson, whose helmet received all the unit calls—but who didn't have the background to understand them.

He didn't have sense enough to keep out of the way, either. Kowacs was very glad that because of the angle, he hadn't swung quickly enough to blow Sitterson away before understanding took over from reflex.

"Not *now*, sir!" he snapped, turning slightly so that Sitterson's head didn't block the pattern of lines dancing across his display as the unit's computer mapped the bunkers and tunnels beneath the village in the echoing shock waves.

There weren't any bunkers or tunnels. The target was as open as a whore's mouth.

"Was that a shot?" the security chief insisted. Hesik lay just back of Sitterson, his face upturned and the big pistol lifted in his right hand.

"Assault elements, *go!*" Kowacs ordered as he rose to his feet himself, so pumped that he wondered but didn't worry whether the wild-eyed Bethesdan colonel was going to shoot him in the back by accident.

First and Third platoons swept into the village clearing from two adjacent sides, forming an L that paced forward with the sudden lethality of a shark closing its jaws.

"Everyone stay where you are!" Kowacs boomed through the loudspeaker built into the top of his helmet. The speaker was damped and had a strong directional focus, but it still rattled his teeth to use the damned thing. Still, *he* was in charge, and the holdouts in the village had to know that.

Even if it meant that he'd catch the first round if the fools tried to resist.

The civilians in plain sight seemed scarcely able to stand up.

Two women—neither of them young, though one

was twenty years younger than Kowacs thought at first glance—were scraping coarse roots on a table in the center of the straggle of huts. Beside them on a straw pallet lay a figure who mig'it have been of either sex; might have been a bundle of rags, save for the flicker of lids across the glittering eyes, the only motion visible as the line of rifles approached.

"*Don't* move, dammit!" Kowacs bawled as a man directly across from him ducked into the hut.

There was a pop and a minute arc of smoke from Bradley's left hand—the hand that didn't hold the leveled shotgun. The smoke trail whickered through the doorway as suddenly as the civilian had—then burst in white radiance, a flare and not a grenade as Kowacs had half-expected.

Bawling in terror, the man flung himself back outside and danced madly as he stripped away the flaming rags of his clothing while the hut burned behind him. A marine knocked him down with his rifle butt, then kicked dirt over the man's blazing hair.

Both platoons were among the huts in seconds. "Empty!" a voice called, and, "Empty!", then, "Out! Out! Out!"

Three of them tried to get out the back way as somebody was bound to do. That was fine, always let 'em *think* they had a way to run. The dazzling whipcrack of a plasma bolt streaking skyward, all the way to the orbit of the nearer moon, caught the trio in plain sight.

They didn't flatten on the ground or raise their hands, just froze in place and awaited the cross fire which would vaporize them if it came. Marines from Second Platoon threw them down and trussed them scornfully.

"He can't move, he's wounded!" a woman was screaming desperately from the hut beside Kowacs.

That didn't sound like an immediate problem, so he glanced around for an eyeball assessment of the situation.

Everything had gone perfectly. The one hut was afire. Several Marines held an extra weapon while their buddies grasped the civilian who'd been carrying it. The woman didn't have to tell anybody that the fellow two of his men were dragging was wounded. Kowacs could smell the gangrene devouring the prisoner's leg.

The only shot fired was the warning round from the plasma weapons placed in ambush. Very slick. So slick that it probably looked easy to Sitterson and Hesik, pounding up from the treeline where they'd been left flat-footed by the Marines' advance.

The elder of the women who'd been preparing food cried shrilly at Kowacs, "Why are you here with guns? We need help, not—"

Then she saw Hesik. Kowacs caught her by one arm and Sienkiewicz grabbed the other when they saw what was about to happen, but it didn't keep the old woman from spitting in Hesik's face.

The Bethesdan colonel slapped her across the forehead with the barrel of his pistol.

The younger of the pair of women broke away from a marine who was more interested in the drama than in the prisoner he was holding. She jumped into the dark entrance of a hut. The three marines nearest lighted the opening with the muzzle flashes of their automatic rifles.

The prisoner flopped down with only her torso inside the hut. Her legs thrashed while one of the Marines, more nervous or less experienced than the others, wasted the rest of his magazine by hosing down her death throes.

The air stank with the oiliness of propellant residues. Hesik looked dazed. He was making dabbing motions with his right hand, apparently trying to put his weapon back in its holster. He wasn't even close.

"Right," said Kowacs, angry that his ears rang and that a screwup had marred a textbook operation. "Get the trucks up here and load the prisoners on while we search—"

"Not yet," ordered Sitterson. Everybody paused.

"Hold him," Sitterson added to the marine gripping the man—boy, he was about seventeen—with his hair singed off. "You too—" pointing at Sienkiewicz. "Make sure he doesn't get loose."

The big corporal obeyed with an expression as flat as those of Kowacs and Bradley while they watched the proceedings. She gripped the boy's left elbow with her own left hand and angled her rifle across her chest. Its muzzle was socketed in the prisoner's ear.

Sitterson took something from his pocket—a miniature shock rod—and said to the boy in a caressing voice, "Now, which of this lot is Milius?"

"Go to—," the boy began.

Sitterson flicked him across the navel with his shock rod. It gave a viper's hiss and painted the midline hairs with blue sparks. The boy screamed and kicked. Sienkiewicz interposed her booted leg, and the security chief punched the prisoner in the groin with the rod.

"Sir!" Kowacs shouted as he grabbed Sitterson by the shoulder and jerked him back. "Sir! People are watching!" He tapped his rifle on the side of his helmet where a chip recorder filed every aspect of the operation for rear echelon review.

Sitterson was panting more heavily than his physical exertion justified. For a moment, Kowacs thought the commander was going to punch him—which wasn't going to hurt nearly as much as would the effort of not blowing the bastard away for doing it.

Instead, the security chief relaxed with a shudder. "Nothing to worry about," he muttered. "Not a problem at all. What's your unit designator?"

"Huh?" Kowacs replied.

Sienkiewicz was spraying analgesic on the prisoner while the other marine stood between the boy and any possible resumption of Sitterson's attack. Maybe they were worried about what their recorders would be saying at a courtmartial.

Maybe they didn't like Sitterson any better than their CO did.

Sitterson stepped behind Kowacs, holding the marine officer steady when he started to turn to keep the security chief in sight. Kowacs froze, waiting for whatever was going to come, but there was no contact beyond Sitterson's finger tracing the serial number imprinted in the back of the helmet rim.

"There," he said as he let Kowacs face around again. "I'll take care of it when we get back. I'll have the file numbers of all the recorders in this company transferred to units in storage on Earth."

Kowacs looked blank.

"That's the way to do it," Sitterson explained with an exasperated grimace. "Don't try to wipe the data, just misfile it so nobody will *ever* be able to call it up."

"Where're those *trucks?*" Bradley demanded to break the sequence of words and events. The vehicles were arriving with their intakes unshrouded for efficiency, howling like demons and easy to hear even for ears deadened by rifle blasts.

Two Marines came out of the hut where the woman sprawled. One of them carried a sub-machine gun he'd found inside. The other held, of all things, an infant whose wails had been lost in the noise and confusion of the raid.

"Check it for bullet splinters," Kowacs ordered with

a black scowl, knowing that if the baby had taken a round squarely it would have bled out by now.

"It just needs changing, sir," said Sienkiewicz unexpectedly.

"Then *change* it!" Kowacs snapped.

"All right," said Sitterson. "I think you're right. We'll take them back to headquarters for interrogation."

Marines faced outward toward the treeline with their weapons ready—just in case. The trucks bellowed in, brushing the upper limbs with thrust and their belly-plates.

Switching to the general unit push because he couldn't trust his unaided voice to be heard as a truck settled in the clearing before him, Kowacs asked, "Bradley, how many we got all told?"

"Thirteen with the kid," the sergeant replied, flashing Kowacs a double hand plus three fingers to reiterate his radio message. "That fits, right?"

Bradley frowned, then added, "Fourteen with the mother."

"Yeah, they'll need that too for identification," Kowacs said with no more emotion than the static hiss of his radio. "But we'll sling it to a cargo rail, all right?"

The draft from the truck exhausts stirred the burning hut into a mushroom of flame, then collapsed it in a gush of sparks spiraling into several of the huts downwind.

"Beta, Delta," Kowacs ordered on the command channel. "Pack up and let's split before it turns out there's an explosives cache where the sensors missed but the fire doesn't."

"Come on, come *on!*" Bradley was demanding on the general frequency. "Three prisoners to a truck. And *secure* them to tie-downs, will you? They're going to tell us things."

Commander Sitterson had begun to sneeze. The

vehicle exhausts were kicking up dust, smoke, and the smell of the corpse being dragged past him.

Kowacs really wanted to be away from this place, though he didn't have any objective reason for the way it made him feel. The only problem was, when they got back to Base Forberry, the interrogations were going to resume.

And if the "Milius" the security chief was looking for was the same woman Toby English had been talking about, Kowacs didn't think he was going to like *that* much either.

As the trucks hovered at the base perimeter, waiting to be keyed through the automatic defenses by the officer of the guard, Commander Sitterson said, "Well, Kowacs. Now that you're under my command, I want you to be comfortable. What can I do for you? Are your barracks satisfactory?"

"Huh?" said Kowacs. He'd been watching the prisoners lashed to the forward bulkhead, the burned kid in the center with an old woman on either side of him. "Barracks? Nothing wrong with them. They leak a bit." *So does the governor's office.* "But you know, there is something you could maybe do . . ."

"Name it," Sitterson said, beaming.

The column got its go-ahead and vectored out of hover mode with a lurch. One of the women called the boy "Andy" when she asked if he were all right.

Andy told her to shut her mouth and keep it shut.

"Well, these trucks," Kowacs explained. "We couldn't decontaminate them properly after we searched the spaceport this morning, just hosed 'em off. If you've got any pull with the yard facilities, maybe you could get us time in a drydock to—"

"Trucks?" gasped the security chief. He half-rose from his bench seat before he realized how far out over the road that left him poised. "*This* truck hasn't been decontaminated?"

"Sir," Sergeant Bradley interrupted with a flat lie, delivered in as certain a tone as that of the Pope announcing Christ is risen. "They've undergone full field procedures and are perfectly safe. But *we* may have to spend twelve hours a day for the next month aboard them, so we'd like to be twice safe."

"Yes, well," Sitterson said, easing back down on the bench with a doubtful expression. "I understand that. Of course I'll take care of it."

Sitterson wanted the prisoners at his headquarters, not the internment facility. The trucks and their heavily armed cargo wallowed through traffic to the parade square, drawing looks of interest or disgust—depending on personality—from the rear echelon types they passed.

The Headhunters were in dual-use vehicles with enough power to keep a full load airborne without using ground effect. They could have flown above the traffic—except that above ground flight was prohibited by base regulation, and Base Thomas Forberry came under Naval control instead of that of the district government. The Shore Police would have been more than happy to cite Commander Sitterson, along with Kowacs and all four of his drivers.

When the trucks grounded in front of the Security Headquarters, dimpling the plastic matting, Kowacs' men began unfastening the prisoners and Sitterson called into his helmet microphone, "Gliere, open the holding cells. We'll keep all the prisoners here for now."

Kowacs couldn't hear the response, but as the building opened, Sitterson added, "Oh—there's a body also. Have someone from forensics work it up for identification and then take care of it, will you?"

"This isn't right!" shouted the boy, Andy, as the

marines to either side of him manhandled him along faster than his burn-stiffened legs wanted to move. "You should be helping us! You should be *helping us!*"

"Come on ahead," Sitterson ordered Kowacs. "I want you with me during the interrogation. They know you mean business."

"Right," Kowacs said on his command channel. "Daniello, you're in charge till I get back. Keep everybody in the barracks, but we're not on alert status till I tell you different."

He strode along beside Sitterson and Hesik. The Bethesdan colonel seemed to be recovering somewhat, but he hadn't spoken since the prisoner made her ill-advised leap for a weapon.

Or for the baby. Well, a bad idea either way.

Sienkiewicz was a half-step behind him. Kowacs looked over his shoulder—looked up—and said, "Did I tell you to come along, Corporal?"

"Yessir," Sienkiewicz said. With her extra bandoliers of ammunition and grenades, and the heavy, meter-long plasma weapon slung behind her hips against need, she looked like a supply train on legs.

Hell, he did want her around.

The cells were open and empty. The guard and the trio of petty-officer interrogators saluted the security chief as he stepped past them, then roughly took the prisoners from the marines and pushed them into the cells—the men alone, the women in pairs. One of the women held the infant. The doors clanged shut when the cells were filled.

In the outer office, Sitterson said, "You can wait here." Not as brusque as "Wait here," but the same meaning. His entourage—Kowacs a big man, Sienkiewicz huge, and Hesik looking thin and trapped—glanced at one another and at the petty officer behind the desk. There wasn't enough room for any of them to sit on the couch.

"Gliere," the security chief said as an afterthought on his way to his private quarters. "Get the number from Kowacs' helmet and see to it that the recordings go to File Thirteen. The whole company. You know the drill."

"Yes *sir*," Gliere replied. "Just a minute while I take care of the cells."

The non-com was watching miniature holos of the holding area. He touched a switch on his desk. Another of the cells closed with a ringing impact.

Sitterson was back within five minutes. He was wearing a fresh uniform; the skin of his face and hands was pink with the enthusiasm with which he had scrubbed himself.

Kowacs hoped the security chief never learned how hot the trucks really were. He'd order a court-martial, beyond any question. It was easy to forget just how nervous rear echelon types got about their health and safety.

"All right," the security chief said brightly. "Let's get down to it, shall we? Gliere, we'll take the man in the end cell."

Andy.

"He thinks he's tough." Sitterson added with a laugh which Hesik echoed.

Kowacs said nothing. He tossed his automatic rifle to Sienkiewicz and gestured her to stay where she was. The corporal's grimace could have meant anything.

Andy tried to walk when they moved him across the aisle into an interrogation room, but he was barely able to stand. He had no clothes to strip off. The sealant/analgesic Sienkiewicz had sprayed on from her first aid kit had dried to mauve blotches like the camouflage of a jungle animal.

When the door shut behind them, the boy wavered and caught himself on the room's small table.

"Attention, damn you!" Sitterson ordered, pulling out his shock rod.

"Why are you doing this to me?" the boy cried. Delirium, drugs, and the decay toxins loosed by his injuries turned his voice into a wail of frustration.

"Why didn't you turn yourselves in?" Sitterson shouted. "Why were you hiding out with your guns?"

"We *did* call in!" Andy said. "And your toady Hesik said wait, he'd send vehicles for us."

"Liar!" Hesik said as he swung the butt of his pistol at the boy's mottled forehead.

You don't learn a damned thing from dead prisoners, and the blow would have killed had it landed.

It didn't land because Kowacs caught the Bethesdan colonel's wrist in one hand and twisted the weapon away with the other as easily as if Hesik were a child.

"Sir," Kowacs said to the security chief. "I think this'll go better if you and I do it alone for a bit, you know?"

"He'll lie!" Hesik said. The marine wasn't looking at him, but his grip was as tight as it needed to be.

Kowacs shrugged toward Sitterson. "He'll talk," he said simply. "Dead, he won't talk."

Sitterson's expression was unreadable. At last he said, "Yes, all right. You and I. Hesik, wait outside. Don't worry."

"He'll *lie!*" the Bethesdan repeated, but the tension went out of his muscles and Kowacs let him go.

Kowacs handed back the pistol. His eyes were on Hesik, and they stayed on him until the door closed again behind the Bethesdan.

"We can have him back anytime," Kowacs said without emotion to the prisoner. "We can leave the two

of you alone, or we can help him with you. If you don't
want that, start talking now."

"You think I care?" the boy muttered.

But he did care. He was naked and hurt, badly hurt.
Kowacs was huge in his helmet and equipment belt,
still black with the grime of the raid; and the marine
was a certain reminder of how thorough and ruthless
that raid had been.

"Tell us about Lieutenant Milius," Sitterson said. He
started to wave his shock rod before he realized that
the threat of Kowacs' presence was greater than that
of temporary pain. "Where is she?"

"Dead, for God's sake!" the boy blurted. "She was
in the terminal building when everything started to go.
Ask the marines we took in there. *They'll* tell you!"

Sitterson slapped him with a bare hand. "You're
lying! You're covering for a traitor who murdered a
fellow officer!"

It wasn't a powerful blow, but it knocked Andy back
against the wall. He would have slumped to the floor
if Kowacs hadn't caught him and jerked him upright.

"Hesik told you that?" the boy said. His lip was
bleeding. "All right, sure—she shot that bastard Bundy.
They came to us, told us to back off—we were stir-
ring up the weasels too badly."

Kowacs released the boy when he felt him gather
himself and straighten.

"Milius told 'em go fuck 'emselves," Andy continued with real venom. "And your precious Bundy, *he*
says, if she won't stop for him, maybe the weasels
will take care of the problem. *That's* why she blew
the bastard away. I just wish we'd taken out Hesik
and the rest of the mothers in that cell then when
we had the chance."

"Lying little swine!" Sitterson cried. He grabbed the
boy by the hair with one hand, throwing him against

the wall while he poked the shock rod toward the prisoner's eye.

The singed hair crumbled. Sitterson's hand slipped in a gooey pad of sealant and serum from the burned skin beneath.

"Sir," said Kowacs as he slid between the collapsing boy and the security chief who stared at his hand with an expression of horrified disgust. "We made a mistake. If these guys are the ones got the Ninety-Second into the port, then they're straight. Even if they did shoot your o.t.s. agent."

"If!" the security chief repeated. "He's a dirty little liar, and he's covering for a traitor who didn't come *near* the port during the assault."

"No sir," Kowacs said. He was standing so close to Sitterson that he had to tilt his head down to meet the eyes of the senior officer. "Milius did lead them in. And she did buy it during the attack."

Sitterson flung himself backward, breathing hard. "Who the hell says?" he demanded. His left hand was clenching and uncurling, but his right held the shock rod motionless so that it did not appear to threaten the marine.

"Toby English," Kowacs said. "Lieutenant English, CO of the Ninety-Second."

Sitterson looked at the Marine. "You're . . ." he began, but his voice trailed off instead of breaking. He swallowed. "Oh, Christ," he said very quietly. "Oh Christ help me if that's true."

"Sure, you can ask Toby," Kowacs said. "The *Haig* lifted off this morning, but you can send a message torp after her for something this important."

"He's off-planet?" the security chief asked. His face regained the color it had lost a moment before.

"Yeah, but—"

"That's all right," Sitterson interrupted, fully himself

again. He opened the door. "We'll adjourn for now, Captain."

Gesturing toward the petty officers waiting for direction, he added, "Two of you, get this one,"—Andy was on the floor, unconscious from shock or the medication—"into his cell and hold him. Just hold them all until I get back to you."

"Sir, I—" Kowacs began.

"Return to your unit and await orders, Captain," Sitterson said crisply. "This operation has been a success thus far, and I don't intend to spoil it."

Kowacs didn't like to think about the implications of that while he and Sienkiewicz hitched a ride back to the barracks on a fuel truck going in the right direction. He didn't like to think about Colonel Hesik's smile, either.

But he couldn't forget either thing.

Kowacs was typing his report, hating the job and hating worse what he was having to say, when Bradley and Sienkiewicz pushed aside the sound-absorbent curtains of his "office."

"Bugger off," Kowacs said, glaring at the green letters which shone demurely against the white background of the screen. "I've got today's report to do."

"Figured you'd get Hoofer to do that," Bradley said. "Like usual."

Kowacs leaned back in the chair that was integral with the portable console and rubbed his eyes. Hoofer, a junior sergeant in First Platoon, was good with words. Usually he'd have gotten this duty, but . . .

"Naw," Kowacs said wearily. "It's knowing how to say it so that nobody back on Tau Ceti or wherever gets the wrong idea. And, you know, burns somebody a new one for shooting a woman in the back."

"She shouldn't have run," Sienkiewicz said.

"Right," said Kowacs. "A lot of things shouldn't happen. Trouble is, they do."

He looked expectantly at the two non-coms. He was waiting to hear why they'd interrupted when they, of all people, knew he didn't like company at times like this.

Bradley eased forward so that the curtain surrounding the small enclosure hung shut. "We went for a drink tonight at a petty officers' club with Gliere, the Tech 8 in Sitterson's office. The Mil Gov bars have plenty of booze, even though you can't find enough to get a buzz anywhere else. He got us in."

"Great," said Kowacs without expression. "If you'd brought me a bottle, I'd be glad to see you. Since you didn't—"

"Thing is," the field first continued as if he hadn't heard his commander speak, "Gliere's boss called him back after the office was supposed to be closed."

Kowacs raised an eyebrow.

"Pissed Gliere no end," Bradley said. "Seems Sitterson wants him to clear the data bank of all records relating to the bunch we brought in today. Wants it just like that lot never existed—and the file overwritten so there aren't any gaps."

Nick Kowacs got up from the console. The chair back stuck; he pushed a little harder and the frame bent thirty degrees, out of his way and nothing else mattered.

He began swearing, his voice low and nothing special about the words, nothing colorful—just the litany of hate and anger that boils from the mouth of a man whose mind is lake of white fury.

"What does he think we are?" Sienkiewicz asked plaintively. "They were on *our* side."

"Right," said Kowacs, calm again.

He looked at his console for a moment and cut its

power, dumping the laboriously created file into electron heaven.

"That's why it's Sitterson's ass if word gets out about what he did." Kowacs continued. He shrugged. "What we all did, if it comes to that."

"They're still in the holding cells," Bradley said. "The prisoners. I sorta figure Sitterson's going to ask us to get rid of that part of the evidence. 'Cause we're conscienceless killers, you know."

"Except the bastard won't ask," Sienkiewicz said bitterly. "He gives orders."

"Right," said Kowacs. "Right. Well, we're going to solve Sitterson's problem for him."

He sat down at the console again, ignoring the way the damaged seat prodded him in the back.

"Sergeant," he said, "book us to use the drydock late tonight to wash the trucks—between midnight and four, something like that."

"Ah, sir?" Bradley said. "The main aqueduct broke this afternoon. I'm not sure if the naval base has water either."

Kowacs shrugged. "Sitterson said he'd get us a priority," he said. "We'll operate on the assumption that he did."

"Yessir," said Bradley.

"Who do you have on guard duty at Sitterson's office tonight?" Kowacs went on.

"I haven't finalized the list," Bradley said unemotionally. "It might depend on what his duties would be."

"The doors to the holding cells are controlled by the desk in Gliere's office," Kowacs said.

"Yessir," Bradley repeated. Sienkiewicz was starting to smile. "I got a lot of paperwork to catch up with. I'm going to take the midnight to four duty myself."

"So get your butt in gear," Kowacs ordered. He powered up his console again.

"Sitterson ain't going to like this," Sienkiewicz said with a smile that looked as broad as her shoulders.

Kowacs paused, glancing up at two of the marines he trusted with his life—now and a hundred times before. "Yeah," he agreed. "But you know—one of these days Toby English and me are going to be having a drink together . . . And when we do, I don't want to look him in the eye and tell him a story I wouldn't want to hear myself."

As his men slipped out to alert the rest of the company, Nick Kowacs started to type the operational order that would be downloaded into the helmets of all his troops. Green letters hung in the hologram field, but instead of them he saw images of what would be happening later in the night.

He was smiling, too.

A jeep, its skirts painted with the red and white stripes of the Shore Police, drove past the District Government Building. Neither of the patrolmen spared more than a glance at the trucks hovering at idle along the four sides of the otherwise empty square.

Kowacs let out the breath he had been holding.

"Hawker Six," Bradley's voice whispered through the helmet phones. "They don't want to come."

"*Get* them out!" Kowacs snarled without bothering about proper radio discipline.

There were more vehicles moving along the main northsouth boulevard of Base Thomas Forberry. Every moment the Headhunters waited was another chance for somebody to wonder why a truck was parked in front of Security Headquarters at this hour.

Eventually, somebody was going to come up with the obvious right answer.

"On the way, Hawker Six," Bradley replied.

They'd raised the sidings on each vehicle, so that you couldn't tell at a glance that the trucks held the entire 121st Marine Reaction Company, combat-equipped.

You also couldn't tell if Kowacs' own truck carried thirteen internees—who would revert to being Bethesdan civilians as soon as the trucks drove through the Base Forberry perimeter on their way to the naval dockyard three kilometers away.

If everything worked out.

"Alpha Six to Hawker Six," reported Daniello, whose platoon waited tensely in its vehicle on the south side of the square. "A staff car approaching with a utility van."

"Roger, Alpha Six," Kowacs replied.

Officers headed back to quarters after partying at their club. Maybe cheerful—and maybe mean—drunks looking for an excuse to ream somebody out. Like whoever was responsible for trucks parking in the parade square.

"Hawker Five—" Kowacs muttered, about to tell Bradley to hold off on the prisoners for a moment.

He was too late. The first of the Bethesdans was coming out between the arms of two Marines, just like he'd been carried in. Andy, a boy trying to look ready to die; and with his injuries and fatigue, looking instead as if he already had.

"What—," Andy demanded.

Sienkiewicz stepped close, ready to club the boy before his shouts could give the alarm. Kowacs shook his head abruptly and laid a finger across his own lips.

The car and van *whooshed* by, their headlights cutting bright swathes through the ambience of Bethesda's two pale moons. The van's axis and direction of movement were slightly askew, suggesting that the driver as well as the passengers had been partying.

"Listen, kid," Kowacs said, bending so that his face was within centimeters of Andy's. "We're going to get you out of the perimeter. What you do then's your own look-out. I don't think Sitterson's going to stir things up by coming looking for you, but Hesik and your own people—that's *your* business. Understood?"

"Whah?" Andy said. The rest of the prisoners were being hustled or carried out. Andy stepped aside so that they could be handed into the back of the truck. "Why are you doing this?"

"Because I'm fucking stupid!" Kowacs snapped.

There was an orange flash to the south. Kowacs' boots felt the shock a moment before the air transmitted the explosion to his ears, it must have been a hell of a bang to people who weren't a couple kilometers away like Kowacs was.

"Motor pool," Sienkiewicz said, making an intelligent guess. "Late night and somebody got sloppy, drove into a fuel tank." Shrugging, she added, "Maybe it'll draw everybody's attention there."

"I'd sooner all the guards were asleep, like usual," Kowacs replied with a grimace.

"Hawker Six," Bradley called. "Some of these aren't in the best of shape. It'll hurt 'em to be moved."

"They'll hurt a lot worse if we leave 'em for Sitterson, Hawker Five," Kowacs replied. "Get 'em out."

"Alpha Six to Hawker Six," said Daniello. "Two vans headed north. They're highballing."

"Roger, Alpha Six," Kowacs said. "No problem."

What *could* be a problem was the way lights were going on in the three-story officers' quarters lining the boulevard in either direction from the square. The blast had awakened a lot of people. The officers gawking out their windows couldn't see a damn thing of the motor pool, now painting the southern horizon with a glow as red as sunrise—

But they could see Kowacs' trucks and wonder about them.

Two marines stepped out of the building with an old man who hung as a dead weight. Bradley followed, kicking the door closed behind him. The sergeant held his shotgun in one hand and in his left arm cradled a six-year-old who was too weak with fever for his wails to be dangerous to the operation.

"Here's the last of 'em, sir," Bradley reported, lifting the child to one of the marines in the vehicle.

Andy looked at the sergeant, looked at Kowacs, and scrambled into the truck himself.

*"Watch it!"* warned Daniello's voice without time for a call sign.

Air huffed across the parade square as the two vans speeding north braked to a halt instead of continuing on. One of the vehicles turned in the center of the square so that its cab faced the District Government Building.

"What the hell?" muttered Kowacs as he flipped his face shield down and switched on the hologram projection from his helmet sensors. His men were clumps of green dots, hanging in the air before him.

The van began to accelerate toward the government building. The driver bailed out, to Kowacs' eyes a dark smudge on the plastic ground sheathing—

And a red dot on his helmet display.

*"Weasels!"* Kowacs shouted as he triggered a long burst at the driver. His tracers gouged the ground short of the rolling target, one of them spiking off at right angles in a freak ricochet.

Most of his men were within the closed trucks. Bradley's shotgun boomed, but its airfoil loads spread to clear a room at one meter, not kill a weasel at a hundred times that range. Where the *hell* was—

The weasel stood in a crouch. The bullet that had waited for Kowacs to take up the last, least increment of trigger pressure cracked out, intersected the target, and crumpled it back on the ground.

—Sienkiewicz?

The square hissed with a moment of dazzling brilliance, false lightning from the plasma gun Corporal Sienkiewicz had unlimbered instead of using the automatic rifle in her hands when the trouble started. Her bolt bloomed across the surface of the van, still accelerating with a jammed throttle and twenty meters from the front door of the District Government Building.

The explosives packed onto the bed of the van went off, riddling the building's facade with shrapnel from the cab and shattering every window within a kilometer.

Kowacs had been steadying himself against the tailgate of his truck. It knocked him down as the blast shoved the vehicle sideways, spilling Headhunters who were jumping out to get their own piece of the action.

But the explosion also threw off the weasels in the second van who were spraying bright blue tracers in the direction from which the marines' fire had come.

Klaxons and sirens from at least a dozen locations were doing their best to stupefy anyone who might otherwise be able to respond rationally.

Kowacs lay flat and aimed at the weasels. There was a red flash from their vehicle. Something flew past like a covey of banshees, trailing smoke in multiple tracks that fanned wider as they passed. Twenty or thirty rooms exploded as the sheaf of miniature light-seeking missiles homed on the folks who were rubbernecking from their barracks windows.

It was the perfect weapon for a Khalian commando to use to spread panic and destruction as they sped away in the night in a Fleet-standard

van—presumably hijacked at the motor pool, where
the previous explosion didn't look like an accident
after all.

The missile cluster wasn't a goddam bit of good
against the Headhunters, blacked out and loaded for
bear.

Only a handful of marines from each platoon was
clear of the hampering trucks, but their fire converged
on the Khalian vehicle from four directions. Tracers
and sparks from bullet impacts flecked the target like
a festival display—

Until Sienkiewicz's second plasma bolt turned it into
a fluorescent bubble collapsing in on itself.

One of the weasels was still alive. Maybe it'd been
in the cab and shielded when the bolt struck the back
of the van. Whatever the cause, the weasel was still
able to charge toward Security Headquarters, firing wild
bursts from its machine pistol.

You expected the little bastards to be tough, but this
one was something special. Kowacs himself put four
rounds into the Khalian's chest, but it had to be shot
to doll rags by the concentrated fire of a dozen rifles
before what was left finally collapsed.

Kowacs rolled to his feet. His whole left side was
bruised, but he couldn't remember how that had happened. He flipped up his face shield and called, "Cease
fire!" on the command frequency.

Sienkiewicz's second target was still burning. Fuel,
plastics, and weasel flesh fed the orange flames. There
was only a crater where the first van had blown up,
but burning fragments of it seemed to have started
their own little fires at a dozen places around the
parade square.

Kowacs switched to the general Base Forberry push
and crashed across the chatter with a Priority One
designator. "All Fleet personnel. The Headhunters are

in control of the vicinity of the Mil Gov complex. Don't fire. Keep your heads down until we've secured the area."

Kowacs turned around.

"Bastards got in through the aqueduct," Bradley snarled beside him. "Sure as shit."

Light from the open door to Security Headquarters blinded Kowacs.

"Kowacs!" shouted Commander Sitterson, a shadow behind his handheld floodlamp with the dimmer shadow of Colonel Hesik behind him. "What are you doing? And where are the—"

Andy stuck his burned face from the back of the truck beside Kowacs.

"You *traitor!*" Sitterson screamed at the marine captain. "I'll have you shot for this if it's the last thing I—" and his voice choked off when he saw that Kowacs had lifted his rifle to his shoulder because that was what you were trained to do, never hip-shoot even though the target's scarcely a barrel's length away.

And Kowacs couldn't pull the trigger.

Not to save his ass. Not in cold blood.

Not even Sitterson.

When Kowacs heard the first shot, he thought one of his men had done what he couldn't. As Sitterson staggered forward, dropping his light, Colonel Hesik fired his pistol twice more into the commander's back and shouted, "I'm on your side! Don't hurt me! I won't—"

The muzzle blast of Bradley's shotgun cut off Hesik's words as completely as the airfoil charge shredded the Bethesdan's chest.

"I was wrong about how the weasels got in," Bradley said in the echoing silence. "Hesik was a traitor who led 'em here before he greased his boss."

Liesl, CO of the Third Platoon, had gotten sorted

out from his men and was standing beside Kowacs. "Gamma Six," Kowacs said, nodding as he slapped a fresh magazine into his rifle, "get aboard and get this truck over to the dock for washing, just like we planned."

"Aye aye, sir," Liesl said. Bickleman was driving again. He boosted engine thrust as soon as he heard the order. The vehicle and its cargo began to move with marines still lifting themselves in over the tailgate.

"Alpha Six," Kowacs said on his command frequency, "secure the boulevard to the south. Maybe there's not another load of bandits, but I don't like surprises. Beta Six, spread your men out and search the trucks we nailed. And *watch* it."

There was a long burst of automatic fire, but it came from a barracks and wasn't aimed anywhere in particular. Somebody whose room had taken a Khalian rocket had survived to add to other people's confusion.

"Headhunter Command to all Fleet personnel!" Kowacs said. "Stop that wild shooting or we'll stop it for you."

All the real problems were over for now. Kowacs didn't think he'd ever be able to tell the true story. Maybe to Toby English over a beer.

That didn't matter.

All that mattered was that he didn't have to admit, even to himself in the gray hours just before dawn, that he'd murdered thirteen civilians to cover an administrative error.

# TEAM EFFORT

## A Story of The Fleet

Most of the Headhunters were experienced enough to know that the *Bonnie Parker*'d been hit—that bone-jarring *clang!* wasn't just re-entry turbulence.

"Instead of coming in on the deck . . . ," Kowacs said, continuing with his briefing. Barely identifiable holographic images wavered in front of his helmet and the helmets of his troops, poised at the cargo bay doors, " . . . the Jeffersonian militia we're supposed to bail out managed to drop straight down into the middle of their objective, a Weasel air-defense installation."

The *Bonnie Parker* was still under control. Not that there was a damn thing the 121st Marine Reaction Company in her belly could do if she weren't. The Headhunters crouched in two back-to-back lines, ready to do their jobs as soon as their ship touched down and her long doors opened.

As it was, there wasn't half enough time for Kowacs to tell his troops exactly what their job *was*.

There wasn't half enough information, either.

The landing vessel bucked. The hull screamed with piercing supersonics like those of a gigantic hydraulic motor—then banged again into the relative silence of re-entry.

Not another hit: a piece tearing loose as a result of the first one.

Not a good sign, either.

Corporal Sienkiewicz, Kowacs' company clerk—and bodyguard—was nearly two meters tall and solid enough to sling a shoulder-fired plasma weapon in addition to her regular kit. She grinned in a close approximation of humor to Bradley, the field First Sergeant, and murmured, "Bet you three to one in six-packs, Top: we don't ride all the way to this one."

"They figured they could keep the Weasel's heads down with suppression clusters until they landed," Kowacs said as he watched the gray, fuzzy holograms his helmet projected for him. Instead of a Fleet hull, the Jeffersonians had used their own vessel—and crew; *that* was bloody obvious—but their cameras and real-time links were to Alliance standard. "And then the missile launchers couldn't depress low enough to hit their ship."

The air-defense installation was a concrete pentagram of tunnels and barracks, with launchers at each point. The crisp outline danced in the holograms with the electric dazzle of anti-personnel bomblets going off. A red flash and mushroom of smoke marked the Khalian's attempted response: as soon as the missile left its hardened launcher, shrapnel exploded it.

In synchrony with the detonating image, the *Bonnie Parker's* hull banged.

This time it *was* another hit.

"Cockpit to cargo," rasped the PA system, distorting

the voice of Jarvi, the Command Pilot. "Three minutes to touchdown."

The Jeffersonians—those dick-headed *anarchists*—must have been carrying five times the normal load of suppression clusters; that and luck were what had saved their asses during the drop.

The extra weight was also why the image of the ground beneath their landing vessel was expanding at such a rate.

"They made it that far," Kowacs continued; his voice cool, his guts cold and as tight as his hand on the stock of his assault rifle. "They landed with the bay doors open, and about half their assault company jumped before the boat was stabilized."

Blurred images degraded a stage further as the editor—an artificial intelligence aboard one of the orbiting support vessels—switched to the feed from the helmet of one of the ground troops. Shouting soldiers, very heavily equipped and logy with the weight of their hardware, lurched to the ground and sprayed streams of tracer into Weasels popping from hatches in the surrounding concrete walls.

The installation had been hardened against air attack. It wasn't intended for defense against infantry landing in its interior.

A shadow fell across the tumbling holograms. The viewpoint changed as the Jeffersonian looked over his shoulder and saw his landing craft balloon away from him with half the troops still hesitating at its doors.

The men who'd jumped weighed at least five tonnes. That sudden release had caused the pilot—already fighting excessive descent speed—to let his craft get away from him.

The ship bounced up ten meters on thrust. Before the pilot could get it back on the ground, one of the launchers had belched a line of smoke. The missile was still accelerating when it hit the landing craft, but its warhead didn't need the boost of kinetic energy to do its job.

Tendrils of burning metal trailed from the edges of the hologram where glare hadn't blanked the camera. Then the entire picture went dead.

"There's a magazine in middle of the installation—" Kowacs said, continuing with the briefing notes assembled from panicked, scrappy messages received in orbit after the landing craft and its booster link were lost.

The light banks in the *Bonnie Parker*'s bay went out. The yellow emergency system came on and the forward doors, port and starboard, started to clam-shell upward. They opened about half a meter, enough to let a frigid, high-altitude wind scream and blast the Marines. Then they jammed.

Somebody started to pray in Kowacs' earphones. Because the system was locked for the briefing, the voice had to be one of the platoon leaders he'd known for *years*—but he didn't recognize it.

"—in which many of the friendlies have holed up awaiting rescue," Kowacs continued as if his palms weren't wet and icy, as if part of his mind didn't wish a flash like the one that ate the Jeffersonian craft would *end* this.

Sergeant Bradley slipped between the lines of Marines, patted one on the shoulder. The high-pitched prayers stopped in mid-syllable. It didn't matter who it'd been, didn't matter at all.

For a moment, Kowacs had thought it might be his own voice.

"We'll land—" he began, speaking louder instinctively though he knew the system would compensate for the wind-rush by raising the gain in the Headhunters' earphones.

The *Bonnie Parker's* emergency lighting flicked out, then back. The starboard rear door, the one which the Weapons Platoon faced, cycled upward without stopping.

"Cockpit to cargo," said the PA system in O'Hara's voice. If O'Hara was speaking, it meant the command pilot had her hands full.

Or was dead.

"Rig to jump in sixty seconds. I say again, rig to jump."

"Headhunter command to cockpit," Kowacs said, tripping his helmet's liaison channel. The four platoon leaders had stepped out of line without needing the orders there was no time to give, checking their units' newer members who might never have made a wire-discharge jump in combat. "Will we be in guidance range of the target?"

There was a clatter as Weapons Platoon jettisoned its belt-fed plasma weapons and their ammo drums out the hatchway. The guns were too heavy to be supported by the emergency wire-discharge packs that were all the Headhunters had available now.

"That's a rog, Headhunter," O'Hara bellowed, his words broken either by static or by the sound of an electrical fire in the cockpit. "Some of you, at least. But you'll need to find your own way home."

First and Third Platoons were reporting ready in the holographic heads-up display in front of Kowacs' eyes. The green dot for Weapons appeared as he switched back to the unit push and said, "We've got one door so we'll jump by sticks, Delta first, then Gamma—"

Second Platoon winded READY but Kowacs continued with what he'd intended to say, "—then Alpha, last Beta. Your helmets have the coordinates downloaded. They'll guide to the intended landing zone—"

"Jump!" screamed the PA system. "Jump, damn you!"

"Go!" said Kowacs.

Weapons Platoon cleared the doorway, one Marine holding back a micro-second until Bradley shoved him from behind. Third Platoon was already pushing into position from the opposite side of the bay, hunched forms fumbling with the reels of wire attached to their equipment harness.

Nobody'd expected to jump until seconds ago. They'd been ready to throw their jump gear away as soon as the *Bonnie Parker* touched down. Now they realized that if the reel unhooked, they'd freefall while the thirty-meter wire floated in the air until its powerpack could no longer polarize the charges at its opposite ends.

"Gamma, *go!*" snapped Lieutenant Mandricard, and Third Platoon was in the air before Kowacs had thought they were ready. A couple of the men were a step behind the others. They dived for the opening, so graceless and massive in their loads of combat equipment that they looked like pianos tipping over a balcony.

He only hoped they'd get their tumbling under control before the dischargers deployed. If two wires fouled, their charges shorted and—

"Alpha—" ordered Lieutenant Seeley over the command net. She was muscling to the hatch one of her Marines who'd stumbled when the *Bonnie Parker* bucked; as the ship did again, making the whole platoon wobble like ten-pins but without falling until Seeley completed, "—*go!*"

The jump door was empty. The bay of the *Bonnie Parker* lighted with crackling brilliance as one of Second Platoon's newbies hit his manual deployment switch while checking his jump reel one last time.

The wire lashed about like a demented cobra,

shorting its juice every time a coil touched metal. Within two seconds, the sparks vanished into a net of purple afterimages. The Marine stood stricken— and his wire lay limp and useless.

"I'll get him, Placido," Kowacs said, stepping to the newbie before the Second-Platoon lieutenant could. Kowacs let the sling hold his assault rifle. His right hand slipped his own jump reel from his belt, fingers working the catches with the ease of smooth practice, while his left stripped the newbie's dead unit.

"*Go!* Beta," Kowacs ordered. Placido hesitated between the door and the newbie. Not all of his platoon was in position; those who were, jumped—and the remainder followed raggedly, each Headhunter lunging out as soon as there was open space before him.

The newbie would have jumped too, jerking himself away from Kowacs before the fresh reel was in place. Instinctively the kid preferred to die rather than to be left behind by his unit.

No problem. Corporal Sienkiewicz gripped the newbie's equipment harness, and nobody she held was going anywhere. Kowacs finished hooking the reel, slapped the kid on the shoulder and shouted, "Go!" as he turned to take the spare unit Bradley had snatched from the equipment locker five meters away.

Sienkiewicz flung the kid across the *Bonnie Parker's* bucking deck, putting her shoulders into the motion. He was bawling as he sailed through the hatch with Lieutenant Placido beside him.

"Here, sir!" Sergeant Bradley shouted, lobbing the replacement discharge reel toward Kowacs because the *Bonnie Parker* had begun to vibrate like the blade of a jackhammer. Kowacs raised his hands, but the gentle arc of the reel that would save his life changed into a cork-screw as the landing vessel tried to stand on her tail.

One of the bay doors torqued off into the airstream. Kowacs couldn't tell where the discharge reel went because all sixteen of the bay's emergency lights blew up in simultaneous green flashes. Kowacs was tumbling, and when he could see anything it was the great cylinder of the *Bonnie Parker* above him, dribbling blazing fragments of itself as it plunged through the dark sky.

The *Bonnie Parker*'d been a good mount, a tough old bird. To the Marines she carried into one part of Hell after another, she'd been as good a friend as hardware could be to flesh and blood. But this was a business in which your luck ran out sooner or later. The *Bonnie Parker*'s luck had run out; and the only difference between the landing vessel and Captain Miklos Kowacs, dropping unsupported through the atmosphere of a hostile planet, was the size of the hole they'd make when they hit the ground.

"Location," Kowacs ordered, and his helmet obediently projected a hologram read-out onto the air rushing past. Three kilometers from the intended target area, which didn't matter now, and, according to the laser altimeter, forty-seven hundred meters in the air.

Very shortly that wouldn't matter either, but the numbers weren't spinning down as quickly as Kowacs would've thought. Spreading his arms and legs slowed him enough that, even with the weight of his gear, he might not be travelling more than, say, thirty meters a second when he hit.

The commo still worked, though there was a hash of static from jamming, other communications, and the band-ripping petulance of plasma weapons.

"Six to all Headhunters," Kowacs said on the unit push. "We're going to be landing south of the target, most of us. Attack the south face. See if you can get some support to knock down a section of the wall. I don't want any unnecessary casualties, but remember—

unless we move fast, the Weasels won't've left us anybody to rescue."

Kowacs took a deep breath without closing the communication. Then he said the rest of what he had to say. "Delta Six, I'm passing command to you. Acknowledge. Over."

"Roger, Six," said Lieutenant Woking in a voice as calm as Kowacs had tried to keep his own. He wasn't the senior lieutenant, but he'd been in the 121st longer than the other three, and Weapons Platoon would be on the ground first.

Nobody was going to argue with Kowacs' final order, anyway.

"Everybody get an extra Weasel for me," Kowacs said, unable to see the useless holograms for his tears. "Headhunter Six out."

Somebody grabbed his right hand.

Kowacs twisted. Another Marine, anonymous with his faceshield lowered, but Bradley beyond doubt. The field first hadn't deployed his own static discharger yet. It wouldn't support two, not heavily-equipped Marines. That'd been tried, and all it meant was that the guy who'd fucked up took his buddy with him.

"Let go!" Kowacs shouted without keying the commo. Bradley's muscles were seasoned to holding his shotgun ready for use through the shock of combat jumps; Kowacs couldn't pull his hand free.

Corporal Sienkiewicz grabbed Kowacs' left hand. As Kowacs looked back in surprise, the non-coms popped their discharge reels simultaneously.

When the long wires were powered up, static repulsion spun them off their reels in cascades of purple sparks. They acted as electrical levers, forming powerful negative charges at the top of the wire and in the air beneath the reel itself. Their mutual repulsion tried to lift the man to whom the reel was attached—for as long as the powerpack could maintain the dynamically-unstable situation.

Static dischargers weren't perfect. Jumping in a thunderstorm was as surely suicide as it would have been with a conventional parachute, though because of lightning rather than air currents. Still, a Marine—or the artificial intelligence in the Marine's helmet—could angle the wire and drop at a one-to-one slant, regardless of wind direction, allowing precision as great as that a landing vessel could provide.

It wasn't safe; but nobody who volunteered for a Marine Reaction Company figured to die in bed.

"This isn't going to work!" Kowacs shouted over the wind-rush.

"It'll work better than remembering we didn't try," Sienkiewicz shouted back. "Start pickin' a soft place to land."

The non-coms were taking a calculated risk which they felt was part of their job; just as Kowacs himself had done when he gave the newbie his discharge reel. Not much he could say about that.

What the hell. Maybe they'd make it after all.

Vertical insertions were scary under the best conditions, and a night drop was that in spades. Though the laser altimeter gave Kowacs a precise read-out, his eyes told him he was suspended over the empty pit of Hell—and his gut believed his eyes.

Dull orange splotches lighted three sections of the blackness, but there was no way to judge the extent of the fires. Burning cities, burning vehicles—or the burning remains of landing vessels like the *Bonnie Parker*, gutted in the air by Weasel defenses.

Occasional plasma bolts jeweled the night with a sudden intensity that faded to afterimages before the eye was aware of the occurrence. Even more rarely, a secondary explosion bloomed at the point of impact, white or orange or raw, bubbling red. Even the brightest of the blasts reached Kowacs' ears as a distance-slowed, distance-muted rumble, barely audible over the rush of air.

They seemed to be plunging straight down. "Top, are you guiding?" Kowacs demanded as his altimeter spun from four into three digits and continued to drop.

"Are you nuts?" Sienkiewicz said before Bradley had time to reply. "We got enough problems keeping the wires from tangling as it is. Sir."

"Oh—roger," Kowacs said in embarrassment. *He* should've thought of that. When he gave himself up for dead, he seemed to have turned off his mind.

And that was a *real* good way to get your ass killed.

They were low enough to see a pattern of lights beneath them, half a dozen buildings within a dimly-illuminated perimeter. A vehicle with powerful headlights carved a swath through the darkness as it drove hell-for-leather toward the compound. For good or ill, the three Marines were going to land within the perimeter at about the time the vehicle entered by the gate.

"When we touch down—" Kowacs started to say.

His altimeter read 312 meters one moment—and 27 a micro-second later as a starship glided beneath them, black-out and covered with radar-absorbent resin.

Somebody—Bradley or Sienkiewicz—swore in amazed horror. Then both non-coms twisted, fighting to keep their lines from crossing and shorting out in the roaring airstream.

Kowacs, hanging from his friends' hands, watched the ship make its landing approach. His mind took in details of the vessel and the movement around it, considering options coolly—

Because otherwise he'd think about a crackle of energy above him and a sickening drop for the last

hundred meters to the ground. Dead as sure as five
kilometers could make him.

"Ready!" he called. The ship had crossed under
them, then slowed to a near halt just above the ground.
They were slipping over it again on the opposite vector, neither descent quite perpendicular. Steam and
smoke rose from the center of the compound, swirling violently in the draft from the ship's passage and
her lift thrusters. The vapors formed a tortured screen
where they were cut by the blue-white headlights of
the ground vehicle that had just raced through the gate.

The ship was Khalian. Her vertical stabilizer,
extended for atmosphere travel, bore the red hen-
scratches that the Weasels used for writing.

"Now!" Kowacs ordered. The three Marines tucked
out of the pancake posture they'd used to slow their
descent, letting the ground rush up at a hell of a clip.
They sailed over a metal-roofed building and hit rolling, short of a second structure—warehouses or something similar, windowless and austere.

Bradley's line still had enough of a charge to splutter
angrily when it dragged the roof and grounded.
Sienkiewicz was thirty kilos heavier than the field first,
even without the weight of her plasma gun and the
other non-standard gear she insisted on adding to her
personal load. Her line popped only a single violet
spark before it went dead.

Close. Real fucking close.

And it wasn't over yet.

Kowacs had been as prepared as you could be to
hit the ground faster than humans were intended, but
Bradley had released his right hand a fraction later than
Sienkiewicz had dropped his left.

Kowacs twisted, hit on his left heel, and caromed
like a ground-looping airplane instead of doing a neat
tuck-and-roll as he'd intended. His left knee smashed

him in the chest, his backpack and helmet slammed
the ground—and when he caught himself, his rifle
sprang back on its elastic sling to rap his hip and
faceshield.

Pain made his eyes flash with tears. His hands, now
freed, gripped and aimed the automatic rifle.

Pain didn't matter. He was alive, and there were
Weasels to kill.

"Helmet," Kowacs said, "translate Khalian," enabling
the program against the chance he'd hear barked orders
soon.

"Clear this way," whispered Bradley, pointing his
shotgun toward one end of the five-meter alley between
warehouses in which they'd landed. He spoke over
Band 3 of the radio, reserved for internal command-
group discussion. The low-power transmission permitted the three of them to coordinate without trying to
shout over the ambient noise.

Which, now that they were down with no wind-rush
to blur other racket, seemed considerable.

"Clear mine," echoed Sienkiewicz, covering the
opposite direction with her rifle while they waited for
their captain to get his bearings.

"Are there doors to these places?" Kowacs asked, pretending he didn't feel a jabbing from his ankle up his
left shin—and praying it'd go away in another couple
steps. He slouched past Bradley to a back corner. The
two males curved around the warehouses in opposite
directions, like the hooks of a grapnel, while Sienkiewicz
covered their backs.

In the other direction, the starship's lift jets snarled
and blew fragments of baked sod into the air. A siren,
perhaps mounted on the vehicle the Marines had seen
arriving, wound down with a querulous note of it own.

The buildings backed up to the perimeter fence.
None of the inhabitants had interest to spare from the

ship that had just landed in the center of the compound.

"No door here," Bradley reported from the back of his building. He spoke with a rising inflection, nervous or just quivering with adrenalin looking for a chance to kill or run.

"We'll go this way," Kowacs muttered to his team as his left hand switched on the forty-centimeter cutting blade he'd unslung in anticipation. The unloaded whine changed to a howl of pure delight as its diamond teeth sliced into the corrugated metal wall of the building.

This was the sort of job for which the cutter was intended, though the 'tools' wouldn't have been as popular in Marine Reaction Companies had they not been so effective in hand-to-hand—hand-to-paw— combat. Kowacs swept the powered blade in a wide arc while the non-coms poised to rake the interior if anything moved when the wall fell away.

Kowacs' mouth was open. To someone outside his head, he looked as if he were leering in fierce anticipation.

In reality, he was stiffening his body to absorb a burst of shots. Weasels inside the warehouse might decide to fire into the center of the pattern his cutter drew, and the first *he'd* know of their intention was the impact of bullets sparking through the sheet metal.

Three quarters of the way around the arc, Kowacs' blade pinged on a brace; the section wobbled like a drumhead. Sienkiewicz leaped at the wall behind the heel of her right boot, burst into the dark warehouse, and sprawled over a pile of furniture stored there.

"Bloody *Hell!*" she snarled as she rolled to her feet, but their helmet sensors indicated the warehouse was cold and unoccupied. Kowacs and Bradley were laughing as they clambered over the accidental barrier.

Kowacs swept his eyes across the clutter, using sonic

imaging rather than white light. Sienkiewicz had tripped
on a sofa. Like the rest of the furniture stored in clear
film against the back wall, it was ornate, upholstered—

And quite clearly designed for humans. Short-legged
Khalians would find it as uncomfortable as humans did
the meter-high ceiling of a Weasel bed alcove.

"Let's go," Kowacs said, but he and his two Marines
were already slipping down the aisle between stacked
cubical boxes of several sizes. The glare of whatever
was going on in the center of the compound flickered
through the louvered windows at the front of the
building.

Sergeant Bradley's load of combat gear bulked his
wiry form, changing the texture of his appearance in
a way that it didn't his heavily-built companions. He
was taking shorter steps with his right leg than his left,
and the twitch of his pack amplified the asymetric
motion.

Kowacs glanced at him.

Bradley looked back, his expression unreadable
behind the faceshield. "No problem, cap'n," he said.
"We ain't holdin' a track meet."

He pulled a five-unit grenade stick from his belt,
poising his thumb above the rotary arming/delay switch
that would tell the bombs when to detonate.

Kowacs didn't have to see Bradley's face to visualize the smile that was surely on it.

The sort of smile a cat wears with its teeth in a
throat. The sort of smile Kowacs himself wore.

The windows were narrow but the full height of the
front wall. They flanked a door whose crossbar had a
manual unlocking mechanism on this side. Sienkiewicz
worked it gently, holding her plasma weapon ready,
while Kowacs and Bradley peered through the louvers.

The only light in the warehouse was what trick-
led through the windows themselves. There was no

possibility that those outside would notice the Head-hunters preparing for slaughter.

The Khalian vessel was small for a starship, a cylinder no more than sixty meters in length; but, unlike the *Bonnie Parker*, it wasn't designed to land outside a proper spaceport. The pilot had given up trying to balance on his lift jets and had dropped to the ground. The narrow-footed landing legs, intended to stabilize the ship on a concrete pad, carved through the flame-blackened sod like knifeblades; the belly of the craft sank deep enough to threaten an explosion when the jets fired again on lift-off.

The hundred or more waiting humans crowded close, some of them yelping as those behind pushed them against still-hot metal. Vapor puffed from the starship as an airlock started to valve open.

A big air cushion vehicle with polished brightwork, its wheeled outriggers lowered for high-speed road travel, pushed close to the airlock with a careless disregard for the clamoring pedestrians. As a ramp extended from the starship, the car's door opened and a plump, self-important man got out. His multi-colored clothing was as rich and obviously civilian as the vehicle in which he'd arrived.

"Say when," Sienkiewicz demanded, her foot poised to shove open the door and fire her plasma weapon. She had no view of what was going on outside. "Say *when*!"

"Sir, what the *Hell* is going on?" Bradley whispered. "These aren't—I mean, they're. . . ."

"Sie," Kowacs said in a calm, soft voice, "fire directly into the airlock, then flatten yourself. Top, you and I will throw grenades with three-second—" his own thumb armed a bundle of mini-grenades just as he knew Bradley was doing with his own "—delay, air burst."

"And duck out the back, cap'n?" asked the field first.

"And rush the ship, Top," Kowacs corrected with no more emotion than he'd shown when going over the munitions manifest three weeks earlier in Port Tau Ceti. "There won't be time for anybody aboard to close the lock. Not after Sie lights 'em up."

The man from the car strode up the ramp. The rest of the crowd—all males, so far as Kowacs could tell—jumped out of his way as if he were still driving his vehicle. The starship's inner lock had opened, because when the fellow reached the top of the ramp, a human in a black-and-silver uniform appeared from inside the vessel and blocked his way.

For a moment the two men shouted at one another in a language Kowacs didn't recognize. The man in uniform unexpectedly punched the civilian in the stomach, rolling him back down the three-meter ramp. The crowd's collective gasp was audible even over the hiss and pinging of the ship's idling systems.

"Sir," begged Sienkiewicz, staring at the blank panel before her. "*Sir*! When?"

The plump man got to his feet, shouting in fury. A figure stepped from the ship and stood next to the man in uniform.

The newcomer was a Weasel. As it barked to the man in uniform, the translation program in Kowacs' helmet rasped, "What are we waiting for? Don't you realize, even *now* a missile may be on the way."

"Ready," said Kowacs, his rifle verticle, gripped in his left hand, and the stick of grenades ready in his right.

The uniformed human turned to the Khalian and *barked*.

"Shoot that one," the helmet translated, "and we'll cram the rest aboard somehow."

The Weasel raised a sub-machine gun. The plump man leaped back into his car with a scream.

"Go," whispered Kowacs.

Sienkiewicz kicked the warehouse door thunderously open an instant before the lightning flash of her plasma bolt lit the night.

The jet of plasma spat between the two figures in the airlock, struck a bulkhead inside the ship, and converted the entrance chamber into a fireball. The blast blew the Weasel and the uniformed human ten meters from the lock, their fur and hair alight.

Anybody inside the starship had burns unless they were separated from the entry chamber by a sealed door. As for the crowd outside—

Kowacs' and Bradley's grenade sticks arced high over the crowd before the dispersion charges popped and scattered the units into five bomblets apiece. The bomblets went off an instant later with the noise of tree-limbs breaking under the weight of ice.

Shrapnel ripped and rang on the front of the warehouse; the crowd flattened like scythed wheat.

Kowacs was up and moving as soon as the last bomblet went off. There was a spot of blood and a numb patch on the back of his right wrist, but nothing that'd keep him from functioning. The grenades spewed glass-fiber shrapnel that lost velocity fast in an atmosphere, but it wasn't completely safe even at twenty meters. Closer up, it—

Sienkiewicz slipped on bloody flesh as she tried to fire a burst from her rifle into the men at the fringe of the grenade explosions. Her shots went off into the night sky, but that didn't matter. The survivors that could move were running away, screaming; some of them blinded; some scattering drops of gore as they waved their arms in terror. . . .

The dispersion charges had spread the bombs well enough that most of the crowd wasn't running.

The Khalian from the ship thrashed in its death agonies on a sprawl of humans. Kowacs' rifle burped three rounds into it anyway as he passed and Bradley—half a step behind—blew off the creature's tusked face with his shotgun.

They weren't so short on ammo that they couldn't make sure of a Weasel.

Kowacs hit the ramp first and jumped it in a single stride despite the weight of his gear. His team faced around reflexively—just as he would have done if one of the others had been in the lead. Bradley fired at the backs of the survivors to keep them moving in the right direction. It was long range for the airfoil loads in his weapon, but one of the targets flung up his hands and dropped a meter short of shelter.

Sienkiewicz put surgical bursts into the windscreen, then the engine compartment of the ground vehicle. The idling turbine screamed, then the fans died and let the skirt flatten. Yellow flames started to flicker through the intake gratings.

A solenoid clacked behind Kowacs as a survivor in the starship's cockpit tried desperately to close the airlock, but the jet of plasma had welded something or fried part of the circuitry.

Kowacs rolled into the ship-center room the plasma bolt had cleansed. A meter-broad circle'd been gouged from the hull metal opposite the lock. Anything flammable at sun-core temperatures was burning or had burned—including a corpse too shrunken to be identified by species. Open hatches lead sternward, toward two cabins and the sealed engineering spaces, and to the left—forward, to the cockpit.

Kowacs fired right and jumped left, triggering a

short burst that sparked off the ceiling and bulkheads of the passageway it was supposed to clear.

None of the bullets hit the Khalian running from the cockpit with a sub-machine gun in one hand.

Kowacs hadn't expected a real target. He tried to swing the nuzzle on, but his right side slammed the deck so his shots sprayed beneath the leaping Khalian. The only mercy was that his opponent seemed equally surprised and tried clubbing the Marine with its sub-machine gun. The Weasel had sprung instinctively on its victim instead of shooting as reason would have told it to do.

"Nest-fouling ape!" shouted the translation program as the sub-machine gun's steel receiver crashed on the dense plastic of Kowacs' helmet. The creature's free hand tore the Marine's left forearm as Kowacs tried to keep the claws from reaching beneath his chin and—

Bradley fired with his shotgun against the Weasel's temple.

Kowacs couldn't hear for a moment. He couldn't see until he flipped up the visor that'd been splashed opaque by the contents of the Khalian's skull.

The hatch at the other end of the short passageway was cycling closed. Kowacs slid his rifle into the gap. Its plastic grip cracked, but the beryllium receiver held even though the pressure deformed it.

Bradley cleared a grenade stick.

"No!" Kowacs shouted. He aimed the Weasel sub-machine gun at the plate in the center of the cockpit hatch and squeezed the trigger. Nothing.

"Sir, they'll be protected by acceleration pods!" Bradley cried. "*This*'ll cure 'em!"

The grenade stick was marked with three parallel red lines: a bunker buster.

There was a lever just above the sub-machine gun's trigger, too close for a human to use it easily but just right for a short-thumbed Weasel. Kowacs flipped it and crashed out a pair of shots.

"We need the ship flying!" he cried as his left hand reached for one of his own grenade sticks and the hatch began to open. He tossed the stick through the widening gap and leaped through behind them.

The bundle wasn't armed. The Khalian pilot was gripping a machinepistol in the shelter of his acceleration pod, waiting to rise and shoot as soon as the grenades went off. He didn't realize his mistake until Kowacs' slugs ripped across his face.

"Get the stern cabins," Kowacs ordered. "The cockpit's clear."

Kowacs glanced behind him at the control panel. Undamaged: no bullet holes or melted cavities, no bitter haze of burning insulation.

No obvious controls either.

"Fire in the hole!" Bradley's voice warned over the helmet link.

Kowacs stiffened. Grenades stuttered off in a chain of muffled explosions; then, as he started to relax, another stick detonated.

"Starboard cabin clear," Bradley reported laconically. He'd tossed in a pair of sticks with a two-second variation in delay. A Weasel leaping from cover after the first blast would be just in time for the follow-up.

Ruined the pelt, of course.

The cockpit's four acceleration pods were contour-to-fit units that, when activated, compressed around the form within them. Three of the pods were shrunken tight to hold Khalians like the corpse in one of them, but a side couch was still shaped for a human.

"Port cabin's locked!" Bradley shouted, his voice from the helmet earphones a disconcerting fraction of a second earlier than the same words echoing down the passageway at merely the speed of sound. "Sir, want I should blast it? Can you back me?"

Humans *could* fly the damned ship.

It was just that none of the humans *aboard* could fly the vessel. And if Kowacs understood the implication of what that Weasel cried a moment before the plasma bolt gave him a foretaste of eternal Hell, the ship was their only prayer of surviving the next—

"Cap'n," Sienkiewicz reported, "I got a prisoner, and he says—"

Kowacs was already moving before the radio transmission cut off in a blast of static, hugely louder than the *crack* of the plasma weapon that caused it.

Sergeant Bradley crouched at the corner of the stern passageway. Bradley's shotgun was aimed at the stateroom he'd found locked, but his head craned back over his shoulder as he tried to see what was going on outside the vessel.

Kowacs skidded in the blood and film deposited on the deck of the central cabin when plasma-vaporized metal cooled. He made a three-point landing, his ass and both bootheels, but the captured sub-machine gun was pointed out the airlock where Sienkiewicz stood.

The plasma weapon was on Sienkiewicz' shoulder; a glowing track still shimmered from its muzzle. One of the warehouses was collapsing around a fireball. A surviving local must've made the mistake of calling Sie's attention to him.

"Move it! Move it, dog-brain!" she bellowed to somebody beneath Kowacs' line of vision. "Or by god the next one's in *your* face!"

As Sienkiewicz spoke, the translation program barked in Weasel through her helmet speaker. She couldn't've captured a—

Kowacs stepped to the corporal's side, then jumped so that the fat civilian scrambling up the ramp in blind panic wouldn't bowl him over. It was the gorgeously-clad fellow who'd strode up the ramp before—and been knocked down it by the human in uniform, with a promise of death if the Headhunter attack hadn't intervened.

"Waved his shirt from the car, Cap'n," Sienkiewicz explained. As she spoke, her eyes searched for snipers, movement, *anything* potentially dangerous in the night and sullen fires. "I thought. . . . Well, I didn't shoot him. And then he barked, you know, that the place was gonna be nuked but he could fly us out."

"Sure, you did right," Kowacs said without thinking it even vaguely surprising that Sienkiewicz apologized for taking a prisoner alive.

"Quickly, the cockpit!" the machine voice in Kowacs' ear demanded while the prisoner's mouth emitted a series of high-pitched barks. "They'll surely destroy this base any moment. They can't allow any sign of our installations!"

The fellow was still in a panic, but the way he brushed past Kowacs proved that he'd regained his arrogance. He looked clownishly absurd: he'd ripped a piece from his shirt-front to wave as a flag, and at some point recently he'd fouled his loose, scintillantly-blue trousers as well.

"Sir!" Bradley cried. He'd enabled his speaker along with the translation program, so barks counterpointed his words. "This cabin! We can't leave it!"

"Watch it, then, for chrissake!" Kowacs snarled as he strode with the prisoner into the cockpit.

The prisoner slipped as he tried to hop over the Weasel in the passageway. He muttered what must have been a curse, but the words were in the unfamiliar language in which he and the uniformed man had argued before the Khalian appeared.

Somebody fired at the ship with a machinegun—from

the side opposite the airlock, so there was no response
from Sienkiewicz. The light bullets were no threat to
hull plating, but the CLANG-CLANG-CLANG,
CLANG-CLANG-CLANG, CLANG-CLANG-CLANG
wound Kowacs' mainspring a turn tighter with each
short burst.

The prisoner flopped down into one of the center
pods. It conformed to his body like a work-piece in
a drop forge, spreading sideways and upward to support him in an upright position. Kowacs knelt on the
deck beside him, holding the muzzle of the sub-
machine gun near the prisoner's ear.

Holographic displays curtained the blank consoles,
meshing unexpectedly with a kaleidoscopic fragment
of Kowacs' memory.

When he'd dived into the cockpit, aiming and firing before the hunched Khalian could respond, there'd
been similar flickers of light over the plastic consoles.
They'd died with the seated pilot—but they came up
automatically as soon as a living intellect sat before
them again.

The prisoner's finger twitched. Six columns of red
light mounted higher. The ship rocked gently, dispel-
ling Kowacs' doubt that an obvious civilian would be
any better able to fly the damned thing than the
Headhunters themselves were. The prisoner was shaking them loose from the soft surface instead of pow-
ering-up abruptly and blowing one or more of the
blocked nozzles.

CLANG-CLANG-whing-*spow-ow-ow*!

The machinegunner had shifted to a position from
which he might be able to accomplish something.
Kowacs hunched lower, but the bullet ripping
through the airlock buried itself in a bulkhead on
the third ricochet. The sniper had moved.

Sienkiewicz was all right: her plasma weapon

crashed out its last charge. The blast that followed was much too great for a belt of ammunition or a few grenades. The machinegunner must've taken cover in a warehouse—without considering what might be in the cases around him.

"The Weasels are going to nuke this place?" Kowacs demanded of the man beside him. His speaker's barking translation was almost as irritating to him as the bullet impacts had been.

"Not them, you fool!" the prisoner snapped, rocking the ship up ten degrees to port. Kowacs clutched the back of the pod for support. "*They* don't have brains enough to be concerned. It's the Clan Chiefs, of course, and they're right—" the ship rocked back to starboard, "but *I* don't intend to die."

"Sir, we're gonna blow the hatch," Bradley reported flatly. Sienkiewicz could back him up, now. The holographic display that took the place of cockpit windows showed one whole side of the compound mushrooming upward in multi-colored secondary explosions.

But a charge heavy enough to blow a bulkhead still wasn't a great idea in the confined space of a ship this small.

"Hold it, Top," Kowacs ordered. "You—prisoner. Can you open and close the door to the port cabin from here?"

"Yes," the prisoner said, grimacing. One of the red columns abruptly turned blue. All six disappeared as the man's finger wagged. The ship settled at a skewed angle.

"Wait!" Kowacs ordered. "Open it a crack for a grenade, then close it again?"

"Yes, yes!" the prisoner repeated, the snarling Khalian vocables seasoning the emotionless translation from Kowacs' headset. "Look, *you* may want to die, but I assure you that your superiors want *me* alive! I'm the

Riva of Riva Clan!" He made a minuscule gear-shifting motion with his left hand.

"Top! Here it comes!" Kowacs shouted.

Bradley and Sienkiewicz had already been warned by Kowacs' side of the cockpit conversation and the *clack* as the hatch's locking mechanism retracted.

The corporal cried, "Got 'em!" Her automatic rifle fired a short burst to keep Weasels clear of the gap while Bradley tossed in the grenade. The hatch hadn't quite cycled closed again when the scattering charge momentarily preceded a quintet of sharp pings—not real explosions.

"Shit, Top!" Kowacs cried, squeezing his helmet tight to his knees and clasping his forearms above it. "Not a—"

The bunker buster went off. The starship quivered like a fish swimming; the holographic display went monochrome for a moment, and flexing bulkheads sledged the vessel's interior like a piston rising on its compression stroke.

"Think we oughta give 'em another, Top?" joked Sienkiewicz with the laughter of relief in her voice.

They were okay, then, and both the ship and its controls seemed to have survived the blast. Kowacs could even hear the hatch start to open again, which said a lot for the solidity of the internal divisions on Weasel ships.

"Idiots!" said the prisoner—the Riva, whatever that was; "clan" might only be as close a word as Weasels had to the grouping The Riva headed. "Suicidal fools!"

Kowacs didn't know that he could argue the point. Thing was, doing the job had always been the Headhunter priority, well above concern for side effects. Bradley's bunker buster would sure as Hell've done the job.

Its bomblets sprayed fuel, atomized to mix

completely with the surrounding air. When the igniter went off, the blast was somewhere between a fire and a nuclear explosion. If the hatch *hadn't* resealed the moment before ignition, the pressure wave could've pulverized more than the contents of one cabin.

The Riva's hands wriggled. Four of the flatlined red holograms blipped upward as he fed thrust to selected jets. The starship lifted a trifle, though not as much as it had when the bunker buster went off.

Sergeant Bradley stepped into the cockpit. Kowacs turned with a smile to greet him. They'd survived thus far, and they were about to shake clear of ground zero as the prisoner played the ship with the skill of a concert pianist on a familiar scherzo.

The ship wasn't going anywhere serious with the airlock jammed open, but they could shift a couple kilometers and start hollering for recovery. A captured ship and a human prisoner who'd thought he could give orders to Weasels—that was enough for anybody, even the Headhunters.

Bradley was a man of average size who looked now like a giant as his left hand lifted The Riva from his seat and jerked his face into the muzzle of the shotgun. Bradley had killed often and expertly. There was utter cold fury in his face and voice as he whispered, "You son of a bitch. Why didn't you tell me? Why didn't—"

"Top," said Kowacs, rising to his feet and making very sure that his own weapon pointed to the ceiling. He'd seen Bradley like this before, but never about another human being. . . .

"—you *tell* me?" Bradley shouted as his gun rapped the prisoner's mouth to emphasize each syllable.

Sienkiewicz had followed the sergeant; her face bore a look of blank distaste that Kowacs couldn't fathom either.

The ship poised for a moment with no hand at its controls. When it lurched heavily to the ground, Bradley swayed and Kowacs managed to get between the field first and the prisoner who was the only chance any of them had of surviving more than the next few minutes.

"I got 'im, Top," Kowacs said in a tone of careless command, grabbing The Riva by the neck and detaching Bradley by virtue of his greater size and strength. "Let's go take a look, you."

He dragged the prisoner with him into the passageway, making sure without being obvious about it that his body was between the fellow and Bradley's shotgun.

Didn't guarantee the sergeant *wouldn't* shoot, of course; but there were damn few guarantees in this life.

The cabin door opened inward, which might've been how it withstood the explosion without being ripped off its hinges. Smoke and grit still roiled in the aftermath of the explosion.

Kowacs flipped down his visor and used its sonic imaging; the ultrasonic projection sources were on either side, and the read-out was on the inner surface of the faceshield. Neither was affected by the fact he'd forgotten to wipe the remains of the Weasel off the outside of the visor.

The cabin'd been occupied when the grenade went off, but Kowacs' nose had already told him that.

Five bodies, all human. They'd been huddled together under the bedding. That didn't save them, but it meant they were more or less recognizable after the blast. Two women—young, but adults; and three children, the youngest an infant.

Weapons would have survived the explosion—stood out against the background of shattered plastic and smoldering cloth. There hadn't been any weapons in the cabin.

"You son of bitch," Kowacs said in a soft, wondering voice, unaware that he was repeating Bradley's words. "Why did you do that? You knew, didn't you. . . ." The sentence trailed off without a question, and the sub-machine gun was pointing almost of its own accord.

"Why should I save the heir of Kavir bab-Wellin?" blurted the prisoner, spraying blood from lips broken by the sergeant's blows. "Kavir would have killed me! Didn't you see that? Just because I became The Riva over his father, he would have *killed* me!"

Somebody shot at the hull again. Either they were using a lighter weapon, or anything seemed mild after the bunker buster had crashed like a train wreck. Sienkiewicz eased to the airlock with her rifle ready, but she wouldn't fire until she had a real target.

"I'll . . . ," Bradley said in a choked voice. He pulled another grenade stick from his belt.

Kowacs was so calm that he could visualize the whole planet, nightside and day, shots and screams and the filthy white glare of explosions.

"No, Top," he said.

He was aware of every one of the ninety-seven Marines in his Headhunters, the living and the dead, even though only Bradley and Sienkiewicz were within range of his helmet's locator. He was walking back to the cockpit, carrying The Riva with him; ignoring the chance of a bullet nailing him as he stepped in front of the airlock—ignoring the burst Sienkiewicz ripped out at the target her light amplifier had showed her.

"Cap'n?" said the field first, suddenly more concerned than angry.

Kowacs dropped the prisoner into the chair out of which he'd been jerked.

"Fly us," he ordered flatly. Then he added, "Helmet. Project. Course to target. Out," and a glowing map hung in front of the ship's holographic controls, quivering when Kowacs' helmet quivered and moved the tiny projection head. The pentagonal air-defense site shone bright green against a mauve background.

"Fly us there. Land us in the middle of it with the airlock facing the pit in the center.'

The Riva's hands made the same initial gestures as before: raising thrust to alternate jets, making the holographic map shiver in wider arcs. He didn't speak.

"Sir, have, ah . . . ," Sergeant Bradley said. He was too good a soldier—and too good a friend—to let anger rule him when he saw his commanding officer in this unreadable mood. "Have our boys captured the place? Because otherwise, the missile batt'ries . . . ?"

He knew Kowacs hadn't gotten any report. Knew also there was no way in hell the One-Twenty-First was going to capture the hardened installation—not after they'd been scattered by the emergency drop and left without the belt-fed plasma weapons that could've taken apart the concrete walls.

The ship see-sawed free with a sucking noise from beneath her hull. All six thrust indicators shot upward. A streak of blue flashed as the vessel shook violently, but the hologram cleared.

They began to build forward speed. Air screamed past the open lock.

"Their computers'll identify us as friendly," Kowacs said.

His eyes were open, but they weren't focused on anything in particular. His left hand was on the prisoner's shoulder as if one friend with another. The muzzle of the sub-machine gun was socketed in The Riva's ear. "There'll be a lock-out to keep 'em from blasting friendlies, won't there, Riva old buddy?"

"There is, but they can override it," barked the prisoner nervously. He was too aware of the gun to turn toward the Headhunters as he spoke. "Look, I can take us to a safe place and you can summon your superiors. I'm very valuable, more valuable than you may dream."

"Naw, we gotta pull out what's left of a Jeffersonian assault company," Kowacs said calmly. "We'll do it fast. Weasels don't think about electronics when you surprise 'em."

"This is madness!" the pilot shouted. "They'll surely kill us all!" There were tears of desperation in his eyes, but his hands kept the ship along the course unreeling on the holographic map.

In two minutes, maybe three, they'd be there. No longer'n that.

"If we can't do it, nobody will," Kowacs said. "The Weasels'll finish 'em off, every damn one of 'em."

Light bloomed with dazzling immediacy a few kilometers behind the ship. The two Marines braced themselves; their prisoner squeezed lower in his acceleration pod.

The vessel pitched. Cabin pressure shot up momentarily as the pressure wave caught them and passed on to flatten trees in an expanding arc.

They were still under control.

Sienkiewicz stepped into the cockpit, moving carefully because of her size and the way the open airlock made the ship flutter in low-level flight. The empty tube of her plasma weapon, slung at buttocks height, dribbled a vaporous fairy-track of ionized metal behind her.

"I just take orders, Miklos," Sienkiewicz said, marking the words as a lie by using Kowacs' first name. "But it was them decidin' to do it their own way that got 'em where they are. I don't see why anybody else needs to die for some anarchist from Jefferson."

"Because it's our *job*, Sie!" Bradley snapped, his anger a sign that the big corporal spoke for at least part of his own mind as well.

"Two *karda* to your goal," whispered Kowacs' earphones, transforming The Riva's nervous chirps without translating the Khalian units into human ones.

"No," said Kowacs. "A job's not enough to die for."

He pulled the sub-machine gun from the grip of the Weasel he'd killed in the next pod. They'd need everything they had to give covering fire while the Jeffersonians scrambled aboard.

Bradley took the weapon from his captain. "Better range to the wall than a scattergun," he said.

"I want you to watch our pilot," Kowacs said.

Bradley dropped his shotgun into a patrol sling with its muzzle forward beneath his right arm. He smiled. "Naw, our buddy here knows what I'll toss into the cockpit if the ship starts acting funny before you tell 'im to move out. A bunker buster'll work just as good on his type as it does on little kids."

"Right," Kowacs said without emotion. "Let's move."

"We're Alliance troops," he went on as they filed down the passageway to their positions at the airlock. "So're the Jeffersonians, whatever they think about it. Maybe if we get this crew out, they'll tell their buddies back home that it's a big universe."

He took a deep breath, "If the Alliance don't stick together," he said, "somebody sure God's going to stick it to all of us. One at a time."

Deceleration stresses made the Headhunters sway. A stream of red tracers—Fleet standard, not Khalian—flicked from the ground and rang on the starship's hull.

Their target's broad concrete rampart slid beneath the airlock.

What Kowacs didn't say—what he didn't have to say—was that there'd always be men who acted for safety or comfort or personal pique, rather than for their society as a whole. The five burned corpses in the cabin behind them showed where that led.

It wasn't anywhere Miklos Kowacs and his troops were willing to go.

Not if it killed them.

# THE END
## A Story of The Fleet

The Red Shift Lounge was the sort of bar where people left their uniforms back in their billet, so the sergeant who entered wearing dress whites and a chest full of medal ribbons attracted the instant attention of the bartender and the half dozen customers.

The unit patch on the sergeant's left shoulder was a black shrunken head on a white field, encircled by the words 121ST MARINE REACTION COMPANY. The patch peeped out beneath a stole of weasel tails, trophies of ten or a dozen Khalians.

The Red Shift was part of the huge complex of Artificial Staging Area Zebra, where if you weren't military or a military dependant, you were worse. Everybody in the lounge this evening, including the bartender, was military: the two men in a booth were clearly officers; the two men and the woman drinking beer at a table were just as clearly enlisted; and the stocky fellow at the far end of bar could have been anything except a civilian.

But no uniforms meant no insignia, no questions about who had the right to go find a mattress with who . . . no salutes.

And none of the problems that occurred when somebody figured a couple hot landings gave him the *right* not to salute some rear-echelon officer.

But down-time etiquette didn't matter when the guy in uniform was a sergeant from the Headhunters, the unit that had ended the war between the Alliance of Planets and the Khalia.

The War between Civilization and Weasels.

"Whiskey," ordered the sergeant in a raspy, angry voice.

"I thought," said one of the officers in diffident but nonetheless clearly audible tones, "that the One-Twenty-First shipped out today on the *Dalriada* at eighteen hundred hours."

The clock behind the bartender showed 1837 in tasteful blue numerals that blended with the dado lighting.

"For debriefing on Earth," the officer continued.

"And the parades, of course," his companion added.

The sergeant leaned his back against the bar. Something metallic in his sleeve rang when his left arm touched the dense, walnut-grained plastic. "I couldn't stomach that," he said. "Wanna make something of it?"

"Another beer," said the stocky man at the other end of the bar. His voice was mushy. The bartender ignored him.

"No, I don't," said the officer. "I don't suppose I would even if I were on duty."

"Bartender," called his companion. "I'll pay for that whiskey. As a matter of fact, sergeant, would you like to—"

He paused. The first officer was already sliding out of the booth, carrying his drink. "Would you mind if we joined you?" his companion said, getting up and heading for the bar before he completed the question.

"Naw, I'm glad for the company," the sergeant said. "I just couldn't take—I mean, *peace* with the weasels? We had 'em where we wanted 'em, by the balls. We shoulda kept going till this—" he tugged at his weasel-tail stole "—was the only kinda weasel there was!"

"I'm proud to meet a member of the Headhunters," said the first officer. "My name's Howes—" he stuck out his hand "—and my friend here is, ah, Mr. Lewis."

Beyond any question, the two men were Commanders or even Captains Howes and Lewis when they were in uniform.

"Sergeant Oaklin Bradley," the Headhunter said, shaking hands with both officers. "Sorry if I got a little short . . . but 'cha know, it tears the guts outa a real fighting man to think that we're going to quit while there's still weasels alive."

The bartender put the whiskey on the bar. Bradley's back was to him. The bartender continued to hold the glass for fear the Headhunter would bump it over.

"You were there at the surrender, I suppose?" Howes said as he picked up the whiskey and gave it to Bradley.

The woman, an overweight 'blonde' in a tank top, got up from the table and made her way to the bar. She was dead drunk—but familiar enough with the condition to be able to function that way.

"Aw, Babs," said one of her companions.

Earlier, the trio at the table had been having a discussion in loud, drunken whispers. Just as Sergeant Bradley entered the lounge, Babs had mumblingly agreed to go down on both enlisted men in an equipment storage room near the Red Shift.

If her companions were unhappy about losing the entertainment they'd planned for the evening, it didn't prevent them from joining her and the two officers in the semicircle around the uniformed hero at the bar.

"Oh, yeah," Bradley said. "I was there, all right." He'd waited to speak until chairlegs had stopped scraping and everyone was close enough to hear easily. "We landed right in the middle of the weasel Presidential Palace or whatever. . . ."

"High Council Chambers," Lewis murmured.

"Yes, yes, I'd heard that," Howes said. His eyes were greedy as they rested on Bradley's fringe of weasel tails. "The Khalians worship strength, so just reaching their capital put the Alliance on top of their dominance pyramid."

The man at the end of the bar stared into his empty mug, turning it slowly and carefully as if to make sense of his distorted reflection in the bottom.

"We killed so many of 'em you could float a battleship in the blood," Bradley said, licking his lips. "Never felt so good about anything in my life. We blew our way into the very fucking center of the place, caught all the weasel brass with their pants down . . . and Cap'n Kowacs, he said we had to let 'em surrender instead of burning 'em all the way we shoulda done."

Bradley tossed down his liquor in a quick, angry motion, then slapped the empty glass on the bar. Babs shifted closer so that one of her heavy breasts lay against the Headhunter's biceps.

"Well, it did end the war," Lewis said, examining his fingernails and looking vaguely embarrassed for disagreeing with the hero.

"*That* part of the war!" Howes retorted sharply. "There's still whoever it was behind the Khalians to begin with."

The bartender refilled the whiskey glass.

*The Headhunter at the bar of the Red Shift Lounge remembered. . . .*

In the belly of Dropship K435, Captain Miklos Kowacs squinted to focus on the image of their target. His holographic display stayed rock-steady as they dived toward the huge Khalian complex, but Kowacs' own eyes and brain vibrated like dessert gelatine.

Speed through an atmosphere meant turbulence, and the lord knew that to survive, the Headhunters were going to need speed as well as electronics that spoofed the Identification: Friend or Foe signal from the weasel fortress.

Every second Marine in the three line platoons carried a man-portable rocket launcher. 'Man-portable' because men were carrying them, not because they were light or handy. Most of the Marines who didn't have launchers lugged three-packs of reloads.

The rockets were to disable the missile launchers of the Khalian base. Even when that job was done, the Headhunters wouldn't have to go underground after the weasels: three of the Marines were strapped under 30-kilo tanks of DPD gas—

Which was designed to sink through the tunnels of a Khalian burrow and kill every living thing that breathed it.

There'd been plenty of room aboard the Attack Transport *Dalriada*, the K435's mothership, but the Headhuters were over-equipped to fit comfortably onto the dropship itself. Marines squatted shoulder to shoulder, bumping one another and cursing bitterly. . . .

Knowing, among other things, that the weight and bulk of the rockets which the mission required meant that they'd had to leave behind the body armor which they'd otherwise have been wearing during an assault like this.

Of course personal armor wouldn't matter a damn if the ship bit the big one while they were all aboard her.

The units aboard the *Dalriada*'s other seven dropships had normal missions: land on the fringe of a defended area and attack. The 121st was different. Last time out, the Headhunters had captured a Khalian courier vessel; now the whole company was shoehorned into a secret weapon that pretended to *be* a weasel ship, telling the target not to fire on them as they raced down to cut Khalian throats.

There were various ways the local weasels could configure their IFF. Faint lines across Kowacs' hologram display recorded the burning tracks of the first two drones sent ahead of K435. At the third try, the fortress hadn't fired, so Operations was betting that K435 could get in untouched if it sent the same IFF response as that last drone.

Operations bet a single hundred-Marine chip. The Headhunters were betting their lives.

" . . . seconds to touchdown!" the flight deck warned. A break in transmission erased the figure, but if they were *seconds* close, K435 was well within the defended envelope.

"Wait for it!" bellowed Sergeant Bradley over the unit frequency as he saw inexperienced troopers rise to jump out before the dropship landed.

No missile explosion, no hammering flares from autoloading plasma weapons. They were all going to live—

Until the weasel ground personnel got done with them. That was fine. Weasels were what the Headhunters had come to meet.

Too many new Marines on this drop. There'd been too fucking many casualties in the Bullseye operation. . . .

Kowacs felt a minuscule lift in K435's bow as the

shock of the vessel's approach was reflected from the ground. An instant later, the braking motors fired at full thrust and hammered the rows of squatting Headhunters down against the deck plating.

"*Now!*" Kowacs, Bradley, and all four platoon leaders shouted as explosive bolts blew away the dropship's hatches and the 121$^{st}$ Marine Reaction Company, the Headhunters, lurched into action.

The world was bright and hot and smelled like brown flames.

An orbital-defense missile roared up from its launcher as the Marines shook themselves out onto the flat roof of the fortress. The sound of the three-tonne missile going supersonic just above the launch tube was ear-splitting.

A Headhunter fired her hand-held rocket launcher while she was still aboard K435. Backblast made that a dangerous trick—but this wasn't a desk job, and starting to shoot instantly was a pretty good response to the shock of landing and the missile launch.

The weasel missile tube was built into the fabric of the fortress. The small Marine round guided for the center of the opening, then fired a self-forging fragment straight down the tube's throat. Even if the armor-piercer didn't penetrate the launcher cap while the next anti-orbital round was being loaded, it was almost certain to jam the cap in place and prevent the weasels from using that tube again.

The weasel fortress was a jumble of huge flat boxes, with point-defense plasma weapons inset at each corner and heavy missile batteries buried deep in their cores. K435 was supposed to have landed on the highest of the twenty to twenty-five cast-concrete prisms, but that hadn't worked out: a box to the west overlooked the one on which the Headhunters were deploying, and the weasel plasma guns could depress at any instant to sweep the whole company to a glowing memory.

"Delta, check 220," Kowacs ordered his Weapons Platoon. His helmet's artificial intelligence put him at the top of the pyramid of lieutenants assigning sectors and sergeants high-lighting specific targets for the Marines of their squad. "Clear the high—"

There was a deafening crash and a blast of static— a plasma discharge radiated all across the radio-frequency spectrum.

Corporal Sienkiewicz stood beside Kowacs because her strength and ruthlessness made her the best body-guard he could find in a company of strong, ruthless Marines. She'd just fired her hand-carried plasma weapon, a heavy tube that looked delicate against her husky two-meter frame.

A Khalian gun position vanished; then the whole top edge of the concrete prism stuttered with dazzling plasma bursts and long tendrils of quicklime burned from the concrete and spewing away in white-hot tendrils. Delta had its own belt-fed plasma weapons set up on tripods, and they didn't need Kowacs' orders to tell them it was everybody's ass if they didn't nail the close-in defenses before some weasel brought the guns under manual control.

The noise of plasma weapons, rockets and rocket warheads made it hard for Kowacs to think, much less hear any of the message traffic on his earphones. Although Kowacs' helmet damped the worst of the racket, shockwaves slapped the skin of his face and hands like huge, hot raindrops.

Squad leaders with echo-location gear were using the noise to map all the surfaces of the Khalian for-tress. When holographic images on a sergeant's helmet visor indicated a missile tube in his squad's sector, he relayed the target to a Marine with a rocket launcher.

The Headhunters' top-attack rockets ripped and snapped all across the concrete jumble. Occasionally a blast of smoky yellow flame indicated that one of the big Khalian missiles had blown up within its launcher.

But the Khalians weren't shooting any more.

Kowacs turned around so that his unaided eyes could confirm what his visor display already insisted. Through the skeletal ribs of K435 and across the fortress, as well as on his side of the landing vessel, nobody was firing except Kowacs' own Marines.

Missiles didn't rise to engage the ships in orbit. Plasma weapons didn't chew themselves new firing slits so that they could bear on the Marine landing force. . . .

Unbefuckinglievable.

There was a momentary lull in the gunfire as the rest of the Headhunters realized the same thing. Then Sergeant Bradley screamed, "Door opening!" on the primary unit push, and three rockets streaked simultaneously toward the northwest corner of the block on which the Marines had landed.

The leaves of the hidden steel trapdoor rang like bells as they flew apart under the impact of the self-forging fragments. There were swatches of fur in the blast debris also.

"Double it!" Kowacs ordered, but there were already three more rockets in the air and three more sharp explosions over the sally-port, chopping weasels into cat's meat before their counterattack had time to get under way.

Kowacs was more agile than most of the Headhunters because he was burdened only with his personal weapons. He began running toward the shattered trapdoor, shouting, "Gas carriers to me!"

You'd've thought the rocket blasts would've kept the weasels down for at least a few minutes. More furry, yellow-fanged heads popped out of the sally-port before Kowacs got out the last syllable of his order.

He shot as he ran, spraying the area with a dozen ricochets for every bullet that counted—but ammo was cheap, and at least a dozen other Headhunters were firing along with their captain. The vivid white fire-ball of a plasma burst hid the target momentarily; Sie had saved back one charge for an emergency like this.

*The weasels had been waving something.*

More weasels rose out of the half-molten pit where the trapdoor had been. They vanished in a maelstrom of bullets and grenade fragments.

Kowacs paused twenty meters from the sally-port to reload. A Marine with one of the green-painted gas cylinders caught up with him. Sienkiewicz was giving the fellow a hand with his load.

More weasels leaped from the fortress. Kowacs aimed but didn't fire. Other Marines ripped the fresh targets into gobbets of bloody flesh.

*The weasels were waving white flags.*

"Cease fire!" Kowacs shouted. Still more weasels were coming up. "Cease fire!"

There were ten or a dozen unarmed Khalians in the next group, all of them waving white flags. Some were females.

A Headhunter fired his assault rifle. One of the tripod-mounted plasma weapons vaporized the weasels with three bolts.

More weasels came up from the crater.

*"Cease fire!"* Kowacs screamed as he ran forward, facing his Marines as he put his body between them and the Khalians.

Facing most of his Marines, because Sie was on one side of him and Sergeant Bradley was on the other. Both non-coms were cursing their captain, but not so bitterly as Kowacs cursed himself and the command responsibility that made him do *this* when he should've been shooting weasels.

Nobody shot. Nobody spoke. Kowacs' panting breath roared behind the constriction of his visor.

Kowacs slowly turned to face the weasels again. His lungs were burning. He flipped his visor out of the way, though that left him without the heads-up display if he needed it.

There were twelve Khalians. They stood on the lip of the crater, waving their small square flags. Each weasel had its nose pointed high in the air, baring the white fur of its throat. Their muzzles were wrinkling, but Kowacs didn't know whether that was a facial expression or just a reaction to the stench of blast residues and death.

Miklos Kowacs had killed hundreds of weasels during his Marine career. He'd never before spent this long looking at a living one.

"Helmet," he said, "translate Khalian."

He splayed the fingers of his left hand, the hand that didn't hold a fully-loaded automatic rifle, in the direction of the weasels. "You!" he said. "Which of you's the leader?" as the speaker on the top of his helmet barked the question in weaseltalk.

None of the Khalians wore clothing or ornamentation. The one on the left end of the line lowered his nose so that he could see ahead of himself, stepped forward, and chattered something that the translation program in Kowacs' helmet rendered as, "Are you Fleet Marines? You *are* Fleet Marines."

"Answer me!" Kowacs shouted. "Are you in charge?" The concrete seemed to ripple. It was solid, but Nick Kowacs wasn't solid just now. . . .

"We wish to surrender to Fleet Marines," the weasel said. He was about a meter forty tall, mid-breastbone level to Kowacs. "Are you Fleet Marines?"

"Goddam," Bradley whispered, his scarred left hand wringing the foregrip of the shotgun he pointed.

"You bet," said Nick Kowacs. His brain was echoing with screams and other memories and screams. "We're the Headhunters, we're the best." *Weasels never surrendered.* "You want to surrender this whole fortress?"

"That too," said the weasel. "You are fighters whom we respect. Come below with us to receive our surrender, Fleet Marine."

Sienkiewicz laughed.

"Bullshit," Kowacs said flatly. "You tell your people to come on out, one at a time, and we'll see about surrender."

"Please," barked the weasel. "You must come into the Council Chamber to take our surrender."

"Bullshit!" Kowacs repeated.

He risked a glance over his shoulder. The three Marines with gas cylinders, kneeling under the weight of their loads, were in the front rank of waiting troops. "Look, get your people up here, or—"

The Khalians had no equipment, but they had been born with tusks and sharp, retractile claws. "Then I have failed," he speaker of the group said. He raised a forepaw and tore his own throat out.

"—almighty!" Bradley blurted as Kowacs choked off his own inarticulate grunt. The weasel thrashed on the seared concrete, gushing arterial blood from four deep slashes. The furry corpse was still twitching when a second Khalian stepped forward.

"Come into the Council Chamber with us, Fleet Marine," the new envoy said. "Only from there can the surrender be broadcast to all."

"No!" shouted Sergeant Bradley. The weasel raised his paw; sunlight winked on the clawtips.

"Yes!" shouted Captain Miklos Kowacs, feeling the ground shiver like the dying weasel before him.

"Ah, sir?" said one of the Marines carrying a gas cylinder. "*All* of us?"

Lieutenant Mandricard, the senior platoon leader, had faced his platoon around to cover the Headhunters' rear while the rest of the Marines were shooting weasel pop-ups. He glanced over his shoulder at the company commander.

Kowacs pointed a finger at Mandricard and said over the general push, "Gamma Six, you're in charge here until I get back, right? If that's not in—" *how long?* "—six zero minutes, finish the job."

He nodded toward the gas cylinders. And smiled like a cobra.

"Sir," said Bradley, "we can't do this."

Kowacs looked at him. "I gotta do it, Top," he said.

"Hold one," said Corporal Sienkiewicz. She'd unharnessed one of the gas carriers and was now—

Godalmighty! She was molding a wad of contact-fuzed blasting putty onto the tank of gas. If she dropped the heavy cylinder, the charge would rupture it and flood the whole area with DPD!

"Right," Sienkiewicz said as she examined her handiwork. "Now we're ready to go down."

Bradley swore coldly, checked his shotgun, and said, "Yeah, let's get this dumb-ass shit over with."

Kowacs hadn't told Sie and the sergeant to accompany him; but he knew they wouldn't accept an order to stay behind. "G—" he said to the Khalian envoy. His voice broke. "Go on, then."

The eleven surviving weasels scrambled into the blasted entrance. Kowacs strode after them.

"I'll lead," said Sienkiewicz.

"Like hell you will," Kowacs snapped as his rigid arm blocked his bodyguard's attempt to push past.

The entrance was a stinking pit. A crowd of weasels, all of them carrying flags, filled the floor below.

The metal staircase had been destroyed by the first volley of rockets; since then, the Khalians had been scrambling up wooden poles to reach the roof and their deaths.

Shattered poles, corpses, and charred white scraps of cloth covered the concrete floor on which living weasels pushed and chittered in a cacaphony that the translation program couldn't handle.

"Back!" barked the Khalian envoy, raising both his clawed forepaws in symbolic threat. "To the Council Chamber!"

The Khalian mob surged down the hallway like a shockwave travelling through a viscous fluid. There were lights some distance away, but the Headhunters' blasts had destroyed the nearest fixtures.

Kowacs looked down, grimaced, and dropped. His boots skidded on the slimy floor.

"Watch—" he said to his companions, but Sie was already swinging herself down. Her right hand gripped the edge of the roof while her left arm cradled her lethal burden like a baby.

Bradley must've thought the same thing, because he said, "Hope the little bastid don't burp," as he followed into the Khalian fortress.

"Come this way!" ordered the envoy as though he and not the Headhunters were armed. The weasels' demonstrated willingness to die made them very hard to control.

Pretty much the same was true of Marines in the reaction companies too, of course.

The ceiling was so low that Kowacs, stocky rather than tall, brushed his helmet until he hunched over. He expected to hear Sie cursing, but the big woman didn't say a word. She was probably concentrating so that she didn't drop the bomb in her arms and end all this before—

Before it was supposed to end. Not necessarily different from the way it was going to end anyway.

The hallway curved. For a moment, Kowacs' helmet picked up the crisp commands of Gamma Six as Mandricard put the Headhunters in as much of a posture of defense as the featureless roof permitted. Reception faded to static, then nothing at all.

They came to a bank of wire-fronted elevators and a crowd of waiting Khalians. "Come with me," the envoy said as he stepped into the nearest cage.

The cage was small and low; three humans in battlegear and a Khalian filled it uncomfortably. As the elevator started the descend, Kowacs saw a horde of weasels pushing into the remaining cages.

Bradley began to shake. The muzzle of his gun wobbled through tight arcs. "It stinks . . . ," he mumbled. "It *stinks*."

He was right, of course. The air circulating in the Khalian burrow smelled of Khalians, and that was a stench worse than death to a man like Bradley, who'd seen what the weasels left of his little daughter on Tanjug . . .

Or to a man like Nick Kowacs, whose family had been on Gravely when the weasels landed there.

Kowacs shivered. "Top!" he said harshly. "Snap out of it. You're not going claustrophobic on me now."

Bradley took off his helmet and squeezed his bald, scarred scalp with his left hand. His eyes were shut. "It's not the fuckin' tunnels," he said. "Not the tunnels. All these weasels. . . . I just, I wanna—"

Bradley's fingertips left broad white dimples on his skin when he took his hand away. The weasel envoy watched the sergeant with bright black eyes.

No one spoke again until the cage stopped and the Khalian repeated, "Come with me," as his paw clashed the door open.

Kowacs couldn't guess how deep in the earth they were now. There was a sea of fur and tusks and chittering weasel voices outside the elevator. Many of this crowd wore ornaments of brass and leather, but Kowacs didn't see any weapons.

He stepped out behind the envoy, watching the passageway clear before them and wondering if the Khalians would close in again behind the three humans.

It didn't matter. They were *in* this, he and Top and Sie, as far as they could get already. At least the tunnel ceiling was high enough for humans, even the corporal with her burden of death.

The envoy led through an arched doorway. The chamber within was huge even by human standards.

The chamber was full of Khalians.

The smell and sound and visual impact stopped Kowacs in his tracks. One of his men bumped him from behind.

Kowacs closed his eyes and rubbed them hard with the back of his left wrist. That made it worse. When he didn't see the room filled with weasels, his mind quivered over the memory of his mother, her gnawed corpse thick with the musk of the furry monsters that had—

"*No!*" Kowacs screamed. The distant walls gave back the echo, cushioned by the soft susurrus of breathing mammals. There was no other sound.

He opened his eyes.

A group of Khalians was coming forward from the crowd. There were twenty or more of them. They wore jewelry and robes patterned with soft, natural colors.

They were very old. Some hobbled, and even those weasels who were able to walk erect had grizzled fur and noticeably worn tusks.

*Weasels don't wear clothing. . . .*

There was a great sigh from the assembled company.

The aged Khalians gripped their robes and tore them
apart in ragged, ritual motions. Some of them were
mewling; their facial fur was wet with tears. They fell
to the floor and began writhing forward, their throats
and bellies bared to the Marines.

The weasel in the center of the groveling line gave
a series of broken, high-pitched barks. The voice of
Kowacs' helmet translated, "Khalia surrenders to you,
warriors of the Fleet Marines. We are your subjects,
your slaves, to use as you wish."

*Come to the Council Chamber, the weasel envoy had
said. The High Council of Khalia. They weren't surrendering this fortress—*

"Khalia surrenders—"

*They were surrendering the whole Khalian race!*

"—to you, warriors of the—"

Bradley's shotgun crashed. Its airfoil charge was
designed to spread widely, even at point-blank range.
The load sawed through the chest of the Khalian
speaker like so many miniature razors. The weasel's
tusked jaws continued to open and close, but nothing
came out except drops of bloody spittle.

The aged Khalian nearest the dead one began to
chant, "We are your slaves, warriors of the Fleet
Marines. Use us as you will. We—"

Sergeant Bradley's face was that of a grinning skull.
He'd dropped his helmet in the elevator cage. There
was no reason left behind his glazing eyes. "You'll die,"
he said in a sing-song voice, "you'll all—"

He fired again. His charge splashed the skull of the
corpse.

"—die, every fucking—"

Kowacs gripped the shotgun barrel with his left
hand. The metal burned him. He couldn't lift the
muzzle against Bradley's hysterical grip.

"Put it down, Top!" he ordered.

The moaning of the crowd was louder. Waves of Khalian musk blended sickeningly with powder smoke.

"—are your subjects, your—"

Bradley fired into the dead weasel's groin.

"—weasel in the fucking uni—"

"*Down!*" Kowacs screamed and touched the muzzle of his assault rifle to Bradley's temple where a wisp of hair grew in the midst of pink scar tissue. Kowacs' vision tunnelled down to nothing but the hairs and the black metal and the flash that would—

There was a hollow *thunk*.

Bradley released the shotgun as he fell forward unconscious. Sienkiewicz looked at her captain with empty eyes. There was a splotch of blood on the green metal of the gas cylinder and a matching pressure cut on the back of Bradley's skull, but the sergeant would be all right as soon as he came around. . . .

"On behalf of the Alliance of Planets," Kowacs said in a quavering voice, "I accept your surrender."

He covered his eyes with his broad left hand. He shouldn't have done that, because that made him remember his mother and he began to vomit.


"Hey, Sergeant Bradley," said one of the enlisted men in the Red Shift Lounge, "let *me* get 'cha the next drink."

The man in whites toyed with his stole of Khalian tails. "We shoulda kept killin' 'em till everybody had a weasel-skin blanket!" he said. "We shoulda—"

Somebody came into the bar; somebody so big that even Sergeant Bradley looked up.

The newcomer, a woman in coveralls, squinted into the dim lounge. She glanced at the group around Bradley, then ignored them. When she saw the stocky man at the far end of the bar, she strode forward.

The sudden smile made her almost attractive.

Bradley's hand closed on his fresh drink. "If there's still one weasel left in the universe," he said, "that's too many."

"Sar'nt?" murmured the drunken blond. "Whyn't you'n me, we go somewhur?"

"Hey, cap'n," said the big woman to the man at the far end of the bar. "Good t' see you."

"Go 'way, Sie," he replied, staring into his mug. "You'll lose your rank if you miss lift."

"Fuck my rank," she said. Everyone in the lounge was looking at them. "Besides," she added, "Commander Goldstein says the *Dalriada*'s engines 're broke down till we get you aboard. Sir."

She laid the man's right arm over her shoulders, gripped him around the back with her left hand, and lifted him in a packstrap carry. He was even bigger than he'd looked hunched over the bar, a blocky anvil of a man with no-colored eyes.

"You're always getting me outa places I shouldn't a got into, Sie," the man said.

His legs moved as the woman maneuvered him toward the door, but she supported almost all of his weight. "Worse places 'n this, sir," she replied.

"They weren't worse than now, Sie," he said. "Trust me."

As the pair of them started to shuffle past the group near the door, the woman's eyes focused on the uniformed man. She stopped. The man she held braced himself with a lopsided grin and said, "I'm okay now, Sie."

"Who the hell are you?" the big woman demanded of the man wearing the Headhunter uniform.

"What's it to you?" he snarled back.

"This is Sergeant Bradley of the 121$^{st}$ Marine Reaction Company," said one of the enlisted men, drunkenly pompous.

"Like hell he is," the big woman said. Her arms were free now. "Top's searching bars down the Strip the other direction, lookin' for Cap'n Kowacs, here."

Kowacs continued to grin. His face was as terrible as a hedge of bayonets.

The group around 'Sergeant Bradley' backed away as though he had suddenly grown an extra head.

The imposter in uniform tried to run. Sienkiewicz grabbed him by the throat from behind. "Thought you'd be a big hero, did ya? Some clerk from Personnel, gonna be a hero now it's safe t' be a hero?"

The imposter twisted around. A quick-release catch *snicked*, shooting the knife from his left sleeve into his palm.

Sienkiewicz closed her right hand over the imposter's grip on his knife hilt. She twisted. Bones broke.

The knife came away from the hand of her keening victim. She slammed the point down into the bar top, driving it deep into the dense plastic before she twisted again and snapped the blade.

"Big hero . . . ," she whispered. Her expression was that of nothing human. She gripped the weasel-tail stole and said, "How much did these cost 'cha, hero?" as she tore the trophies away and flung them behind her.

The bartender's finger was poised over the red emergency button that would summon the Shore Police. He didn't push it.

Sienkiewicz' grip on the imposter's throat was turning the man's face purple. Nobody moved to stop her. Her right hand stripped off the uniform sleeve with its Headhunter insignia and tossed it after the stole.

Then, still using the power of only one arm, she hurled the imposter into a back booth also. Bone and plastic cracked at the heavy impact.

"I'm okay, Sie," Kowacs repeated, but he let his corporal put her arm back around him again.

As the two Headhunters left the Red Shift Lounge, one of the enlisted men muttered, "You lying scum," and drove his heel into the ribs of the fallen man.

Kowacs found that if he concentrated, he could walk almost normally. There was a lot of traffic this close to the docking hub, but other pedestrians made way good-naturedly for the pair of big Marines.

"Sie," Kowacs said, "I used to daydream, you know? Me an old man, my beard down t' my belt, y'know? And this little girl, she comes up t' me and she says, 'Great Grandaddy, what did you do in the Weasel War?'"

"Careful of the bollard here, sir," Sienkiewicz murmured. "There'll be a shuttle in a couple of minutes."

"And I'd say to her," Kowacs continued, his voice rising, "'Well, sweetheart—I survived.'"

He started to sob. Sienkiewicz held him tightly. The people already standing at the shuttle point edged away.

"But I never thought I *would* survive, Sie!" Kowacs blubbered. "I never thought I would!"

"Easy, sir. We'll get you bunked down in a minute."

Kowacs looked up, his red eyes meeting Sienkiewicz' concern. "And you know the funny thing, Sie," he said. "I don't think I did survive."

"Easy. . . ."

"Without weasels t' kill, I don't think there's any Nick Kowacs alive."

# SMASH AND GRAB
## A Story of The Fleet

The receptionist facing Captain Kowacs wasn't armed, but there was enough weaponry built into her desk to stop a destroyer. Her face was neutral, composed. If she was supposed to do anything besides watch the Marine captain, she was fucking off.

This was like going through a series of airlocks; but what was on the far end of *these* doors was a lot more dangerous than vacuum.

The inner door opened to admit a guide/escort—Kowacs' third guide since hand-delivered orders jerked him out the barracks assigned to the 121st Marine Reaction Company.

*His* company, his Headhunters. And would to God he was back with them now.

"If you'll come this way, please, Captain Kowacs," said the guide.

This one was a young human male, built like a weightlifter and probably trained as well as a man could

be trained. Kowacs figured he could take the kid if it
came to that . . . but only because training by itself
wasn't enough against the instant ruthlessness you
acquired if you survived your first month in a reaction company.

Captain Miklos Kowacs had survived seven years.
If that wasn't a record, it was damn close to one.

Kowacs was stocky and powerful, with cold eyes and
black hair that curled on the backs of his wrists and
hands. The Fleet's reconstructive surgeons were art-
ists, and they had a great deal of practice. Kowacs was
without scars.

On his body.

"Turn left at the corridor, please, sir," said the
escort. He was walking a pace behind and a pace
to Kowacs' side. Like a well-trained dog . . . which
was about half true: if the kid had been *only*
muscle, he wouldn't have been here.

*Here* was Building 93 of the Administration Annex,
Fleet Headquarters, Port Tau Ceti. That was the only
thing Kowacs knew for sure about the place.

Except that he was sure he'd rather be anywhere
else.

Building 93 didn't house clerical overflow. The doors
were like bank vaults; the electronic security system
was up to the standards of the code section aboard a
Command-and-Control vessel; the personnel were cool,
competent, and as tight as Nick Kowacs' asshole during an insertion.

"Here, please, sir," said the escort, stopping beside
a blank door. He gestured. "This is as far as I go."

Kowacs looked at him. He wouldn't mind seeing how
the kid shaped up in the Headhunters. Good material,
better than most of the replacements they got . . . and
Marine Reaction Companies always needed replacements.

He shivered. They'd needed replacements while there were Weasels to fight. Not any more.

"Have a good life, kid," Kowacs said as the blue highlights in the doorpanel suddenly spelled SPECIAL PROJECTS/TEITELBAUM with the three-stars-in-circle of a vice admiral.

The door opened.

Nick Kowacs was painfully aware that he was wearing the pair of worn fatigues he hadn't had time to change when the messenger rousted him; also that the best uniform he owned wasn't up to meeting a vice admiral. He grimaced, braced himself, and strode through the doorway.

The door closed behind him. The man at the desk of the lushly-appointed office wore civilian clothes. He was in his mid-40s, bigger than Kowacs and in good physical shape.

Kowacs recognized him. The man wasn't a vice admiral. His name was Grant, and he was much worse.

*I thought he was dead!*

The man behind the desk looked up from the hologram projector his blunt, powerful fingers toyed with.

He grinned. "What's the matter, Kowacs?" he said. "You look like you've seen a ghost."

Grant gestured. "Pull a chair closer and sit down," he said. He grinned again. There was no more humor in the expression the second time. "Hoped I was dead, huh?"

Kowacs shrugged.

The chair along the back wall had firm, user-accommodating cushions that would shape to his body without collapsing when he sat in them. The one Kowacs picked slid easily as his touch reversed magnets to repel a similar set in the floor.

*Keep cool, learn what hole you're in, and get the hell out.*

Nobody likes to talk to the Gestapo.

Though if it came to that, reaction company Marines didn't have a lot of friends either.

Assuming the office's owner was the vice admiral in the holographic portrait filling the back wall, Teitelbaum was a woman. In the present display, she wore a dress uniform and was posed against a galactic panorama, but there were probably other views loaded into the system: Teitelbaum and her family; Teitelbaum with political dignitaries; Teitelbaum as a young ensign performing heroically in combat.

Special Projects.

"You work for Admiral Teitelbaum, then?" Kowacs said as he seated himself carefully.

"I'm borrowing her office," Grant said without apparent interest. He spun the desk projector so that the keyboard faced Kowacs, then tossed the Marine a holographic chip. "Go on," he ordered. "Play it."

Kowacs inserted the chip into the reader. His face was blank, and his mind was almost empty. He hadn't really felt anything since the Weasels surrendered.

The message was date-slugged three days before, while the $121^{st}$ was still on the way to Port Tau Ceti. An official head-and-shoulders view of Kowacs popped into the air beneath the date, then vanished into another burst of glowing letters:

FROM: BUPERS/M32/110173/Sec21(Hum)/SPL
TO: KOWACS, Miklos Alexievitch
SUBJECT: Promotion to MAJOR
*Effective from this date. . . .*

Kowacs looked across the desk at the civilian. The air between them continued to spell out bureaucratese in green letters.

Grant's face was too controlled to give any sign that

he had expected the Marine to react visibly. "Here," he said. "These are on me."

He tossed Kowacs a pair of major's collar tabs: hollow black triangles that would be filled for a lieutenant colonel. "Battledress style," Grant continued. "Since it doesn't seem that you have much use for dress uniforms."

"I don't have much use for any uniforms," said Nick Kowacs as his tongue made the decision his mind had wavered over since the day he and his Headhunters had taken the surrender of the Khalian Grand Council. "I'm getting out."

Grant laughed. "The hell you are, mister," he said. "You're too valuable to the war effort."

The data chip was reporting Kowacs' service record to present. Part of the Marine's mind was amazed at the length of the listing of his awards and citations. He supposed he'd known about the decorations when he received them, but they really didn't matter.

His family had mattered before the Khalians massacred them.

And it mattered that the 121st Marine Reaction Company had cut the tails off more dead Weasels than any other unit of comparable size.

"Fuck you," said Nick Kowacs distinctly. "The war's over."

"Don't you believe it, mister," Grant replied. There was only the slightest narrowing of his cold blue eyes to indicate that he'd heard *everything* the Marine had said. "We've got a real enemy, now—the Syndicate. The humans who've been using the Weasels for their cannon fodder. The people *behind* the whole war."

Kowacs shut off the projector. The list was reminding him of too much that he usually managed to forget while he was awake: hot landings . . . civilians that neither god nor the Headhunters had been able to save

from the Khalians . . . Marines who hadn't survived—
or worse, who mostly hadn't survived.

"I don't . . . ," Kowacs muttered.

"We'll be raising mixed units of our best and the
Khalians' best to go after the Syndicate," Grant said.
"You'll want to be in on the real kill, won't you?"

From his grin, Grant knew *exactly* how Kowacs
would feel about the suggestion of working with
Weasels. It was the civilian's response to being told to
fuck himself.

"Besides," Grant went on, "What would *you* do as
a civilian, Kowacs?"

"I'll find something," said the Marine as he stood
up. "Look, I'm leaving now."

"Siddown, mister!" Grant said in a tone that Kowacs
recognized because he'd used it often enough himself;
the tone that meant the order would be obeyed or the
next sound would be a shot.

Kowacs met Grant's eyes; and smiled; and sat in the
chair again.

"Let's say that you're here because of your special
knowledge," the civilian said. Grant could control his
voice and his breathing, but Kowacs saw the quick
flutter of the arteries in the big man's throat. "If you
know who I am, then you know too much to think you
can just hang up your uniform any time you please."

*But I wouldn't have to work much harder to be
buried in that uniform.*

Aloud, Kowacs said, "You didn't call me in here to
promote me."

"You got *that* right," Grant said, his voice dripping
with the disdain of a man who doesn't wear a uniform
for a man who does. "We've got a job for you and your
Headhunters."

Kowacs laughed. "What's the matter? Run out of
your own brand of sewage workers?"

"Don't push," said the civilian quietly.

After a moment, Grant resumed, "This is right up your alley, Kowacs. The Syndicate used cut-out bases in all their dealings with the Khalians, so the Weasels don't have the locations of any of the Syndicate home worlds. But we think we've got the coordinates of a Syndicate base—so you're going to grab prisoners and navigational data there before the Syndicate realizes they're at risk."

Kowacs frowned as he considered what he'd just been told. *There had to be a catch. . . .*

"All right," he said. "What's the catch?"

Grant shrugged. "No catch," he said.

"If there wasn't more to this job than you're telling me," Kowacs said, unsure whether he was angry, frustrated, or simply confused, "we wouldn't be briefed by the fucking Eight-Ball Command, *mister*. Is this some kinda suicide mission, is that what you're telling me?"

*But that couldn't be right either. Normal mission-control channels hadn't shown any hesitation about sending the Headhunters on suicide missions before.*

*And the Headhunters hadn't hesitated to go.*

"Nothing like that," said Grant. "It's safer than R&R—you won't even risk catching clap."

Kowacs waited.

"You see," Grant continued, "you're going to use A-Potential equipment for the insertion. All points are the same point to the device you'll ride in. The Syndicate won't have any warning."

*That was the fucking catch, all right.*

The 92nd MRC had tested A-Pot equipment on Bull's-eye. Sometimes it worked, sometimes it got them dead. *Dead* wasn't the scary part of the stories Toby English and his Marines had brought back from that operation, though. . . .

"I . . . ," Kowacs said. ". . . don't know how the guys are going to react to this. Seems to me that maybe a unit that's already got experience with—"

"Wrong, Major Kowacs," Grant said. He didn't shout because he didn't have to shout. "You know exactly how you and your company are going to react. Because it's orders, and everybody knows what happens to cowards who disobey orders in wartime."

For a moment, Kowacs couldn't see anything for the red film in front of his eyes. When his vision cleared, he noticed that one of the civilian's hands had dropped out of sight behind the desk.

There was no need for that. The room's automatic defensive system which would trip faster than a human could if somebody tried to attack the man in Admiral Teitelbaum's chair; and anyway, Nick Kowacs wasn't out of control, was *never* out of control. . . .

"As a matter of fact," Grant said in what was almost a conciliatory tone, "the Ninety-Second was the original choice for the mission, but they're still in transit. They've been switched with the back-up company. Yours."

Kowacs swallowed. "You got the coordinates from a captured Syndicate ship?" he said, sure that he'd be told that sources and methods were none of his business. He had to change the subject, or—or else.

Grant smiled again. "From the mind of a prisoner. Before he died. The prisoner you captured on Bull's-eye, as a matter of fact."

"From his *mind*?" the Marine repeated. "How did you do that?"

"Pray you never learn, mister," Grant said.

"Right," said Kowacs as he got to his feet. He wondered whether his escort was still waiting outside the door. Probably. "I'll alert the company. I assume formal briefing materials are—"

Grant nodded. "Already downloaded to the One-Twenty-First data bank," he said. "I'll take the lock off them immediately."

"Right," Kowacs repeated. He reached for the latchplate of the door, then changed his mind and turned.

"Just one thing, *Mister* Grant," he said. "My Headhunters aren't cowards. If you think they are, then come on a drop with us some day."

"Oh, I will," the civilian said with the same mocking, terrible smile as before. "As a matter of fact, Major Kowacs—I'm coming with you on this one."

"Our job," said Nick Kowacs in the personnel hold of the intrusion module, "is to—"

The high-pitched keening of a powerful laser cutter rose, drowning out his voice and thought itself.

Sergeant Bradley glanced around flat-eyed, looking for the source of the noise. It came from somewhere between the module's double hulls. He started for a hatch, wiping his palms on his fatigues to dry the sudden rush of sweat.

Kowacs grabbed the sergeant with one hand as he put his helmet on with the other.

"Right," Kowacs said over the general frequency. "Lids on." He looked to see which of the new replacements needed to be nudged by their neighbors before they figured out that the rest of the briefing would be conducted by radio even though the Headhunters were all in one room together.

"Our job," Kowacs went on, "is to capture personnel, data banks, and anything that looks like it might be navigational equipment. We *aren't* going in to blow the—"

The laser shut off. A woman with commander's collar pips on the uniform she wore under her lab coat

walked into the bay with two male technical represen-
tatives, speaking among themselves in low voices. Heads
turned to watch them.

Sergeant Bradley grimaced.

"—place up, we're going in to gather information
before the *enemy* blows it up. We've only got seventeen minutes. That's one-seven minutes, period. Anybody who—"

The trio in lab coats gestured Marines away from
a portion of deck and knelt down. One of the tech reps
took an instrument from his pocket and placed it cup-
end down on the decking. He frowned at the result;
the commander growled at him.

"—loses sight of the mission will have me to answer
to," Kowacs continued.

"And they'll wish they'd never been born!" added
Sergeant Bradley. The field first sergeant got enough
venom into the justified threat to take out some of his
frustration about the way the briefing had to be held.

And the way the mission was shaping up.

Kowacs was holding the briefing here because the
module's hangar was the only space in the huge headquarters complex both big enough to hold a hundred
Marines—*and* cleared for this particular dollop of
Sensitive Compartmentalized Information. Unfortunately, the module was still under test, and the technical crews dialing in the hardware had precedence
over the briefing.

The Marines who were about to ride the hardware
into the middle of enemies worse than the Khalians
couldn't argue with the priority, but it didn't make life
simpler.

Kowacs touched a stud on the control wand a
Grade P7 Fleet technician had given him. For a
wonder, the system worked perfectly. The hold's
circular bulkhead was replaced by a holographic

display, the simulated interior of the Syndicate base the Headhunters would be attacking.

"We'll be landing inside the docking bay," Kowacs said as a slow hammering sound began to work its way across the ceiling above him. "In all likelihood it'll be under atmosphere, but we'll be wearing ten-minute airpacks for an emergency."

The two tech reps got up and walked toward the hatch, a rectangle with rounded corners in the midst of a holographic gantry. The commander followed them, shaking her head. She turned in the hatchway to frown at the deck she'd been examining.

"Suits?" asked Laurel, a squad leader in 3rd Platoon.

"Weapons Platoon will be in suits," said Kowacs. "They'll provide security for the module. The remainder of us'll be travelling light. We'll fan out in three-man teams. You'll all have pre-briefed objectives, but don't hesitate to divert to grab anything that looks like it might be valuable."

Something *popped* within the hulls. The encircling holograms vanished. All the lights in the bay went out. First the display, then the lights, came back on moments later.

Somebody swore bitterly.

Corporal Sienkiewicz—the tallest, possibly the strongest, and certainly the toughest member of the 121st— looked bored as she lounged against a bulkhead covered by the image of an open corridor. She knew what the Headhunters' job was this time out—and she knew her own job on every operation, to cover Kowacs' back and keep him alive till the next time. The whys and hows of the operation didn't matter to her beyond that.

"Sir," said a newbie named Bynum—five years a Marine but on his first operation with the Headhunters. "I looked this boat over and she don't have engines. No shit."

"The ship," said Kowacs harshly, "is none of our business. Do you hear? The ship just gets us there and brings us back."

"S'posed to bring us back," somebody muttered in what should have been general silence.

"Listen!" Kowacs snarled. He had to take a tough line, because they all knew this could be a rat-fuck, and the only way his Headhunters were going to go through with it was by rigid obedience. "If there's any of you who don't think you want to chance life in a reaction company any more, I'll approve your transfer *now*. Want to be a cook? A recruiter? Just say the word!"

Nobody spoke. A number of the Marines looked down, at the deck, at their hands.

*They were a good bunch, the very best. They'd charge Hell if he ordered it . . . only in part because they knew if it came to that, Nick Kowacs would be leading from the front.*

The laser cutter shrieked as it bit into an interior bulkhead again.

"Is this an Eight-Ball Command job?" ask Lieutenant Timmes of Weapons Platoon.

"Yes, it is," Kowacs said flatly.

He looked around the crowd of hard faces and the blank visages of Marines who had opaqued their helmet visors. "If anybody's got a problem with that, the transfer offer still stands."

"No problem," said Timmes. "Just wanted to know."

"*Them* bastards," said a sharp-featured trooper named Fleur. "You never know what they're playing at."

Kowacs suspected Fleur had been a disciplinary enlistment—volunteer for a reaction company or face a court martial—but Kowacs had no complaint to make of the Marine. He didn't guess any of the Headhunters, himself included, were good civilian material.

"You don't know what anybody who's got any real authority is playing at," Kowacs said. He was restating the argument by which he'd more-or-less convinced himself. "It's just that people like you and me at the sharp end, we don't see the regular sort, the admirals and Sector Commandants. The boys in Interservice Support Activity, they may be bastards but they're willing to put themselves on the line."

"Gotta give 'em credit for that," chuckled Bradley.

The laser cutter had stopped. The sergeant removed his helmet to knuckle the bare scar tissue of his scalp.

"I don't gotta give 'em a fuckin' thing but a quick round if I get one in my sights," muttered Fleur.

Kowacs opened his mouth to react, because you weren't supposed to shoot putative friendlies and you *never* talked about it, neither before nor after.

Before he could speak, Sergeant Bradley changed the subject loudly by asking, "D'ye mean we don't gotta wear those fucking A-Pot hardsuits that the Redhorse had all the trouble with on Bull's-eye?"

Kowacs looked at his field first. Bradley gave Kowacs a half wink; Bradley and Corporal Sienkiewicz would straighten out Fleur, but it didn't have to be now and in public.

A man in a white lab coat entered the hold and began making his way through the listening Marines. For a moment he was anonymous, like the noises in the hull and the other intruders who'd been focused on their technical agenda.

"I don't know," the newly-promoted major said. "I'll have to—"

The big technician in the corner of Kowacs' eyes suddenly sharpened into an identified personality: the man in the lab coat was Grant.

"Fuckin' A," Sienkiewicz muttered as she drew herself alert.

"I'll take over now, Kowacs," the spook said with as much assurance as if the Headhunters had been his unit, not Nick Kowacs'.

Grant wore a throat mike and a wireless receiver in his right ear, though he had no helmet to damp out the ambient noise if the laser started cutting again.

He stared around the assembled Marines for a moment, then looked directly at Kowacs' bodyguard and said, "No, Corporal, for this one you'll be using the same stone-axe simple equipment you're used to. If you tried to open an A-Potential field inside an existing field—the intrusion module. . . ."

He smiled at the big woman. "You wouldn't like what happened. And I wouldn't like that it screwed up the operation."

Grant met the glares and blank globes of the waiting Headhunters again. "For those of you who don't know," he said, "my name's Grant and you all work for me. You'll take orders through your regular CO here—" he jerked his left thumb in Kowacs' direction without bothering to look around "—but those orders come from me. Is that clear?"

Beside the civilian, Kowacs nodded his head. His eyes held no expression.

"And since you work for me . . . ," Grant resumed as he reached beneath his lab coat, "I've got a little job for one of you. Private Fleur—"

Grant's hand came out with a pistol.

"Catch."

Grant tossed the weapon to Fleur. It was a full-sized, dual-feed service pistol, Fleet issue and deadly as the jaws of a shark.

The Marines nearest to Fleur ducked away as if Grant had thrown a grenade. Kowacs, Bradley, and Sienkiewicz were up on the balls of their feet, ready to react because they'd *have* to react; they were responsible for the unit and for one another.

"Private Fleur," Grant said, "I'm afraid for my life. There's somebody planning to kill me. So I want you to clean my gun here and make sure it's in perfect working order for when I'm attacked."

Nobody spoke. Other Marines eased as far away from Fleur as they could. Even without combat gear, the Headhunters packed the hold. English's 92nd MRC was a demi-company half the size of the 121st. . . .

Fleur stared at the civilian, but his hands slid over the pistol in familiar fashion. He unlatched one magazine, then the other, and slammed them home again.

"Careful," added Grant as he grinned. "There's one up the spout."

"I . . . ," said Fleur

If Fleur's trigger finger tightened, Kowacs would get between the private and Grant . . . but he'd have to be quick, since Sie would be going for *him* and Bradley was a toss-up, Kowacs or Grant or Fleur, the only thing sure being that the sergeant would do something besides try to save his own hide.

"My cleaning kit's back at the billet," Fleur said. He swallowed. "Sir."

"Then you'd better return the gun, boy," said Grant. "Hadn't you?"

Fleur grimaced. For a moment he looked as though he were going to toss the weapon; then he stepped forward and presented the pistol butt-first to its owner. Fleur's hand was dwarfed by that of the civilian.

The laser started cutting again. Grant aimed his pistol at the open hatch. Marines ducked, though nobody was in the direct line of fire.

Grant pulled the trigger. The flash*crack* and the answering *crack* of the explosive bullet detonating somewhere out in the hanger removed any possibility

that the weapon had been doctored to make it harmless.

The cutter shut down. Technicians shouted in surprise, but nobody stuck his head in through the hatch.

Grant put the pistol away under his lab coat. "All
right, Fleur," he said. "You're relieved. Go back to
your quarters and pack your kit. Your orders are
waiting for you there."

Kowacs felt exhausted, drained. Sienkiewicz gripped
his shoulder for the contact they both needed.

"Your new assignment's on an intra-system tug,"
Grant added. Then, as harshly as the pistol shot of a
moment before, "*Get* moving, mister!"

Fleur stumbled out of the hold—and the Headhunters. A few of the Marines flicked a glance at his back;
but only a glance.

Grant exhaled heavily.

"Right," he said. "This is going to be a piece of cake,
troops. The bastards won't know what hit them. There's
just one thing I want to emphasize before your major
here gets on with his briefing."

He grinned around the bay. Sphincter muscles tightened.

"The module will be on-site for seventeen minutes,"
Grant went on. "That's not eighteen minutes, it's not
seventeen minutes, one second. Anybody who isn't
aboard on time spends the rest of his life in Syndicate hands."

"You see," the smiling civilian concluded, "I couldn't
change the extraction parameters. Even if I wanted to."

An electronic chime warned that the Headhunters
were three minutes from insertion.

The hatches were still open. The intrusion module's
bulkheads were hidden by images, but the hologram
was not a simulation this time. The present view was

of the hangar in which the vehicle had been constructed and the twelve sealed black towers surrounding the module at the points of a compass rose. The towers would presumably launch the module . . . somehow.

"Everybody's aboard," prompted Sergeant Bradley, stating what the green bar in Kowacs' visor display already told him.

"Grant isn't aboard," Kowacs said, finger-checking the grenades which hung from his equipment belt.

"I don't get this," complained a Marine to no one in particular. "We can't ride all the way from Port Tau Ceti packed in like canned meat. Can we?"

"Fuck Grant," said Sienkiewicz.

The eighteen members of Weapons Platoon carried the tubes, tripods and ammunition of their belt-loaded plasma weapons. Their rigid hardsuits of black ceramic stood out from the remaining, lightly-equipped Marines like raisins in a pound cake.

Kowacs saw Grant's image coming across the hangar floor with long strides. The civilian wore fatigues, but he carried what looked like a briefcase. His commo helmet was non-standard.

Grant's pistol hung muzzle-up in a harness beneath his left armpit.

"Right," said Kowacs. "Six to all team leaders—" his helmet's AI switched him automatically from the private channel he shared with Bradley and Sie to the general command frequency "—administer the gas antidote to your teams, then dose yourselves."

Grant entered the module. The hatches closed.

There was barely enough room for equipment and the ninety-three personnel aboard the spherical vessel; if the Headhunters' line establishment had been at full Table of Organization strength, Kowacs would have had to cut some people from the operation.

What the Marine who'd complained didn't

understand—what *Kowacs* didn't understand, though he accepted it—was that the Headhunters weren't traveling through space, not even sponge space, on this operation. They were using the Dirac Sea underlying the universe, *all* universes and all times, to create congruity between a top-secret hangar in Port Tau Ceti and the Syndicate base they were about to attack.

At least that's what they were doing if the notion worked. The closer Kowacs came to the event, the less likely it seemed that the notion *could* work.

"Hold still, sir," said Bradley, the administrative head of the team to which Kowacs belonged operationally. He jerked the tab on the front of the major's blouse.

The integral injector pricked Kowacs as it filled his bloodstream with chemicals. The drug would provide a temporary antidote to the contact anesthetic sprayed from bottles which every third Headhunter carried for this operation.

The chime announced *two minutes*.

Grant turned his briefcase sideways and extended its legs. When he opened the lid to expose the keyboard and display, the case became a diaphragm-high workstation. Despite the crowding in the bay, the Marines gave the civilian plenty of room.

A Third Platoon team leader pulled his own tab. He collapsed jerking as reaction to the drug sent him into anaphylactic shock.

Lieutenant al-Habib, the platoon commander, pushed toward the casualty, swearing in a combination of concern and fear. Everybody was supposed to have been reaction-tested before now; and testing was a platoon responsibility.

Kowacs' eyes narrowed, but he said nothing. If he and al-Habib both survived the operation, al-Habib was out of the Headhunters.

If.

The warning chimed one minute. The holographic displays vanished, leaving the bulkheads bare for the moment before the hold's lighting flickered and went off. Grant's face was lit from below by his workstation, making him look the demon Kowacs was sure he really was.

The lights came on again, but they were red.

Kowacs opaqued his visor. He figured he could keep his expression neutral, but he didn't want to bother any of his people if by chance they correctly read the terror behind their major's eyes.

The module drifted. It was more than weightlessness. Kowacs had the horrible feeling that he was rushing *somewhere* but had neither control nor even sensory input, as though his vehicle were skidding on ice in pitch darkness. He heard some of his troops screaming, and he didn't blame them.

The world switched back with the abruptness of a crystal forming in a supersaturated solution. The lights became normal; holograms covered the bulkheads again.

The holograms didn't show the hangar. They didn't show anything at all, just a gray blur without even a spark to pick it out.

Grant was talking angrily, but his helmet contained his words. His big, capable fingers rapped a code into the keyboard. The gray blur shifted slowly through violet to a green like that of translucent pond scum. Though the color changed, it remained featureless.

"What's hap'nin to us?" somebody demanded sharply. "What's—"

Sergeant Bradley's knife poised point-first in front of the panicked Marine's right eyeball. The blade wouldn't penetrate her visor, but its shock value was sufficient to chop her voice off . . . and if she'd taken time to reflect, she would have known that the edge could be through her windpipe before she got out the next syllable.

"Hey, Grant," Kowacs called.

Grant continued talking to someone on the other side of his communications link. His anger was obvious even though his words were inaudible.

Kowacs raised his visor and leaned across the workstation from the opposite side, putting his face where the civilian couldn't ignore him.

Grant's fist clenched. Kowacs grabbed his wrist and squeezed.

For a moment the two powerful men struggled, as motionless as neighboring mountains. Sienkiewicz moved just out of the range of Kowacs' direct vision, but Kowacs didn't need help.

The civilian relaxed. His mouth formed a command, and the shield of silence dropped away from his helmet. "What the fuck do *you* want?" he snarled.

"Where are we?" Kowacs whispered. Everyone in the module was watching them, but only the nearest Marines could hear the leaders over the hiss of nervous breathing. He shook his hand, trying to get feeling back into it.

"There's nothing wrong," Grant said. "We're not where we're programmed to be—or *when* we're programmed to be—but there's nothing wrong. If they can't straighten it out, we'll just return when the seventeen minutes are up."

*We hope*, Kowacs' mind added, but that wasn't something even for a whisper.

"Right," he said aloud. "I'm going to calm everybody down; but Eight-Ball Command pays, understand?"

*Grant probably* didn't *understand . . . yet.*

Kowacs didn't key the helmet intercom, opting for the more personal touch of his direct voice.

"All right, Marines," he bellowed. "We're on R&R for the next fifteen minutes or so, courtesy of the Special Projects Bureau. But you all know the Fleet— what we get's one room and no sandy beaches."

Sienkiewicz laughed loudly.

"Hey," called al-Habib, "you can keep your sand if you find me a cathouse!"

Kowacs grinned broadly at the lieutenant whose quick understanding had just reinstated him in the Headhunters. "Naw, Jamal," he said. "When you join the Marines, you get fucked over—but you don't get laid."

This time the laughter was general. The holographic light bathing the walls shifted slowly back to gray.

Kowacs lifted his helmet to scratch his close-cropped scalp.

"Okay, now listen up," he resumed in a tone of command. "This is a good time for you all to go over your missions again by teams. The delay doesn't mean that we're off the hook. Even Special Projects—"

Kowacs waved toward Grant, bent over his workstation. "—and Eight-Ball Command are going to get things right eventually. I want us *sharp* when the times comes. Understood?"

"Yes *sir!*" came from a dozen throats, and no more eyes filled with incipient panic.

"Then get to it!" ordered Sergeant Bradley.

Helmet-projected maps began to bloom in the midst of three-Marine clusters, teams going over the routes they expected to take through the hostile base.

Kowacs leaned toward Grant again. He expected the civilian to be visibly angry at being made a laughing-stock to defuse tension, but there was no expression on the big man's face.

Which proved that Grant was a smart bastard as well as a bastard; and that wasn't news to Kowacs.

"I'm in contact with echelon," Grant said. "Everything is proceeding normally."

"Except we're not where we're supposed to be," Kowacs said. Bradley and Sienkiewicz were close behind him—everything was close in the module's hold—but they were facing outward, watching the company for their major.

"They've refined the parameters," Grant said. "We should be able to turn around at the end of seventeen minutes and go in immediately, without docking."

"Fine," said Kowacs without expression. "That's almost as good as having the shit work right the first time."

"Just have your troops ready to go, mister!" the civilian snapped. "Got that?"

"You bet," said Kowacs as he straightened. "You just get us to the target; we'll take it from there."

And they did.

The alarm chimed, the interior lights went red, and the intrusion module was within a cylindrical bay large enough to hold a liner—or a battleship. The trio of courier vessels docked there at present were dwarfed by the volume surrounding them.

"Artificial gravity and standard atmosphere!" Kowacs shouted, relaying the information that other Headhunters might not think to check on their visors, as the hatches—*only two fucking hatches, as though this were a bus and not an assault craft!*—opened and the dozen Syndicate maintenance people visible in the bulkhead displays gaped at the module that had appeared in their midst.

Bradley was through the hatch first because he had the shotgun and it was the close targets who were dangerous—though none of the Syndicate personnel, all of them human, seemed to be armed. The woman a hundred meters away, running for a courier vessel, was probably the biggest problem because she'd been smart enough to react.

Kowacs shot her. He was second through the hatch because the 121$^{st}$ was *his* company, not Sie's, however much the corporal might want to put her body out there first when the action was going to start.

The target flopped on the walkway with her limbs flailing. There were dots of blood on the back of her tunic, and a great splash of scarlet and lung tissue blown by the keyholing bullets onto the walkway where she thrashed.

Taking prisoners had to wait until there were enough Headhunters out of the module to secure the area.

Bradley ran for the corridor marked D on the maps from Eight-Ball Command and 6 in yellow on the girdered lintel. Kowacs followed his field first toward what was the transient wing of the base according to data sucked from the prisoner's brain. The major fired a short burst into a glazed office, shattering the clear panels and sending the staff to cover behind banks of short-circuiting equipment.

As usual, Corporal Sienkiewicz carried the considerable weight of a shoulder-fired plasma weapon in addition to her regular gear. She lighted the bay with a round of plasma into the nose turret of both courier vessels on her side of the intrusion module.

The dazzle and *crack!* of the miniature fusion explosions forced their reality onto the huge room. One of the turrets simply slagged down, but ammunition detonated in the other. Balls of ionized gas bubbled through the vessel's open hatches.

The navigational computer of *that* boat wasn't going to be much help to the spooks back at Port Tau Ceti, but the raiders couldn't risk somebody arming the turrets before teams detailed for vessels in dock got aboard the couriers.

Coming back without the desired information was better than not coming back. Even Grant, monitoring all the teams from the belly of the module, would agree with that.

Bradley carried a bottle of stun gas. It was a volatile liquid intended for contact application, though the fumes would do the job if they had to. The sergeant directed the bottle's nozzle into the office Kowacs had shot up, angling the fine jet so that it sprayed the terrified personnel hiding behind their bullet-riddled equipment.

Pickup teams would secure the prisoners later, though they'd be stacked like cordwood beneath Headhunter boots during extraction. *Provided casualties didn't clear too much of the module's hold.*

The corridor formed a Y. Bradley followed the left branch, as planned.

There were rooms on both sides. The third door down quivered as though in indecision. Kowacs riddled it. He was switching to a fresh magazine when the fat man in garish silks and ribbons tumbled out into the corridor, still clutching his pistol.

He'd have been a good one to capture—if that had been an option compatible with Kowacs staying alive.

Belt-fed plasma weapons fired short bursts from the docking bay. Timmes' platoon was taking an active definition of perimeter security. Light reflecting down the corridor angles threw momentary harsh shadows.

The docking bay was out of Kowacs' direct sight. He could have viewed the module by switching his visor to remote images, just as he could follow the progress of any of his Marines either visually or by a digital read-out.

He didn't bother. The Headhunters were too experienced to need their major looking over their shoulders—

And anyway, their major had enough on his own plate.

An emergency barrier began to slide across the corridor twenty meters ahead.

"Down!" Kowacs shouted as his left hand snatched a grenade from his equipment belt. He flung the bomb sidearm as he flattened.

A pair of security men in helmets and uniforms ran from a cross-corridor just beyond the sliding barrier. They leveled sub-machine guns. Bradley sent an arc of stun gas in their direction, but the bottle didn't have quite enough range and Kowacs, sliding on his right shoulder, couldn't twist his assault rifle on-target fast enough to—

The anti-tank grenade struck the barrier, clung for an instant, and went off with a deafening crash. The barrier bulged inward, jamming in its track. The shaped-charge warhead blew a two-centimeter hole through the metal and cleared the corridor beyond with a spray of fragments and molten steel.

The shockwave skidded Kowacs back a meter from the blast area. The frangible casing powdered harmlessly, as it was intended to do, and commo helmets saved the Headhunters' hearing.

"Go!" Kowacs cried.

Sienkiewicz was already on her feet and past the barrier, the near limit of the station's transient accommodations. The corporal paused beside the first door to make sure Bradley was ready with his stun gas, then smashed the panel open with her boot.

Bradley sprayed the interior with his nozzle set on mist. The gas glowed like a fluorescent rainbow in the flicker of distant plasma discharges.

Another team sprinted past Kowacs and broke left at the cross-corridor. Automatic fire blasted.

The team leader spun and fell. His Number Two

dropped her bottle of gas and dragged the leader beyond the corner of the main corridor, across from Kowacs.

The Number Three, under cover also, started to lean out to return fire with his automatic rifle. Kowacs waved him back, then whipped a cluster of fragmentation grenades around the corner with a motion that exposed none of his body.

The cluster rebounded as a unit from the far wall of the cross-corridor, separated into its component sections with a triple pop, and detonated in a white sleet of flame and glass shrapnel.

Kowacs dived into the corridor in the shadow of the blast. Bradley was beside him and Sie covered their backs, facing the opposite direction in case company tried to intervene down the other leg of the cross-corridor.

There were three uniformed Syndicate personnel in the corridor, two sprawled on their faces and a third staggering toward safety as a barrier ten meters away slid to seal the hall. Kowacs and Bradley both fired.

The security man flung his arms out and lurched forward. His back was splotched with slits from the airfoil charge of Bradley's shotgun; there were three neat holes between his shoulders—Kowacs' aiming point.

The barrier ground to a halt. The security man's body might not have been enough to stall out the motor, but his helmet was. There was just about enough room for a man to squeeze through the opening between the barrier and its jamb.

Somebody on the far side of the barrier fired. The bullets ricocheted through the gap, howling like banshees and all the more dangerous for the way they buzzsawed after deforming on the corridor wall.

"Cover me!" screamed the other team's Number

Two. She bolted past Kowacs and Bradley, snatching up her bottle of gas as she ran.

Kowacs poured the remainder of his rifle's magazine through the opening. Bradley unhooked a grenade cluster. His shotgun's pattern was too wide to get much of the charge through the opening at that range, and the airfoils wouldn't ricochet effectively anyway.

A bullet zinged past the running Headhunter, close enough to pluck a pouch of ammo from her belt and half-spin her, but she reached the dead zone behind the barrier without injury. She fumbled with her bottle of gas. Bradley's arm went back with a grenade cluster.

"D—" Kowacs shouted, but he didn't finish the "Don't" because there wasn't much chance the sergeant would miss the risky throw—and anyway, Bradley was going to do what he pleased in a firefight, whether Nick Kowacs thought it was a good idea or not.

The grenade cluster arced through the narrow slot and burst with a triple flash waist-high above the corridor floor. At the blast, the Number Two poked her gas bottle into the opening and began to spray a mist of anesthetic into the other side of the barrier.

The firing slackened. A woman in the bright, loose clothing favored by Syndicate bigwigs slumped across the opening and lay still. A pistol slipped from her hand.

Unexpectedly, the Headhunter dropped her gas bottle and collapsed also.

*The fucking seventeen-minute delay. The gas antidote was wearing off!*

"Headhunter Six to all personnel," Kowacs said as he lurched to his feet and another Syndicate bullet whanged through the slot. "Stop using gas! The antidote's—"

Sienkiewicz fired the last round from her plasma

weapon through the opening. The wall thirty meters down the corridor bloomed in a sun-hot fireball as the jet of directed plasma sublimed the metal-and-ceramic structure into vapor in a microsecond.

"—wearing off!" Kowacs completed as he hit the slot a step ahead of Bradley, who'd been that much slower getting to his feet, and two steps before Sie, who rocked back with the violence of the bolt she'd unleashed.

The major went through sideways. His equipment belt hooked on the edge of the barrier anyway, twisted but didn't hold him.

The corridor dead ended. The four rooms on the left side were glowing slag from the plasma charge. A security man knelt in an open doorway across from where the bolt had hit. He'd dropped his rifle and was pawing at his eyes, possibly blinded already and certainly dead when Kowacs walked a one-handed burst across his chest.

*The shooters didn't know anything worth carrying back to Tau Ceti.*

The end door on the right side was a centimeter open when Kowacs saw it, slamming shut an instant thereafter. He hit its latch bootheel-first, springing fasteners that were intended for privacy rather than security.

The interior lights were on. There were two people inside, and a coffin-sized outline taped to the back wall of the room. The people were a man and a woman, both young, and they were starting to lock down the helmets of their atmosphere suits.

The man's gauntleted hand reached for the submachine gun across the bed beside him. Kowacs fired, but Bradley fired also and at point-blank range the rifle bullets were lost in the plate-sized crater the shotgun blew in the target's chest.

The back wall exploded outward. The outline had been drawn with adhesive-backed explosive strips, and the vaguely-familiar woman detonated it as she finished fastening her helmet.

The other side of the wall was hard vacuum.

The rush of atmosphere sucked the woman with it, clear of the Headhunters' guns. Loose papers, bedding, and the helmet from the corpse sailed after her.

The mask of Kowacs' emergency air supply slapped over his nose and mouth, enough to save his life but not adequate for him to go chasing somebody in a proper suit. The suit's maneuvering jets would carry the woman to a regular airlock when the raiders left and it was safe to come back.

The room lights dimmed as the atmosphere that scattered them into a useful ambiance roared through the huge hole. Kowacs reached for the male corpse, lost his balance and staggered toward death until Sie's huge hand clamped the slack of his equipment belt.

"Let's go!" she shouted, her voice attenuated to a comfortable level by the AI controlling Kowacs' headphones. "We're timing out!"

"Help me with the body!" Kowacs ordered as the three of them fought their way back into the corridor. The wind was less overmastering but still intense.

"We don't need dead guys!" Bradley shouted, but he'd grabbed the other leg of the body, clumsy in its bulky suit.

"I got it," said Sienkiewicz, lifting the corpse away from both men. She slammed it through the gap at the barrier in what was half a shove, half a throw.

"We need this one," Kowacs wheezed.

The corridor was empty except for Syndicate corpses. Headhunter pickup teams had gathered the casualties as well as the loot and headed back to the

module. It'd be close, but Kowacs' team would make
it with ten seconds to spare, a lifetime. . . .

"We need this deader . . . ," he continued as they
pounded down the hallway against the lessening wind-
rush. Sie had the body. "Because he's wearing . . .
ensign's insignia . . . on his collar."

The module was in sight. A man stood in the open
hatch, Grant, and goddam if he didn't have his arm
outstretched to help jerk the latecomers aboard.

"*Fleet* ensign's insignia!" Kowacs gasped.

The receptionist looked concerned, and not just by
the fact that Major Kowacs carried a full load of
weapons and equipment into her sanctum.

Or as much of his weapons and equipment as he
hadn't fired off during the raid.

The escort, rising and falling on the balls of his feet
at the open door of these third-tier offices, was evi-
dently worried. "Come this way, please, sir," the young-
ster said. Then, "He's been waiting for you."

"I been waiting for a hot shower," Kowacs rasped.
Powdersmoke, ozone, and stun gas had worked over
his throat like so many skinning knives. "I'm still
fucking waiting."

The escort hopped ahead of Kowacs like a tall, per-
fectly-groomed leprechaun. Kowacs could barely walk.

The adrenaline had worn off. He seen the preliminary casualty report—*with three bodies not recovered.*
There was a ten-centimeter burn on the inside of his
left wrist where he must have laid the glowing barrel
of his assault rifle, though goddam if he could remember doing that.

There were bruises and prickles of glass shrapnel
all over Nick Kowacs' body, but a spook named Grant
insisted on debriefing him *at once, with your full
equipment, mister.*

The door flashed SPECIAL PROJECTS/TEITELBAUM an instant before it opened.

"Where the hell have you been?" snarled Grant.

His briefcase lay open on the desk. A gossamer filament connected the workstation to the office's hologram projector. Fuzzy images of battle and confusion danced in the air while the portrait of Admiral Teitelbaum glared down sternly.

"I had to check out my people," Kowacs said as he leaned his blackened rifle against one of the leather-covered chairs. He lifted one, then the other of the crossed bandoliers of ammunition over his head and laid them on the seat cushion.

"I said *at once*," the civilian snapped. "You've got platoon leaders to baby-sit, don't you?"

"I guess," said Kowacs. He unlatched his equipment belt. It swung in his hands, shockingly heavy with its weight of pistol and grenades. He tossed it onto the bandoliers.

*God, he felt weak. . . .*

Grant grimaced. "All right, give me your helmet."

Kowacs had forgotten he was wearing a commo helmet. He slid it off carefully. The room's filtered air chilled the sweat on the Marine's scalp.

The civilian reversed the helmet, then touched the brow panel with an electronic key. Kowacs knew about the keys but he'd never seen one used before.

Line Marines weren't authorized to remove the recording chips from their helmets. That was the job of the Second-Guess Brigade, the rear-echelon mothers who decided how well or badly the people at the sharp end had behaved.

Grant muttered to his workstation. The ghost images shut down. He put the chip from Kowacs' helmet directly into the hologram reader. His own weapon and shoulder harness hung over the back of his chair.

"Didn't your equipment echo everything from our helmets?" Kowacs asked.

He remained standing. He wasn't sure he wanted to sit down. He wasn't sure of much of anything.

"Did a piss-poor job of it, yeah," the civilian grunted. "Just enough to give me a hint of what I need."

He scrolled forward, reeling across the seventeen-minute operation at times-ten speed. Images projected from Kowacs viewpoint jerked and capered and died. "Too much hash from the—"

There was a bright flash in the air above the desk.

"—fucking plasma discharges. You know—" Grant met the Marine's eyes in a fierce glare, "—it was bughouse crazy to use a plasma weapon in a finger corridor. What if the whole outer bulkhead blew out?"

"It didn't," said Kowacs. "You got complaints about the way the job got done, then you send somebody else the next time."

Grant paused the projection. The image was red with muzzle flashes and bright with pulmonary blood spraying through the mouth of the man in the tattered spacesuit.

"Smart to bring back the body," Grant said in a neutral voice. "Too bad you didn't capture him alive."

"Too bad your system didn't work the first time so we could've kept using the stun gas," Kowacs replied flatly. The parade of images was a nightmare come twice.

Grant expanded the view of the dying man's face. "We've got a hard make on him," he said. "There was enough residual brain-wave activity to nail him down, besides all the regular ID he was carrying. Name's Haley G. Stocker, Ensign . . . and he disappeared on a scouting mission."

"A Syndicate spy?" Kowacs said.

"That's what the smart money's betting," the civilian agreed.

He backed up the image minusculy. The blood vanished like a fountain failing, the aristocratic lips shrank from an O of disbelieving horror into the sneer the ensign bore an instant before the bullets struck.

"Only thing is," Grant continued, "Ensign Stocker disappeared thirty-five years ago."

He looked at Kowacs and raised an eyebrow, as if he were expecting the Marine to come up with an explanation.

"Bullshit," said Kowacs. "He's only about twenty. He was."

"Close," the civilian agreed. "Twenty and a half standard years when you shot him, the lab says."

He let the projector run forward. The spy, the *boy*, hemorrhaged and died again before his mind could accept what was happening.

"I don't get it," said Nick Kowacs. He heard a persistent buzzing, but it came from his mind rather than the equipment.

Grant looked . . . tired wasn't the right word, lonely wasn't the right word, but. . . . Grant had paid a price during the operation too—

Or he'd never have been talking to a line Marine this way.

"It looks like we still don't have all the bugs out of the A-Pot intrusion system," Grant said. "The best we can figure now, the second pass was early. Thirty-five years early."

He spoke to the voice control of the holographic reader. The image paused, then expanded.

The face of the woman who'd escaped was slightly distorted by the faceshield of her helmet, and she was considerably younger—

But the features were beyond doubt the same as those lowering down from the portrait of Vice-Admiral Teitelbaum on the wall behind.

# MISSION ACCOMPLISHED

## A Story of The Fleet

*Nick Kowacs laughed to imagine it, him sitting at a booth in the Red Shift Lounge and saying to Toby English, "That last mission, the one that was supposed to be a milk run? Let me tell you what really went down!"*

"Come on, come on, come on," begged the Logistics Officer, a naval lieutenant. "Your lot was supposed to be in the air thirty minutes ago, and I got three more convoys behind it!"

"Keep your shirt on, sailor," said Sergeant Bradley. "We'll be ready to move out as soon as Major Kowacs gets this last set of voice orders—"

Bradley nodded toward the blacked-out limousine which looked like a pearl in a muckheap as it idled in a yard of giant excavating machinery. The limousine was waiting for the Headhunters when they pulled into the depot. Bradley didn't know what the major was hearing inside the vehicle, but he doubted it was anything as straightforward as verbal orders.

"That's faster than you'll have your equipment airborne even if you get on with your job," he concluded.

Bradley acted as first sergeant for the field element of the 121st Marine Reaction Company, Headhunters, while the real first sergeant was back with the base unit on Port Tau Ceti. Bradley knew that before the lieutenant could punish him for insubordination, the complaint would have to go up the naval chain of command and come back down the marine side of the Fleet bureaucracy . . . which it might manage to do, a couple of lifetimes later.

As if in answer to Bradley's gibe, drivers started the engines of the paired air-cushion transporters which cradled a self-contained excavator on the lowboy between them. The yard had been scoured by earlier movements by heavy equipment, but the soil of Khalia was stony. As the transporters' drive fans wound up, they shot pebbles beneath the skirts to whang against the sides of other vehicles.

One stone hit a Khalian wearing maroon coveralls. He was one of thousands of Weasels hired to do scut work in the wake of the Fleet's huge logistics buildup on what had been the enemy home planet—when the Khalians were the enemy. The victim yelped and dropped to the ground.

Sergeant Bradley spit into the dust. If the Weasel was dead, then the universe was a better place by that much.

Drivers fired up the engines of the remainder of the vehicles the 121st was to escort. Four lowboys carried 3-meter outside-diameter casing sections. The final piece of digging equipment was a heavy-lift crane to position the excavator initially, then feed casing down

the shaft behind the excavator as it burned and bur-
rowed toward the heart of the planet.

All of the transporters were ground effect. The noise
of their intakes and the pressurized air wailing out
beneath their skirts was deafening. The lieutenant
shouted, but Bradley could barely hear his, "You won't
be laughing if the planetwrecker you're sitting on top
of goes off because you were late to the site!"

Corporal Sienkiewicz, Kowacs' clerk/bodyguard, was
female and almost two meters tall. This yard full of
outsized equipment was the first place Bradley
remembered Sie looking as though she were in scale
with her surroundings. Now she bent close to the
Logistics Officer and said, "We won't be doing anything, el-tee. It's you guys a hundred klicks away
who'll have time to watch the crust crack open and
the core spill out."

The Syndicate had mined Khalia. If the planet
exploded at the crucial moment when Syndicate warships swept in to attack, the defenders would lose the
communications and logistics base they needed to win.

But most of the Weasels in the universe would be
gone as well. . . .

The door of the limousine opened. Bradley keyed
the general-frequency override in his commo helmet
and ordered, "Five-six to all Headhunter elements.
Mount up, troops, it's time to go play marine." His
voice was hoarse.

As Bradley spoke, his fingers checked combat gear
with feather-light touches. His shotgun was slung
muzzle-up for boarding the vehicle. The weapon's
chamber was empty, but he would charge it from the
box magazine as soon as the trucks were airborne.

Bandoliers of shotgun ammo crossed his back-and-
breast armor. From each bandolier hung a container
of ring-airfoil grenades which Bradley could launch

from around the shotgun's barrel for long range and a high-explosive wallop.

Hand-flung grenade clusters were stuffed into the cargo pockets of either pants-leg. Some gas grenades; some explosive, some incendiary, some to generate fluorescent smoke for marking. You never knew what you were going to need. You only knew that you were going to need more of *something* than you carried. . . .

A portable medicomp to diagnose, dispense drugs, and patch the screaming wounded. If you could reach them. If they weren't out there in the darkness being tortured by one Khalian while the rest of a Weasel platoon waited in ambush; and you still had to go, because she was your Marine and it didn't matter, you had to bring back whatever the Weasels had left of her.

Sergeant Bradley lifted the rim of his commo helmet with one hand and knuckled the pink scar tissue that covered his scalp. He didn't carry a fighting knife, but a powered metal-cutter dangled from his left hip where it balanced his canteen. He'd killed seven Weasels with the cutting bar one night.

Bradley was twenty-eight standard years old. His eyes were the age of the planet's molten core.

"Come on, Top," Sienkiewicz said, putting her big hand over the tension-mottled fingers with which the field first gripped his helmet. Major Kowacs sprinted toward them as the limousine accelerated out of the equipment yard. "We got a taxi to catch."

"Right," said Bradley in a husky voice. "Right, we gotta do that."

He prayed that the Headhunters would be redeployed *fast* to some planet where there weren't thousands of Weasels running around in Fleet uniforms. . . .

Sergeant Custis, a squad leader with three years service in the Headhunters, pulled Kowacs aboard the truck while Sie and Bradley hooked themselves onto seats on the opposite side of the vehicle's center spine.

"Cap'n?" said Custis as his head swung close to his commanding officer's helmet. "Is it true the Weasels are going to blow up their whole planet if we don't deactivate the mines first? Ah, I mean, Major?"

Kowacs grimaced. One of the problems with latrine rumors was that they were only half right.

He checked to see that the flat box was secured firmly to his equipment belt. He'd clipped it there as soon as he received the device in the limousine.

Another problem with latrine rumors was that they *were* half right.

"Don't sweat it, Buck," Corporal Sienkiewicz offered from the bench seat on which she sat with her back against Custis' back. "It's gonna be a milk run this time."

The lead truck was out of the gate with 1$^{st}$ Platoon aboard. A lowboy followed the Marines; the truck with Weapons Platoon and Kowacs' command team lifted into the number three slot.

There was enough cross-wind to make the vehicles skittish. At least that prevented the gritty yellow dust which the fans lifted from coating everybody behind the leaders.

The Marine transporters had enough direct lift capacity to fly rather than skimming over a cushion of air the way the mining equipment had to do, but for this mission Kowacs had told the drivers to stay on the deck. After all, the Headhunters were supposed to be escorting the excavating machinery . . . or something.

"Six to all Headhunter elements," Kowacs said, letting the artificial intelligence in his helmet cut through the conversations buzzing through the company. Everybody was nervous. "Here's all the poop *I* know."

But not quite everything he was afraid of. He instinctively touched the special communicator attached to his belt. . . .

"A presumably hostile fleet is approaching Khalia," Kowacs resumed aloud.

"Weasels!" a nearby Marine snarled. The AI blocked radio chatter, but it couldn't prevent people from interrupting with unaided voice.

"The enemy is human," Kowacs said firmly. "Any of you replacements doubt that, just talk to a veteran. *This* outfit has met them before."

That ought to shut up the troops who were convinced the Khalians had broken their surrender terms. Kowacs' words told the Headhunter veterans *they* knew better, so they'd hold to the CO's line as a matter of status. And no replacement, even a Marine with years of service, would dare doubt the word of a full-fledged Headhunter.

It was only Nick Kowacs who still had to fear that the incoming warships were crewed by Khalians like the hundreds of millions of other bloodthirsty Weasels all around him on this planet. He looked around him.

The fast-moving convoy was three klicks out of the Fleet Logistics Base Ladybird—one of hundreds of depots which had sprung up within hours of the successful invasion of Khalia. The countryside was a wasteland.

The local foliage was brown and dun and maroon, never green. Even granting the difference in color, the vegetation was sparse and signs of habitation were limited to an occasional hut shaped like an oversized beehive.

How could the Alliance *ever* have believed a race as primitive as the Khalians was capable of sustaining an interstellar war—without someone else behind them, arming the Weasels and pointing them like a sword at the heart of the Alliance?

"FleetComSeventeen believes that the human enemy, the Syndicate . . . ," Kowacs said as his eyes searched terrain that was already being scanned to the millimeter from orbit, " . . . has used its past association with the Weasels to plant a chain of thermonuclear devices at the planet's crustal discontinuity. If the weapons go off together, they'll crack Khalia like an egg and destroy everything and everyone the Fleet has landed here."

Corporal Sienkiewicz chuckled and said to Bradley in a barely-audible rumble, "Including us."

The convoy was rolling at over 100 KPH. The lowboys accelerated slowly, but they could maintain a higher speed than Kowacs had expected. The Marine trucks had their side armor lowered so that the outward-facing troops could shoot or deploy instantly, but the wind buffeting was getting severe.

"*We're* not aboard a ship because we'd be as useless as tits on a boar in a space battle," Kowacs continued. "Anyway, the naval boys don't have near the lift capacity to get even Fleet personnel clear in the time available. Our engineering personnel are going to destroy the Syndicate mines instead."

*Destroy the mines—or detonate them out of sequence, making the result a number of explosions rather than a single, crust-splitting surge. Asequential detonation was a perfectly satisfactory solution—for everyone except those directly on top of the bang.*

"We're just along to protect the hardware," Kowacs concluded. "It's a milk run, but keep your eyes open."

A yellow light winked on Kowacs' raised visor, a glow at the frontier of his vision. One of his platoon leaders had a question, and the major's AI thought he ought to listen to it.

"Go ahead, Gamma Six," Kowacs said.

"Nick . . . ?" said Horstmann of 3rd Platoon, aboard the last vehicle in the convoy. "What are we s'posed to be protecting *against*?"

"Right, fair question," Kowacs agreed.

He'd asked the same thing when the orders came over the squawk box in the Headhunters' temporary barracks. The voice on the other end of the line said, "Any fucking thing! Get your asses moving!" and rang off.

Which was pretty standard for headquarters staff scrambling line marines; but not the way Nick Kowacs liked to run his own outfit.

"I presume—"

"I *guess*," spoken with an air of calm authority that implied the CO knew what was going on, there was no need to panic.

"—that headquarters is concerned about Weasels who haven't gotten the word that they've surrendered. And maybe there's some locals who think we're planting mines instead of deactivating them. You know how rumors start."

Bradley laughed. Kowacs laughed also.

Another light winked: Sergeant Bynum, who was running Weapons Platoon until another lieutenant transferred in to replace Woking. Woking had died of anaphylactic shock on a Syndicate base that Fleet HQ swore the Headhunters had never seen.

"Go ahead, Delta Six."

"Capt—Major?" The veterans had trouble remembering the CO's promotion. Kowacs had trouble with it himself. "How did they locate these planet-wreckers, anyhow?"

*Well, somebody was bound to ask that. Would've been nice if they hadn't, though. . . .*

"They used A-Potential equipment," Kowacs answered flatly. The wind rush made his eyes water. "Toby

English's Ninety-second is in orbit aboard the *Haig*. The destroyer's got the new hardware, and they've done subsurface mapping."

"A-Pot shit," said Bynum. "Like the stuff that left us swinging in the breeze on the last mission? The mission the brass said didn't happen—only we took fourteen casualties."

The only thing Nick Kowacs really understood about A-Potential equipment was that he never wanted to use it again. No grunt had any business tapping powers to which all points in time and space were equivalent. Maybe it wasn't such a bad idea if some other friendly used the technology, but. . . .

The artificial intelligence in Bradley's helmet should not have been able to emulate Kowacs' unit and enter this discussion without the CO's stated approval . . . but it could. The field first broke in to state with brutal simplicity, "If savin' your ass is the only thing you're worried about, Bynum, you sure shouldn't've volunteered for the Headhunters."

Kowacs took his hand away from the special communicator. The plastic case felt cold.

Bynum muttered something apologetic.

"Alpha Six to Six," said the 1st Platoon leader laconically from the leading truck. "Hill One-Six-Fiver is in sight. Over."

"Right," said Kowacs. "Okay, Headhunters, we've arrived."

If anything, this landscape of pebble-strewn hills and wind-carved vegetation was more bleakly innocent than any of the countryside the convoy had passed through on its way here.

"Dig in, keep your eyes on your sensors, and be thankful we've got a cushy job for a change."

*And while you're at it, pray that Fleet Vice-Admiral Hannah Teitelbaum, whom Kowacs suspected to be a traitor in the pay of the Syndicate, hadn't gotten the Headhunters sent here for reasons of her own.*

Corporal Sienkiewicz surveyed the landscape, flipping her helmet visor from straight visuals through infra-red to ultra-violet, then back. Nothing she saw repaid her care—or explained her nervousness.

In addition to her massive pack and slung assault rifle, Sie cradled a three-shot plasma weapon lightly in her arms. She had no target as yet for its bolts of ravening hell, but *somewhere* out there. . . .

"Gamma Six to Six," said the commo helmet. "We're dug in. Over."

The rock in 3rd Platoon's sector was a little more friable than that of the others, so they'd finished ahead of 1st and 2nd. Probably wasn't enough difference to make it worthwhile sending Horstmann's powered digging equipment over to help Lanier and Michie's men, though.

The excavation site, Hill 165, was one of a series of low pimples on a barren landscape. The crane was swinging the excavator into final position, nose down. Occasionally Sienkiewicz heard a bellowed curse as a variation in wind velocity rotated the machine out of alignment—again.

The Headhunters dug in by three-Marine fire teams, just below the hillcrest so that they wouldn't be silhouetted against the sky. Each platoon, stiffened by two of Weapons Platoon's belt-fed plasma weapons, was responsible for a 120-degree wedge—

Of wasteland. There was absolutely no chance in the world that this empty terrain could support more than the Weasel equivalent of a goatherd. Sie had imagined a Khalian city from which furry waves might surge toward the humans; but not here.

And not from a tunnel complex, either. If the

*Haig*'s A-Potential equipment had located planet-wreckers lying just above the asthenosphere, it would have spotted any large abnormality lying close enough to the surface to threaten the Headhunters.

So what the *Hell* was wrong?

The self-contained excavator touched the ground. Its crew switched on their cutters with a scream that became a howl, then dropped into bowel-loosening subsonics.

The huge device disappeared into rock with the jerky suddenness of a land vehicle sinking in a pond. Just before the stern vanished from sight, a thirty-centimeter gout of magma spurted from it and spun 90° in the magnetic deflector positioned above the pithead. The molten rock crossed a swale to splash and cool against a gravel slope three kilometers away.

Ten-second pulses of glowing waste continued to cross the $2^{nd}$ Platoon sector every minute or so. Lanier's troops had left a corridor as the engineering officers directed, but they'd still be glad for their dugouts' overhead cover.

Nick and Top walked over from where they had been talking to the engineers. Bradley was carrying a communications screen of unfamiliar design in one hand. He looked okay again. Sienkiewicz had to watch the field first pretty careful nowadays, any time there might be Weasels around.

"Anything out there, Sie?" the major asked, casual but obviously ready to react if his big bodyguard could put a name to her forebodings.

Sienkiewicz shrugged. "Not that I can find, anyway," she admitted. Her palms sweated against the twin grips of the plasma weapon.

The crane lowered the first section of casing to follow the excavator. Rock didn't simply go away because you heated it gaseous and slung it out the back of your equipment at high velocity. Pulses rising along the casing's magnetic field focused the waste in the center of the bore until it could be deflected to a tailings pile on the surface.

Kowacs must have been feeling the same thing Sienkiewicz did—whatever *that* was—because he touched the unfamiliar black object clipped to his equipment belt.

Sienkiewicz noted the gesture. "You know," she said, "it sorta looked like the guy who called you over to the car in the yard there . . . like he was Grant."

"Fucking spook," Bradley muttered. His fingers began to check his weapons and ammunition, as though he were telling the beads of a rosary.

"Yeah, that was Grant," Kowacs agreed. He started to say more, then closed his mouth.

The three members of the command team spoke over a commo channel to which only they had access. The wind that scoured these hills also abraded words spoken by unaided voices.

Bradley touched the black monomer case of the object Kowacs had gotten in Grant's limousine. It was ten centimeters to a side and very thin. The outside was featureless except for a cross-hatched voiceplate and a small oval indentation just below it.

"I thought," the field first said, articulating the same assumption Sienkiewicz herself had made, "that all this A-Potential stuff was supposed to be turned in after the last mission?"

Kowacs' face worked. "It's a communicator," he said. "Grant says it is, anyhow. He thought . . . maybe we ought to have a way to get ahold of him if, if something happened out here."

He stared grimly at the stark hills around them. "Doesn't look like there's much to worry about, does there?"

Sie's right hand began to cramp. She spread it in the open air. The wind chilled and dried her calloused palm.

"What's Grant expecting, then?" Bradley said, as though he were asking for a weather report. Wispy clouds at high altitude offered no promise of moisture to the sparse vegetation.

Kowacs shrugged. "We didn't have time to talk," the stocky, powerful officer said. His eyes were on the horizon. "Except, the other twelve excavators got sent out with Shore Police detachments for security. This is the only one that's being guarded by a reaction company."

"Anybody know who gave the orders?" Sienkiewicz heard herself ask.

"With a flap like this on, who the hell could tell?" Kowacs muttered. "Grant said he'd check, but it'll take a couple days . . . if there's anything left after the Syndicate fleet hits."

Then, as his fingers delicately brushed the A-Pot communicator, Kowacs added, "There's no reason to suppose somebody's trying to get rid of the Headhunters because of what we saw on that last mission."

"No reason at all," Sienkiewicz said, repeating the lie as she continued to scan the bleak horizon.

Bradley stared at the pattern on the flat-plate screen. He adjusted the focus, but the image didn't go away.

"Major!" he said sharply. "We got company coming!"

Bradley had borrowed the screen from the engineers so the Headhunter command team could eavesdrop on the excavator. A peg into rock fed seismic vibrations to the screen's micro-processor control for sorting.

Though the unit was small, it could discriminate between words vibrating from the sending unit on the excavator's hull and the roar of the cutters and

impellers. Thus far, the only words which had appeared
on the screen in block letters were laconic reports:

> PASSING TWO KILOMETERS. IN THE
> GREEN.
>      PASSING   FIVE   KILOMETERS.
> REPLACING HEADS FIVE-THREE AND
> FIVE-FOUR WITH BACKUP UNITS.
>      PASSING EIGHT KILOMETERS. . . .

When there were no words to decode from vibrations travelling at sound's swifter speed through rock,
the screen mapped the surrounding hills. It had found
a pattern there, also.

The command team's dugout was as tight and crude
as those of the remaining fire teams: two meters on
the long axis, a meter and a half in depth and front-
to-back width. The walls were stabilized by a bond-
ing agent, while a back-filled sheet of beryllium
monocrystal on thirty-centimeter risers provided top
cover.

Kowacs bumped shoulders with the field first as he
leaned toward the screen. Sie scraped the roof when
she tried to get a view from the opposite end of the
dugout.

"What is it?" Kowacs said. Then, "That's just Hill
Two-Two-Four in front of us, isn't it? Vibration from
the excavater makes the rock mass stand out."

"No sir," Bradley said. "There was a pattern, and it's
changed."

His lips were dry. He'd never used a screen like this
before and he might be screwing up, the way a newbie
shoots at every noise in the night. But . . . years of surviving had taught Bradley to trust his gut, to flatten
*now* or to blast *that* patch of vegetation that was no
different from the klicks of jungle all around it.

Something here was wrong.

**PASSING TWELVE KILOMETERS**, the screen said, blanking its map of the terrain. **HEADS RUNNING EIGHTY PERCENT, STILL IN THE GREEN.**

The quivering map display returned to the screen. It shifted, but the clouds changed overhead and the planet surely trembled to its own rhythms besides those imposed on it by human hardware. . . .

"The digger's getting deeper, so the vibrations don't look the same up here," Sienkiewicz muttered. She looked out the firing slit toward Hill 224 and manually adjusted her visor to high magnification.

"Headhunter Six to all elements," Kowacs ordered in a flat, decisive voice. "Full alert. Break. Alpha elements, watch Hill Two-Two-Four. Break. Delta Six, prepare to redeploy half your weapons to Alpha sector on command."

Metal glinted on the side of the hill a kilometer away. Bradley centered it in the sighting ring of his visor and shouted, "Support, target!" so that his AI would carat the object for every Headhunter within line of sight of it.

"Break," continued the major, his voice as bored but forceful as that of a roll-call sergeant. "Knifeswitch One-Three—" Regional Fire Control "—this is Headhunter S—"

The transmission dissolved into a momentary roar of jamming. Bradley's artificial intelligence cut the noise off to save his hearing and sanity.

The glint on Hill 224 vaporized in the sunbright streak of a plasma weapon. A ball of gaseous metal rose, then cooled into a miniature mushroom cloud.

"—arget for you," Kowacs continued beside Bradley.

So long as he was transmitting out, the major couldn't know that his message was being turned to garbage by a very sophisticated jammer. Instead of a brute-force attempt to cover all frequencies, the enemy used an algorithm which mimicked that of the Headhunters' own spread-frequency transmitters. The low-level white noise destroyed communication more effectively than a high-amplitude hum which would itself have called regional headquarters' attention to what was going on.

"You're being jammed!" the field first said, slipping a RAG grenade over the barrel of his shotgun.

Airflow through the center of the grenade kept the cylinder on a flat trajectory, even though it was launched at low velocity. The warhead was hollow, but its 12-cm diameter made it effective against considerable thicknesses of armor.

**PASSING EIGHTEEN KILOMETERS**, said the borrowed screen. Sound—through rock or in air—was unaffected by the jamming. Bradley heard the fire teams to either side shouting because their normal commo had been cut off.

The side of Hill 224 erupted in glittering hostility. Bradley adjusted his visor to top magnification as Kowacs' rifle and Sie's plasma weapon joined the crackling thunder from all the 1$^{st}$ Platoon positions.

The enemies were machines. Individually they were small, the size of a man's head—small enough to have been overlooked as crystalline anomalies in the rock when the *Haig* scanned for planet-wreckers.

There were thousands of them. They began to merge into larger constructs as they broke through the surface and crawled toward the Headhunters on Hill 165.

Bradley clapped Sie on the shoulder. Light shimmered across the track of ionized air from the muzzle of her weapon to the patch of molten rock across the swale. "Save your ammo!" Bradley shouted.

He pushed himself through the tight opening between the ground and the dugout's top cover, then reached back inside for his shotgun. RAG grenades had a maximum range of 500 meters, and the aerofoil charges in the shotgun itself were probably useless against *this* enemy even at point blank.

Bradley ran in a crouch toward the crew-served plasma weapon in the second dugout to the right. He expected bullets—bolts—*something*, but the enemy machines merely continued to roll down the slope like a metal-ceramic sludge.

Even at a thousand meters, bullets from Marine assault rifles seemed to have some effect on the individual machines. An object in a marksman's killing zone flashed for a moment within a curtain of rock dust cast up by deflected bullets. After the third or fourth sparkling hit, the machine slumped in on itself and stopped moving.

When two or more machines joined, the larger unit shrugged off bullets like a dog pacing stolidly through the rain. Only a direct hit from a plasma bolt could affect them—and Weapons Platoon had only a hundred rounds for each of its belt-fed plasma weapons.

Bradley knelt at the back of the gun pit. "Raush!" he ordered. "Blair!"

The crew triggered another short burst. Air hammered to fill the tracks burned through it, and ozone stripped the protecting mucus from Bradley's throat.

He reached through the opening and prodded the gunner between the shoulder blades with the shotgun's muzzle. "Raush, damn you!" he croaked.

The gunner and assistant gunner turned in surprise. Their eyes widened to see the gun and Bradley's face transfigured into a death's head by fear.

"Single shots!" the field first ordered. "And wait for three of the bloody things to join before you shoot! Don't waste ammo!"

Bradley rose to run to the other 1$^{st}$ Platoon gun pit, but Kowacs was already there, bellowing orders.

*Nick understood. You could always count on the captain.*

Raush resumed fire, splashing one and then a second of the aggregated creatures into fireballs with individual bolts.

Not every aimed shot hit. The machines moved faster than they seemed to. The survivors had covered half the distance to the Headhunter positions.

Bradley loped across the hilltop. His load of weapons and ammunition weighed him down as if he were trying to swim wrapped in log chain. Without radio, face-to-face contact was the only way to get plasma weapons from distant gun pits up to where they could support 1st Platoon.

Bradley thought of dropping the bandoliers of shotgun ammo he was sure were useless, but his hand stopped halfway to the quick-release catch.

This didn't seem like a good time to throw away any hope, however slim.

"Grant!" Kowacs shouted into the A-Pot communicator as a shining, five-tonne creature lumbered up the slope toward the dugout. It was the last of the attacking machines, but it was already too close for either of the crew-served plasma weapons to bear on it. "We need support fast! Bring the *Haig* down! We need heavy weapons!"

Sienkiewicz fired three-shot bursts from her assault rifle. The bullets disintegrated as orange-white sparkles on the creature's magnetic shielding, a finger's breadth out from the metal surface.

Sie's plasma weapon lay on the floor of the dugout behind her. The muzzle still glowed a dull red. She'd fired her last two plasma rounds an instant apart when a pair of low-slung creatures lunged suddenly from dead ground to either side.

Those targets now popped and bubbled, melting across the face of the rock from their internal energies; but there was one more, and Sienkiewicz was out of plasma charges.

Kowacs dropped the communicator and aimed his rifle. The creature was fifty meters away. It was shaped roughly like an earthworm, but it seemed to slide forward without quite touching the rock.

The dark patch just above the rounded nose might be a sensor window. Anyway, it was Sie's aiming point, and maybe two rifles firing simultaneously—

Kowacs squeezed the trigger, leaning into the recoil. He watched through the faint haze of powder gas as his bullets spattered vainly.

The fat black cylinder of a RAG grenade sailed toward the target in a flat arc. Kowacs and Sienkiewicz ducked beneath the dugout's rim. The hollow *whoomp!* of the armor-piercing charge rippled the ground and lifted the Marines a few millimeters.

Kowacs looked out. Wind had already torn to rags the black smoke of the explosion. There was a thumb-sized hole through the machine's skin. The cavity widened as the creature's snout collapsed inward like a time-lapse image of a rotting vegetable.

Bradley knelt beside the dugout, sliding another RAG grenade over his shotgun's barrel to the launching plate. It was the last of his four rounds: the ammo cans dangled empty from his bandoliers.

"Have you raised Grant?" the field first demanded. "Do we got some help coming?"

"I'll settle for an extraction," Sienkiewicz muttered. She looked down at the grenade stick she'd plucked from her equipment belt to throw if necessary. The grenade was a bunker buster, devastating in enclosed spaces but probably useless against an armored opponent in the open air.

"The trucks won't crank," Bradley said flatly. "The power packs are still at seventy percent, but current won't flow through the control switches to the fans."

There was a moment of silence relieved only by the vibration of rock which spewed out of the pithead and hurtled across the sky. The stream cooled only to yellow-orange by the time it splashed on the tailing pile.

A plasma weapon began to thump single shots at a fresh target.

Fireballs flashed and lifted from Hill 224. Every time the residue of the bolt's impact drifted away, something fresh and metallic lifted from the same glassy crater. After the sixth bolt, the gun ceased fire.

"I don't know if I'm getting through," Kowacs said. He picked up the communicator and stared at it for a moment. Then he turned and shouted over to the next dugout on the right, "All plasma weapons to the First Platoon sector! Pass it on."

"All plasma weapons to First Platoon sector!" Sienkiewicz echoed toward their left-hand neighbors. "Pass it on!"

The dugouts were within voice range of one another. It was risky to strip the other sectors, but movement on Hill 224 proved there would be another attack here. The two plasma weapons which had not been engaged against the first attack were the only ones in the unit that still had sufficient ammo to blunt a second thrust.

Kowacs' throat was swollen. He couldn't smell the foul smoke drifting from the creatures smashed just in front of the dugout, but he felt the tissues of his nose and mouth cringe at further punishment.

He put his thumb on the shallow depression beneath the communicator's voiceplate and said hoarsely, "Grant, this is Kowacs. Please respond. We need destroyer-class support *soonest*. We're being attacked by machines."

Part of Kowacs' mind wondered whether the

creatures had their own internal AI programs or if some Syndicate operator controlled them through telerobotics. What did the operation look like from *that* bastard's point of view?

"We could use ammo resupply and a little extra firepower."

His voice broke. He cleared it and continued, "For God's sake, Grant, get Toby English and the *Haig* down here now!"

Kowacs lifted his thumb from the depression. Nothing moved when he squeezed down. No sound—from Grant, of static, *nothing*—came from the voiceplate when he released the 'key'.

Maybe there wasn't a key. Maybe there wasn't even a communicator, just a plastic placebo that Grant had given Kowacs so the spook could be sure Headhunter Six would accept the mission that would mean the end of his whole company. . . .

"Bloody hell," Top muttered as he stared toward what was taking shape on the furrowed side of Hill 224.

A gun crew staggered over from 2nd Platoon with their plasma weapon on its tripod, ready to fire. They grounded beside the command dugout. The gunner slid behind his sights, while the assistant gunner helped the team's Number Three adjust the hundred-round belt of ammunition she carried while her fellows handled the gun.

Masses of shimmering metal oozed through the soil across the swale as if the hillside was sweating mercury. The blobs were larger than those which had appeared at the start of the first attack, and they merged again as soon as they reached the surface.

Clattering rifle fire had no affect on the creatures. None of the command team bothered to shoot.

Three plasma weapons, then a fourth, sent their

dazzling radiance into the new threat. Blazing metal splashed a hundred meters skyward. The whole hillside glowed with an auroral lambency.

The ball of metal continued to grow. It was already the size of a cathedral's dome. Plasma bolts no longer touched the creature's shimmering skin.

It slid forward. The crater it left in the side of Hill 224 was the size a nuclear weapon would make.

Only two plasma weapons were still firing. The one nearest the command team had run almost through its belt of ammunition. The weapon's barrel glowed, and the rock a meter in front of its muzzle had been fused to glass.

Sergeant Bradley aimed his RAG grenade and waited. Sie arranged all her grenade clusters on the forward lip of the dugout so that she could throw them in quick succession as soon as the target rolled into range.

Kowacs emptied his assault rifle into the shining mass. It was halfway across the swale. Because of its size, the creature moved with deceptive speed.

As Kowacs slid a fresh magazine into his weapon, his eye caught the message on the excavator screen:

**THIRTY-SEVEN KILOMETERS. TARGET DESTROYED WITHOUT INCIDENT. A PIECE OF CAKE. BEGINNING ASCENT.**

Top fired his RAG grenade. The shaped-charge explosion was a momentary smear against the monster's shielding, nothing more.

Heatwaves shimmered from Kowacs' gunbarrel. He fired the entire magazine in a single hammering burst and reloaded again. When the creature got within forty meters, he'd start throwing grenades.

*And I'll say to Toby English, "Boy you bastards cut*

*it close! Ten seconds later and there wouldn't have been anything left of us but grease spots!"*

Nick Kowacs laughed and aimed his rifle again at a towering monster framed by a sky that was empty of hope.

# FACING THE ENEMY

Oval membranes along the Ichton's lateral lines throbbed as the creature writhed against the table restraints. Two audio speakers flanked the observation screen which Sergeant Dresser watched in the room above. One speaker keened at the edge of ultrasound, while a roll of low static cracked through the other.

"What's the squeaking?" Dresser asked tensely.

"Just noise," said Tech 4 Rodriges, looking up from his monitor. "Moaning, I guess you'd say. Nothing for the translation program—" he nodded toward the hissing second speaker "—to translate."

He hoped Dresser wasn't going to nut, because the fella didn't have any business being here. That was how the brass would think, anyway. So long as the Ichton was alone, Rodriges' job was to flood it with knockout gas if something went wrong. That didn't seem real likely; but if the creature damaged its *so*-valuable body, there'd be hell to pay.

Dresser's lips were dry, but he wiped his palms on the thighs of his fresh utilities. The uniform felt light compared to the one he'd worn during the most recent mission on *SB 781*. The scout boat's recycling system had cleaned away sweat and body oils after every watch, but there wasn't anything machines could do about the fear which the cloth absorbed just as surely. . . .

That was thinking crazy. Had to stop that *now*.

"Don't worry," he said aloud. "I'm fine."

"Sure an ugly bastard," Rodriges commented in a neutral voice.

Upright, the Ichton would be the better part of three meters tall. The creature's gray body was thin, with a waxy glow over the exoskeleton beneath. By contrast, the six limbs springing from the thorax had a fleshy, ropy, texture, though they were stiffened internally by tubes of chitin. Now they twitched against invisible restraints.

"First good look I really had of him," Dresser said softly. "Of it."

He wasn't sure how he felt. He wiped his hands again.

"Huh?" said Rodriges in amazement. "But—it was you caught him, right? I mean—you know, the real one. Wasn't . . . ?"

Light winked from the Ichton's faceted eyes as the creature turned its head mindlessly from one side to the other.

"Hey, no sweat," Dresser said. A grin quirked a corner of his mouth. The first thing that had struck him funny for—

From since they'd made landfall a month and a half ago. Rodriges thought the Ichton *looked* ugly, but he hadn't seen what the creatures did. . . .

The Ichton on the screen relaxed. One speaker squealed plaintively; the other asked in an emotionless voice, "Where . . . ? Where am I?"

"Sure, that was us," Dresser said. "*SB 781*, not just

me; but my boat, my crew, you bet. Only you don't . . . I didn't really look at it, you know? Bundled it up and slung it into a stasis field before we bugged out. Scout boats don't have what you'd call great passenger accommodations."

A separate chirping punctuated the sounds the Ichton made. In a voice identical to that provided for the prisoner, the translator said, "Please relax. The restraints are simply to prevent you from injuring yourself upon waking. When you relax, we will loosen them."

"That's Admiral Horwarth, the project head," Rodriges said knowingly. "Don't know jack shit about medicine or biochem, but she sure can make a team of prima donna medicos get on with the program."

Dresser was lost in memory. He said, "When we landed, I was watching on my screen, and there was this city, a Gerson city it turned out. . . ."

Thomson was at the center console, watching the ground swing toward *SB 781* with the leisured assurance of a thrown medicine ball. Occasionally her fingers scissored over the controls without touching them.

The approach was nerve-wrackingly slow, but that was the way it had to be. Staying out of Ichton warning sensors was the only way the scout boat was going to survive. The turbulence and friction heat of a fast approach would have pointed a glowing finger straight toward them.

"Lookit that sucker!" muttered Codrus.

Dresser and Codrus didn't bother to back up Thomson, but the chance that she would have to take over from the boat's artificial intelligence was a million to one—and the chance that a human could do any good if the AI failed was a lot worse than that.

Codrus was watching the nearest Ichton colony, a

vast pimple of blue light projecting kilometers into the stratosphere. Ichton strongholds began as hemispheres of magnetic force. The flux was concentrated enough to sunder the molecular bonds of projectiles and absorb the full fury of energy weapons. As each colony grew, the height of its shield decreased in relation to the diameter.

This colony was already a hundred kilometers across. It would not stop growing until its magnetic walls bulged against those of other Ichton fortresses.

*Lookit that sucker.*

The scout boat quivered and bobbed as the AI subtlely mimicked the patterns of clear air turbulence, but the computer-enhanced view on Dresser's screen remained rock solid. It had been city of moderate size—perhaps 15,000 inhabitants if human density patterns were applicable.

The buildings tended to rounded surfaces rather than planes. The palette was of earth tones, brightened by street paving of brilliant yellow. From a distance, the soft lines and engaging ambiance of the city as it originally stood would have suggested a field of edible mushrooms.

The tallest of the surviving structures rose about ten meters. The ragged edges in which the tower now ended were the result of Ichton weapons.

A column of Ichtons had passed through the community. The invaders' weapons, derivatives of their defensive shields, had blasted a track across the center of the inhabited area and gnawed apart most of the rest of the city as well.

"Hang on," warned Thomson.

"What gets me," said Dresser, "is they didn't attack the place. It was just there, and they went through it rather than going around."

"They took out major urban centers with anti-matter

bombs," Codrus said. "Musta had a scale of what they blitzed and what they ignored unless it got in the way. Of course—"

"Touchdown!" Thomson said.

*SB 781* fluffed her landing jets—hard twice, while there were still twenty meters of air beneath the boat's belly, then a softer, steady pulse that disturbed the soil as little as possible. No point in inserting stealthily through a hundred kilometers of atmosphere and then kick up a plume of dirt like a locating flag.

"—sooner or later, they cover the whole land surface, so I don't guess they worry about when they get around t' this piece or that."

The scout boat shuddered to a halt that flung Dresser against his gel restraints. His display continued to glow at him with images of the wrecked city, enhanced to crispness greater than what his eyes would have showed him at the site.

Ichton weapons fired beads the size of matchheads which generated expanding globes of force. Individual weapons had a range of only three hundred meters or so, but their effect was devastating—particularly near the muzzle, where the density of the magnetic flux was high. The force globes acted as atomic shears, wrenching apart the molecules of whatever they touched. Even at maximum range, when the flux formed an iridescent ball a meter in diameter, it could blast the fluff off the bodies of this planet's furry natives.

Dresser was sure of that, because some of the Ichtons' victims still lay in the ruins like scorched teddy bears.

"They're Gersons," Dresser said to his crew. "The natives here. One of the races that asked the Alliance for help."

"Too late for that," Codrus muttered. His slim, pale hands played over the controls, rotating the image of the Ichton fortress on his display. From any angle, the blue glare was as perfect and terrible as the heart of a supernova. "Best we get our asses back to the *Hawking* and report."

This was Dresser's first mission on *SB 781*; the previous team leader had wangled a commission and a job in Operations. Thomson and Codrus came with the boat . . . and they were an item, which sometimes worked and sometimes didn't.

It didn't work on *SB 781*. Both partners were too worried about what might happen to the other to get on with the mission.

"Not till we've done our jobs," Dresser said softly. He raised the probes, hair-thin optical guides which unreeled to the height of twenty meters above *SB 781's* camouflaged hull. His display immediately defaulted to real-time images of a wind-sculpted waste.

The immediate terrain hadn't been affected by the Ichton invasion—yet. Eventually it too would be roofed by flux generators so powerful that they bent light and excluded the blue and shorter wave lengths entirely. Within their impregnable armor, the Ichtons would extract ores—the rock had a high content of lead and zinc—and perhaps the silicon itself. The planet the invaders left would be reduced to slag and ash.

Thomson tried to stretch in the narrow confines of her seat. Her hands trembled, though that might have been reaction to the tension of waiting above the flight controls against the chance that she'd have to take over. "No job we can do here," she said. "This place is gone. *Gone*. It's not like we've got room t' take back refugees."

Dresser modified his display. The upper half remained a real-time panorama. The glow of an Ichton colony stained the eastern quadrant in a sickly blue counterfeit of the dawn that was still hours away. The lower portion of the display became a map created from data *SB 781*'s sensors gathered during insertion.

"Command didn't send us for refugees," he said. He tried to keep his voice calm, so that his mind would become calm as well. "They said to bring back a live prisoner."

"We *can't* get a prisoner!" Codrus said, maybe louder than he'd meant. "Anything that'd bust open these screens—"

He gestured toward the Ichton fortress on his display. His knuckles vanished within the holographic ambiance, then reappeared like the head of a bobbing duck.

"—'d rip the whole planet down to the core and let *that* out. The place is fucked, and we need to get away!"

"They're still sending out colonies," Dresser said.

His fingers raised the probes ten meters higher and shrank the image area to 5° instead of a full panorama. The upper display shuddered. The blue glow filled most of its horizon.

Five Ichton vehicles crawled across terrain less barren than that in which the scout boat hid. Trees grew in serpentine lines along the boundaries of what must once have been cultivated fields. For the most part, the land was now overgrown with brush.

"About twenty klicks away," Dresser continued. He felt the eyes of his subordinates burning on him; but he was in charge, and *SB 781* was going to carry out its mission. "We'll take the skimmers and set up an ambush."

"Take the boat," Thomson said through dry lips. "We'll want the firepower."

Dresser shook his head without taking his eyes off his display. "The boat'd get noticed," he said. "You guys'll be in hard suits with A-Pot weapons. That'll be as much firepower as we need."

"Lookit that!" Codrus cried, pointing across the cockpit to Dresser's display. "Lookit that!"

A family of Gersons bolted from the row of trees just ahead of the Ichton column. There were four adults, a pair of half-grown children, and a furry infant in the arms of the female struggling along behind the other adults.

The turret of the leading vehicle rotated to follow the refugees. . . .

"You okay, Sarge?" Rodriges asked worriedly.

Dresser crossed his arms and kneaded his biceps hard. "Yeah," he said. "Sure." His voice was husky. "Seein' the thing there—"

He nodded toward the screen. The Ichton was sitting upright. The voice from the speaker said, "Don't try to use your conscious mind to control your muscles. You wouldn't with your own body, after all."

"You can't imagine how cruel they are, the Ichtons," Dresser said.

"Naw, it's not cruel," the technician explained. "You're only cruel to something you think about. The bugs, they treat the whole universe like we'd treat, you know, an outcrop of nickel ore."

"So cruel . . . ," Dresser whispered.

The Ichton's tympanic membranes shrilled through the left speaker. The translation channel boomed, "Where the hell am I? Thomson? Codrus! What's happened to my boat!"

Sergeant Dresser closed his eyes.

"Where's 781, you bastards?" demanded the Ichton through the machine voice.

## 2

"The sub-brain of your clone body will control the muscles, Sergeant Dresser," said the voice from a speaker in the wall. "You can't override the hard-wired controls, so just relax and let them do their job."

The words were compressed and harshly mechanical; the room's lighting spiked chaotically on several wavelengths. Were they torturing him?

Who were *they*?

"Where's my crew?" Dresser shouted. He threw his feet over the edge of the couch on which had awakened. His legs splayed though he tried to keep them steady. He collapsed on his chest. The floor was resilient.

"Your men are all right, Sergeant," the voice said. The speaker tried to be soothing, but the delivery rasped like a saw on bone. "So is your human self. Your memory will return in a few minutes."

Memory was returning already. Memory came in disorienting sheets that didn't fit with the real world. Images that Dresser remembered were sharply defined but static. They lacked the texturing of incipient movement that wrapped everything Dresser saw through the faceted eyes of his present body.

But he remembered. . . .

The male Gerson—the tallest, though even he was less than a meter-fifty in height—turned and raised an anti-tank rocket launcher. The rest of the family blundered past him. The juveniles were hand in hand, and the female with the infant still brought up the rear.

"Where'd he get hardware like that?" Codrus muttered. "I'd've figured the teddy bears were down to sharp sticks, from the way things look."

The Ichton vehicles moved on air cushions; they didn't have the traction necessary to grind through obstacles the way tracked or even wheeled transport could. The leader's turret weapon spewed a stream of projectiles like a ripple of light. The hedge row disintegrated in bright flashes.

"They sent a starship to the Alliance, after all," Dresser muttered. "The ones left behind still have some weapons, is all."

Brush and splintered wood began to burn sluggishly. The leading Ichton vehicle nosed into the gap.

"Much good it'll do them," said Thomson.

The Gerson fired. The rocket launcher's flaring yellow backblast enveloped twenty meters of brush and pulsed the hedge on the other side of the field. The hypervelocity projectile slammed into the Ichton vehicle.

Slammed, rather, into the faint blue glow of the defensive shield surrounding the Ichton vehicle. The impact roared across the electro-optical spectrum like multicolored petals unfolding from a white core.

The vehicle rocked backward on its bubble of supporting air. The projectile, flattened and a white blaze from frictional heating, dropped to the ground without having touched the body of its target.

The turret traversed. The male Gerson knew what was coming. He ran to the side in a desperate attempt to deflect the stream of return fire from his family. His head and the empty rocket launcher vanished into their constituent atoms as the powerful turret weapon caught him at point blank range. The high-temperature residue of the sundered molecules recombined an instant later in flashes and flame.

The Ichton gunner continued to fire. Projectiles scythed across the field, ripping smoldering gaps in the vegetation.

The refugees threw themselves down when the shooting started. As the gun traversed past, a juvenile leaped upright and waved his remaining arm. Before the gunner could react, the screaming victim collapsed again.

The turret weapon ceased firing.

The entire column entered the field. The leading and trailing vehicles were obviously escorts, mounting powerful weapons in their turrets. The second and third vehicles in the convoy were hugely larger and must have weighed a hundred tonnes apiece. They didn't appear to be armed, but their defensive shielding was so dense that the vehicles' outlines wavered within globes of blue translucence. The remaining vehicle, number four in the column, was unarmed and of moderate size, though larger than the escorts.

Dresser's mind catalogued the vehicles against the template of his training and experience: a truck to supply the new colony en route . . . and a pair of transporters, armored like battleships, to carry the eggs and larvae which would populate that colony.

The Ichton convoy proceeded on a track as straight as the line from a compass rose. For a moment, Dresser thought that the Gerson survivors—if there were any—had been overlooked. Then the supply truck and the rear escort swung out of the column and halted.

A Gerson jumped to her feet and ran. She took only three steps before her legs and the ground beneath her vanished in a red flash. Heat made the air above the turret gun's muzzle shimmer.

The supply truck's sidepanel slid open, and the defensive screen adjacent to the door paled. A pair of Ichtons stepped out of the vehicle. Heavy protective suits concealed the lines of their bodies.

"Big suckers," said Thomson. Her hands hovered

over the console controls. Flight regime was up on the menu.

"Three of us 're gonna take on a whole army of *them*?" Codrus asked.

Dresser thought:

*It's not an army.*

*It doesn't matter how big they are—we're not going to arm wrestle.*

*You guys aren't any more scared than I am.*

He said aloud, "You bet."

One of the Ichtons tossed the legless Gerson—the body had ceased to twitch—into the bag he, *it*, dragged along behind. The other Ichton spun abruptly and sprayed a 90° arc of brush with his handweapon.

Though less powerful than the turret gun, the projectiles slashed through the vegetation. Branches and taller stems settled in a wave like the surface of a collapsing air mattress.

The Ichton with the bag patrolled the swath stolidly. He gathered up the bodies or body parts of three more victims.

"Don't . . . ," Dresser whispered. Codrus and Thomson glanced sidelong, wondering what their commander meant.

The armed Ichton pointed his weapon. Before he could fire, the Gerson female with the infant in her arms stood up.

"*Don't.* . . ."

Instead of shooting, the Ichton stepped forward and reached out with its free hand. It seized the Gerson by the shoulder in a triaxial grip and led her back toward the vehicle. The remaining Ichton followed, slowed by the weight of the bag it was dragging.

Dresser let out the breath he had been holding longer than he realized.

➤    ➤    ➤

"Now relax, Sergeant Dresser," said the mechanical voice. "Let the backbrain control your motions."

Dresser got to his feet, his four feet. His eyes stared at the ceiling. He wanted to close them, but they didn't close. A part of his mind was as amazed at the concept that eyes could close as it had been at the flat, adamantine images from Dresser's memory.

"You're doing very well, Sergeant," the voice cajoled. "Now, I'm going to open the door in the end of the compartment. Just follow the hallway out. Don't be in a hurry."

Dresser's right front leg bumped the table, but he didn't fall. He was terrified. His mind tried to focus on anything but what his legs were doing. The doorway lurched closer.

It was like being in freefall. But he knew there was no landing possible from this mental vacuum.

## 3

Rodriges manipulated his controls. The screen split. Its right half showed the back of the cloned Ichton shambling through the doorway, while a frontal shot of the creature approached down the hallway on the left.

"He's gonna get t' meet the brass," the technician muttered. "Horwarth and Doctor del Prato. Bet you never thought you'd be meeting an admiral and a top biochemist personal-like, did you, sarge?"

Dresser grunted.

Rodriges touched the controls again. The right image leapfrogged to the interior of a three-bed medical ward which included a well-appointed office. The admiral, seated behind a desk of what looked like real wood, was a stocky female. She wore a skull & crossbones ring in her left ear, and her right ear was missing. To her right sat a florid-faced civilian whose moustache flowed into his sideburns.

The door to the ward had been removed and a section of bulkhead cut from the top of the doorway. Even so, the Ichton lurching down the corridor would have to duck or bang its flat head.

"Why didn't they wake him up here?" Dresser asked. He made a tight, almost dismissive, gesture toward the medical ward.

Rodriges looked sidelong at the scout. "Umm . . . ," he said. "They didn't know quite how you'd—how he'd react when he woke up, y'know? They got me here for protection—"

The technician tapped carefully beside, not on, a separate keypad. It was a release for the weapons whose targeting was slaved to the screen controls.

"—but they don't want, you know, to lose the work. There's five more clones on ice, but still. . . ."

Dresser's face went hard. He didn't speak.

The Ichton paused in the doorway and tried to lower its head. Instead, the creature fell forward with its haunches high, like those of a horse which balked too close to the edge of a ditch.

"That's all right," said Admiral Horwarth brusquely. Her voice and the hypersonic translation of her voice echoed from the paired speakers of the observation room. "You'll soon have the hang of it."

"Part of the reason he's so clumsy," Rodriges said as he kept his invisible sight centered on the clone's chest, "is the body's straight out of the growth tank. It hasn't got any muscle tone."

His lips pursed as he and Dresser watched the ungainly creature struggle to rise again. "Of course," the technician added, "it could be the bugs're clumsy as hell anyhow."

"The ones I saw," said Dresser tightly, "moved pretty good."

The leading Ichton vehicle started to climb out of the dry wash; the nose of the last vehicle dipped to enter the end farthest from Dresser.

The scout boat's artificial intelligence planned the ambush with superhuman skill. It balanced the target, the terrain, distance factors, and the available force—the lack of available force—into a 70% probability that some or all of the scout team would survive the contact.

The AI thought their chance of capturing a live Ichton was <.1; but that wasn't the first thing in any of the scouts' minds, not even Dresser's.

The convoy's inexorable progress led it to the badlands site within two minutes of the arrival time the AI had calculated. A wind-cut swale between two tilted sheets of hard sandstone had been gouged deeper by infrequent cloudbursts. The resulting gully was half a kilometer long. It was straight enough to give Dresser a clear shot along it from where he lay aboard his skimmer, on higher ground a hundred meters from the mouth.

The Ichtons could easily have gone around the gully, but there was no reason for them to do so. From what Dresser had seen already, the race had very little tendency to go around anything.

"Team," he said to his distant crewmen, "go!"

Codrus and Thomson fired from the sandstone ridges to either flank. Their weapons tapped energy from the Dirac Sea underlying the real-time universe, so the range—less than three hundreds meters in any case—was no hindrance.

Sightlines *could* have been a problem. Since Dresser had only two flankers, it didn't matter that they had clear shots at only the first and last vehicles of the convoy. The tops of the huge egg transporters were visible from the crewmen's positions, but the supply truck had vanished beneath the sharp lips of the gully.

The beams from the A-Potential weapons were invisible, but at their touch the magnetic shielding of the escort vehicles flared into sparkling cataclysm. Dresser's helmet visor blocked the actinics and filtered the visual uproar. He continued to have a sharp view of the vehicles themselves—undamaged at the heart of the storm.

The A-Pot weapons could focus practically limitless amounts of power on the magnetic shields, cancelling their effect—but the beams couldn't focus *through* the shields. The escort vehicles stopped dead. Their power supplies shunted energy to the shields—to be dumped harmlessly back into the Dirac Sea—but as soon as the A-Pot beams were redirected, the escorts would be back in the battle.

"Mines," Dresser said to the audio controller in his helmet, "*go!*"

The gossamer, high-explosive mesh the scouts had spread across the floor of the gully went off. There was a green flash, a quick shock through the bedrock which slapped Dresser ten centimeters in the air, and—a heartbeat later—the air-transmitted blast that would have deafened the sergeant without the protection of his helmet.

The explosive's propagation rate was a substantial fraction of light speed. The blast flattened the two escorts from the underside before it lifted them. Their wreckage spun into the air.

Though the supply truck's shields were unaffected, the shockwave bounced the lighter vehicle against the side of the gully. It caromed back and landed on one side. Its shields hissed furiously, trying to repel the washed stone. The generators didn't have enough power to levitate the truck, and the ground wasn't going to move.

Mass and magnetic shielding protected the egg transporters. The huge vehicles lurched, but neither showed signs of damage. The leading transporter plowed through the wreckage of the escort. The driver of second transporter cut his controls to the right. Bow weapons, their existence unguessed until this moment, blasted an alternate route into the sandstone wall.

The mine's unexpected groundshock lifted Dresser, then dropped him back on the hard-padded couch of his skimmer. He tried to aim his weapon.

The bow of the leading egg transporter pointed directly at him. A panel had recessed to clear the muzzle of an axial weapon like the one carving a ramp through kilotonnes of rock. Its bore looked big enough for a man to crawl down.

Codrus caught the Ichton vehicle with his A-Pot weapon. The beam held the huge transporter as rigid as a moth on a pin. The screens' watery glare vanished.

Dresser raked the undefended target lengthwise with his drum-fed rocket launcher.

The launcher cycled at the rate of two rounds per second. It was easy for an experienced gunner like Dresser to control the weapon during short bursts, despite the considerable recoil: though the barrel was open at both ends, highly-accelerated exhaust gas gave a sharp backward jolt to the sides of the tube.

Dresser's first rocket exploded on the muzzle of the Ichton gun. The next two green flashes shredded the bow of the transporter as recoil shoved Dresser and lifted his point of aim.

He lowered his sights and fired again, probing

deeper into the Ichton vehicle through the damage caused by his initial burst. His helmet dulled the slap*bang*! of the shots and protected his retinas from the bright explosions. The rocket backblast prickled like sunburn on the backs of his bare hands.

A sulphurous fireball mushroomed from the rear of the transporter, far deeper than Dresser had been able to probe with his rockets. The shield generators failed. Codrus' weapon now cut spherical collops from the vehicle.

Dresser shifted his aim to the remaining transporter. He thought he had half the twenty-round drum remaining, but he knew he was too pumped to be certain.

A pair of Ichtons jumped from a hatch in the side of the transporter stalled in the beam of Thomson's weapon. Codrus, bulky and rounded in the hard suit which was an integral part of the A-Pot system, stood up on his ridge to rip the vehicle while Thomson's beam grounded its shield.

Dresser punched three rockets into the transporter's broadside. Green flashes ate meter-diameter chunks from the plating. The individual Ichtons turned together and fired their handweapons at Codrus.

The rock beneath the crewman blurred into high-temperature gas. The Ichton projectiles were near the range at which the flux expanded beyond coherence and the miniature generators failed. If Codrus hadn't been shooting, his A-Pot suit might have protected him against the attenuated forces—

But an aperture to fire through meant a gap in the opposite direction also. Circuits in the A-Pot suit crossed, then blew in a gout of sandstone so hot it fluoresced.

"Ship!" Dresser shouted into the audio controller. He slammed a pair of contact-fuzed rockets through a hole blown by the previous burst. "Go!"

Ten klicks away, *SB 781* was lifting from her camouflaged hide. The AI would execute the flight plan the AI had developed. Dresser could override the machine mind, but he wouldn't have time—

And anyway, he might not be alive in five minutes when the boat appeared to make the extraction.

Bright gray smoke rolled in sheets out of the two lower holes in the transporter's plating. Flame licked from the highest wound, sullenly red, and the smoke *it* trailed was sooty black.

The transporter began to slip back down the ramp its gun had carved. The forward half of the vehicle was shielded, but smoke and flame continued to billow beneath the blue glow.

Thomson shrieked uncontrollably on the team frequency as she lashed the two Ichtons with her weapon. The creatures' personal shields deflected the beam— to Dresser's surprise, but if you couldn't *touch* the target, it didn't matter how much energy you poured into the wrong place.

Dresser kicked the bar behind his left boot to power up his skimmer. It induced a magnetic field in the rock with the same polarity as that in the little vehicle's own undersurface.

The skimmer lurched a centimeter upward, throwing off Dresser's aim. The last rocket in his magazine missed high. The transporter was beginning to sag in the center.

"Thomson!" Dresser shouted. "We want a prisoner!"

The rock beneath the Ichtons first went molten; then froze and shattered into dust finer than the sand that had once been compacted to make stone; and finally expanded into a white fireball that drank the Ichtons like thistledown in a gas flame. When transformed into a real-time analog, Thomson's A-Potential energy easily overwhelmed the Ichton defenses.

The skimmer wobbled downhill. Dresser steered with his feet on the tiller bar while he lay on his left side and fumbled a fresh magazine onto his rocket launcher. The Ichtons fired at movement. . . .

"Kill the fucking bastards!" Thomson screamed.

The front half of the damaged transporter began to crumple like overheated foil beneath its magnetic shielding. High-voltage arcs danced across the plates, scarring the metal like fungus on the skin of a poorly-embalmed corpse.

"K—" said Thomson as her A-Pot beam drew a streak of cloudy red sky from another universe into the heart of the transporter. The back half of the vehicle blew up with a stunning crash even louder than that of the minefield that initiated the contact.

Because Dresser's skimmer was in motion, he was spared the groundshock. The airborne wave was a hot fist that punched fire into his lungs and threatened to spin his little vehicle like a flipped coin. The skimmer's automatic controls stabilized it as no human driver could have done, then shut down. Dresser kicked the starter again.

"Bastards!" shouted Thomson as she rode her own skimmer forward in search of fresh targets.

The explosion slammed the overturned supply truck into the gully wall again. The magnetic shielding failed; one side of the vehicle scraped off on the rock. A living Ichton, suited and armed, spilled out along with other of the truck's contents. Another of the creatures was within the gutted vehicle, transfixed despite its armor by a length of tubing from the perimeter frame.

Protein rations, bundled into transparent packets weighing a kilogram or so, littered the gully floor. The mother Gerson was only partway through processing. Her legs and the lower half of her furry torso stuck out the intake funnel in the truck body. The apparatus had stalled from battle damage.

The baby Gerson lay among the ration packets, feebly waving its chubby arms.

Thomson fired from her skimmer. She didn't have a direct sightline to the supply truck, but her suit sensors told her where the target was. The A-Pot beam ripped through the lip of stone like lightning in a wheat field.

Rock shattered, spewing chunks skyward. At the end of the ragged path, visible to Dresser though not Thomson, the damaged truck sucked inward and vanished like a smoke sculpture.

*SB 781* drifted across Thomson, as silent as a cloud. The vessel was programmed to land at the center of the gully, since the team didn't have the transport to move an Ichton prisoner any distance from the capture site.

"Ship!" Dresser cried, overriding the plan. "Down! Now!"

The living Ichton got to its feet. Dresser, twenty meters away, grounded his skimmer in a shower of sparks and squeezed his trigger.

The rocket launcher didn't fire. He'd short-stroked the charging lever when the transporter blew up. There wasn't a round in the chamber.

The baby Gerson wailed. The Ichton spun like a dancer and vaporized the infant in a glowing dazzle.

*SB 781* settled at the lip of the gully, between Thomson and the Ichton. She wouldn't shoot at their own ride home—and anyway, the vessel's A-Potential shielding should protect it if she did.

The team's *job* was to bring back a prisoner.

Dresser charged his launcher and fired. The warhead detonated on the Ichton's magnetic shield. The green flash hurled the creature against the rock wall.

It bounced back. Dresser fired again, slapping the Ichton into the stone a second time. The creature's weapon flew out of its three-fingered hands.

At Dresser's third shot, a triangular bulge on the Ichton's chest melted and the shield's blue glow vanished.

The Ichton sprawled in an ungainly tangle of limbs. Dresser got off his skimmer and ran to the creature. He dropped his rocket launcher and drew the powered cutting bar from the boot sheath where it rode.

Dresser's vision pulsed with colors as though someone were flicking pastel filters over his eyes. He didn't have time to worry whether something was wrong with his helmet optics. Thomson's shouted curses faded in and out also, so the damage was probably within Dresser's skull. Fleet hardware could survive one hell of a hammering, but personnel were still constructed to an older standard. . . .

The Ichton twitched. Dresser ran the tip of his 20-cm cutter along the back of the creature's suit. The armor was non-metallic but tough enough to draw a shriek from the contra-rotating diamond saws in the bar's edge.

Dresser wasn't going to chance carrying the prisoner with in-built devices still functioning in its suit, not even in the stasis bay of *SB 781*. The tech mavens on the *Hawking* could deal with the network of shallow cuts the cutter was going to trace across the chitin and flesh. There wasn't time to be delicate, even if Dresser had wanted to be.

The air in the gully stank, but that wasn't why Dresser took breaths so shallow that his oxygen-starved lungs throbbed.

He couldn't help thinking about the baby Gerson vaporized a few meters away.

**4**

There were two humans in the room with Dresser in his new body. The one behind the desk wore blue; the other wore white.

He wasn't sure what the sex of either of them was.

"As your mind reintegrates with the cloned body, Sergeant," said the mechanical voice, "you'll achieve normal mobility. Ah, normal for the new body, that is."

White's mouth parts were moving. Dresser knew—remembered—that meant the human was probably speaking; but the words came from the desk's front corner moldings. Ears alternated with the speech membranes along Dresser's lateral lines. He shifted position instinctively to triangulate on the speakers' precise location.

"I want to tell you right now, Sergeant, that the Alliance—that all intelligent life in the galaxy is in your debt. You're a very brave man."

The voice and the location were the same—the desk speakers—but it was the other mouth that was moving. A translation system in the desk piped the actual speech out in a form Dresser could understand.

Now that he concentrated, he could hear the words themselves: a faint rumble, like that of distant artillery. It was meaningless and scarcely audible. He would have to watch to determine which of the pair was speaking—

But watching anything was easy. Dresser could see the entire room without turning his head. He noticed every movement, no matter how slight—nostrils flaring for a breath, the quiver of eyelashes at the start of a blink. His new brain combined the images of over a hundred facet eyes and sorted for the differences in the views they presented.

"It was obvious before we started that the enemy's numbers are enormous," Blue continued. "We now realize that Ichton weapons are formidable as well. In some ways—"

The desk translated Blue's throat clearing as a burst of static.

"Well, anyway, they're quite formidable."

The difficulty was that almost all Dresser now saw *was* movement. The background vanished beyond ten meters or so. Even closer objects were undifferentiated blurs until they shifted position. Though Dresser knew—remembered—the physical differences between human males and females, he couldn't see details so fine, and he lacked the hormonal cues that would have sexed individuals of his own kind.

Ye Gods, his own kind!

"You'll be landed back near the site where your original was captured, Sergeant Dresser," Blue went on.

The machine translator rasped Dresser's nerve endings with its compression. Its words lacked the harmonics that made true speech a thrill to hear no matter what its content.

"You shouldn't have any difficulty infiltrating the Ichton forces," interjected White. "The natural recognition patterns of your body will appear—*are* real, are totally real."

Dresser suddenly remembered the last stage of the firefight in the gully. He perceived it now through the senses of his present body. The Ichton flung from the vehicle, under attack but uncertain from where—

*Sound and movement close by, a threat.*

*Spinning and blasting before the enemy can strike home.*

*Reacting before the higher brain can determine that the target was merely a part of the food supply which hadn't been processed before the attack occurred.*

Dresser screamed. Both humans flinched away from the high-frequency warble.

"I'm not a bug!" he cried. "I won't! I won't kill babies!"

"Sergeant," said White, "we realize the strain you're under—"

"Though of course, you volunteered," Blue said.

"—but when your personality has fully integrated with the body into which it's been copied," White continued, "the—dichotomies—will not be quite so, ah, serious. I know—that is, I can imagine the strain you're experiencing. It will get better, I promise you."

"Sergeant . . ," said Blue, "I'll be blunt. We're hoping you can find a chink in the Ichtons' armor. If you can't, the mission of the *Stephen Hawking* is doomed to fail. And all lifeforms in at least this galaxy are, quite simply, doomed."

"Except for the Ichtons themselves," White added.

The machine couldn't capture intonation; memory told Dresser that the bluster of a moment before had vanished.

Dresser's memory tumbled out a kaleidoscope of flat-focus images: a wrecked village; cancerous domes scores of kilometers in diameter, growing inexorably; an Ichton—Dresser's body in every respect—blasting a wailing infant by mistake, a waste of food. . . .

"I can't l-l-live like this!" Dresser cried.

"It's only temporary," Blue said. "Isn't that right, Doctor? I'm not denying the risk, Sergeant Dresser, but as soon as the mission's been completed, you'll be returned to your own form."

"Ah," said White. "Yes, of course, Sergeant. But the main thing is just to let your mind and body integrate. You'll feel better shortly."

"I think the best thing now is for you to start right in on the program," said Blue. "I'll bring in your briefing

officers immediately. You'll see that we've taken steps
to minimize the risk to you."

Blue continued to speak. All Dresser could think of
was that tiny Gerson, like a living teddy bear.

**5**

The screen showed six personnel entering the ward
where the Ichton clone hunched. One of the newcomers was a Gerson.

In the observation room, Dresser turned his back
on the screen. "How much does he remember?" he
asked Rodriges harshly.

The technician shrugged. "Up to maybe thirty-six
hours before the transfer," he said. "There's some loss,
but not a lot. You okay yourself?"

"Fine," said Dresser. "I'm great."

On the screen, a uniformed man without rank tabs
outlined the physical-training program. The clone's new
muscles had to be brought up to standard before the
creature was reinserted.

Dresser shuddered. Rodriges thumbed down the
audio level, though the translation channel remained
a distant piping.

"When I volunteered . . . ," Dresser said carefully. "I
didn't know how much it'd bug—bother me. To see
myself as an Ichton."

"Naw, that's not you, Sarge," Rodriges said. "Personalities start to diverge at the moment the mind scan
gets dumped in the new cortex—and in *that* cortex,
the divergence is going to be real damn fast. None of
the sensory stimuli are the same, you see."

Dresser grunted and looked back over his shoulder.
"Yeah," he said. "Well. Bet he thinks he's me, though."

"Sarge, you did the right thing, volunteering," Rodriges soothed. "You heard the admiral. Using somebody who's seen the bugs in action, that improves the chances. And anyway—it's done, right?"

The clone was moving its forelimbs—arms—in response to the trainer's direction. The offside supporting legs twitched unexpectedly; the tall creature fell over. A civilian expert jumped reflexively behind a female colleague in Marine Reaction Unit fatigues.

"It's going to be just as hard for him when they switch him back, won't it?" Dresser said. He turned to the technician. "Getting used to a human body again, I mean."

"Huh?" Rodriges blurted. "Oh, you mean like the admiral said. Ah, Sarge. . . . A fast-growth clone—"

He gestured toward the screen. Dresser didn't look around.

"Look, it's a total-loss project. I mean, in the tank we got five more bodies like this one—but the original, what's left of that's just hamburger."

Dresser stared but said nothing.

Rodriges blinked in embarrassment. He plowed onward, saying, "Cost aside—and I'm *not* saying it's a cost decision, but it'd be cheaper to build six destroyers than a batch of fast-growth clones. Anyway, cost aside, there's no *way* that thing's gonna be back in a body like yours unless yours . . . You know?"

The technician shrugged.

"I guess I was pretty naive," Dresser said slowly.

Rodriges reached over and gripped the scout's hand. "Hey," the technician said. "It's not you, you know? It's a thing. Just a thing."

Dresser disengaged his hand absently. He looked toward the screen again, but he didn't see the figures, human and alien, on it. Instead, his mind filled with the image of the baby Gerson, stretching out its chubby hands toward him—

Until it vanished in tears that diffracted light into a dazzle like that of the weapon in Dresser's three-fingered hands.

# FAILURE MODE

In the mirror-finished door to the admiral's office, Sergeant Dresser saw the expression on his own face: worn, angry, and—if you looked deep in the eyes—as dangerous as a grenade with the pin pulled.

"You may go in, sir," repeated Admiral Horwarth's human receptionist in a tart voice.

Dresser was angry:

Because he'd gone through normal mission debriefing and he should have been off-duty. Instead he'd been summoned to meet the head of Bureau 8, Special Projects.

Because it had been a tough mission, and he'd failed.

And because he'd just watched a planet pay the price *all* life would pay for the mission's failure. Even the Ichtons would die, when they'd engulfed everything in the universe beyond themselves.

216

"The admiral is *waiting*, Sergeant," said the receptionist, a blond hunk who could have broken Dresser in half with his bare hands; but that wouldn't matter, because bare hands were for when you were out of ammo, your cutting bar had fried, and somebody'd nailed your boots to the ground . . .

Dresser tried to stiff-arm the feral gray face before him. The doorpanel slid open before he touched it. He strode into the office of Admiral Horwarth, a stocky, middle-aged woman facing him from behind a desk.

On the wall behind Horwarth was an Ichton.

If Dresser had had a weapon, he'd have shot the creature by reflex, even though his conscious mind knew he was seeing a holographic window into the Ichton's cell somewhere else on the *Stephen Hawking*. The prisoner must be fairly close by, because formic acid from its exoskeletal body tinged the air throughout Special Projects' discrete section of the vessel.

People like Dresser weren't allowed weapons aboard the *Hawking*. Especially not when they'd just returned from a mission and the Psych read-out said they were ten-tenths stressed—besides having to be crazy to pilot a scout boat to begin with.

"Sit down, Sergeant," Admiral Horwarth said. She didn't sound concerned about what she must have seen on Dresser's face. "I'm sorry to delay your down-time like this, but—"

She smiled humorlessly.

"—this is important enough that I want to hear it directly from you."

Dresser grimaced as he took the offered chair. "Yeah, I understand," he said. "Sir."

And the hell of it was, he did. Even tired and angry—and as scared as he was—Dresser was too disciplined not to do his duty. Scouts without rigid self discipline didn't last long enough for anybody else to notice their passing.

"I suppose it was a considerable strain," Horwarth prodded gently, "having to nursemaid two scientists and not having a normal crew who could stand watches?"

Dresser had been staring at the Ichton. He jerked his gaze downward at the sound of the admiral's voice. "Sorry, sir," he muttered. "No, that wasn't much of a problem. For me. The trip, that's the AI's job. There's nothing for human crews to do. I—"

Dresser looked at his hands. He waggled them close in front of his chest. He'd been told you could identify scouts because they almost never met the eyes of other human beings when talking to them. "Scouts, you know, anybody who's willing to do it more than once. Scouts keep to themselves. The boat isn't big enough to, to interact."

He raised his eyes to the Ichton again. It was walking slowly about its cell on its two lower pairs of limbs. The top pair and their gripping appendages were drawn in tight against the creature's gray carapace.

"The scientists," Dresser continued flatly, "Bailey and Kaehler . . . they weren't used to it. I think they were pretty glad when we got to the landing point, even though it didn't look like the right place . . ."

"You've done something wrong, Dresser!" snarled Captain Bailey as *Scout Boat 781*'s braking orbit brought the vessel closer to the surface of the ruined planet. "This place hasn't beaten off an Ichton attack. It's been stripped!"

"At this point, sir," Dresser said, "I haven't done anything at all except initiate landing sequence. The artificial intelligence took us through sponge space to the star that the—source—provided. There's only one life-capable planet circling that star, and we're landing on it."

He couldn't argue with Bailey's assessment, though. MANTRA—properly, the name of the project file rather than the nameless planet itself—was utterly barren. Only the human-breathable atmosphere indicated that the planet's lifelessness resulted from an outside agency rather than incapacity to support life.

The agency had almost certainly been a swarm of Ichtons. The chitinous monsters had devoured the surface of the planet, to feed themselves and to build a fleet of colony ships with which to infect additional worlds. The Ichtons were a cancer attacking all life . . .

MANTRA was gray rubble, waterless and sterile. Before they left, the invaders had reduced the planet to fist-sized pellets of slag, waste from their gigantic processing mills. The landscape over which the scout boat sizzled contained no hills, valleys, or hope.

"Chance wouldn't have brought us to a solar system, Captain," Kaehler said. She was small for a woman, even as Bailey was large for a man; and unlike her companion, she was a civilian without military rank. "It must be the correct location."

When Dresser thought about Kaehler, it appeared to him that she'd been stamped through a mold of a particular shape rather than grown to adulthood in the normal fashion. Events streamed through the slight woman without being colored by a personality.

Dresser thought about other people only when they impinged on his mission.

Dresser remembered that he wasn't dealing with scout crewmen. "Hang tight," he said. Even so, he spoke in a soft voice.

The AI pulsed red light across the cabin an instant after Dresser's warning. A heartbeat later, the landing motors fired with a harsh certainty that flung the three humans against their restraints.

Approach thresholds for scout boats were much higher than the norm for naval vessels, and enormously higher than those of commercial ships. The little boats might have to drop into a box canyon at a significant fraction of orbital velocity in order to survive. The hardware was stressed to take the punishment, and the crews got used to the experience—or transferred out of the service.

*SB 781* crunched down at the point Dresser had chosen almost at random. They were in the mid-latitudes of MANTRA's northern hemisphere. That was as good as any other place on the featureless globe.

"Well, sirs . . ." Dresser said. The restraints didn't release automatically. Scout boats were liable to come to rest at any angle, including inverted. The pilot touched the manual switch, freeing himself and the two scientists. "Welcome to MANTRA."

"Was there a problem with the equipment?" Admiral Horwarth asked. "The Mantra Project was the first field trial, as I suppose you know."

She gave the scout a perfunctory smile. "I don't imagine that information stays compartmented within a three-man unit."

The Ichton turned to face the pick-ups. It seemed to be staring into the admiral's office, but that was an illusion. The link with the prisoner's cell was certainly not two-way; and in any case, the Ichtons' multiple eyes provided a virtually spherical field of view, though at low definition by human standards.

"The equipment?" Dresser said. "No, there wasn't any difficulty with the equipment."

He laughed. He sounded on the verge of hysteria.

➤      ➤      ➤

"There," Kaehler called as the pole set a precise hundred meters from the imaging heads locked into focus on her display. "We have it."

"I'll decide that!" Captain Bailey replied from the support module twenty meters away. He shouted instead of using the hard-wired intercom linking the two units.

The breeze blew softly, tickling Dresser's nose with the smell of death more ancient than memory. He watched over Kaehler's shoulder as the image of the pole quivered and the operator's color-graduated console displays bounded up and down the spectrum—

Before settling again into the center of the green, where they had been before Bailey made his last set of adjustments.

"There!" Captain Bailey announced with satisfaction.

They'd placed the imaging module twenty meters from *SB 781*'s side hatch. The support module containing the fusion power supply and the recording equipment was a similar distance beyond. A red light on top of the fusion bottle warned that it was pressurized to operating levels.

Though there was a monitor in the support module, Bailey had decreed that in the present climate they needn't deploy the shelters which would have blocked his direct view of the imaging module's three-meter display. If Kaehler had an opinion, the captain didn't bother to consult it.

Kaehler folded her hands neatly on her lap. "What has this proved?" Dresser asked, softly enough that he wouldn't intrude if the scientist was really concentrating instead of being at rest as she appeared to be.

Kaehler turned. "We've calibrated the equipment," she said. "We've achieved a lock on the target post, one second in the past. We'll be able to range as far back as we need to go when the artificial intelligence harmonizes the setting with the actual output of the power supply."

"That's what the captain's doing?" Dresser asked with a nod.

"The artificial intelligence is making the calculation," Kaehler said. "Captain Bailey is watching the AI while it works. I presume."

Dresser looked from Kaehler to the pole, then to the horizon beyond. "I don't see how it could work," he said to emptiness. "A second ago—the planet rotates on its axis, it circles the sun, the *sun* moves with its galaxy. Time is distance. Time isn't—"

He gestured toward the distant target.

"—the same place on a gravel plain."

Kaehler shrugged. "In this universe, perhaps not," she said. "We're accessing the past through the Dirac Sea. The normal universe is only a film on the—"

She shrugged again. It was the closest to a display of emotion Dresser had seen from her.

"—surface. Time isn't a dimension outside the normal universe."

"Kaehler!" Captain Bailey shouted. "Stop talking to that taxi driver and begin the search sequence. We've got a job to do, woman!"

The target pole hazed slightly in Dresser's vision, though the holographic image remained as sharp as the diamond-edged cutting bar on the scout's harness.

"I wanted to learn what it did," Dresser said in the direction of the image on the admiral's wall display. "I don't like to be around hardware and not know what it does. That's dangerous."

Admiral Horwarth glanced over her shoulder to see if anything in particular was holding the scout's attention. The Ichton rubbed its upper limbs across its wedge-shaped head as though cleaning its eyes. It raised one of its middle pair of legs and scrubbed with it also.

Horwarth looked around again. "Captain Bailey was able to find the correct time horizon, then?" she prompted.

"Not at first," Dresser said in his husky, emotionless voice. "You said five thousand years."

"The source believed the event occurred five thousand standard years ago," the admiral corrected. "But there were many variables."

"Kaehler went back more than ten thousand," Dresser said, "before she found anything but a gravel wasteland . . ."

"There," Kaehler said. Bailey, watching the monitor in the support module, bellowed, "Stop! I've got it!"

Dresser was watching the display when it happened. He might not have been. The search had gone on for three watches without a break, and MANTRA's own long twilight was beginning to fall.

The pulsing, colored static of the huge hologram shrank suddenly into outlines as the equipment came into focus with another time. The score of previous attempts displayed a landscape which differed from that of the present only because the target pole was not yet a part of it. This time—this Time—the view was of smooth, synthetic walls in swirls of orange and yellow.

Kaehler rocked a vernier. The images blurred, then dollied back to provide a panorama instead of the initial extreme close-up. Slimly conical buildings stood kilometers high. They were decorated with all the hues of the rainbow as well as grays that might be shades beyond those of the human optical spectrum. Roadways linked the structures to one another and to the ground, like the rigging of sailing ships. Moving vehicles glinted in the sunlight.

"Not that!" Bailey shouted. "Bring it in close so that we can see what they look like."

Kaehler manipulated controls with either index finger simultaneously. She rolled them—balls inset into the surface of her console—off the tips and down the shafts of her fingers. The scale of the image shrank while the apparent point of view slid groundward again.

Dresser, proud of the way he could grease a scout boat in manually if he had to, marvelled at the scientist's smooth skill.

"Get me a close-up, dammit!" Bailey ordered.

The huge image quivered under Kaehler's control before it resumed its slant downward. "We're calibrating the equipment," she said in little more than a whisper. "We're not in a race . . ."

Pedestrians walked in long lines on the ground among the buildings. Vehicles zipped around them like balls caroming from billiard cushions instead of curving as they would have done if guided by humans.

The locals, the Mantrans, were low-slung and exoskeletal. They had at least a dozen body segments with two pairs of legs on each. They carried the upper several segments off the ground. A battery of simple eyes was set directly into the chitin of the head.

Kaehler manually panned her point of view, then touched a switch so that the AI would continue following the Mantran she had chosen. The alien was about two meters long. Its chitinous body was gray, except for a segment striped with blue and green paint.

"They have hard shells too," Kaehler commented. "You'd think the Ichtons might treat them better."

"The Ichtons don't spare anything," Dresser said softly. He had once landed on a planet while an Ichton attack was still going on. Then he added, "On our bad days, humans haven't been notably kind toward other mammaliforms."

"Kaehler, for god's sake, start bringing the image forward in time!" Captain Bailey shouted. "We aren't here as tourists. We won't see the locals' superweapon until after the Ichtons land. Get with the program, woman!"

Kaehler began resetting the controls on her console. Her face was expressionless, as usual.

"Humans," Dresser said, looking over the stark landscape, "haven't always done real well toward other humans."

Dresser glanced at Admiral Horwarth, then shifted his gaze to the captive again. He continued to watch the admiral out of the corners of his eyes.

"They had a high tech level, the Mantrans," Dresser said. "I made myself believe that they could have built something to defeat the Ichtons. But I knew they hadn't, because—"

Dresser swept both hands out in a fierce gesture, palms down.

"—I could *see* they hadn't," he snarled. "There was nothing. The Ichtons had processed the whole planet down to waste. There was nothing! Nothing for us to find, no reason for us to be there."

"Our source was very precise," Horwarth said gently. "The Ichtons have genetic memory, which our source is able to tap. MANTRA was a disaster for them which has remained imprinted for, you say *ten*, thousands of years."

The 'source' was an Ichton clone, controlled by a human psyche. Dresser knew that, because the psyche was Dresser's own.

The scout began to shiver. He clasped his hands together to control them. With his eyes closed, he continued, "It took Kaehler an hour to get dialed in on the moment of the Ichton assault. Bailey badgered her the whole time . . ."

"I think—" Kaehler said.

A bead of blue fire appeared at the top of the image area. The terrain beneath was broken. The Ichton mothership had appeared in the southern hemisphere. *SB 781*'s navigational computer told Dresser that the vector was probably chance. The Ichtons didn't appear to care where they made their approach.

The display turned white.

"Kaehler!" Bailey shouted. "You've lost the—"

"No!" Dresser said. "They follow an anti-matter bomb in. That's how they clear their landing zones."

The white glare mottled into a firestorm, roaring to engulf a landscape pulverized by the initial shockwave. For an instant, rarefaction from an aftershock cleared the atmosphere enough to provide a glimpse of the crater, kilometers across and a mass of glowing rock at the bottom.

The Ichton mothership continued to descend in stately majesty. A magnetic shield wrapped the enormous hull. Its flux gradient was so sharp that it severed the bonds of air molecules and made the vessel gleam in the blue and ultraviolet range of the spectrum.

Kaehler's right hand moved to a set of controls discrete from those which determined the imaging viewpoint in the physical dimensions. As her finger touched a roller, Captain Bailey ordered, "Come on, come on, Kaehler. Advance it so that we can see the response! It's—"

The display began to blur forward, if Time had direction. Bailey continued to speak, though it must have been obvious that Kaehler had anticipated his command.

"—the response that's important, not some explosion."

The glowing mothership remained steady. The Mantran reaction to being invaded was violent and sustained. War swirled around the huge vessel like sparks showering from a bonfire.

Kaehler advanced the temporal vernier at an increasing rate, letting the ball roll off her finger and onto the palm of her hand. She reached across her body with the other hand and switched a dial that increased the log of the rate.

A convoy of Ichton ground vehicles left the mothership while the rock of the crater still shimmered from the anti-matter explosion. The twenty vehicles had not escaped the frame of the display when the Mantrans engaged them from air and ground.

Ichton weapons fired flux generators like those which served the creatures as armor. The shearing effect of their magnetic gradients—particularly those of the heavy weapons mounted on the mothership— wreaked havoc with the defenders, but the quickly-mounted Mantran counterattack nonetheless overwhelmed the convoy vehicle by vehicle. The last to disintegrate in a fluorescent fireball was a gigantic cylinder carrying the eggs that were to be the basis of a new colony.

The Ichtons didn't send out further convoys. Instead, they ripped at the defenders with their flux generators. At intervals, the mothership lofted missiles that exploded with the flash and actinics of anti-matter when the Mantrans blew them up. Very rarely, a missile disappeared from Kaehler's display without being destroyed.

Mantran earthworks grew around the mothership like mosaic virus expanding across a tobacco leaf. The defenders' weapons bombarded the vessel ceaselessly, but the Ichton armor absorbed even fusion bombs without damage.

"This isn't where they'll develop it," Bailey said abruptly. "We need to check their arsenals, their laboratories."

Kaehler didn't react. She continued to move the image in time without changing the spatial point of focus.

"This is where they'll deploy any weapon," Dresser snapped. "This is where we need to be for now."

Bailey was in command of the expedition and the scout's superior by six grades. Dresser didn't care. The command had been foolish. One of the reasons Dresser was a scout was his inability to suffer fools in silence, whatever the fools' rank.

On the display, seasons blurred between snow and baked, barren earth. All life but that armored within the mothership and the defenders' lines was blasted away by the mutual hellfire. The sky above *SB 781* darkened, but the huge hologram lighted the boat and the watching humans.

"Stop playing with the scale, Kaehler," Captain Bailey ordered. "I'll tell you if I want a close-up."

Kaehler looked startled. Her hands were slowly working the temporal controls, but she hadn't touched the spatial unit since she initially focused on the mothership.

"It's not the scale that's changing," Dresser said. "It's the ship. It's expanding the volume covered by its shields, despite anything the Mantrans can do."

The innermost ring of Mantran defenses crumbled as the blue glare swelled, meter by meter. Seasons washed across the landscape like a dirty river . . .

Dresser unclenched his hands. He looked at Admiral Horwarth in embarrassment for being so close to the edge. "It was like gangrene, sir," he said. "Have you seen somebody with gangrene?"

She shook her head tautly. "No," she said. "I can imagine."

"You can't cure it," the scout said, speaking toward the Ichton again. The creature was huddled in a corner of its cell. "They just keep cutting pieces off and hope they got it all. Which they probably didn't."

"But the Mantrans *were* able to hold?" Horwarth prompted.

The scout shrugged. "For years," he said, "but it didn't matter. The fighting was poisoning the whole planet. The atmosphere, the seas . . . The land for hundreds of kilometers from the mothership was as dead as the floor of Hell. The Ichtons didn't care. The whole Mantran infrastructure was beginning to break down."

Dresser laced his fingers again. "Then the Ichtons sent out another convoy . . ."

Dresser looked from Kaehler to Bailey. Both scientists were glassy-eyed with fatigue.

"Ah, Captain Bailey?" Dresser said.

Bailey didn't reply. He may not even have heard.

The display was a fierce blue glare which sparkled but never significantly changed. It was like watching the play of light across the facets of a diamond, mesmerizing but empty.

"Cap—"

Thousand-meter fireballs rippled suddenly at the north side of the mothership's shields. Through them, as inexorable as a spear cleaving a rib cage, rocked a column of Ichton vehicles.

The leading tank spewed a stream of flux projectiles that gnawed deep into the Mantran defenses until a white-hot concentration of power focused down on the vehicle. The tank ripped apart in an explosion greater than any of those which destroyed it, widening the gap in the Mantran defensive wall.

The convoy's second vehicle was also a tank. It continued the work of destruction as it shuddered onward. The defenders' fire quivered on the Ichton shield, but the Mantrans couldn't repeat the concentration that had overwhelmed the leader.

"They can't stop it." Dresser whispered. "It's over."

The image volume went red/orange/white. The dense jewel of the mothership blazed through a fog that warped and almost hid its outlines. The blur of seasons was lost in the greater distortion.

"Kaehler, what have you done, you idiot?" Bailey shouted. He stepped out of his module; hands clenched, face distorted in the light of the hologram. Except for the blue core, the image could almost be that of the display's stand-by mode—points of light in a random pattern, visual white noise.

*Except* for the Ichton mothership at the blue heart of it.

"It wasn't . . ." Kaehler said as her hands played across her controls with a brain surgeon's delicacy, freezing the image and then reversing it in minute increments.

" . . . me!" The last word was a shout, the first time Dresser had heard Kaehler raise her voice.

The image froze again in time. A disk of the planet's surface, hundreds of kilometers in diameter, slumped and went molten. Its center was the Ichton vessel. Vaporized rock, atmospheric gases fused into long chains, and plasma bursting upward from subterranean thermonuclear blasts turned the whole viewing area into a hellbroth in which the states of matter were inextricably blended.

The scout understood what had happened before

either of the scientists did. "They blew it down to the mantle," Dresser said. "The Mantrans did. Their weapons couldn't destroy the Ichtons, so they used the planet to do it."

*And failed,* but he didn't say that aloud.

Kaehler let the image scroll forward again, though at a slower rate of advance than that at which she had proceeded before. The Ichton convoy vanished, sucked into liquescent rock surging from the planet's core. Plates of magma cooled, cracked, and upended to sink again into the bubbling inferno.

Sulphur compounds from the molten rock spewed into the stratosphere and formed a reflective haze. The sky darkened to night, not only at the target site but over the entire planet. Years and decades went by as the crater slowly cooled. Night continued to cloak the chaos.

"Bring it back to the point of the explosion, Kaehler," the captain said. Bailey spoke in what was a restrained tone, for him. For the first time during the operation he used the intercom instead of shouting his directions from the support module. "Freeze it at the instant the shockwave hit them. That must have been what destroyed the ship."

"It didn't destroy the ship," Kaehler said. Her voice had even less affect than usual. The image continued to advance.

The magnetic shields of the Ichton vessel provided the only certain light. The ship floated on a sea of magma, spherical and unchanged.

"They're dead inside it!" Bailey shouted. "Focus on the microsecond of the first shockwave!"

"You damned fool!" Kaehler shouted back. "I don't have that degree of control. We've got a hundred-millimeter aperture, or have you forgotten?"

Dresser watched Kaehler's profile as she spoke. She

didn't look angry. Her face could have been a death mask.

The display continued to crawl forward. Lava crusted to stone. Cracks between solid blocks opened less frequently to cast their orange light across the wasteland. Century-long storms washed the atmosphere cleaner if not clean.

Bailey blinked and sat down in his module. Kaehler turned back to her controls.

"Their own people," she said in a voice that might not have been intended even for Dresser. "There were thousands of them in the defenses. They all died."

*There had been millions of Mantrans in the defense lines.*

"They couldn't pull them out," the scout said softly. "The defenses had to hold until the last instant, so that the mantle rupture would get all the Ichtons."

"Did they know they were going to die?" Kaehler whispered.

"They knew they'd all die anyway," Dresser said.

*Everything in the universe would die.*

The mothership released a sheaf of missiles, bright streaks across the roiling sky. Their anti-matter warheads exploded in the far distance, flickers of false dawn.

Three convoys set out from the mothership simultaneously. Mantran forces engaged one convoy while it was still within the display area, but the vain attempt lighted the hummocks of lava as briefly as a lightning flash . . .

"I knew it was over then," Dresser said to his hands in the admiral's office. "I'd *known* it before. They don't quit. The Ichtons don't quit."

He looked at the captive again. It now lay on its

back. Its six limbs moved slowly, as though they were separate creatures drifting in the currents of the sea.

"It may have been the failure of conventional techniques that forced the Mantrans to develop their superweapon," Horwarth suggested. She wasn't so much arguing with the scout as soothing him.

Dresser shook his head. "There was never a superweapon on MANTRA, Admiral," he said. "Just death."

"Move us forward faster, Kaehler," Captain Bailey ordered over the intercom. "And—change the spatial viewpoint, I think. Follow a moving column."

For once, Dresser thought the captain had a point. There was nothing useful to be seen in the neighborhood of the mothership.

Three more convoys set out across the cooling lava. These met no resistance.

Kaehler remained fixed, as though she were a wax dummy at her console.

*There was nothing useful to be seen anywhere on the planet.*

"Kaehler?"

The female scientist began to change settings with the cool precision of a machine which had just been switched on again. She did not speak.

The images on the display flip-flopped through abrupt changes in time and place. An image of all MANTRA hung above the console. Half the planet was in sunlight. Yellow-lit cities of the indigenes and the blue speckles of Ichton colonies studded the remaining hemisphere.

For the moment, the colonies were small and there were only a few of them visible. For the moment.

Kaehler's fingers searched discrete blocks of time and space like an expert shuffling cards, throwing up images for a second or less before shifting to the next:

A barren landscape with neither Ichtons nor Mantrans present.

A distant nighttime battle, plasma weapons slamming out bolts of sulphurous yellow that made Ichton shields pulse at the edge of the ultra-violet. Just as Kaehler switched away, an anti-matter warhead obliterated the whole scene. Ichton machinery with maws a kilometer wide, harvesting not only a field of broad-leafed vegetation but the soil a meter down. Enclosed conveyors snaked out of the image area, carrying the organic material toward an Ichton colony. The invaders' tanks oversaw the process, but their waiting guns found no targets.

A Mantran city looming on the horizon—

"There!" Bailey called. "There, hold on that one!"

Kaehler gave no sign that she heard her superior, but she locked the controls back to a slow crawl again. Perhaps she'd intended to do that in any case.

Mantran resistance had devolved to the local level. This city was ringed with fortifications similar to those which the planet as a whole had thrown up around the Ichton mothership. Though the defenses were kilometers deep, they were only a shadow of those which the invaders had breached around their landing zone.

The Ichton force approaching the city was a dedicated combat unit, not a colonizing endeavor. Turreted tanks guarded the flanks and rear of the invaders' column, but the leading vehicles were featureless tubes several hundred meters long. They looked like battering rams, and their purpose was similar.

The city's defenders met the column with plasma bolts and volleys of missiles. A tank, caught by several bolts and a thermonuclear warhead simultaneously, exploded. The failure of its magnetic shields was cataclysmic, rocking nearby vehicles as the Mantran bombardment had not been able to do.

For the most part, Ichton counterfire detonated the missiles before they struck. Plasma bolts could at best stall an Ichton target for a few moments while the vehicle directed the whole output of its power supply to the protective shields.

The tubular Ichton vehicles were built around flux generators as large as those of the mothership's main armament. Three of them fired together. A section of the Mantran defenses vanished in a sunbright dazzle. It shimmered with all the hues of a fire opal.

The gun vehicles crawled closer to the city. The height of the flux gradient of their projectiles was proportional to the cube of the distance from the launcher's muzzle. Even at a range of several hundred meters, the weapons sheared the intra-atomic bonds of the collapsed metal armoring the defenses.

All the available Mantran weaponry concentrated on the gun vehicles. The ground before their treads bubbled and seethed, and the nearest of the indigenes' fortifications began to slump from the fury of the defensive fire.

The Ichtons fired again; shifted their concentrated aim and fired again; shifted and fired. The gap before them was wide enough to pass the attacking column abreast. Counterfire ceased, save for a vain handful of missiles from launchers which hadn't quite emptied their magazines.

The column advanced. An inner line of plasma weapons opened up—uselessly.

In the ruins of the outer defenses, a few Mantrans thrashed. Muscles, broiled within their shells by heat released when nearby matter ionized, made the Mantrans' segemented bodies coil and knot.

Sergeant Dresser turned his head. He was a scout. He was trained to observe and report information.

There was nothing new to observe here.

"Kaehler!" Captain Bailey shouted from the edge of Dresser's conscious awareness. "Bring us forward by longer steps, woman! This isn't any good to us."

When Dresser faced away from the holographic display, he could see stars in the sky of MANTRA. He wondered if any of them had planets which had escaped being stripped by the Ichton ravagers . . .

"Bailey figured," Dresser said in a voice too flat to hold emotion, "that we'd be able to tell when the superweapon was developed by its effect on the Ichtons. When we saw signs of the Ichtons retreating, of their colonies vanishing, then we'd know something had happened and work back to learn what."

Admiral Horwarth nodded. "That sounds reasonable," she said.

"They should've taken a break, Bailey and Kaehler," the scout added in a non sequitur. His mind, trapped in the past, bounced from one regret to another. "Going straight on, I knew it was a mistake, but I wasn't in charge."

Horwarth looked over her shoulder at the captive Ichton. The movement was a way of gaining time for her to decide how to respond. The Ichton still lay full length on the floor of its cell. Its limbs wrapped its torso tightly.

Horwarth turned again. "Should we have sent more than one team?" she asked. "Was that the problem?"

"No," Dresser said sharply. The harshness of his own voice surprised him.

"No sir," he said, meeting the admiral's eyes in apology. "I don't think so. Time wasn't that crucial. Bailey

got focused on finding the superweapon. The more
clear it was that no such weapon existed—"

Dresser's anger blazed out unexpectedly. "The planet
was a wasteland!" he snarled. "We knew that from the
pre-landing survey!"

"The Mantrans could have developed their weapon
when it was too late to save their planet, you know,"
Horwarth suggested mildly. "What we have is evidence
that the Ichtons were traumatized by the contact—not
that the Mantrans survived it."

Dresser sighed. "Yeah," he said to his hands, "I told
myself that. But Bailey—and I think maybe Kaehler
too, though it didn't hit her the same way. They weren't
focused on the long-term result any more."

He shook his head at the memory. "They were too
tired, and it was getting close to dawn . . ."

Captain Bailey walked toward them from the support module. For a moment, Dresser saw his head
silhouetted against the telltale on top of the fusion
bottle. The red glow licked around the captain's features like hellfire.

Bailey didn't speak. Kaehler had ignored the last several of his commands anyway.

On the display, two Mantrans huddled together on
a plateau as invaders approached from all sides. There
were probably fewer than a thousand indigenes surviving at this time horizon.

Kaehler waited like a statue. Her fingers poised
above the controls. The apparatus scrolled forward at
one second/second.

"How long has it been since the Ichtons landed?"
Dresser asked quietly. He wasn't sure she would
answer him either.

"Six hundred standard years," Kaehler replied without moving more than her lips. "At the time we're

observing, the Mantran year was at two-eighty-one standard. The Ichtons took so much mass with them that the planet shifted to an orbit longer by forty days."

The atmosphere on the holographic display was so foul that the sun shone wanly even at noon. Nevertheless the image area was lighted vividly by the six Ichton colonies visible from this point. Each colony had grown as large as the mothership was when it landed.

When the time was right—when everything useful on MANTRA had been processed into Ichton equipment or Ichton flesh—the myriad colonies would blast off from the stripped planet. Each would be the mothership of a fresh brood, capable of destroying a further world in logarithmic progression.

"What sort of equipment do the defenders have?" Captain Bailey asked. He was looking at Kaehler.

"They don't have anything, sir," Dresser replied. He knew—all three of them knew—that Kaehler wasn't going to speak. "I thought they were dead, but a few minutes again, they moved a little."

Military operations on MANTRA had ceased generations before. The Ichton columns grinding away the rock on which the pair of indigenes sheltered were miners, not troops.

"Pan back a little ways, Kaehler," Bailey said. "I want to get a view of the enemy."

Kaehler didn't respond.

The Mantrans were life-sized images above the purring console. One of them coiled more tightly. Bright yellow blotches of fungus were the only color on either body. Illumination from the Ichton colonies turned the hue to sickly green.

Bailey cursed under his breath. He stamped back toward the support module.

When her superior was halfway to his proper position, Kaehler adjusted her controls. The apparent viewpoint lifted, giving Dresser a view of the approaching Ichtons.

The plateau on which the pair of Mantrans lay was artificial. Mining equipment ground away the rock from six directions, lowering the surface of the plain—of the planet—by twenty meters. A snake of tubing connected each of the grinding machines to one of the Ichton colonies which squatted on the horizon. There the material would be sorted, processed, and built into the mothership growing at the heart of each colony.

The closed conveyors gleamed with magnetic shields. Such protection was now unnecessary. Not even rain fell. Separate conveyor lines carried tailings, the waste that not even Ichton efficiency could use, into the ocean basins already drained by the invaders' requirements.

Cutting heads snuffled up and down the face rock, then moved in a shallow arc to either side with the close of each stroke. An Ichton in shimmering body armor rode each machine, but there was no obvious need for such oversight. The cutters moved like hounds casting, missing nothing in a slow inexorability that was far more chilling than a cat's lithe pounce.

Bits of the upper edge of the plateau dribbled into the maw of a cutter rising to the top of its stroke. One of the Mantrans coiled because the ground was shifting beneath its segmented body. Dresser wasn't sure that the movement was conscious. Certainly the indigene made no concerted effort to escape.

Not that escape was possible.

Kaehler touched her controls, focusing down on the two Mantrans. The images swelled to larger than life size. Edges lost definition.

One of the creatures was chewing on a piece of cloth. Its chitinous jaws opened and closed with a sideways motion. The fabric, a tough synthetic, remained unaffected by the attempt to devour it.

"The left one has a weapon!" Captain Bailey suddenly cried. "Increase the resolution, Kaehler! This must be it!"

Dresser could see that the Mantran, writhing as the plateau disintegrated beneath it, didn't have a weapon. The yellow fungus had eaten away much of the creature's underside. Most of its walking legs were withered, and one had fallen off at the root. That, hardshelled and kinked at an angle, was what Bailey's desperation had mistaken for a weapon.

Kaehler turned toward her superior. "I can't increase the resolution with a hundred-millimeter aperture," she said in a voice as empty as the breeze.

Bailey stood at the edge of his module. His head was silhouetted by the telltale behind him. "You could if you were any good at your job!" he shouted. "I'm tired of your excuses!"

The cutting head rose into sight on the display. The Ichton riding it pointed his weapon, a miniature version of the flux generators which had devoured armor denser than the heart of a star.

Kaehler stared at Bailey. Her left hand raised a panel on the front of her console. She didn't look down at it.

Dresser touched the woman's shoulder with his left hand. He was icy cold. "Ah, ma'am?" he said.

"All right, Captain," Kaehler said in a voice like hoarfrost. "I'll enlarge—"

"Wait!" Bailey shouted.

Dresser didn't know what was about to happen, but he wouldn't have lived as long as he had without being willing to act decisively on insufficient data. He gripped Kaehler and tried to lift her out of her seat.

Kaehler's hand yanked at the control which had

been caged within the console. Dresser saw Captain
Bailey's face lighted brilliantly in the instant before
another reality enveloped the imaging module and
the two humans within it.

The Ichton fired, knocking the head off the nearer
indigene with the easy nonchalance of a diner opening a soft-boiled egg. Rock beyond the Mantran disintegrated also, spraying grit into Dresser's face as his
right hand snatched his cutting bar.

The air was foul with poisons not yet reabsorbed
by ten thousand years of wind blowing through a filter of porous waste. The sky was black, and the horizon gleamed with Ichton colonies gravid with
all-destroying life.

Kaehler had opened the viewing aperture to the
point that it enveloped herself, her equipment—

And Sergeant Dresser, who hadn't carried a gun on
a lifeless *desert*, for god's sake, only a cutting bar that
wouldn't be enough to overload Ichton body armor.
Dresser lunged for the monster anyway as it turned
in surprise.

A stream of flux projectiles blew divots out of stone
as the Ichton brought its weapon around. Kaehler didn't
move.

Dresser's powered, diamond-toothed blade screamed
and stalled in the magnetic shielding. He tried to grab
the Ichton weapon but caught the limb holding it
instead. The scout's fingers couldn't reach a material
surface. Though he knew his arm was stronger than
the exoskeletal monster's, his hand slipped as though
he was trying to hold hot butter.

Dresser looked down the muzzle of the Ichton
weapon.

He thought, when he hit the ground an instant later,
that he was dead. Instead, he was sprawled beside *SB
781*. Plasma spewing from the fusion bottle formed a

plume that melted the upper surfaces of the support module. It was brighter than the rising sun . . .

Dresser met Admiral Horwarth's eyes. "He'd vented the containment vessel," the scout said. "Bailey had. He knew it'd kill him, but it was the only way to shut the apparatus off fast enough from where he was."

"I've recommended Captain Bailey for a Fleet Cross on the basis of your report, Sergeant," Horwarth said quietly. "The—cause of your transition through the aperture will be given as equipment failure, though."

Dresser shrugged. His eyes were wide and empty, with a thousand-meter stare that took in neither the admiral nor the image of the motionless Ichton on the wall behind her.

"It wasn't Kaehler's fault," the scout said. His voice sank to a hoarse whisper. "She cracked, people do that. It wasn't a fault."

He blinked and focused on Horwarth again. "Is she going to be all right?" he asked. "She wouldn't talk, wouldn't even move on the trip back."

"I'll have a report soon," Horwarth said, a bland placeholder instead of an answer.

Dresser wrapped his arms tightly around his torso. "Maybe it wasn't Bailey's fault either," he said. "I figure he cracked too. Even me, I'm used to the Ichtons, but it bothered me a bit. He wasn't ready to see the things he saw on MANTRA."

"A bit" was a lie obvious to anyone but the man who said it.

Dresser's smile was as slight and humorless as the point of a dagger. "I brought his feet back in cold storage. Everything above the ankles, that the plasma got when he dumped the bottle."

"There doesn't appear to have been any flaw in the

equipment itself, though," Horwarth said. "Until the damage incurred in the final accident."

"I was the one who screwed up," Dresser said to his past. "I should've grabbed her quicker. *I* was supposed to be the scout, the professional."

"When the equipment can be rebuilt," Admiral Horwarth said, clamping the scout with the intensity of her gaze, "there'll have be a follow-up mission to complete the reconnaissance."

"No," said Dresser.

Horwarth ignored the word. "I'd appreciate it if you would consent to pilot the mission, Sergeant," she said. "You know better than almost anyone else how impor—"

"No!" Dresser shouted as he lurched to his feet. "*No*, you don't need a follow-up mission! We'd completed the mission, and we'd *failed*. That's why it happened, don't you see?"

"What I see is that the incident aborted Captain Bailey's mission, before it reached closure," the admiral said.

She rose also and leaned forward on her desk, resting on her knuckles. Her voice rose as either her facade cracked or she let some of her real anger and frustration out as a means of controlling the scout. "What I see is that we *have* to find the weapon the Ichtons fear, because you've proved that no conventional weapon can defeat them in the long term."

"Admiral," Dresser begged.

He turned to the closed door behind him, then turned again. He didn't realize that he was crying until a falling tear splashed the back of his hand. "Sir. The coordinates were wrong, something was wrong. The only thing left to learn on MANTRA was whether the last of the indigenes died of disease or starvation before the Ichtons got them."

Horwarth softened. She'd skimmed the recordings the expedition brought back. She didn't need Psych's evaluation of the two survivors to understand how the images would affect those who'd actually gathered them.

"Sergeant," she said, "something happened to the Ichtons before they spread from MANTRA. It made memory of the place a hell for them ten thousand years later. We have to learn what."

"Sir . . ." Dresser whispered. He rubbed his eyes angrily, but he was still blind with memory. "Sir, I'll go back, I'll do whatever you want. But we failed, sir, because there was nothing there to succeed with. And since I watched MANTRA eaten, I know just how bad we failed."

"We've got to try, Ser—" Admiral Horwarth began.

The electronic chime of an alarm interrupted her. Horwarth reached for a control on her desk.

Dresser's gaze focused on the holographic scene behind the admiral. Three humans wearing protective garments had entered the Ichton's cell. They stumbled into one another in their haste.

"Duty officer!" Admiral Horwarth snarled into her intercom. "What the hell is going on?"

Two of the attendants managed to raise the Ichton from the floor of the cell. The creature was leaking fluid from every joint. It was obviously dead.

The chitinous exoskeleton of the Ichton's torso was blotched yellow by patches of the fungus whose spores had travelled with Sergeant Dresser from the surface of a dying planet.

# THE TRADESMEN

*Author's note: I'm indebted to Wilkeson O'Connell, whose work showed me the way to solve a problem that had been exercising me for some time.*

*—DAD*

Colonel Evertsen heard voices in the outer room of his office in the Tactical Operations Center. An outbound convoy—a convoy headed from the interior to the front—had reached Fort Burket a half hour before; District Administrator Kuyper, Evertsen's civilian counterpart, would be coming to discuss the latest dispatch from Capetown.

Evertsen turned, closing the maintenance log he'd been studying in a vain attempt to change the numbers into something Capetown would find more acceptable. The roads in this Slavic hinterland had been a joke before they were made to bear the weight of mechanized armies. Now they'd been reduced to dust, mud, or ice. Take your choice according to the season, and expect your engines and drive trains to wear out in a fraction of the time that seemed reasonable in an air-conditioned office in Capetown.

Instead of the rumpled Kuyper, a tall, slim officer turned sideways to enter the narrow doorway and threw a salute that crackled. He was wearing battledress in contrast to Evertsen's second-class uniform, but the clean, pressed garments proved he was a newcomer to the war zone.

"Janni!" said Evertsen in pleasure. He rose to his feet, stumbling as he always did when he tried to move quickly and his right knee betrayed him.

"Lieutenant Jan Dierks reporting to the base commander, *sir*," the newcomer said. He broke into a grin and reached across the desk to clasp Evertsen by the arm. "You live in a maze here, Uncle Jan. Is the danger so great this far from the front lines?"

Evertsen bit back the retort—because Dierks was his nephew, and because anyway Evertsen should be used to the attitude by now. He got it every time he went home on leave, after all. *I see, colonel, you're not in the fighting army any more . . .*

"Not so dangerous, not now," Evertsen said, gesturing Dierks to a chair. The room's only window was a firing slit covering the east gate. There were electric lights, but Evertsen normally didn't bother with them until he'd shuttered the window for the night. "The fort was laid out two years ago, after all. But although the danger has receded, one gets used to narrow doorways and grenade baffles more easily than one might to a sapper in one's bedroom."

"Oh, I didn't mean to imply . . ." Dierks said in sudden confusion. He was a good boy; the sort of son Evertsen would have wanted if things had worked out differently.

"No offense taken, Janni," he said easily. "Though in fact the constant advance causes its own problems.

The point elements always bypass hostiles, and some of those are going to decide that a logistics base guarded by cripples and transients is a better choice for resupply than trying to get back to their own lines."

Evertsen tried to keep the bitterness out of his voice when he said, "cripple," but he knew he hadn't been completely successful.

Dierks looked through the firing slit, perhaps for an excuse to take his eyes off his uncle, and said, "There's a convoy from the front arriving. Do they usually come in at the same time as an outbound one?"

"Not usually," Evertsen said in a dry voice, "though they're supposed to. We won't be able to send your trucks forward without the additional escort that accompanies the inbound convoy."

He rotated his chair to view the east gate. There were about forty vehicles, meaning a score or more were deadlined at one of the forward bases. That was par for the course, but Christ! why couldn't Capetown see the Russian Front needed mechanics worse than it did more riflemen? Around and beyond the convoy, the plains rolled on forever.

The leading truck was a standard 6x6, empty except for the load of sandbags that would detonate any pressure-fuzed mine. The duty of driving that vehicle changed every fifteen minutes.

Two armored cars followed. There should be four more at the middle and end of the line, but Evertsen saw only two. The four guntrucks, each with quad-mounted heavy machine guns behind walls of mortar boxes filled with gravel, were spaced evenly among the non-combat vehicles.

"I suppose returning convoys are to reposition the trucks?" Dierks said.

"That," Evertsen said. He turned from the window. "And for casualties and leave-men. Mostly casualties."

He cleared his throat. "A fit young man wouldn't be posted to Fort Burket, Janni. Where do your orders take you?"

"The Fourth Independent Brigade, sir," Janni said with pardonable pride. The Four Eye was a crack unit whose neck-or-nothing panache made it a fast route to promotion . . . for the survivors. "I could choose my itinerary, and when I saw an officer was needed to escort specie to the District Administrator at Fort Burket, well, I volunteered."

There was an angry mutter in the outer office. Administrator Kuyper squeezed through the doorway with a document in his hand and shouted, "Evertsen, do you know what those idiots in Capetown have done? They've—"

Janni jumped to his feet. Kuyper noticed his presence and said more mildly, "Oh, good afternoon, Lieutenant. I didn't realize . . ."

"You've met the Lieutenant Dierks who brought the discretionary fund supplement, Kuyper," Evertsen said from his chair. "Allow me to present my nephew Janni, who's been posted to the Four Eye."

"It's about the damned discretionary fund that I've come, Evertsen," Kuyper said. "They've reduced the bounty authorization from a hundred aurics to sixty, and they've made an immediate cut in the supplement to the discretionary fund."

Evertsen's fist clenched. "Do they give a reason?" he asked, more so he had time to think about the implications than because any reason could justify Capetown's action in his mind. He wished Janni wasn't present for this, but he couldn't very well order the boy out.

Kuyper waved the document, obviously the one Janni had brought with the paychest. " 'At this crisis in national affairs,' " he quoted, " 'the fighting fronts must take precedence for resources over the lines of communication.' By Christ, Evertsen! How much use do they think those greater resources will be if the convoys carrying them are looted by guerrillas?"

Dierks looked from one man to the other, hearing without enough background to understand the words. The hefty administrator was between him and the doorway. Because he couldn't easily leave, Dierks said, "The specie I escorted was to pay the Slav irregulars, then, the Ralliers? Rather than your own troops?"

"Yes," Kuyper said, "and there'll be hell to pay when they—"

Kuyper's eyes were drawn to the viewslit because it was the brightest thing in the room. "Oh, *Christ!*" he said, staring toward the gate. "It never rains but it pours. There's Bettina Crais, in with the convoy and coming toward the TOC. Three guesses what she's going to want!"

"And how she's going to react," Evertsen agreed grimly. He'd rather have had a few weeks to figure a way out of the impasse; but if he'd been a lucky man, he wouldn't be commanding a line-of-communication base. "Well, we may as well get it over with."

"Lieutenant, give me a hand with the paychest if you will," Kuyper said. "Even in its present anemic state, that much gold is a load for me. Besides, it won't hurt to have a fit young officer like you in the room when Crais gets the news."

The two men started out. Evertsen said, "Kuyper, perhaps Lieutenant Dierks shouldn't be . . . ?"

Janni stiffened in the doorway. "Sir," he said, "I'm cleared at Most Secret level. I'll obey any order from a superior officer, of course; but I remind you that to treat me as a child because of our relationship would dishonor the uniform I wear."

*He thinks I'm trying to protect him from violence*

*by an angry Rallier,* Evertsen thought. *And he's young enough to worry about honor!*

"Yes, of course," Evertsen said with a curt nod. "You'll find the experience instructive, I'm sure."

The colonel stared at his hands while he waited. Once he'd dreamed of commanding a unit like the Four Eye himself. He'd had a lot of dreams. Once.

Janni and Kuyper returned from the latter's office with a metal chest which they set on the corner of Evertsen's desk. The administrator waited beside it; Janni stood at parade rest on the other side of the desk, facing the door.

The maintenance log was still out. Evertsen sighed and slipped it into a bookcase behind him as voices murmured in the outer office.

Bettina Crais entered.

She was a petite woman; that was obvious even though a felt camouflage cape, worn dark-side out in this season, covered her from neck to ankles. She'd slung her long-barreled Moisin-Nagant rifle muzzle-down over her right shoulder; a swatch of rabbitskin, bound fur-side in, protected the bolt and receiver against the elements. Mounted on a stud in her left ear was half a gold coin the size of a thumbnail, so worn that the fractured portrait of George III was barely a shadow on the surface.

"Colonel," Crais said, nodding. "Mister Administrator. I've come for my pay."

Dierks blinked in amazement. Despite Crais' fine features and short blond hair, he'd assumed she was Slavic until she spoke—with a Vaal-District accent you could cut with a knife.

"Mistress Crais," Evertsen said, "allow me to present my nephew, Lieutenant Jan Dierks."

She turned her head. Janni drew himself to attention reflexively. Crais grinned and said, "A pretty boy you've got here, Colonel. Want to send him out with me to blood him?"

"Lieutenant Dierks is on his way to take up a combat appointment," Evertsen said, trying hard to keep the disgust out of his voice. He didn't want to anger Crais, particularly not now.

"And d'ye think what I do isn't combat, Colonel?" she sneered. "Without me and the Ralliers, the truck drivers and invalids you've got staffing this place would find out what combat really is."

"Well, Crais," said Kuyper with false warmth, "you'll probably want to relax for a few days before you head back. I'll arrange a room for you in the transient officers' billets so you won't have to doss down in the civilian lines. You can run a tab at the O Club as well until we get the finances straightened out."

Crais turned her ice-blue eyes on the civilian. "I don't owe anybody, Mister Administrator," she said in a voice that came straight down from the Arctic Circle. "And I'll find my own bed. It's for the one night only, because I'm heading back at dawn with the inbound convoy. I've got my husband Lute up with the three kids, and I want to get back to them."

"You've brought your family to the Zone?" Evertsen said in amazement. "Good God, I didn't know that!"

"I shouldn't wonder if a lot goes on around here that you don't know about, Colonel," Crais said with not quite a sneer. "We've got a dugout as snug as you please with paneling inside. Lute doesn't hunt with me—it's no more his thing than it would be your nephew's here, I reckon—but he takes care of the kids and the garden. We'll have all our own food come this time next year."

"Where is it you live, Mistress Crais?" Janni asked with careful politeness. He was too much a gentleman to allow Crais' belittling to affect him openly, though

Evertsen had seen a vein throb in the boy's throat a time or two during the conversation.

"Nowhere, now," Crais said, turning her cold eyes onto him, "but it'll be an estate in a few years when things settle down. Me and mine'll be here on the land, and no rich party-boy from Capetown will take it away from us. There'll be no more scraping a crop from sunbaked clay the way my family's always had to do."

She caught the line of Janni's eyes and tapped the broken sovereign. "This, you mean?" she said. "This came from Lute's family. My folks arrived at the Cape without a pot to piss in, but that'll change, boy. My son and the girls, they'll be folk as good as any walking the streets of Capetown!"

Crais looked out the viewslit. Vehicles were still grunting and snarling through the entrance baffles. It might be an hour before the last of the convoy was safely within the perimeter of Fort Burket.

"The outbound convoys drop me on the road and I hump my goods home myself," she said. She was obviously pleased to tell a young aristocrat how hard her life was and how well she succeeded. "From a different spot each time. Most of the hostiles couldn't track a tank over a grass lawn, but I don't make it easy for them. When I come in, I wait at Depot Seven-niner for an inbound convoy."

She grinned. "You don't stand out in the middle of the road and flag a convoy," she said. "Not even me."

"How do you get into the fuel depot?" Evertsen asked, both from interest and because he saw that the chance to talk—to brag—put Crais in a better mood. "I'd have thought the garrison would be just as quick to shoot as the convoy escorts are."

Crais shrugged. Even the simplest of her movements were as graceful as a gymnast's. "We have click signals on the radio so they know I'm coming," she said. "And they know they need me. Depot Seven-niner would do better to take down its barbed wire than to lose me patrolling the district."

Her left hand reached under her cape and came out with objects on a string. "That's talk enough," Crais said. "I've got six hundred aurics coming. Pay me and I'll arrange for my needs."

She tossed the string onto the center of the desk. There were six items tied on a strand of sinew. Shrivelled up the way they were, they could be mistaken for mushrooms or nutmeats, but of course they were—

"Those are human ears!" Janni said. "Good God! Some of them are from children!"

"Your uncle don't trust nobody, boy," Crais said with a sly grin toward Evertsen. "Not the Ralliers and not even a fellow citizen from the hardscrabble part of his own country. He wants proof, so we bring him the left ear from every kill."

She looked at Evertsen. "So here they are, Colonel. Want to soak them open so you can be sure I'm not trying to cheat you with a right ear or two?"

"That won't be necessary," Evertsen said without inflection. He and Kuyper had seen more ears than Crais had, many more of them. They were experts by now, well able to make sure the State wasn't cheated by the irregulars in its service.

"The lieutenant's right," Kuyper said. "Four of these are children. Stay-behinds, and all the men able to carry a gun off with the guerrillas."

"Aye, that's right," Crais said; her voice calm but the look in her eyes as she gazed at the administrator . . . less calm. "A family, still working their plantings from a cave-in in the wall of a ravine. Pretty well hid, too. I wouldn't have found them, I guess, without the smell of wood smoke to draw me. That's why I pack in block alcohol for our fire, you see."

Janni didn't speak again, but neither could he draw his eyes away from the wizened trophies. Crais grinned more broadly and went on, "I hid at the treeline for three hours till I got the woman and the older girl, she was maybe twelve, together. Nailed them both with one round. The grampa came out of the house with a rifle and I shot him too. Thought I could use his ammo belt, but he had an old single-shot Berdan, so I was out another round. Cartridges cost money in the Zone, Lieutenant."

Janni stood iron-faced. It was hard to tell whether he even heard what the woman was saying.

Vaguely disappointed at the lack of response, Crais continued, "I tossed a smoke bomb into the dugout and waited to see if anybody more come out. I use sulphur and tar and enough gunpowder to keep it going if they try to douse it, but nobody did this time. They all choked. I went in when it aired out and found a girl of eight and a boy of six. And a baby, but I didn't bother to sex that one."

Her left index finger, as delicate as carved ivory, indicated the tiny last lump on the string.

Crais looked directly at Janni again. "You may wonder why I used a smoke bomb instead of a grenade, Lieutenant," she said. "I'm a working girl and can't afford to lose a trophy. Your uncle wouldn't have paid me for the baby if all I'd been able to bring him back was the foot and a few toes. Would you, Colonel?"

"Good Christ, woman!" Evertsen said. "We have to do this; we don't have to like it."

"*Some* of us have to do this, Colonel," Crais said. "Some of us don't have estates we could retire to if we felt like it."

"Ashkenazy's band brought twenty units to Fort Schaydin last week," Kuyper said. "All of them were real guerrillas, too."

Crais turned to the administrator like a weasel preparing to spring. "Real, were they? Aye, I suppose they were—if you want to call people who get drunk around an open fire in the Zone real guerrillas. They were under a political officer from Berlin who was going to show the locals how to do it."

The woman stood like an ice pick stuck into soft flesh, looking disdainfully at the three men. "You know the real danger's locals from the Zone who filter back and hide with stay-behinds till they're ready to cut throats, Kuyper," she said. "Ain't that so, Colonel?"

Evertsen nodded curtly. "Yes," he said, "I suppose it is."

Kuyper peered toward the viewslit. "There's a lone truck following the convoy," he said. "I think it's Bruchinsky's lot."

Colonel Evertsen stood and looked, in part because it gave him a chance to turn away from Bettina Crais. A 6x6 truck had caught up with the convoy just as the last armored car grunted through the gates. It was originally a German Horch, Evertsen thought, but with a wood-burning gasogene adapter and repairs which used parts from many other vehicles. At least twenty Ralliers filled it, already whooping with anticipation of their next few days.

One man jumped out of the cab and started purposefully toward the TOC, however. Unfortunately.

"Yes, that's Bruchinsky," Evertsen said heavily. "I'd have appreciated some time to untie the knot Capetown's bound us with; but if there's any luck, it doesn't come to poor bastards with gimp legs that keep them out of field commands."

"I'm not holding you up, Colonel," Crais said, misunderstanding the comment. "I'll take my pay now and leave, so you needn't to share your pretty office with me and Bruchinsky both."

Evertsen turned. "Explain the new situation to Mistress Crais, Kuyper," he said.

Kuyper nodded calmly; the plump civilian had never flinched from the unpleasant duties of his position. "We've received a dispatch from Capetown changing the amount of the bounty," he said. "From now on we'll be paying you sixty aurics per assessed unit instead of the hundred you've received in the past. That means three hundred and sixty aurics will be paid for the present string."

"The hell you say, lardbelly!" Crais shouted. Her left hand moved beneath her cape and clenched on something hidden. "The *hell* you say."

She looked venomously at the men, her lips working without sound. The flesh was drawn so tight across Crais' cheekbones that her face might almost have been a skull. "Do you know what it costs me to live in the Zone? Nobody issues *me* food and fuel. Do they think I could patrol every day and tend crops besides?"

"Capetown believes that since the threat has diminished," Kuyper said, "the bounty can also be cut. In my capacity as District Administrator I'll make representations to Capetown about the changed policy, but—"

"How diminished will the threat look if me and the Ralliers stop hunting the Zone, *mister*?" Crais said. "In a month, in a week even? And what happens if some of us start hunting for the other side, hey? How many ears are there on a convoy inbound with a load of wounded, hey?"

"You can swallow that sort of nonsense, for a start!" Evertsen said. "Berlin might be willing to take on the Ralliers—for the duration only, of course— if they decided to turn their coats again; but the only use they'd have for you, Crais, is the same one they have for every Draka they capture. And if they were going to make distinctions among Draka—that wouldn't be to the advantage of any of the three of us, would it?"

"Damn you, it ain't right!" Crais said, but there was more despair than anger in her voice this time.

In a gruffly conciliatory tone Evertsen said, "It isn't my job to explain Capetown's policies, Mistress Crais. That's just as well, because sometimes I find those policies completely inexplicable."

"See here, Crais," Kuyper said mildly, "I think there's a way we can work with you. Capetown's right about the number of units dropping these past months. The guerrillas have been steering clear of the district, and you've rooted out most of the stay-behinds. I think there'll be enough in the account to pay you at the old rate for adults; but children will have to go at sixty aurics per unit, I'm afraid."

Crais looked at the two older men. Her expression couldn't be said to have softened, but Evertsen no longer felt there was a real chance that she was going to lunge for his throat with a skinning knife.

"I understand your concern about the cost of supplies, Crais," he said. "I'll give you a chit for my steward, directing him to sell you food and fuel from my personal stock at the delivered cost to me. I think you'll find that more reasonable than dealing with drivers for supplies that've fallen off the back of quartermaster trucks, so to speak."

"Still ain't right," Crais muttered. "But I guess I oughta be used to the short end of the stick. All right, I'll take your bargain."

Evertsen stripped an order blank off the pad and began writing directions to his steward on the back of it before Crais had an opportunity to change her mind. She added in a mixture of explanation and defiance, "It won't matter so much next year because we'll have the crops in. But we need to make it through the season, you see."

A heavy Slavic voice sounded at the entrance to the TOC. Kuyper had already raised the lid of the strongbox. He paused and said, "Say, Crais? Would you mind waiting a moment to be paid? I want Bruchinsky to see that everybody's being treated the same, if you see what I mean."

"Afraid Bruchinsky might fly hot when you tell him to bend over, hey?" Crais said with a cold smile. She straightened her trophy string on the metal desktop. "Yeah, all right, I'll help you with him."

She frowned in concern and added, "Bruchinsky keeps pretty good discipline in the field, you know. You only see his lot when they come in to tie one on, but it'd take a battalion to replace them."

"But you bring in two units for every three we get from Bruchinsky's whole band, Mistress Crais," Evertsen said. He was flattering her, but the words were still the cold truth.

Crais grinned. "That's so," she said. "Hunting's a job best done alone, *I* think."

There was a boom of laughter and a huge Slav squeezed through the entrance. His hair and beard were matted into a sheepskin vest worn fleece-side out, and a large rosary hung from his neck. "It is I, the great Bruchinsky, Colonel!" he said. "Eight hundred gold you owe us! We celebrate tonight!"

Evertsen saw his nephew's nostrils flare, then tighten. The Rallier's effluvium was a shock even to those prepared for it by experience. Well, Janni would smell worse things when he first stood on a battlefield fought over for several days in high summer; as he surely would, if he survived.

Crais and the Rallier exchanged brief comments in Zone Pidgin, a mixture of English, German, and several

Slavic dialects. The two irregulars respected one
another, though Evertsen knew there were under-
currents of mutual disdain as well: for a Slav on the
one hand, for a woman on the other.

"We'll be with you in a moment, Captain
Bruchinsky," Kuyper said. "We were just paying off
Mistress Crais."

He took out a roll of ten-auric coins and broke the
paper on the edge of the strongbox. He stacked ten
pieces of new-minted gold behind each of the larger
ears. "That's a hundred apiece for the two adults,
and . . ."

Kuyper set six coins beside the first, the second, and
the third of the small ears, then paused to break
another roll. "And the last," he said. "Sixty aurics apiece
for each of the children, two hundred and forty in all."

"What?" Bruchinsky said in amazement. "What's this
fucking shit? You pay for ear, not fucking man ear and
kid ear!"

"Not any longer, Captain Bruchinsky," Evertsen said
coldly. "Capetown has decreed a change in the bounty,
and of course we're bound by their decision."

"No fucking way I let you Draka bastards cheat me!"
the Rallier shouted. "No *fucking* way!"

He flung back the sheepskin, exposing the sub-
machine gun he slung beneath it. Like Crais' rifle it
was of Soviet manufacture, a Shpagin with a 71-round
drum. Soviet weapons had a rugged willingness to
function that made them favorites among troops who
operated without the luxury of a unit armorer.

Neither Evertsen nor Kuyper spoke. Janni stood like
a statue, his face unreadable. The only sign that the
boy was aware of his surroundings was the way his eyes
traversed the room: back and forth, taking it all in.

Bettina Crais bent forward and scooped her coins,
stack by stack, into a calfskin purse. The gold chimed

musically. She folded Evertsen's note to his steward and stuck that in her purse as well.

"Crais!" said Bruchinsky. "You let them shit on you this way? You take their fucking sixty?"

Crais looked at the Rallier. Evertsen had seen gun muzzles with more expression. "It doesn't look to me like there's much choice, Bruchinsky," she said. "You want to buy my string off me at the old price?"

"Fuck!" the big Slav said. "Fuck all fucking Draka!"

He laughed as explosively as sudden thunder and slapped his string down on the desk beside that of Crais. There were eight units, four of them so fresh that a drop of blood oozed from the adult's torn lobe.

"Sure, pay me the fucking money," he said cheerfully. "The boys all be so drunk in the morning they don't know how much money we get. Me too, by Jesus!"

Crais settled the purse back under her cape. She gave a nod; more a lift of her chin. "I'll be on about my business, then," she said. "See you in a week or two, I reckon, Colonel."

She stared at Janni again with her expressionless eyes. "Watch how you go, boy," she said. "It'd be a pity if ears as cute as yours wound up hanging from a string."

Bruchinsky laughed uproariously as Crais left the room.

Kuyper began stacking coins with unobtrusive precision. The administrator made a show of every payout. Partly that was because the Slavs generally liked a bit of ceremony, but Kuyper himself was the sort of man who wanted order and dependability in all things. It was difficult for Kuyper to be stuck in this wilderness with Capetown's whimsies grinding him from one side against the flint realities of the Zone on the other, but he served the State as well as humanly possible.

So did Colonel Evertsen; but it was hard to remember that as he read the disgust under his nephew's blankness.

"Shit on Capetown," the Rallier said cheerfully. "We still richer than I think when we start in. We break down and get lucky."

"A breakdown in the Zone lucky?" Evertsen said, frowning slightly. "Lucky you survived, you mean."

"Aw, our fucking shitpot motor, you know," Bruchinsky said. "Still, she not fancy but she get the job done okay. Just like me and the boys, that's right?"

He laughed and fumbled a bottle out of a side pouch. It was empty, as Bruchinsky decided after frowning at it for some moments. He cursed and deliberately shattered it on the floor.

Evertsen said nothing. His batman would sweep up the glass. It was the colonel's duty to the State to deal with the irregulars. . . .

"Naw, the luck's good because we walk around while Oleg fixes the motor," Bruchinsky resumed, sunny following the momentary squall of the empty bottle. "Pedr thinks he sees a track. I don't see shit, but Pedr, he good tracker. Near as good as your blond bitch-dog, Colonel, that's right?"

Evertsen offered a thinly noncommittal smile. He didn't like to hear a Slav animal refer that way to a Draka, but more than policy might have kept him from reprimanding Bruchinsky in this particular case.

"We go a little ways in and I think 'a rag,' but we look at it and it's a doll," the Rallier continued. "So Pedr's right, and six of us we follow up fast while the rest stays with the truck."

Kuyper broke another roll of aurics with a golden tinkle. There were five adults and three children in the string. The latter were very fresh.

"We find the place three miles, maybe, off the road,"

Bruchinsky said. "It's hid good, but a kid's crying before
we see anything and we crawl up close. There's a man
hoeing squash and corn planted together, but he's pat-
ting a kid who's bit on the neck by a big fucker horsefly.
One burst—" he slapped the sub-machine gun "—and
I get them both. Not bad, hey, even though the boy
wiggles till we twist his neck."

Kuyper set six coins behind the first of the small
ears, then looked at the Rallier with an expression
Evertsen couldn't read. The administrator resumed
counting, his fingers moving a little slower than before.

"There's two girls in the dugout," Bruchinsky said.
"They got good gun like this—"

He pumped his sub-machine gun in the air for an
example.

"—but they little girl, they cry and cry but they can't
cock it, you see?"

Bruchinsky racked back his charging handle. *His*
weapon was already cocked, so it spun a loaded round
out onto the floor.

Evertsen managed not to wince. He supposed being
shot by accident in his office by a drunken Slav would
be a fitting end to his career.

"Pedr finish them with his knife after he have a little
fun, you know?" the Rallier said. "So we run back with
four more kills, the truck fixed, and we drive like hell
to catch up with the convoy almost. Lucky, not so?"

"That completes the count, Captain Bruchinsky,"
Kuyper said, closing the lid of the strongbox. "Six
hundred and eighty aurics."

"Shitload of money," the Rallier said admiringly. "It
all be shit gone soon, but we party tonight!"

"If that's all . . . ," Evertsen said. It had gone better than he'd dreamed a few minutes before. Not that
his superiors would care about the skill with which he
and Kuyper had covered Capetown's idiocy. . . .

"One thing," Bruchinsky said, fumbling in another of his pouches. "This I get from the farmer today. Does it spend? It's broke, but it's real gold by Jesus!"

He held it out for the others to see. It was a sovereign, snapped in half and mounted for an ear stud. The legend and lower portion of the bust of George III were worn to shadows.

Janni began to laugh. The sound started normally but rose into hysterical peals.

Bruchinsky, the only man in the room who didn't get the joke, looked in growing puzzlement at his Draka companions.

# COMING UP AGAINST IT

The Grantholder's Palace was five hundred meters ahead of Milligan when the artillery prep landed, just as planned. The first rounds were high-capacity shells detonated by zero-delay nose fuzes, so that the blasts blew chunks from the exterior walls instead of going off inside the six-story building. The shockwaves rocked Milligan about a second after the orange flashes.

The shells were to provide entry for the assault squad, not to kill the occupants. The squad would do the killing.

The city's power grid went out at the same time, though occasional vehicle headlights marked the streets Milligan skimmed over. The AI of Milligan's suit sharpened the amplified-light view of the palace with mapped images from the data bank. So far as the squad was concerned, this mission was a scramble with no time for practice, but the intelligence base was remarkably complete. *Somebody'd* known what was coming.

The windmilling figure in powered battle armor flung skyward by the ground-floor shellburst wasn't part

264

of anybody's plan. The cyborg who was supposed to go in low on the south face while Milligan hit the top floor had hot-dogged. He got to the target just as the entry salvo did, and the shockwave flung him out of control.

The cyborg had a name, all four of them did, but the humans of the squad's Fire Team One used letter calls in the rare instances they had anything to say to members of the other fire team. This cyborg was Gamma. He was at roof height, flailing in smoke and the debris of terra-cotta cladding, when the remainder of the artillery prep arrived: cargo shells delivering anti-armor sub-munitions to clear the palace-roof defenses.

The Grantholder had a small particle-beam weapon and a pair of powerful lasers, all in separate turrets. The sub-munitions chose specific targets and punched self-forging fragments through them, destroying the weapons and killing the crews.

The blast-formed uranium projectiles riddled Gamma's powered battle armor with similar ease. The scuttling charge sucked the suit in with a white flash and a blast more powerful than those of the artillery rounds.

"My shell was a dud!" shouted Porter. "Cap'n, shall I cut my own?"

A shell that didn't burst would only knock a head-sized hole in the light brick that covered the building's load-bearing concrete frame. Porter could blow an entrance in the wall herself, but she'd have to hover on her jets while she did so. That would make her an easy target for everybody in the Gendarmery camp adjoining the palace to the north and east.

"Hit the ground floor south, Porter!" Milligan called. He paused before the smoke-streaming hole, a rectangle three meters wide framed by concrete beams, revectored his jets, and jumped for his own entrance five stories up.

"Roger that, Porter!" Wittvogel agreed. Porter was already correcting her curved approach to bring her around to the south of the building.

Porter had been supposed to go in on the east side of the fifth story. Captain Wittvogel had the roof and Platt—who was new, plenty of simulator time but no combat missions—would take the fourth story, believed to be servants quarters.

The cyborgs had the three lower stories and the basements, as much as anything to keep them out of the way of the humans of Fire Team One. The cyborgs weren't really squad members any more than they were really human. They didn't take orders well, and they didn't worry about damage to friendlies so long as their own kill rate stayed high. Putting Porter in with Fire Team Two was dangerous, but not as dangerous as wobbling fifteen meters in the air like a shooting-range pop-up.

The hole into the top floor was identical to the one at ground level. Because the building's cladding didn't support any weight, it was the same thickness at all levels. The palace had its own generator. Lights were on inside, though they merely backlit swirls of smoke from bedding ignited by the shellburst. The suit switched to Imaging Infra-Red before Milligan had a chance to.

Milligan hesitated in the air, letting gravity and his upward inertia come into balance before he made the next move. He jetted his suit forward, chopping the fuel-feed with the same motion. When his foot touched the crossbeam, he was walking rather than flying.

There were three doors into the huge bedchamber by which Milligan entered the palace. The explosion had blown off the doorpanels. Somebody stepped into the center doorway, shouting a question. Milligan riddled him/her with the railgun in his right forearm. He meant it for a short burst, but he fired a full hundred rounds before the AI shut the circuits down to cool.

OK, he'd been spooked, but he was all right n—

Movement in both the other doorways. Snap-shot *right*, railgun again but the trigger-pull as gentle as a mother's kiss. The target was wearing a breastplate that absorbed kinetic energy from Milligan's ring penetrators. As a result, they flung the body backward instead of simply killing him/her.

The local in the left doorway fired an electron beam. Milligan's sensor displays flared white, though the internal read-outs didn't jump.

Later in the mission there might have been a problem, but for the moment Milligan's suit was in blueprint condition. The shielding held. His weapon switches were live, however. A transient tripped a pulse from the laser in Milligan's left forearm, pointed at nothing in particular.

The palace's interior walls had a cinder block core. That glowed white when the laser ripped the sheathing away. Upholstery and ornate wooden furniture exploded into flame. The local ducked or was driven back by the fireball. Freed from the electron beam's overload, Milligan's sensors clicked back on.

He fired a short burst waist-high through the wall—the core was tough, but it wouldn't stop depleted-uranium ring penetrators moving at 5.5 KPH. The local staggered into the open again, stumbling over his/her dropped electrogun.

This time Milligan's laser was aimed and waiting. His pulse ripped the target.

Milligan strode through the corpse, burst by its own super-heated body fluids, and into the large office beyond. His shoulder jounced the edge of the doorway, deforming the metal jamb and crumbling cinder blocks.

The suit had switched back to straight optical. The carets Milligan didn't have time for indicated there were people in the office, half a dozen of them, ducking behind desks and consoles. Trying to hide, trying to find cover from which to snipe at the unexpected intruder . . .

Milligan toggled his weapons' switch to FRAG, pointed with his left little finger to select a five-meter range, and twitched the finger six times across the arc of the room.

The anti-personnel grenades *choonked* from the launcher on his left shoulder. They burst in the air with saffron flashes, hurling out a sleet of glass whiskers. The shrapnel wouldn't do more to powered battle armor than buff the paint, but it carved flesh from the bones of unprotected humans.

When screaming figures leaped from where they'd hidden, Milligan snapped railgun projectiles through them to finish the job. Because of Ambassador Razza's orders, he didn't want to rake the consoles themselves with his penetrators.

Porter had a friend in the Earth Embassy here on Monticello. For 'friend' read 'lover'. Milligan didn't know which sex, and that sure-hell wasn't a question he was going to ask Porter.

While the squad suited up for the mission, Porter said, "You *bet* Razza wants to keep this operation secret. She wants to secretly transfer Dupree's credit accounts to her own bank."

The cyborgs must have heard the comment, but none of them reacted. Even if true, it was non-essential information so far as they were concerned, like the color—gray-green—of the walls here in the embassy basement.

Milligan looked at her. "Do you know that?" he'd asked.

"Do I *know* the sun's going to come up tomorrow?" Porter sneered. She was blond, stocky and very short—less than a meter-fifty. Maybe because of that, Porter made a point of being the toughest person in any group. With the force multiplier of her powered battle armor, she could come pretty close.

Platt stared at Porter and said, "No, Corporal. It's a secret mission because until we get the proof that the Grantholder is communicating with the Throgs, Grant Dupree is still an ally so we can't move openly. Don't you remember? The ambassador explained it all herself."

Even Milligan blinked at that. Porter shook her head and said, "My God, kid, you really *are* as stupid as you look." She rapped her knuckles on the concrete wall. "Here, I'd like to sell you this building, hey? A nice, solid place. You can make a bundle on resale."

Platt blushed. "There's no call to insult me just 'cause I'm new," he said.

"Porter, Platt," Captain Wittvogel said. "Get your gear on, all right? We load on the truck in one-five minutes, and I want time to bring everything up to spec if it doesn't check out."

A plus of the mission was that they didn't have to insert from orbit. A slightly modified civilian semi-trailer would carry the squad to within a klick of the unsuspecting target.

"You won't have to wait for me," Porter muttered, slapping closed the inspection port on her railgun magazine. As she tested joint movement manually, she went on, "Look, Platt, there's no way Razza would come in on this drop with us if it was Hegemony intelligence we were after. This is for her bank account, pure and simple, and she doesn't trust anybody else to oversee that."

"Corporal," Captain Wittvogel said.

Porter grimaced but didn't turn to face him.

"*Corporal,*" Wittvogel repeated.

The captain was tall and rangy. The gray in his reddish hair could have been a genetic quirk, but he certainly wasn't a kid. He didn't raise his voice often, but neither did he expect to be ignored.

Porter turned and braced to attention. "Sir," she said.

"Politics aren't our job, Corporal," Wittvogel said softly. "OK?"

"Sorry, sir," Porter agreed. "I—mission nerves, I guess. I talk too much."

Captain Wittvogel grinned tightly. "If you weren't nervous," he said, "I'd think you didn't have the sense God gave a goose. But don't let's go spooking the newbie, OK?"

The squad finished check-out and suiting up without further discussion, except for the cyborgs. Two of them argued about whether or not the greater hardness of tungsten penetrators was a good trade-off for the higher sectional density of depleted-uranium railgun ammo.

If there'd ever been a time to worry about the why of this mission, that time had ended when the sides of the semi fell down and the assault squad launched from the heart of Dupree City. Right now, Sergeant Terrence Milligan shared a building with over a hundred people who wanted him dead. It wasn't just Ambassador Razza's orders to 'Leave no witnesses!' that kept his trigger fingers twitching.

The office proper was clear. Enhanced IIR, reading body temperatures through the walls, indicated a swarm of locals in the chamber beyond. Heat from the grenade blasts had melted a fusible link, sliding an armored fire door across the double-width archway joining the rooms.

"Milligan!" Captain Wittvogel ordered. "Prep an entrance down to five, but don't blow it yet!"

"Sir, I haven't cleared—" Milligan began, though his hands were already unlimbering one of the three frame charges he carried for this mission.

"Now, dammit!" Wittvogel ordered. "I know what's clear, and I know *nobody's* dealt with five yet!"

Milligan flopped the charge on the flooring, hardwood over a base of structural concrete. He spaced his weapons' selector down one and toggled on EXTERNAL.

A local fired an anti-armor grenade that punched a head-sized mousehole from the other side of the cinder block wall. Milligan looked up from an echosound of the floor, making sure that he wasn't setting the frame charge above an internal wall on the fifth story. He spat three railgun rounds to either side of the mousehole.

Folded for carriage, the frame charge deployed into a meter by two-meter rectangle of explosive tape as soon as Milligan pulled it from its holder. The objective side was convex, with capsules of adhesive which the operator could release with a slap to the top if the charge had to be tacked in place.

A local with a back-pack laser fired through the hole, searing away half Milligan's helmet sensors and sending his armor's environmental system into overload before he could lurch away from the swept area. The office was full of smoke. The suit went back on IIR, and the short laser pulse Milligan directed at the mousehole diffused badly in the murky atmosphere.

"Fire the frame charge, Milligan!" Captain Wittvogel ordered.

*Was he standing on the rectangle of explosive?* He hopped sideways again. Bullets raked the office, harmless but sawing on Milligan's nerves when they ricocheted from his armor. Locals were prising back the firedoor. He triggered his railgun toward the wall and detonated the frame charge with his left index finger.

Though the trough shape focused the explosive's effect against the flooring, the blast still knocked Milligan another step sideways. That was good, because a local used the mousehole to fire a kinetic-energy hittile that wasn't a damned bit affected by the smoke which shrouded Milligan's laser into near uselessness. The rocket-driven tungsten slug snapped at Mach 5 through where Milligan should have been, through the block wall, through a concrete beam with a blast of sparks from the reinforcing rods, and out into the night.

The hittile would have punched at least *into* the powered battle armor if Milligan had been in its path.

The rectangle of floor sagged from one short side instead of falling cleanly. The concrete was reinforced by wire mesh, not rods. Strands the charge hadn't severed acted as a hinge, popping one by one under the weight of the 15-cm thick slab. A laser blazed up through the hole.

"Get him!" screamed a local as the firedoor jerked up its sloping track against the force of gravity a handspan at a time. The next room must be huge to have allowed the hittile's backblast to expand without the overpressure killing everybody enclosed with it.

Milligan placed short bursts through the door opening and the riddled wall. His left hand snatched an incendiary bomb from the carrier on his right hip which balanced the frame charges. He didn't dare let the railgun overheat or he was fucked for good and all.

He dropped the bomb through the opening onto the fifth story. As he did so, the chamber from which the locals fired at him belched flame past the firedoor, out the mousehole, and through every hole Milligan's penetrators had picked in the block wall.

"Coming through!" Captain Wittvogel called. The

hypersonic *crack* of his railgun firing single shots punctuated the words. "Coming through, Milligan. Don't shoot!"

The firedoor, driven by the full strength of a suit of powered battle armor, shot along its track and banged against the stops. Wittvogel strode through the archway, troll-huge and the most beautiful thing Milligan had ever seen. The door slid down again, shutting off the sea of fire beyond.

Captain Wittvogel surveyed the office. The chamber from which he'd entered was a conference room, wrapped now in flame but no danger to a fully-armored soldier. Air sucking through the mousehole helped to clear smoke from the office.

"Clear to come down, sir," he called on the general channel. Switching to line-of-sight laser commo, he added to Milligan alone, "The pick-up boat's on the roof, and Razza's in it."

Wittvogel's bomb satchel hung empty. He must have thrown his load of three incendiaries together. The railgun merely brought mercy to the locals still twitching in the flames. "Your charge and the missile backblast covered the hole I put in their ceiling," he explained. "It doesn't do to get too focused in this sort of business."

The steel emergency hatch to the roof beside the building-center elevator shaft opened. A rope-and-batten ladder dropped. Two men carrying locked cases, technicians of some sort, wobbled down into the office. Their eyes through the goggles of their respirators looked terrified.

Milligan's incendiary bomb had driven back the shooters on the fifth story briefly, but now a laser probed the hole in the office floor again. A workstation, constructed primarily of inert plastic, burst into flame. The technicians were hunched beneath an unbearable weight of fear. They crawled to a console served by armored leads.

Milligan leaned toward the hole. He pulsed his own laser twice without bothering to aim. Wittvogel laid a frame charge on the floor three meters from the existing hole. "Wait till I go," the captain said. "Then come in, but *don't* forget I'm down there too."

"No!" Ambassador Razza ordered as she dropped from the roof wearing a light powered suit. Because the ambassador didn't have experience with the servos, she overcorrected and banged into the elevator/utility column. "Wittvogel, you stay here and guard me."

She glanced at the cowering technicians. They'd opened their cases and were attaching leads to the console's input slots. "Get to work, damn you!" she added.

Milligan looked up. He couldn't make eye contact with his captain through their armored suits. As he tried, he realized there weren't any options anyway. He swore softly.

Wittvogel took a bomb from Milligan's satchel. A lanyard jerked loose the safety pin. The charge would go off at its next contact. A fragmentation grenade, dangerous to the techs and the equipment, bounced up out of the hole but fell back onto the fifth story before it exploded.

"Your choice," the captain said.

"Mine," Milligan replied. With luck, the locals would concentrate on the new opening while Milligan dropped in through the original one. He fired his laser through the hole, keeping to an angle that protected him from a direct reply but might bounce his beam usefully from the wall of the chamber below.

All hell was breaking loose in the Gendarmery camp. Somebody there had been alert enough to fire at

Kappa, the cyborg who was supposed to enter the palace from the north and clear the basement while his partner—Porter, as it turned out—took care of the ground floor.

The shot hadn't damaged Kappa, but it deflected him from his orders, never a hard result to achieve with a cyborg. Kappa was rampaging through the Gendarmery camp, blowing up tanks and other heavy equipment. The gendarmes' attempts to engage the swift-moving target only increased the carnage in their own dense ranks.

Milligan pulled the last incendiary from his satchel. "Ready!" he called.

Wittvogel blew the frame charge. Milligan hurled his bomb into the hole before him. He leaped into the inferno with his laser arm outstretched. Three railgun projectiles rang on his suit before he hit the floor.

He was in it *bad*. The fifth story was a single room built around the utility shaft. It was a barracks for the Grantholder's bodyguard, and there were at least a dozen soldiers in or getting into powered battle armor. The local suits weren't up to Hegemony spec, but they were plenty good enough to win at twelve to one odds.

"Scrambler! Scrambler!" Milligan screamed as his laser ripped a local point-blank and two more powered suits spun from the empty fireball of Wittvogel's bomb to engage the real threat. The entrance round had broken up when it hit the solid casing of the utility shaft. Strewn explosive burned red, adding color to the spluttering white of the incendiaries.

Milligan curved his right middle finger back to his palm to bring up his weapons display. A rocket banged into his breastplate and ricocheted off. He staggered. The warhead didn't have time to arm before it hit him, but it went off with an orange flash and a huge *Wham!* on the wall it struck next.

The display read EMP. Milligan fired the scrambler grenade toward the armored local twenty meters away, across the big room. Another scrambler spat down from Wittvogel on the sixth floor an instant after Milligan got his away.

There was nothing in particular to see when the electromagnetic pulse generators went off. The cold reaction didn't even burst the scrambler's thermoplastic casing. Milligan couldn't see anything anyway, because the EMP shut down his powered battle armor as surely as it did the local suits.

Everything went black. Milligan's terrified breathing roared in the absence of the normally-hissing environmental system.

Scrambler grenades burned out circuits, whether the electronics were operating or on standby but connected to a power source. Equipment on the floors above and below five, shielded by wire mesh/concrete barriers, wouldn't be affected. All circuitry on the fifth story fried.

Milligan reset his suit by forcing his left index finger against his thumb. When the mechanical switch connected, the suit's duplicate control boards, then the sensors, came back to life.

Wittvogel leaned down through the hole shooting. Local battle armor, frozen in weird postures when the metallic muscles lost power, were easy targets. Suits blazed in the laser flux. The redundant circuitry of Hegemony powered battle armor was expensive, beyond the ability or desires of Grant Dupree's financial arbiters. The local suits would be cold metal until someone carried them to a major repair facility.

Nobody was going to get a chance to do that. A telltale indicated Milligan's weapons were live again. He ignored the suits and aimed instead at movement, soldiers scrambling out of their useless armor. Railgun slugs picked the locals off before they could find hand-held weapons with which to reply.

The last bodyguard pounded at the elevator's call-plate, though he must have known that the EMP had burned out those circuits too. Milligan's projectiles snapped through the body and sparked red against the elevator's metal door beyond.

"All clear, Captain!" Milligan called. His voice was a shrill squeal that reminded him of how frightened he'd been.

"Fourth story clear!" Platt reported an instant later. "But it was soldiers, not servants."

Special duty gendarmes, Milligan presumed. The newbie wasn't good enough to have handled a room-ful of powered battle armor by himself.

"Captain, I've got the ground floor clear," Porter said, her voice a half-step higher than usual, "but there's something in the base—"

The palace shook. Porter's voice cut out.

Milligan switched to a remote view from Porter's display. The upper left quadrant of his screen fuzzed with empty static, telling him what his gut already knew: nothing was broadcasting on that channel.

There was a white flash from the middle of the Gendarmery camp. A hypervelocity missile had skewered Kappa like a butterfly on a pin. The cyborg's scuttling charge destroyed the evidence of Hegemony involvement.

The projectile was much more powerful than the one which had narrowly missed Milligan on the sixth story. It had been launched from the ground floor of the Grantholder's Palace.

"I'll get the bassid!" rumbled Alpha, the cyborg covering the second story; a statement rather than a report, and purely rhetorical.

"Alpha, hold where you are until—" Captain Wittvogel ordered.

A laser fired on a lower floor, then metal belled. Alpha had cut through the elevator door, then kicked the tags of metal away so that he could jump into the shaft. You might as well pray as give orders to a cyborg who'd already made up his/her/its mind. There was at least a chance that God would listen to you.

Milligan pulled the second of his frame charges free of its holder and deployed it on the scarred concrete floor. A quick echo-sound indicated the fourth story of the palace was laid out on the same pattern as the fifth: a single room divided by frail partitions rather than structural walls.

Whoever was in the palace basement had proved they could take out Hegemony soldiers one at a time. That meant—to anybody but a kill-focused cyborg— that the squad's survivors had to join in order to meet the threat with massed firepower.

Milligan, Platt, and Beta could link on the fourth story, moving through the floor of the fifth story and the ceiling of the third. Elevators and staircases were easy: easy ways to die. You *never* used them in a hostile building.

Unless you were a cyborg in a hurry. Alpha dropped on his jets to ground-floor level. The palace rocked with the backblast of another powerful hittile, punching through the elevator door and Alpha's breastplate before the cyborg could even start to cut his way clear with his laser. White fire flashed up the shaft and bulged the doors beside Milligan.

A frame charge went off on a lower story. Platt or Beta, probably Beta because Platt was too shook, yammering to the captain for direction. All the kid needed to do was hold what he'd got, help was coming.

Milligan triggered his frame charge. The blast shocked dust waist-high across the open room. The slab sagged but didn't fall cleanly. Milligan stamped on it, breaking one side loose.

He switched his remote to Beta. It took a moment of disorientation before Milligan realized the cyborg was looking down, not up, through a freshly-blown entrance hole. Instead of forming with Platt on the fourth story, Beta had decided to go after the unseen hostiles alone.

Milligan kicked at the hanging slab again. It broke apart. Half of the concrete sandwich swung to either side of the hold before tearing loose to fall.

In the upper left quadrant of Milligan's display, a ten-square meter section of the second-story's flooring lifted to a frame charge fired from below. Beta, poised on the third story, aimed both laser and railgun. The cyborg's arms, extended to fire, showed at the lower edge of the remote viewpoint.

Shattered concrete crumbled beneath a blanket of roiling dust. Metal glinted. The cyborg opened fire.

Milligan dropped through his opening to the fourth story. On the remote image, powdered lime blazed fiercely white as it drank energy from the cyborg's laser.

The hostile hurled itself upward, firing a hypervelocity missile as it came. Beta's laser flux deformed but could not deflect the projectile. The cyborg, struck squarely, lurched back from a hammerblow instead of a penetrating rapier thrust.

The hostile was a Throg in powered battle armor, tripodal and seemingly the size of a dump truck. Either the operator was twice as big as any Throg Milligan had ever seen before, or the aliens who built the suit had retained their natural shape while constructing something more nearly akin to a tank than powered battle armor.

As Beta tumbled away from the hittile's punch, the Throg finished the job with the laser in one of its triple arms. The remote image degraded momentarily, then blanked into the snowy emptiness of death.

Milligan switched off the remote channel. "Captain," he called, surprised that his voice didn't quiver, "we've got a Throg in armor, a mother-huge one. Platt and me are going to need help soonest. Soonest!"

Platt had cleared most of the unarmored locals on this story with laser and fragmentation grenades. The single room was a sea of ruddy flame. Smoke veiled the optical spectrum while the heat played hell with Milligan's IIR, despite low-pass filters which excluded the fire proper.

The building shuddered. A suit as massive as the Throg's made things jump just by walking. Milligan launched an Eye Fly in vague hope that he could thread it down to the third story to watch what the Throg was doing.

That was silly. He didn't have time to control the little remote sensor. Anyway, the reinforced-concrete flooring would limit the information it sent by spread-band radio as badly as it did Milligan's direct sensor inputs.

"Platt, up to the sixth floor," Captain Wittvogel ordered. "Milligan, cover him and follow. If it's just one Throg, then three of us can handle him."

"That's a lie!" Ambassador Razza broke in unexpectedly. Milligan had forgotten she was present, with a suit that gave her full access to the squad's commo net. "There aren't any Throgs here! You're trying to trick me so that I don't get the, the data!"

Platt, halfway across the big room, slapped a frame charge against the ceiling above him. "No you idiot!" Milligan shouted. "Use the hole I've—"

"Ambassador, you'd better withdraw n—" the captain began.

The floor directly under Platt quaked upward in a

gush of flames fanned to multiple brightness by the
Throg's frame charge. Shattered concrete avalanched
away, leaving a black square instead of support.

Platt reacted fast, firing his jets, but he didn't have
the instinctive control that was the only thing that
might have saved him. The newbie's powered battle-
armor banged into the concrete ceiling and ricocheted
down to the blazing floor.

Milligan's laser licked the Throg's central arm as the
alien aimed another hittile. The rocket motor blew up
in the launching tube with a spew of yellow flame.

The Throg lifted through the hole it had blown in
the floor. Its laser, pulsing with a flux so dense that
airborne particulate matter exploded from the beam's
path, caught Platt on his second bounce. Bits of the
newbie's armor flew off in sparkling arcs before the
scuttling charge devoured the remainder.

The Throg's third arm flailed in Milligan's direction,
ripping out railgun projectiles. Though the Throg had
three weapon stations, the single mind controlling them
couldn't split its attention any better than a human's
could. The slugs plowed the ceiling and blazing floor,
but none of them touched Milligan as he leaped for
the only shelter sturdy enough to withstand his
opponent's power: the utility shaft, a square-section
tube of structural concrete.

Milligan fired as he moved, lighting one of the
Throg's leg joints white for the instant it took to
punch part of the railgun's hosing burst through the
weakened armor. The Throg stumbled, skewing the
creature's laser response into a touch of scarlet pain
across Milligan's buttocks rather than a finishing
blow.

It took luck to wreck the Throg's knee while shooting
on the fly, but you didn't *get* that kind of luck unless
you were good to begin with. Milligan crouched beside

the utility shaft, aware that neither luck nor skill would preserve him much longer.

The Throg's heavy armor would be clumsy in open terrain, an easy target for a human who knew what he was doing. In a point-blank slugfest, though . . .

The hovering Eye Fly's signal in Milligan's remote quadrant showed the Throg edging clockwise around the shaft, slowed by injury but still mobile. Milligan matched the creature centimeter by centimeter. Both armored figures were close to the concrete.

"Captain Wittvogel," Milligan said. "I really need some support down here."

He couldn't break for the hole in the ceiling or through an exterior wall. The alien would catch him on the fly, as it had Platt and the cyborg out in the Gendarmery camp. Milligan and the Throg were here on the fourth story together until one of them died.

If the ambassador didn't believe there were Throgs in Grant Dupree, then the purpose of the mission was just what Porter had claimed: to loot the Grantholder's credit accounts. But Razza had been wrong—

So Porter was dead, and they were all going to be dead very shortly. The only good thing about the situation was that the Throg had weaponry powerful enough to flick the pick-up boat out of the air. The ambassador couldn't abandon her armored infantry and expect to survive herself.

The Throg tried a bank shot with its laser, ceiling to support beam. The backsplash bathed Milligan unpleasantly, but the surfaces weren't good enough reflectors to make the attempt dangerous. Concrete glowed white, fading slowly as it cooled.

A laser slapped briefly on an upper story. Milligan didn't know what Wittvogel was shooting at, but eventually the surviving gendarmes were going to get organized enough to take a hand. "Captain—" Milligan said.

"Back from the shaft, Milligan!" Wittvogel ordered. "Now!"

So far as Milligan could see, moving away from the concrete shelter would be suicide. He obeyed anyway, in a soldier's reflex. Captain Wittvogel didn't give orders just because he liked the sound of his own voice; and anyway, there wasn't a good choice available.

Milligan jumped for a corner, his back to a support beam. The Throg sprang awkwardly around the edge of the utility shaft, its railgun and laser pointing. The missile Milligan detonated had wrecked the launcher as well.

The sensors of Milligan's suit quivered but didn't fail in an attenuated electromagnetic pulse. The Throg collapsed in a pile of battle armor, no longer powered because the scrambler had destroyed its control circuits.

Milligan heated the back of the Throg's neck joint with his laser, then sent three penetrators through like icepicks into the alien's brain before it could reset its suit. Scuttling charges began to destroy the armor, working inward from the limbs.

Milligan's helmet recorder had full evidence of Grantholder Dupree's treasonous congress with the Throgs. He lifted through the fifth story and back up to the smoke-wrapped office on the sixth.

The technicians hugged one another instinctively. Wittvogel and the ambassador were faceless in their armor.

"Captain, how did you do that EMP?" Milligan blurted, using modulated laser to keep the discussion private.

Wittvogel picked up a technician bodily and tossed him through the roof hatch. On spread-band radio, audible to Razza as well as Milligan, he said, "I cut the shielding on a power lead with my laser and popped a scrambler beside it. The EMP travelled down the cable trunk in the central shaft. The conduit gave the pulse a linear form, so it didn't fry your suit too."

Razza headed for the hatch, climbing rather than trusting her control of the suit's jets. Holding the remaining technician in his arms, Wittvogel added loudly, "That trick was the only way I could save Ambassador Razza's life."

As soon as the ambassador's legs were clear, Wittvogel jetted upward. Milligan followed the captain so closely that exhaust turbulence banged him into the hatch coaming as he exited. He scarcely noticed the shock after everything he'd been through.

The boat was ready to go, its thrusters puffing a mist of ionized reaction mass. The small craft's hull was armored, but its real protection tonight was the sparkling chaos in the Gendarmery camp. Cooked-off rockets and projectiles lofted by the explosion of their neighbors drew glowing arcs across the sky. Warheads which landed in Dupree City set off secondary blasts among the house and vehicles.

Ambassador Razza jumped into the boat. Wittvogel set his armored hand in the hatchway, unblocking the track only when he and Milligan were aboard also.

Acceleration flung them all to the rear of the compartment. The technician Wittvogel held was moaning with relief.

"Sir," Milligan said. The hot surface of his armor raised a wisp of haze from the plastic liner of the bulkhead against which he leaned. He was still using laser commo. "Why did you have to cut a lead? The EMP would've travelled down the conduit sheath itself, wouldn't it?"

The boat's rhythmic buffeting implied that the pilot

was holding them so close to the deck that the terrain-avoidance system had to boost them to clear trees. Grant Dupree's air defenses weren't likely to be a danger, but there was no point in taking chances.

The captain turned so that his helmet-top laser communicator pointed directly at Milligan. "If I hadn't cut the input lead to the data bank," Wittvogel said deliberately, "then the scrambler wouldn't have cleared the main accounts as well as the copy these techs had already made. They could have retrieved it again."

Wittvogel opened his arms. The technician scrambled free on all fours, sobbing loudly.

"Nothing I could do was going to bring back Porter and Platt," the captain said. "And anyway, soldiers die."

Ambassador Razza had opened the faceplate of her helmet. Her skin was white; sweat glittered on her cheekbones and upper lip. Milligan wondered if she realized yet that the scrambler grenade had converted her plans of wealth into electromagnetic garbage.

"But I didn't think anybody ought to get rich off my people's death," Captain Wittvogel added, in a whisper as harsh as a leopard's cough.

# WITH THE SWORD
# HE MUST BE SLAIN

*"If anyone slays with the sword, with the sword he must be slain."*

—Revelation 13:10

The Colonel had never met this tasking officer, but he was a Suit and the Colonel figured all Suits were the same. The fact that this particular Suit was part of Hell's bureaucracy rather than Langley's didn't make a lot of difference.

"Good to see you, Colonel," the Suit said as he studied the folder in front of him. "Please sit down."

He didn't get up from behind his desk, and he didn't offer to shake hands. Probably afraid he'd transfer sweat to the fine wool/silk blend of his garment. This particular Suit fancied English tailoring instead of Italian, but that was pretty standard for the Company boys too. The left half of the Colonel's lips smiled.

"Yes?" said the Suit.

"I was wondering," the Colonel said, "whether Hell is a CIA proprietary operation. Or vice versa."

"I think we'd best use our time to productive ends, Colonel," the Suit said dismissively. "The schedule is rather tight for jokes."

There was a look of disdain in his eyes. The Colonel would have liked to put the muzzle of a pistol in the Suit's mouth and watch those hard black eyes bulge when he pulled the trigger, but he wouldn't do that.

He'd never done that, much as he'd wanted to, every fucking time. The Suits with their clean hands and clean clothes were all the same. . . .

The Suit frowned again at the red-bordered folder in front of him, then transferred his attention to the Colonel. "What's your physical condition?" he said. "This says you were—"

"I'm fit," the Colonel said curtly. His ribs were taped. He'd blocked the obsidian-fanged club, but the blow had driven the flat of his own weapon, a similar club, into his side. Adrenaline had hidden the pain while the Colonel buried the butt of his club in the solar plexus of the squat giant who'd struck him and then broke his neck with the edge of his hand; but the pain was back now, every time he breathed.

"Colonel, if you're not—"

"I said I was fit!" the Colonel said. "I can execute your Goddamned operation better than anybody else you can hand the job to!"

The Suit gave him a cold smile. "Yes, you will have your joke, won't you?" he said. "Very well."

He shifted one, then two sheets from the right side of the folder to the left and said, "You'll be inserted with a twenty-man team to eliminate an Enemy base. We believe it's a medical unit, but there'll doubtless be a security element attached. You should be fine if you execute a quick in-and-out."

The Suit flipped another page. *You'll be fine, you smug sonuvabitch*, the Colonel thought, *because you won't be within a hundred klicks of the sound of gunfire. You'll be drinking in a bar with your Savile Row and Armani colleagues, talking solemnly about the strain of your position.*

The Colonel had gotten the job through an Australian friend, Macgregor. Mac was dead now, killed trying to start the motor of his Zodiac boat during some goatfuck in the Seychelles, the Colonel had heard. Maybe true, maybe not. Rumors hadn't gotten any more accurate than they'd been before things started to come apart.

The Colonel doubted Mac had known any more about the employer than he had himself. Suits were looking for people with special skills for work in the international security field—just like always. The pay was good.

The Colonel wasn't stupid; he wouldn't have survived this long without more raw brainpower than most of the Suits who tasked him. He'd realized a long time ago that the pay was just an excuse. He was doing this work because the only time he felt alive was when he *was* doing the work, and he wasn't ready to die.

When the Colonel figured out who his employer was, he didn't much like it. But neither did the knowledge make any real difference in what the Colonel did or how well he did it.

"Here's the map of the terrain," the Suit said, handing over a folded document. "You can study it as long as you wish, but it can't leave the room, of course."

"Of course," the Colonel said. Suits were always jealous of their secrets, their Sources and Methods. A captured map might tell the Enemy what we knew and how we'd learned it. In this particular case, the Enemy being who He was, that was even funnier than the usual Suit bullshit.

The map was satellite imagery overlaid with contour lines and elevations noted in meters. A hollow triangle marked the objective. The satellites hadn't been up for the past six months, though the Colonel was losing track of time. Still, the mountainous terrain itself wasn't likely to have changed much.

There were no landmarks familiar to the Colonel. He waved a corner of the map to the tasking officer. "Where is this?" he asked.

"The operation doesn't require that you have that information," the Suit said coolly.

The Colonel looked at him and smiled. *Eyes bulging outward. A spray of blood from the nostrils as the bullet acts as a piston in the chamber of the skull.*

He went back to studying the map.

"You'll insert by air," the Suit said. "The vehicle will remain under your operational control and will extract you at the completion of the mission."

"Enemy forces?" the Colonel said, his eyes on the map.

"In the region as a whole, considerable," the Suit said. He shrugged. "Brigade strength, we believe. But the site you're to eliminate should have no more than a platoon present for security. The Enemy won't be able to bring greater forces to bear in the time available—if you do your job properly."

"Yes, all right," the Colonel said. He stood up and handed back the map. The right knee caught him as it always did, the calling card of a paradrop into bamboo when he was nineteen and thought he was indestructible. "I'm ready to meet my unit."

The Suit replaced the map within the folder. "Very well," he said. "One of the service personnel is waiting outside the door. He'll lead you to your men."

The Colonel paused before touching the doorknob and looked back. Maybe it was the "if you do your job properly" that made him angry enough to say, "Does it bother you to be working for the losing side?"

"I beg your pardon?" the Suit said. He looked genuinely puzzled.

"This is the battle of Good against Evil," the Colonel said. "Evil loses, right? And don't try to tell me we're the forces of Good!"

"Certainly not that," the Suit said with a faint smile. "What a concept."

His smile hardened. "But for the rest, Colonel, you're quite wrong. Good doesn't defeat you." The Suit shook his head. "What a concept!" he repeated.

The Colonel stepped into the hallway where the silent servitor waited. He didn't know how to take what the Suit had just told him, so he didn't think about it.

He had a lot of experience with not thinking about things.

The troops were camped under a metal-roofed shelter at the edge of thorny scrubland. Fiber matting hung from the rafters on the south side as a sun shade. There were low platforms around the edges where the men would lay out their bedrolls at night. Now they used the platforms as seats as they cooked on a pair of small fires burning on the dirt floor in the center.

The man who noticed the servitor guiding the Colonel toward the shelter jumped up and called to the others. Chattering with high-pitched enthusiasm, the troops spilled out to stand in a single rank to greet their new commander.

The air was hot and dry. The outline of the mountains in the eastern distance was as unfamiliar to the Colonel as the topographic map had been.

"Sir!" said the man at the left end of the line of troops. He threw the Colonel a British-style salute, palm outward. "I am Captain Sisir Krishnamurtri of the Telugu Resistance Army. My men and I know you by reputation. We are honored to serve with you!"

The Colonel returned the salute with the edge of his hand out the way he'd learned it too many years ago. Instinctively he sucked in his gut. He was in good shape—"great shape for a man of his age," people said—but he knew the difference between that and nineteen.

The servitor knew the difference too. They never spoke, these hairless, sexless nude figures who performed administrative duties for the fighting forces, but they had minds and personalities. This one smirked when he saw the Colonel pretending to be more than the decayed remnants of what he once had been.

What made it worse was that the troops were so absurdly young themselves. Captain Krishnamurtri was probably twenty-five, but the Colonel doubted any of the others were out of their teens. Several on the far end of the line were fourteen at the oldest, boys hopping from one foot to the other with their eagerness to go out and kill.

Telugus were South Indians, the Colonel thought, though he'd never heard of a Telugu Resistance Army. They were small, dark folk, barefoot and wearing dhotis wrapped around their loins. Krishnamurtri had put on a short-sleeved khaki shirt as a sign of his rank when the Colonel arrived. Their red sweatbands were probably a uniform.

"I'm pleased to be working with you too, Captain," the Colonel said. That was a lie, but it was a very familiar lie; and God knew he'd commanded worse. In Sierra Leone, for instance . . . "Send the men back to their meal while you brief me on your unit."

God knew. The Colonel smiled at his accidental joke.

Black humor was the only kind of humor there was in the field.

The platform at the east end of the shelter was eight inches high, twice that of the others. It provided a dais on which Krishnamurtri and the Colonel sat—the Telugu squatting, the Colonel with his left leg crossed and the right straight out in front of him because the knee hadn't bent properly since the day bamboo splintered its way through the connective tissue.

"First off," the Colonel said, "how many of your men speak English?"

A young soldier came over with two small glass cups of tea on a brass tray. There was a sprig of mint in either cup. He bowed, set the tray down between the officers, and scuttled off.

Krishnamurtri picked up a cup and offered it to the Colonel. "Them?" he said. "None, they only speak Telugu. They're merely field workers. I am a Brahmin. Without me they would be nothing. You will tell me what to do, Colonel, and I will see that they do it."

The Colonel sipped his tea. It was sweet and hot, hotter even than the steady wind out of the west.

He'd seen it too often to be surprised any more: local officers who thought their men were dirt. That's what they were in truth, often enough, thugs good for nothing but to smoke *khat* or whatever the local drug of choice was and carry off girls to rape for the next week or so until they got tired of them.

But the officers were even worse to any eyes but their own. If the Colonel could speak Telugu or the troops knew English, he wouldn't have kept Krishnamurtri around even to wipe his feet on. That wasn't an option—it usually wasn't—and anyway, the other side was usually just as badly off.

Even now. This was the Colonel's third operation for his present employer, and the quality of the opposition had been well short of divine. He smiled again.

Before the Colonel could ask about the unit's training and experience, a vehicle sailed out of the western sky as slowly as a vulture and landed beside the shelter in a shimmer of static electricity. It was a narrow, flat-bottomed craft more like a toboggan than an aircraft. It was open-sided except for the exiguous cockpit in front where a kneeling servitor drove. The Colonel had never seen anything like it before.

The servitor got out, pointed an index finger at the weapons lying on the rear deck, and walked away without a backward glance. The Telugus chirped with amazement as they gathered around the vehicle.

"An air sled!" Krishnamurtri said. "And look, they're giving us ion guns too, enough for all of us! This is because we serve with you, Colonel. We are honored, greatly honored!"

The Colonel got to his feet with the care his ribs and his many previous injuries required. He kept a straight face as he stepped out of the shelter. He'd never heard of air sleds *or* the ion guns which the delighted Telugus were now waving in the air. He didn't suppose it mattered.

On his first operation for the present employer the Colonel's troops had been mostly Nigerians. They'd been armed with a variety of World War II weapons: Enfield rifles and Tommy guns, with American pineapple grenades and a Danish light machine gun, a Madsen, that took 8-mm ammunition instead of the .303 that the rifles used.

Riddle had been assigned as his XO on that operation. The Colonel had worked with him before, on Bouganville. Riddle knew his business, right enough, but he was a nasty piece of work. He liked his boys as young as possible and screaming, even when they were prostitutes and already, as Riddle put it, stump-broke. The Colonel hadn't been sorry when the bunker Riddle threw a grenade into blew up and took him with it. There must have been a ton of explosives stored inside.

You could call the operation a success: they'd destroyed the Enemy base camp. Only the Colonel himself and a handful of his troops had survived, though.

The second operation was supposed to eliminate an Enemy command post. The Colonel had been assigned to a unit of Amerinds armed with clubs and spears. He'd worked in Latin America often enough in the past, but he didn't speak the language his troops did and they had only a smattering of the Spanish that had to serve as his command language.

They'd done their job, caught the hostile commander in his hammock with one of his wives and hacked them both to bloody fragments. Enemy forces had kept up the pursuit to where the canoes were stashed, however; only the Colonel himself and two paddlers had made it all the way back for pickup.

The Colonel examined the ion gun. It had a short barrel, a long tubular receiver, and a pistol grip with a normal trigger and a three-position safety above it. The weapon had no other controls.

He extended the telescoping buttstock, walked around the end of the shelter, and aimed through the disk-shaped optical sight toward the mountains. Telugus crowded behind him, jabbering in excitement.

The Colonel pulled the trigger. Nothing happened. He was deliberately ignoring Captain Krishnamurtri's offered suggestions, though it was going to be embarrassing if the Colonel couldn't figure the weapon out himself.

He thumbed the rotary safety to its middle position

and squeezed the trigger again. A sunburst carved a crackling path through the air. The beam traveled several kilometers, though it dissipated in a foggy cone well short of the mountains. The gun recoiled hard, like a shotgun with heavy loads.

The sighting disk went black at the instant of discharge, but purple ghost images danced on the retina of the Colonel's left eye. He'd have to remember to close it in the future, fighting a lifetime's conditioning to shoot with both eyes open in order to be aware of his surroundings as well as his sight picture.

He turned the safety straight back, to its third position. He sighted, closed his left eye, and squeezed. His feet were braced and the butt was firmly against his shoulder. Even so the discharge rocked him backward.

The flash lit the entire vicinity. The Colonel had aimed well above the nearby vegetation, but it still exploded into flame. The weapon ejected a silvery tube from a port in the underside.

The Colonel lowered the weapon carefully; its muzzle was white hot. "All right," he said to Krishnamurtri as the other troops capered behind him, thrilled by the display. "Do we have a driver for the air sled?"

The Colonel checked moonrise against his watch, then velcroed the field cover over its face. The fabric both protected the crystal and concealed the luminous dial. This was a bright night, but habit and the awareness of how often little things were the difference between life and death kept the Colonel to his routine.

He settled onto the right front of the vehicle beside Rao, the pilot. There were no seats. The Colonel's stiff right leg stuck out the side at an angle.

"All right," the Colonel said. "Take us up."
Krishnamurtri, squatting immediately behind Rao,
relayed the order as a short bark.

Rao had circled the base camp alone to prove he
could fly the air sled. As they staggered into the air
with a full load of troops and equipment, though, the
Colonel knew they were in trouble.

Because they weren't rising as fast as Rao thought
they should, the Telugu shouted at the vehicle and
jerked back on the simple joystick control. The bow
came up—too sharply. The sled apparently couldn't stall,
but it *could* slide backward if the angle of attack was
too sharp. It started to do that.

Krishnamurtri pounded Rao on the top of the head.
The troops in back babbled with surprise and fear.

The Colonel put his big right hand over the pilot's
and rolled the joystick forward. The stick slid in on its
axis also. That in-and-out motion controlled the sled's
speed, as the Colonel realized when they slowed.
They'd almost mushed out of the air before he hauled
up on Rao's hand and the stick.

The sled's nose dipped. They accelerated in a rush
toward the ground. The Colonel eased the stick back
carefully, fighting Rao's urge to haul them up hard. The
vehicle lifted smoothly instead of crashing through the
scrub, shedding pieces of itself and the men aboard.

They leveled out and started to climb gently. The
Colonel took his hand away from the joystick. He
patted Rao on the shoulder.

He turned toward Krishnamurtri. "Tell him that easy
does it," he said. "With a load like this it's important
not to overcorrect."

Krishnamurtri shouted another string of Telugu
abuse at Rao. The Colonel couldn't do anything about
that, but when Krishnamurtri raised his hand to hit the
pilot again he caught the captain's wrist.

"Stupid peasant!" Krishnamurtri muttered as he subsided.

The Colonel rode with his right leg sticking out in the airstream. His ion gun pointed at the scrubland, ready to fire individual bolts. Because of where he sat in the vehicle, he held the grip with his left hand. The right was his master hand, but he'd learned long ago to use either as circumstances dictated.

The Colonel had flown helicopters in the past. He'd never had formal training, just a quick-and-dirty grounding in the basics. There'd been time to spare and the pilot wanted somebody who could grab the stick if he was shot in a place that was incapacitating but not fatal. (The pilot didn't care *what* happened to the bird if he'd already bought the farm.)

That particular operation had been a dream—the team extracted before anybody on the ground knew they'd had company. Three months later, though, a different pilot took a .51-cal round through the throat and sprayed his blood all over what was left of the cockpit while the Colonel flew them back to the base. They'd pancaked in from twenty feet up, but that wasn't the Colonel's fault: another round had opened the tank. The turbine died when the last of the jet fuel leaked out in the airstream.

The Colonel figured he could fly the air sled if he had to—fly it better than Rao, at any rate—but he couldn't both fly the bird and conn them in at low level the way this insertion had to be made. Besides, the controls were on the left side of the cockpit; they'd have to land for him and Rao to change places, which meant circling back to the base to find a cleared area. The number of ways that could go wrong made the risk at least as significant as letting Rao continue as pilot.

The Telugu seemed to have gotten things under

control after the rocky start. The sled's speed built up until they were belting along at close on ninety knots by the Colonel's estimate. They could have done with a proper windscreen, though the reverse curve of the sled's dash panel did a remarkably good job of directing the airflow over the pair in the immediate front of the vehicle. Buffeting was much worse for the common soldiers farther back.

The Colonel gave his usual half-mouthed smile. Rank hath its privileges. In this case, the privilege of taking the first round himself if they happened to overfly an Enemy outpost. God knew Enemy troops should've been patrolling well out from their bases in the mountains.

But even if the local commander knew what he was doing, his subordinates might still have ignored his orders or simply done a piss-poor job of executing them. You couldn't assume that the Enemy was ten feet tall, any more than you could count on the Enemy not knowing his ass from a hole in the ground.

The air sled continued slowly climbing. He'd told Rao—told Krishnamurtri, at any rate—that they needed to stay within ten feet of the treetops; they were up to thirty by now and going higher. Rather than go through the Brahmin, the Colonel tapped on the top of the dashboard to get Rao's attention and mimed a gliding descent with his right hand.

Krishnamurtri immediately shouted at the pilot and slapped the back of his head. Rao looked around in wide-eyed amazement. The air sled yawed; the troops in the back cried out with fear. They had a right to be afraid: the sled didn't even have a grab rail. The Colonel was more than a little surprised that they hadn't lost somebody during the wobbling takeoff.

He put his hand over Rao's again, steadying the Telugu instead of trying to take control, and said to

Krishnamurtri in a clipped, very clear voice, "I'll handle this if you please, Captain. And I suggest that you not hit our pilot again while we're in the air. A Claymore mine isn't in the same league as an air crash for shredding human bodies. As I've seen many times."

God knew he had.

The air sled stabilized. They flew on without further incident until the ground beneath changed abruptly from rolling scrubland to fractured terrain where rocks stood up in sheer-sided walls from the softer earth beneath. Rao pulled back on the joystick. He was adjusting his altitude instinctively by the mountains on the horizon rather than the broken hills immediately below the air sled.

The Colonel tapped the dashboard and again mimed a descent. Rao glanced at him sidelong and adjusted the stick only minusculely. The sled continued to rise, though at a flatter angle.

"Tell him to follow the gully to our left!" the Colonel said to Krishnamurtri. The sled's drive mechanism made no sound other than a low-frequency hum and an occasional pop of static electricity, but wind rush meant words had to be shouted to be heard. "We need to be down below the level of the gully's walls!"

The Brahmin nodded several times as though he understood, but he didn't say anything to Rao. "Well, tell him!" the Colonel said, wishing he spoke Telugu.

But why stop with a little wish like that? He could wish that he had a team of Special Forces instead of Third World farm boys qualified as soldiers by the fact that they wouldn't fall over if you leaned a rifle against them. He could even wish that he'd lived his previous life in a fashion that didn't have him now commanding troops on the side of Hell in Armageddon.

The Colonel smiled. "Tell him," he repeated. His voice was no longer harsh, but Krishnamurtri looked even more frightened than before. Maybe it was the smile.

Krishnamurtri spoke to the pilot without his usual hectoring violence. Rao looked at the Colonel with a desperate expression. The Colonel put his hand over Rao's and gently forced the joystick forward.

"Tell him he can slow down if he has to," the Colonel said to Krishnamurtri. "But not too much. Remember, if we don't do this fast, they're going to do us."

He smiled. "Just as sure as Hell."

It was mostly bad luck.

The Colonel had a phenomenal talent for correlating maps with real terrain at ground level; practice had honed an innate skill. Nevertheless he had to concentrate to guide them along the route he'd planned after ten minutes with an aerial photograph, and he wasn't paying much attention to the Telugus. After the fact, he wished that he'd remembered to warn Rao that the gorge they were following took a hard jog to the left, but there was only so much you could do.

Rao tried to go over the sudden barrier instead of banking with it. That might have been all right if the sled hadn't been so heavily loaded; as it was, they were going to clear the rock but not the thorny trees growing on the creviced top.

The Colonel acted in a combination of reflex and instinct, two of the supports that had kept him alive longer than even he could credit when he looked back on his life. He thumbed the ion gun's safety to position three, rock and roll, and triggered the weapon.

The ion gun's discharge dazzled the night. Trees vanished and the limestone slope beyond glowed white under the lash of the beam. The air sled sailed through a momentary Hell of furnace-hot air. The troops were screaming.

Ash flew into the Colonel's eyes when he opened them after shooting. He blinked furiously to clear them so he could see again.

Rao fought the sled under control, then clapped the Colonel on the shoulder with a cry of delight. The Telugu was thrilled to still be alive.

"Watch your—" the Colonel said, unable to see clearly himself but aware that this was no time for the pilot to be thinking about dangers already past.

Rao curved back over the lip of the gorge they'd been following. The air sled dropped precipitately as it left the updraft from rock heated by the ion blast. The back end ticked the ground hard enough to throw the rearmost Telugus overboard. Without their weight, the nose tilted sharply down.

Rao screamed; the Colonel hauled his hand fiercely back on the joystick. Neither man's action made any useful difference. The sled scraped along the rocky soil, disintegrating as it threw its passengers off to either side.

The Colonel bailed out at the first hop, before the sled started to tumble. He curled into a ball and hit rolling; there wasn't a good way to smack the ground at forty knots, but he'd done it before and survived.

He clamped the ion gun to his belly. The barrel was searingly hot from firing, but the Colonel's instinct to cling to his weapon was stronger than any pain.

He skidded to a halt well down the slope and paused a moment before he got to his feet. He'd once seen a man leap from a C-47 as it bellied in on a grass strip. The fellow would probably have been all right if he hadn't tried to stand up before he'd come to a complete stop. Momentum flipped him in an unexpected cartwheel; he broke his neck when he came down again.

The Colonel had seen people die in some of the *damnedest* ways. God knew he had.

He checked himself over. He didn't seem to have broken any bones. His left elbow had taken a knock, but it bent and straightened all right. His ribs felt like there was a white-hot sword in his side every time he took a breath, but there was no blood in the phlegm when he cleared dust and soot from his lungs in a wracking cough. Pain had never kept the Colonel from moving when his life depended on it. His life certainly depended on moving now.

There'd been a box of six reloads along with the ion guns; five remained after the Colonel tested the weapon. He thrust one of the silvery tubes into the receiver now and turned the safety back to single shot. The Colonel had taken all the reloads himself since he hadn't been with his troops long enough to know which men might be trusted with extra ammo.

Probably none of them. Christ, what a mess. Ten klicks into hostile territory with twenty farmers, no commo, and no transport but their own feet. The Telugus—Krishnamurtri included—didn't even have boots.

The Brahmin sat weeping. He seemed healthy enough except for scrapes.

Rao lay on his back, whimpering as he tried unsuccessfully to breathe. The pilot had separated from the air sled only moments after the Colonel did, but a blow from the joystick had crushed his ribs. Rao's chest quivered, but without the rib cage for an anchor his diaphragm couldn't suck air into his flailing lungs.

The Colonel shook Krishnamurtri. When that didn't rouse him, the Colonel slapped him hard. "Get the men together," he ordered. "Tell them we're hiking back to base. Anybody who can't march gets to make his own peace with the Enemy, but I haven't seen much sign of heavenly mercy in the past."

Krishnamurtri looked at the Colonel in sick amazement. The Brahmin's teeth had cut his upper lip in two places, either during the crash or when the Colonel slapped him.

"Look," the Colonel said in a soft voice. He slid out the double-edged knife he wore in a sheath sewn to his right boot. "If you can't talk to these people, you're no good to me at all."

Krishnamurtri crawled backward in a sitting position, his eyes on the Colonel. He shouted orders in high-pitched Telugu.

The Colonel half walked, half slid, the twenty feet down to Rao. The Telugu watched in sick desperation. His lips moved, but he had no breath to form words. He couldn't have spoken a language the Colonel could understand anyway.

The Colonel had heard the words often enough, in at least a score of languages. God knew he had.

The Colonel thrust the bootknife behind Rao's left mastoid and drew it expertly around to the right, severing the Telugu's throat to the spine. He stepped back, clear of the spurting blood, and tugged the pilot's dhoti off to wipe his blade while the body was still thrashing.

It wasn't the kind of help Rao had wanted, but it's all the help there could be: a quick death in place of the slower one of suffocation.

Krishnamurtri was on his feet, calling orders with increasing confidence. Men were moving among the trees and brush. At the bottom of the gorge, vegetation burned with an occasional blue electrical splutter to mark where the air sled had come to rest.

That fire and the one the Colonel had lit with his ion gun would mark his unit for the Enemy, too. They didn't have a prayer of getting out of this goatfuck. Not a prayer.

The Colonel smiled at his joke. He sheathed his knife as he waited for his surviving men to gather.

There were thirteen of them left, twelve Telugus and the Colonel himself. Four of the troops hadn't showed up after the crash; three more had been too badly injured to march. And there was Rao, of course.

Only eight Telugus were armed. Ion guns had gone skidding off into the night when the sled tumbled. Unlike the men, the weapons hadn't walked back up the slope looking battered and worried. The Colonel didn't have time to waste searching for guns in the moonlight.

He'd left the wounded men as they were. He couldn't do anything to help them, and they couldn't tell the Enemy anything that wasn't obvious: the survivors were hiking home.

The Colonel would have killed his wounded if he'd had a reason to do so, but he'd never been one of those who liked killing for its own sake. That kind wasn't good for much. Like the looters and rapists, they were so absorbed in their desires that they didn't pay attention to the real business—till they took a charge of buckshot in the back, or a pitchfork up the bum, or a roofing tile splashed their brains across the pavement.

The Colonel had seen all those things and more. God knew he had.

He didn't hear any night birds, but frogs of at least a dozen varieties clunked and chirped and trilled from the bottom of the gorge. There must be open water, at least in pools.

The Colonel kept his unit just below the crest. It would have been easier to walk either on the ridge or down the center of the gorge. The first would have left them exposed to observers and very possibly silhouetted to a sniper; the latter was, like a trail in hostile jungle, an obvious killing ground.

Krishnamurtri objected to having to march on a surface so steep that frequently a man slid until he grabbed a spiky tree branch. The common soldiers didn't seem to mind, or at any rate they didn't bother to complain that life wasn't fair. Maybe they thought it was.

The Colonel smiled. Maybe they were right. Maybe everybody got exactly what he deserved.

Through Krishnamurtri he'd told the troops to keep two meters' interval. That plan had broken down immediately, as the Colonel knew it would. The stronger men bunched at the front of the line while the weaker half dozen straggled farther and farther behind. The Colonel had called a halt after the first hour—measured by the moon, not his watch—to regroup, and it was about time to call another.

The Colonel marched at the rear. The gorge itself provided the direction, so he was best located where he could keep stragglers from falling out of the column altogether. Krishnamurtri was immediately ahead of him.

"We'll halt in three minutes," the Colonel said. Krishnamurtri had lost his weapon in the crash. "Pass it on."

The Colonel's boot slipped; he dabbed a hand down and caught himself, but a thorn hidden in the gritty soil jabbed fire up his middle finger. The pain in his ribs had subsided to a background awareness, dull because of its familiarity.

A metallic whistle trilled behind them; how far behind the Colonel wasn't sure, but it couldn't be more than a kilometer even with the breeze carrying the sound. Not far enough.

"Cancel that order," the Colonel said, checking his

weapon again by reflex. "We'll keep going till we get there."

Another whistle—this one was pitched a half-tone higher than the other—called. It was from the righthand distance, either on the opposite ridge or from somewhere within the gorge itself.

The Telugu just ahead of Krishnamurtri had been using his ion gun as a crutch; he'd torn his right thigh badly during the crash, but he was managing to keep up with the column reasonably well. Now he turned, balancing on his left leg, and aimed his weapon across the valley.

"Stop—" the Colonel said, lunging forward. He fell over Krishnamurtri who was trying to dodge back.

The soldier triggered six wild shots into the night. The first two bolts hit the tops of trees on the other slope. Recoil lifted the muzzle with each shot so that the last four drew quivering tracks toward the stratosphere.

The Telugu shot with both eyes closed. He'd probably never been told to shoot any other way.

The Colonel knocked him silly with a sidewise swipe of his ion gun. The Telugu's own weapon flew out of his hand and bounced down the slope. Plant matter as dry as the air itself caught fire at the touch of the glowing muzzle.

The ionization tracks of the six bolts trembled in the air, dissipating slowly. Each was an arrow of light pointing back toward the shooter.

"Let's go!" the Colonel said as he broke into a shambling run. Their only chance was to stay ahead of the pursuit, and God knew that was no chance at all.

As usual, the Colonel was more agile in a crisis than he could ever be with greater leisure to choose his footing. Krishnamurtri was wailing somewhere behind him, but the common soldiers stayed ahead with the ease of youth. The Colonel could see a few of his troops bounding like klipspringers across a stretch of slope scoured by a rockslide.

Despite the need for haste, the Colonel went downslope to stay covered by the trees. Nobody shot at the exposed Telugus. Another whistle called, this one seemingly from over the ridge to their left.

They didn't have a prayer. Not a prayer.

The Colonel had the map in his mind. A second crack in the rock, a crevice only ten or twenty feet wide, joined the gorge a few hundred meters ahead. Just beyond that junction was the tumbled edge of the hills, then the scrubland where an evader could choose his own direction without being channeled by the terrain. If they could make it out of the hills alive—

If the Colonel could make it out of the hills alive. He'd lost control of his unit, and anyway it had come to "Save what you can!"

It always came to that. The Colonel remembered an overloaded helicopter struggling off the roof of the American Embassy in Saigon and many similar scenes. Scenes he'd survived.

But of course, there'd come the scene he didn't survive, as sure as the sun would rise.

The Colonel smiled. Even surer than that, maybe, in these days.

An automatic weapon fired from dead ahead. It wasn't an ion gun. The distant, spiteful, muzzle blasts syncopated the projectiles' bursting charge, *Whack/ crack/Whack/crack/Whack/crack*.

Ion guns replied, two or maybe three of them. Bolts traced across the sky, as ineptly aimed as those of the Telugu the Colonel had left unconscious after the second whistle blew.

The Enemy weapon fell silent after firing three rounds. The shellbursts had flickered blue-white

through the vegetation, more like a short circuit arc-
ing than any explosive the Colonel had seen before.

He understood the trap as surely as if he were
within the mind of the Enemy commander.

"Go straight ahead!" the Colonel shouted. The
Telugus couldn't hear him, couldn't understand the
words if they did hear, and wouldn't obey if they did
understand. "Shoot your way through! Don't turn!"

He reached the crevice. It led off to the left, trailing back into the hills before it ended in a spring and
a pair of sheer cliffs. Rock dust still swirled where the
Enemy gunner had scarred the main slope, driving the
Telugus like a sheep dog snapping at the ears of his
flock.

The gunner was somewhere out in the narrow wedge
of rolling scrub that the Colonel could see beyond the
mouth of the gorge. He might be as much as a kilometer distant. He wasn't there to stop the Telugus but
merely to turn them.

The Colonel switched his safety to position three.
He triggered the ion gun toward the empty landscape
ahead.

The weapon spun out of his hand with a roar. Firing a third full-charge blast down the bore had eaten
through the side of the barrel. Flame washed the right
side of the gorge as well as the intended target.

The Colonel flung the useless gun away. He drew
his bootknife and plunged into the blaze his plasma
had ignited. His left hand held the tail of his fatigue
shirt over his mouth and nose.

He heard the incoming artillery when he'd gotten
about a hundred meters into the hell of burning shrubs.
The ground was so hot it blistered him through his
boots and socks.

He ran on, navigating by instinct and his memory
of what the terrain ahead had looked like in the

moment before he fired. The night lit blue behind him and the earth shuddered. The Enemy had blown the crevice shut, killing everyone who had tried to shelter within its narrow walls. Rocks continued to fall for more than a minute after the explosion.

The Colonel ran and then walked and finally crawled. He was crawling when a pair of servitors pried the bootknife from his hand and loaded him onto an air sled like the one that had brought him into the hills.

One of the voiceless creatures held the Colonel while the other flew. The Colonel's arms and legs continued to move because instinct, all that remained, told them to.

The Suit debriefing the Colonel was the one who'd tasked him for the mission. He made another notation in the folder on his desk and said in a detached voice, "Well, these things happen. It doesn't appear that the blame lies with you."

He put down his pen and went on, "So. How would you rate your present physical condition, Colonel?"

All Suits were the same anyway. They stamped them out with cookie cutters in Ivy League colleges and sent them on to CIA and Hell.

The Colonel smiled.

"I'm fit," he said. Pus leaked through his mittens of bandage. The damage wasn't serious: he'd just scraped the thick skin of his palms down to the flesh while crawling. His knees were in similar shape, but the bandages there didn't show beneath the loose trousers of his jungle fatigues.

His hands hurt remarkably, an enveloping throb every time his heart beat. For the first twenty-four hours after regaining consciousness the Colonel had eaten Percodans like candy.

He hadn't taken any drugs in the past six hours, though. Pain was something you got used to.

The Suit sniffed. "Well, I'm not going to argue with you," he said. "We're getting rather shorthanded, as you can imagine."

He glanced down at the folder, then closed it decisively. He looked at the Colonel with an expression as hard and detached as that of a falcon in a winter sky. "Very well," the Suit said. "Return to your quarters. I can't say precisely when you'll be called for the next mission, but I'm afraid that your stand-down this time will be relatively brief. We're approaching endgame."

"Yes, all right," the Colonel said. He stood with the care a lifetime of injuries made second nature to him.

Endgame. It was funny to think about it all being over, after a lifetime. . . .

The Colonel put his bandaged fingers on top of the desk and leaned forward slightly. The Suit looked up with the false smile that Suits always got when they thought their attack dogs might be about to slip their leashes. The Colonel had seen that look often enough before.

The Colonel smiled back. "Tell me," he said. "Tell me the truth. Do we really defeat Good?"

The Suit looked puzzled. "Excuse me?" he said. "I don't understand your question."

The Colonel blinked. He straightened, taking his hands away from the desk. He didn't know what response he'd expected, but honest confusion on the Suit's part certainly wasn't it.

"You said the Bible was wrong," the Colonel said. "You said that the armies of Good don't defeat us."

He felt the air-conditioned room pulse red with a sudden rage that wasn't directed at this Suit or even every Suit: the Colonel hated the universe and he hated himself.

The door behind him opened. Servitors slipped in quickly, ready to wrestle the Colonel down and sedate him if necessary.

"Didn't you say that?" the Colonel shouted.

"The Bible doesn't say the armies of Good will defeat you," the Suit said, giving the pronoun a slight emphasis. His expression had returned to its usual faint sneer. "What a concept!"

The Colonel began to shiver. He supposed it was the air conditioning.

"Good doesn't have armies, Colonel," the Suit said, tenting his fingers over the closed folder. "Everyone who's fighting is on our side. You of all people should understand that."

The Colonel turned around. The servitors stood to either side of the doorway. There were four of them.

"I suggest you get as much sleep as you can," the Suit behind him said in a professional replica of concern. "There won't be much time, you know."

"Yes, all right," the Colonel said. He walked out of the room, ignoring the smirks of the servitors.

He had a lot of experience with not thinking about things.

# NATION WITHOUT WALLS

The blast echoed much farther and faster than the sound waves alone could have.

Level 17 was to State Standard Floorplan, a sixty-meter circle crammed with almost five hundred desks. The computer was guided by psychiatric profiles and performance analyses to the same instant decision a human director would have made by gut reaction: Lacey's mastoid implant rang him to alert.

This one was too big to be dropped.

"Ready," Lacey said by reflex, swinging away the counterweighted scanner helmet under which he had been hunched at his desk. He was a squat man and as grim as a wolf, dark except for a jagged scar from his right ear to his collarbone. His expression was that of a hunter who had seen much of the world and found little humor in it. Over his net jumpsuit he wore a jacket, opaque and slightly unfashionable; it pouted to hide the needle stunner holstered high on his right hip.

"Bomb explosion in the Follard Tower," said the

voice behind Lacey's jawbone. "A car and driver are
assigned to you. There are currently three dead." After
a pause that would have been meaningful in a human,
the computer added, "One of the dead has been identified as Loysius Follard."

Lacey was already moving in a quick shuffle that
took him around other U-shaped desks and their occupants, men and women sexless under their enveloping scanner helmets or staring blank-eyed beyond the
circular confines of the room. A few chatted low-voiced
with their neighbors. Few took notice of Lacey's haste:
to these investigators, "private" business was no more
interesting than naked skin to a Turkish bath attendant.

Over the door to the pad a light panel was flashing the number of the car assigned to Lacey. He
ignored the six-digit display, knowing that on a priority run the car would already be swinging toward the
doorway to pick him up.

It was, lift fans shrieking as it hopped a row of sta-
tionary vehicles to get to him. The driver was a blob
of orange in a crash suit, loose fabric that would inflate
at a 10-g impact, and a polarized face shield. The
passenger compartment behind him was an open box
with low bulkheads, a bench, and a scanner helmet for
the occupant. The vehicle's own single camera was on
a meter-high pole above the nose, a vantage that caught
both driver and passenger and was legally adequate so
long as they faced it except when grounded and thus
in the field of other scanners.

Lacey leaped aboard, slapping the driver on the
shoulder as he hit the seat. The car's quick acceleration urged the agent back as, helmet already settled
over him, he willed an upward twitch of his ring finger. The nerve had been cut and rerouted to trigger
his implant for his commands to the Crime Service data
net.

"Explosion site," Lacey directed. In his helmet screen smoke eddied in what had been a ten-meter cubicle before the explosion had blown out the two partitions separating it from the greater office of which it had been one corner. Two of the dead were victims of a wall fragment which had cartwheeled through the banks of desks in the main office. The third corpse lay across the cubicle's own gleaming console of polished mahogany. Incredibly, the dead man had been the only occupant of the smaller room despite the fact that it had the full complement of three scanning cameras and the heavy tax burden that went with them. Lacey realized why the computer had singled out the third man. "Loysius Follard," he told his implant, "Economic highlights."

Instead of an immediate answer, the link made a faint clicking noise like lock tumblers clearing and asked, "Access code, please."

"Access code" from the computer because Lacey had just requested information proscribed even to Crime Service personnel unless they had a particular need. The data were available in a special bank, probably that of the Security Police, to which outside access was rigidly controlled. And the computer had added "Please" because it is easier to program in politeness than it is to defend its absence to people of the stature that sometimes queried the Sepo net.

Blocks like that were unusual, though Lacey had suspected power when he saw Follard's office. Flipping the helmet away from his eyes, Lacey punched his code, B-D-Q, M-E-Z, O-P, on the plate built into the driver's seat back. It was the one portion of the car deliberately hidden from the scanner, just as desk code plates were shrouded from room cameras—one secret in a State dedicated to eradication of all others.

Another faint clicking. Then, "Loysius Follard, controls Kongo Holding Corporation, controls—"

"Cancel," Lacey said. Kongo Holding was, for all practical purposes, the nation of Argentina. He had hoped knowledge of the primary victim's business would be a line on the assassin. Business at Follard's eminence opened, literally, the whole of Earth's seventeen billion people as potential enemies.

It also explained why economic data were on the Sepo list. The omnipresent scanners recorded every act and cut through the sham of straw men and proxy voting. Even a man of Follard's power could not avoid them, but he could arrange that availability of the data be sharply restricted. There would always be friends, contacts, favors. The Thirty-first Amendment and the Open Truth Act implementing it had not been what many saw them to be, an abandonment of the fight for individual privacy against the flood of technological intrusion. Rather, they were an attempt to utilize and control the information-gathering which eighty years of unsuccessful prohibition had proved to be an ineradicable part of American life. When everything became open to a few, much could be forbidden to the generality.

Lacey dropped the helmet over his eyes again. His blocky face was tightening with concentration and the scar had tensed to a line of white fire. On the internal screen appeared the private office at the moment of explosion, images recorded by the scanning cameras and recalled for Lacey from the huge electronic vaults beneath Atlanta. Follard was sprawled across the smooth intarsia of his desk top. His eyes were open and the lighter skin of his right palm was visible through his half-clenched fingers. The bubble of flame which wrecked the room burst from a ventilator duct just as the louvers began to quiver to signal that the fan had switched on.

Lacey requested the scanner on the outer wall, three minutes before the explosion. Follard was slumped even then, a message capsule visible beneath his shoulder from the new angle.

"Give me the third scanner," Lacey said, "explosion minus four." The camera behind Follard's desk should have displayed the capsule's contents when it was opened; instead there was nothing. The camera was out of order, had been out of order minutes before the blast might have damaged it. No object is eternal, but scanning cameras were Man's nearest present approach to that ideal. Lacey switched to the first scanner and a sight of Follard speaking a quick affirmative into a wall microphone—sound simulacra could be developed by the net, but no investigator of Lacey's experience needed them when the subjects' lips were visible. The desktop burped the thin 10-cm-square container, examined in the bowels of the Tower for concealed dangers after a courier service had delivered it. Follard touched the tab of the stiff foil capsule with his signet. The radioactive key within the ring caused the tab to roll back without incinerating the contents as any other means of opening would have done. Then Follard collapsed across his desk.

Lacey's face spread in a grin that bared his prominent eyeteeth. "Technical request," he directed his implant. "I want a desk print-out on lethal gases, instantly fatal and explosive in low concentration."

"Define 'low concentration'," croaked the computer link.

"Bloody hell!" Lacey spat, then considered. "However much an unreinforced 50-cc message capsule could hold, distributed in a . . . twenty-five-cubic-meter office."

The driver's hand touched Lacey's forearm, "Sir, we've got the site—but there's a Sepo on the pad and—"

Lacey cocked up the scanner helmet, glaring past the half-turned driver to the roof pad of the Follard Tower. The massive block of concrete and vitril was of standard design, a landing pad on the roof for the top executives—those with air cars—and fifteen floors beneath linked by open stairs. Rank among chiefs would go with altitude, an inversion of that among the lower orders who entered at ground level and climbed stairs to their desks. Follard's top-floor window gaped emptily instead of reflecting from a polarized surface. Seven private cars with closed cabins and luxurious appointments were ranked about the open stairhead. There, one hand on the stair rail and the other holding a modulated-laser communicator, stood a drab, weedy man who had pulled the blue skullcap of the Security Police from his pocket to assert his authority.

Three news-company cars were in sight but keeping a respectful five-hundred-meter distance from the Sepo. Lacey snorted, knowing that if only Crime Service had been present the reporters would have been swarming over the site. He had once knocked a pair of them down with his stunner when they ignored his demand to keep clear. The microscopic needles and their nerve-scrambling charges had done no permanent harm to the newsmen, but Lacey had been threatened with the Psycomp if he ever did it again. It was surprising that the Sepos were already at the scene. It was almost as if—

The security man raised his communicator and aimed it at the pickup cone on the nose of Lacey's car. The microphone shroud covered the Sepo's lips and the beam itself had too little scatter to be intercepted. The message rumbled out of the car's loudspeaker perfectly audibly: "Shear off, you! This area is under Security control."

The vehicle hesitated in the air, ten meters from the

Sepo and slightly above him. The driver was balancing his fans as best he could, but the frail craft still wobbled as Lacey leaned forward with no attempt at secrecy and shouted, "Keep your pants on, friend, I'm from Crime Service and a murder site damned well isn't closed to me."

The Sepo lowered the communicator from his convulsing face and snarled, "I said shear off, bead brain! Don't you know what 'Security' means?"

"Set me down," said Lacey tightly to his driver. His face was gray and dreadful. Without hesitation the driver canted forward his twin joy sticks. The Sepo's communicator fell as his right hand slashed down to his belt holster. Lacey's driver tramped the foot feed, sending the car howling straight at the blue skullcap. The Sepo shouted and ducked as the screaming lift fans plucked away a bit of his jacket which billowed into their arc. The car hit the pad. It bounced from excess velocity but Lacey had timed the impact to leap clear at the instant steel scraped concrete. The Sepo was on his knees, scrabbling for the weapon he had dropped. Lacey took a half step forward and kicked. The gun was a silvery glitter that spun far over the roof edge and away.

"Oh dear Lord," the security man blurted, sitting back and in his nervousness wiping his face with his skullcap. "If some civilian g-gets that—don't you know what it was? That was a powergun!"

"No it wasn't, friend," said Lacey, satisfaction beginning to melt his face back into human lines. "Powerguns are approved for military use in war zones; not for police, not even for Sepos. And I sort of doubt that anybody's going to use your toy after it fell thirty meters, anyway." Then, with the same precision as before, Lacey's toe caught the Sepo in the temple.

The stairs were open-work which scarcely interfered

with the cameras in the big room below. The three hundred workers, mostly clerks and minor supervisors, were crowded into the western half of it while two technicians and the Tower's medical unit worked hastily on the score of living casualties. The line of demarcation was not chance but another blue-capped Sepo whose nervousness evaporated when he saw Lacey and mistook him for a superior in the same organization. "I'm Agent Siemans, sir," he announced with a flat-handed salute. "Kadel and I took over right away and kept everybody off the—him."

Sieman's gestures indicated the desk and body visible through the torn partition. Lacey nodded crisply, quite certain that "everybody" in the Sepo's mind had included Crime Service investigators too. Sieman's cross-draw holster was visible through his unclipped jacket. It held a fat-barrelled powergun.

Lacey quickly covered the private office with his hand scanner. The blast had seared everything in it so that the synthetic fibers of Follard's suit had shrunk over his limbs and left the uncovered skin of his face and hands crinkled. The routing slip on the message capsule was clear, however, protected by the body which had fallen across it. Lacey flicked it upright to record the sender-recipient information. The name of the former—Lyall Mitchelsen, within Richmond Sub-region—meant nothing to Lacey. Presumably it had meant a great deal to Follard or the magnate would not have opened the message out of sight of even his personal staff.

Out of sight of the scanning cameras, too—but that had to be a chance malfunction.

Heavy shoes clattered behind Lacey. As he turned, a savage voice cried, "Freeze!" His scar again beginning to flame but a quizzical smirk on his face, the investigator rotated only his head toward the newcomers. Two of them were big men capped with Sepo blue and crouching over automatic powerguns. The third, stepping daintily across a flattened wall-panel, was slim and glittered in a suit like cloth of gold. His hair was white or blond, a determination which the smooth pallor of his skin did nothing to aid. Skin like that meant wealth as often as it did youth, and the slim man radiated wealth.

There was another aura as well: he was unarmed, but he was deadly in a way neither of the gunmen flanking him could equal.

"Good morning, Field Agent Lacey," he said with a smile. His delicate fingers—the nails perfectly matched the sheen and color of his wrist-to-ankle suit—raised the needle gun far enough from Lacey's holster to be sure it was no more than it seemed, then slid it back disdainfully. "I am Sig Hanse, Agent Lacey. I am of the Security Police."

Hanse's tone, his smile, both implied a great deal more than the words alone said.

"You're in the presence of a major Security offense" Lacey said. At Hanse's quick blink he added, "Lethal weapons in non-military hands."

The Sepo's fingers trembled. "Get out of here, Lacey," he said softly. "You've been recalled. This isn't a wife-stabbing, a drunk with a chair-leg bludgeon. It's a Security matter; and if you aren't too stupid to grasp this concept, try to realize that you aren't cleared at a high enough level to be told exactly why. I might add that there is now a Security block over all the records of this crime. No data will be released without my code—just to remind you of your duty to the State."

"I can be expected to do my duty under the Constitution and the Code, Citizen Hanse," Lacey said. He took an easy, unconcerned step between the two gunmen and then glanced back at their leader. "And you? The powerguns?"

"A needle can bounce from a stud, can fail to discharge when it hits—can just not stun a man instantly unless it gets a ganglion," Hanse snapped. "Our targets are too dangerous—to the State!—to allow that."

"Good hunting," Lacey murmured as he walked out of the room. His shoes whispering on the stair treads were the only other sound his exit made. His eyes were as empty as those of the Sepo now lying among the blast casualties as the technicians and their computer worked to repair the skull fractured by Lacey's foot.

Two new vehicles squatted on the roof: an open car like Lacey's with a blue-capped Sepo on the driver's saddle, and an older but luxurious closed car of a quality equal to that of the private ones already parked there. Lacey jerked a thumb at the Sepo. "Hanse says take your car down and block the front entrance, friend."

The Sepo blinked. "Hey, but how about the roof?" he demanded.

Lacey climbed into his own car. "Well, what about it?" he mimicked. "He's your bleeding boss—you go grill him about it."

The Sepo grunted as though punched in the stomach. He booted his fans to life and sailed over the parapet as soon as their double whine had begun to lift the car. "Hold it," Lacey said to his own driver. He jumped back out and crossed to the superb car beside it. Hanse's vehicle seated three, but he had taken his bodyguards down with him to confront Lacey. There were no loose objects within the cabin. Its design was unusual for a police vehicle in that the scanner helmet was pivoted for use only by the front seat passenger, not for the one on the soft leather bench on which Hanse himself surely rode. That was ostentation of a sort which Lacey, who viewed the helmet as a tool and not a symbol of punishing drudgery, honestly could not understand.

There was a code panel, too, built flush with the seat back. Lacey's hand scanner recorded the banks of letters from several angles. Then he swung quickly back aboard his own assigned craft.

"What're your orders, anyway?" he asked his driver's back.

"Just to remain at your disposal, sir. This was a first-priority call."

"Bleeding right it is," Lacey said. He tried to blank the rage from his voice before he added, "Look, find an empty pad somewhere—an office building too run down to get air traffic, something like that. Set down there and let me think."

As the car rose smoothly, Lacey said to his implant, "Run me life stats on Lyall Mitchelsen, Richmond Subregion."

There was a pause, followed by a crunch of static and a metallic voice stating, "The information you have requested is under Security block. Please punch your access code."

"Cancel," Lacey said so sharply that the syllables clicked. He paused a moment, then said, "Technical request."

"Ready," replied the implant.

"I ran a code board on my hand scanner two minutes ago. Retrieve that and analyze the buttons for wear patterns by group." Using the alphabet rather than Arabic numerals gave more than $2 \times 10^{11}$ possibilities in an 8-digit figure, hopelessly beyond the realm of chance discovery; however, the buttons would wear with use. If the board was used only by one man, that left 64 combinations to eliminate. Assuming, of course, that the Technical Section had not been programmed to alert Security when a request like Lacey's was received. It was the first time Lacey had tried to break a Security code, but he had gotten where he was by his total unwillingness to stop when he had started something. He wasn't going to back off now.

"Degree of wear is as follows. First group, S. Second group, A-E-G-H-I-N. Third group, remaining buttons, with no significant wear."

"Now—" Lacey began. He planned to set up a dummy query through the CS net to insulate his identity from Security when he began running his potentially 63 incorrect access codes. The pattern of the seven letters—S doubled—struck him suddenly. Barking a laugh of vicious triumph, he keyed his implant and repeated, "Run me life stats on Lyall Mitchelsen, Richmond Subregion."

*Crunch.* "The information you have requested is under Security block. Please punch your access code."

Lacey's index finger picked out S-I-G-H-A-N-S-E. It would not have been ease of recall that possessed the Sepo to pick that code—no one with trouble remembering eight letters would have risen to Hanse's level. But it could well have been the silent joke of arrogance between Hanse and the computer; proving that he, alone among the .8 billion people of Southern Region, the State-ruling Sun Belt, had not lost his identity.

"Lyall Mitchelsen, 56, industrialist, murdered 4-28-02 in Greater—"

Yesterday. "Method of murder?"

"Air car crash. Controls locked at 500 meters when a rogue circuit was triggered by a tight-beam radio signal."

"Bleeding martyrs! How did a circuit like that get into Mitchelsen's car?"

"The circuit was designed into all 01 and 02 Phaeton

Specials. Investigation has as yet failed to identify the member of the design team actually responsible. There is an increasing possibility that it was somehow imported from beyond the team."

The computer had halted, but it added as a seeming afterthought, "The murder technique was discovered through analysis of seven identical accidents yesterday within a 21-minute period. The other victims were . . ."

With the scanner helmet down, using it and his implant simultaneously, Lacey continued to run his data oblivious to his external surroundings. The Security computer had already linked eighteen assassinations in the Southern Region during the past day and a half, Follard's being the most recent of them. Aside from their style of death, the only known factor unifying all eighteen was their enormous private power. None had been in government directly—bureaucrats and elected officials both could be scanned at public booths by any citizen at any time—but the wealth of these men and women had given them influence beyond that of all but a handful of those in open authority. Their lives were open to licensed reporters, but reporters—or their superiors—were amenable to pressure unless an incident was too striking to ignore.

And of course, even the most powerful of men could be scanned from all angles by investigators like Lacey, except when a camera went out.

"Give me office scanner repair records for all victims," Lacey demanded with a non-flick of his ring finger.

"The information you have requested is under Security block. Please punch your access code."

Lacey paused, shocked for the first time in the investigation. That the Security terminal had again come on the line meant that the data was covered by a block not associated with the assassinations—which would have seemed absurd, had he not already begun to realize that Security—at least for the Southern Region—had been involved in something very strange which the deaths had begun to make public. Lacey lifted his helmet in order to punch the unfamiliar letters of Hanse's name. He caught the eyes of his driver on him.

"Bleeding idiots!" Lacey screamed, "They know I can't work with women!" He fell back against his seat, his body trembling and his complexion a sudden yellow-green. She had touched him, hadn't she? Though her sexlessness beneath crash suit and mirrored visor had kept the act from immediate impact, memory now sifted nausea through Lacey's body. He leaned over the side of the halted car. After a minute he got his blurring vision focused on the asphalt of the landing pad without having had to vomit first.

"Will you please put your visor down?" Lacey asked in a small voice. A thump indicated that he had been obeyed. It had been an attractive face in many ways, high cheekbones and blue eyes framed by jet hair. His mind still superimposed it on the hard plastic of the helmet.

"Why?" the driver asked. Her throaty voice was slightly camouflaged by the shield, but Lacey could no longer understand how he had imagined it to be masculine.

He turned to the now-blank visor. "I want you out of the car, please. I'll have them send another with a male driver and you can switch with him."

"No, I'm your driver and the people who determined that won't be overruled," she said calmly. "But why does it matter?"

"Why?" whispered Lacey, his face as hard as a headsman's axe. "Because my brain got wet-scrubbed, friend. Because I was frozen in a nutrient bath for three months while a Psycomp made sure that I never raped another woman. Never willingly touched another woman, as a matter of fact, though that may have been a little farther than the computer meant to go." He had the trembling of his hands under control and the bright sun was baking the sweat off his face now.

The driver considered him silently. After a moment she said, "I'm the best in your section, you know. I can do things with a car that none of the others can. Or would try to."

"You dropped us on that Sepo like you were reading my mind," Lacey agreed. "But I still don't want to share a car with you."

"Look, you don't have to touch me, you know." There was an odd tension in her voice, a need that went beyond anything the situation seemed to call for. "Can you work with a driver who drives and who takes orders like nobody else you'll find?"

He looked away, up at a sky that had become blue and pleasant again. Belatedly he punched Hanse's access code. "Do you have a name," he asked, "or do I just call you Fireball?"

"You can call me anything you please," the girl said quietly, "but my name is Tamara Damien."

The data began to fire out of Lacey's implant and he let it carry him out of his personal situation. Of the fifty-four cameras in the victims' offices, only one had ever malfunctioned up to five years before. After that, one after another, brief failures began to show up in the maintenance records. Two to five minutes at a time, ten or a dozen times a year. Long enough to read and memorize a note, enough even to scribble one off. Three victims had no scanner failures at all until Lacey followed up with records of their vehicle units.

"Okay, what other scanners have similar malfunction

records?" Lacey asked, his voice still a flat purr with only a trace of hoarseness.

"Vehicle unit, Southern Regional Pool Car 138814; vehicle unit, Southern Regional Pool Car 759541; vehicle unit, Southern Regional Pool Car, 294773. No other units."

Lacey touched his tongue to his lips. "Who were the cars checked to at times of malfunction?" he asked.

"Alvin Hormadz, Director for Security, Atlanta Subregion; Willa Perhabis, Director for Security, Richmond Subregion; Sig Hanse, Security Coordinator, Southern Region."

Which by that time was no surprise.

"Uh-hmm," Lacey sighed, showing his teeth like a satisfied tomcat. He blinked, seeing Tamara for the first time since the data had begun coming in. She was as tense as he had been when he faced the guns of Hanse's bodyguards. "Oh, hell," he said. "Take your helmet off. We're going to be here a while."

She unsnapped the chin strap and slid the gear away from hair that sweat had stuck to her cheeks. It fluffed in the breeze as she freed it. Lacey's stomach roiled but he grinned wider. If he had not been able to laugh at the irony of the situation, he would have committed suicide within days of his psychic remake.

"Can I ask you a personal question?" Tamara said, her eyes on the helmet as she placed it on the seat beside her.

"Sure," Lacey agreed unconcernedly.

"Why did you commit rape? You aren't . . . you aren't cool, but you seem to act as though you were. How did you come to lose control like that?"

"Oh, my," said Lacey, kneading the back of his neck with his eyes closed. "The people *I* pick up talk about losing control, as if that could make me feel sorry for them. I raped the bitch because it was the only way

I could punish her as much as I thought she deserved. For this—" he touched his scar—"for a lot of things. I had to find an empty, unfinished dwelling unit with doors I could wedge against the Red Team that was going to come as soon as the scanners picked up what I was doing. You aren't going to successfully rape anybody nowadays if you just lose control, my friend."

Tamara's face was blank. "And you kept your job as an investigator?"

"No, that's not quite what happened," Lacey explained. His grin interrupted him by turning into an open chuckle. "I sold insurance before they got into my mind. The Psycomp seems to have decided that single-mindedness and an ability to plan could be useful to the State—in the right channels, that is."

He nodded at the scanner helmet. "Trouble is, it's not something I can turn off because somebody decided to change the rules. I think I've already gotten deeper in this channel than some folks are going to like, both Hanse and his bunch and the folks who are knocking them off."

"I don't see why the Sepos haven't already arrested you this morning," the girl said. She was facing Lacey, the scanner staring over the top of her head like a one-eyed crow. The sky beyond was empty: Tamara had set them on an older building, designed for elevators and individual offices. When power for the elevators became prohibitive, the upper floors were left untenanted. The view from the room was clear and had because of its stability an emotional impact unequaled by that of an air car at the same height.

"Would you rather I didn't ask—?" the girl said awkwardly.

Lacey blinked. "Sorry, I was drifting," he said with a nicer smile than before. He scratched his ribs where his jumpsuit clung to them. "No, I can explain it. Hanse wasn't going to arrest me for disarming his thug, he had too much to explain on that one himself. What he was doing here in person, for instance. Given the timing and the fact his office is in Atlanta, I'd bet that he was on his way to warn Follard that somebody had gotten onto whatever game they were playing. . . ." The smile broadened, then faded. "There was a chance that he might have had me shot, of course. That would have been a little easier to clear."

"But you searched his car, you broke his access code," Tamara blurted. She was using both hands to gesture toward Lacey, too agitated to notice that he slid back away from them. "I saw you, the car scanner saw you, the three roof scanners saw you. Why are you still loose?"

"Maybe when Hanse gets around to checking me, I won't be," Lacey said, motioning the girl to calmness. "But the things you're talking about don't flag the computer automatically, friend Tamara. Certain patterns will be kicked up to a human observer by the circuit that watch-dogs all scanner inputs—a room exploding, a CS investigator kicking an armed Sepo in the head— that sort of thing. But Loysius Follard falling asleep at his desk didn't set any lights flashing, and neither did a fellow opening the door of a car, then closing it and walking away. The data's there in the vaults under Atlanta; but until somebody retrieves it, I'll still be walking free.

"Riding free," he corrected with another smile. "And I think I'm ready, now, to ride back to the State Building. There's some data there for me, and I've had my dose of open space for the day."

He had lied about his purpose. He walked into Level 17 from the landing pad but glanced at the print-out without great interest. The lethal agent had almost certainly been PDT, a volatile liquid explosive/toxin supposedly in military hands only. Anything that exists can be had by a man who knows what to offer the right people.

"Support request," Lacey said to his implant.

"Ready."

"I want a check on PDT stockpiles. Track down any losses and report the results to me."

"Accepted at third priority."

Lacey unlocked the lowest drawer of his desk and took a cylindrical package from it. His face was set but looked ready to explode like a Prince Rupert drop if touched by anyone's glance.

17 was the roof level—government offices were built a little higher, on the average, than new private ones (complaints about "the hogs at the public trough" continued to be useful campaign rhetoric) and Crime Service had to be alongside the pad. Lacey walked the sixteen flights to the ground through offices of identical size and equal crowding. The stairs were a broad helix, thin-railed and with treads which were almost freestanding. They were supposed to deaden sound, but the material creaked. In late afternoon, Lacey was alone on the staircase and drew occasional eyes. None of them remained on him long.

He had over a kilometer to go but he did not take a bus. It was easier to feel that he was anonymous, stepping into a doorway from a sidewalk—there one moment, then gone—than it would have been when getting off a bus at an address that other passengers might recognize.

Ground floor of the old building which was his destination held a food bazaar that smelled frowsty and sweet. It was unpartitioned with its internal load-bearing pillars replaced by transparent myrmillon, but a greasy coating had opaqued them and no one seemed to care.

The second through eighth levels were housing of poor and successively-degenerated quality. The ground plan was marked off into eighty dwelling units by waist-height vitril panels on the lower floors, rusted hog-fencing on the upper ones. The center of the big room was a bank of coin-operated hot plates. Other furniture depended on the whim and wealth of the units' occupiers: chairs and frequently a table, beds on floor-spread mattresses, and occasionally an electric light to supplement the dozen glow-strips in the ceiling. These would go on at sunset and out promptly three hours later, rain or shine. The only sight barriers in the room were the sheets fronting the latrines at either end, so placed that the stools were shielded from viewers in the belly of the room but were swept by one of the three scanners. Need for the law to make that concession to privacy was thrown in doubt by the unrepaired damage to several of the screens, ignored both by users of the latrines and the others in the room. Lacey climbed through the wretched dwelling levels without expression and, just possibly, without notice.

The ninth floor was empty save for a browned, youngish man on a stool at the base of the winding stairs. "Hey, back already?" he cackled, his grin combining cameraderie and condescension. A woman and three men, one of them well-dressed and very drunk, clattered down the stairs together.

Lacey moved aside. He held out three large bills to the doorman. "Which stall?" he asked.

"One a these days you'll want the Honeymoon Suite and I'll fall right off this chair," the seated man chuckled.

"Which stall?"

The doorman blinked up at dark eyes and a neck bright with scarred lightning. His hand twitched toward the length of pipe behind him, but wisely he controlled the motion and took the proffered money instead. "Sixty-one's empty," he said, looking away. "I'll mark you down for it."

Lacey turned without nodding and began to climb the last flight of steps. Under his breath the doorman muttered, "Bet I don't see *you* many more times, buddy. Ones like you they don't let walk around very long."

The tenth floor was sweaty, stinking bedlam, far darker than the lower levels because the canvas cubicles spaced around the walls blocked most of the windows. Studding the ceiling at two-meter intervals were 150 separately-controlled scanner units. They stood like the sprinkler heads of an earlier day in which fire had been thought a greater danger to society than privacy. Beneath them, divided by narrow aisles, were arrayed the cribs that bumped and swayed to the activities of their occupants which the cameras impassively recorded. The accommodation house catered to those who did not want their neighbors in their own dwelling units to learn what they were doing, or who they were doing it with.

In Lacey's case, *what* he was doing it with.

"What stall?" boomed the floor boss, a huge albino with Negroid features who stood in front of a control panel.

"Sixty-one."

"Right, sixty-one," the albino echoed, checking the panel. "Two hours of scanner time. You want company?" His doughy fingers indicated the north wall, the Mourners' Bench, along which waited apathetically a score of haggard prostitutes of both sexes.

"No."

"S'okay, sixty-one," the bigger man repeated. "We rent you four walls and a private scanner. What you do with them's between you and the data bank."

Lacey strode down the jostling aisle to the crib marked 61 in red numerals on the tile floor. He stepped inside and drew the curtain shut. The scanner above him beeped and an orange telltale came on, indicating the unit was in operation. The cubicle was dim enough that the supplementary infra-red system was probably on. Without haste, Lacey stripped off his coveralls and folded them, laying his pistol on top of the garment. He opened the package he had brought and removed the artificial vagina from its foam nest. He switched it on, sat down on the cot, and affixed it to himself.

Lacey's eyes were as empty as the lens of the scanner they stared up toward as his body shuddered. Beneath the emptiness was a rage that bubbled like lava-filled calderas.

He walked back to the State Building, this time from a desire for walking rather than from shame. The shame had drained out of him along with some of the other emotions he was trying to void. Lacey's mind was working again, using the rhythm of his feet to shuffle patterns in the information he had collected. The dusky street was quiet enough and as clean as is only possible in a society in which all litter has value to someone. At alternate blocks stood uniformed police with gas guns and banana-clipped stunners, ready for their computer links to direct them to trouble. For the most part they appeared as bored and logy as the vagrants with whom they shared the evening. There was infrared for the omnipresent scanners, but no power was wasted for men to see by. The night is an irksome companion.

The squad at the gate of the building passed Lacey without hesitation. Several of the red-hatted men recognized him, while the rest ignored him because their implants told them it was safe to do so. On several floors only the stairway was lighted by glow strips, since government offices tended to close at nightfall like everything else. Level 16, where uniformed monitors wore helmets to direct squads to trouble spots, was a bright exception; and Level 17 was about a quarter occupied also. An investigator could run his subject at any time—the data bank would wait—but many of the hunters were like Lacey. They stuck to the unusual criminal who had eluded the first rush of a Red Team; stuck with him until they had drunk his blood.

Lacey sat at his desk and pulled down the scanner helmet to begin checking back the message capsule. In all likelihood the assassin had not believed that would be possible. In general his assumption would have been correct; but this case had been handed to Lacey. The capsule had popped onto Follard's desk from the Tower's security system, hidden from the scanners as it ran past a battery of useless fluoroscopes and radiation testers. For his own reasons, Follard had not allowed a subordinate to open the capsule; he had paid for secrecy with his life. Lacey picked up the capsule where it had entered the system, delivered ten minutes before then with a mass of others like it in the hold of an air car. Lacey switched to a roof camera showing two bored guards with batons and the green uniforms of a private message service standing around while the white-haired driver dumped armloads of capsules into the chute. Lacey magnified by ten, then by a hundred, as he focused the image on the tumbling rectangles.

And then the computer took over. With time and even greater magnification, Lacey might himself have been able to catch the routing slip on the metal and identify the death capsule. The precise machinery of the police net scanned the object for tiny imperfections and for details of the routing slip so slight that even the corner of a letter in a camera field would be an identification. Lacking that, the capsule's albedo alone could identify it where the light intensity was known. Technology made practical a job that was otherwise only a theoretical possibility. It was like giving a bloodhound an escapee's sock to sniff.

The capsule had been in the morning's delivery. Had it not been, Lacey would have traced through the Tower looking for the point at which an insider had slipped it into the normal flow. He gave quick directions to his implant and the delivery car jerked backward across the city in a series of ten-second jumps in the helmet. They stopped when it had run back to its loading point, the internal dock of a regional distribution center.

All but three floors of the huge granite building were lifeless, filled with sorting machinery and endless belts studded with hundreds of thousands of capsules of identical shape and size. Odd-sized packages were handled by humans on the two lowest floors, and the charge for such service was enough to guarantee its use only in cases of necessity. The third level received packages by dumbwaiter and capsules by chute, integrating them into the bins from which the delivery cars were loaded.

The computer needed further guidance at that point, for the chutes themselves were inaccessible to men and thus unscanned. The conveyors on each floor, however, with their complex system of shunts, feeds, and crossfeeds that sorted each capsule toward its proper drop chute, were as open to cameras as any other room. Lacey moved floor by floor, focusing each time on the aperture which dropped capsules into the Follard Tower bin. His voice had grown husky with giving directions and his fingers stiff from flexing on his chair arms, but if anyone could have seen his face behind the helmet they would have cringed back from a smile more fitted to a tiger than a man. Even a man like Lacey.

Mail to the Follard Tower was delivered at twelve-hour intervals. Lacey ran each floor back to the time the previous load had gone out, then switched up one level. The speeded up, reversed flow of images would have driven mad anyone less used to it than he was; and perhaps—a possibility that Lacey had never denied to himself—he withstood it only because he was already mad.

On the eighth floor he picked up the capsule again, part of a shipment brought from Richmond Subregion by high-altitude airliner. It was not too long afterward that Lacey's helmet focused on a Petersburg street and a man, slim and fiftyish with tight-rolled hair and a skin so black it looked purple, who dropped the capsule into a collection box and then thumbed in coins until the postage light glowed green.

"Name and data," Lacey croaked to his implant.

"William Anton Merritt, age 54, on dole for past thirty-seven months. Eight years Chief of Operations, Security, for Southern Region. Previously—"

Lacey cut off the flow and returned to his man. It was without surprise that he back-tracked Merritt to a counter in the General Delivery room of the Petersburg mail depot where he had peeled off a routing slip addressed to him and replaced it with the one that would carry the toxin to Follard. There was no reason, after all, that the murder device should have been prepared in the subregion from which it had to be mailed in order to pass as coming from the conspirator Mitchelsen. Back a step further, then; Merritt punching his I. D. on a code board and waiting the few seconds for the capsule to drop into the delivery slot. From there back through a mirror image of the previous routings—no less arduous, but no less possible to follow—for they led straight back to Greensboro Subregion in which sat Lacey hunched under his helmet and the body of Loysius Follard lay on a teak slab with a thousand torchlit mourners howling around it like the damned.

This time, Lacey did not need the data bank to identify the girl who jumped from an air car to mail the capsule to Merritt in Petersburg.

For the moment he did not trace the capsule to the point at which it was filled with explosive and sealed, or back even earlier when the PDT had been removed from some government stockpile. That information was safe in the data bank until he chose to retrieve it, and the people concerned—the scores or perhaps hundreds it had taken to bring off so many simultaneous assassinations—would be just as easy to find a few hours or days later. Only death had ever saved a target from Lacey. Instead of searching for other names now, he twitched the finger no wedding ring would ever grace and said, "Give me a current location on William Anton Merritt."

Information that far-reaching required a delay for computer time to check literally hundreds of thousands of scanner images in a pattern of concentric probabilities; but for Lacey it was only seconds before the data squeaked back into his mastoid. He grunted as he considered it. "Estimated time of arrival?" he asked.

"Forty-three minutes."

How does an ex-bureaucrat, supposedly on State Subsistance Allowance, come to be piloting a private stratosphere craft from Toronto to Greensboro? Friends, doubtless, like everything else Merritt had arranged. Lacey gave a few specific instructions, then asked, "My driver from yesterday—Tamara Damien. Is she on duty?"

"She will report at 0700. Do you wish another driver assigned or should she be given an emergency summons?"

"Hmm. What time is it?" The windows were, Lacey noticed as he swung up the scanner helmet, beginning to pale.

"0637."

"Fine, I'll be in the target range. Tell me when she gets in."

The range was a quadrant of Level 15, separated by opaque partitions despite the added scanner cost. Experience had proven that peripheral images of men raising guns destroyed the efficiency of the clerical unit sharing the floor, even though a myrmillon divider would have been more than adequate to stop the tiny needles.

There were already a dozen shooters using the 20-meter range, standing with their backs to the outside windows and firing inward toward the point of the wedge where the target screen stood. Jacket open, Lacey took a vacant station. His stance comfortable and his fingers curved loosely on his thighs, he announced, "Ready."

A target image visible only from his station flashed, a tawny woman raising what might have been either a length of pipe or a shotgun. Lacey's weapon was in his right hand, then locked with his left as he crouched and fired three shots so sudden they appeared to have been fully automatic.

The target disappeared and a silhouette of it formed on the spotting screen just above Lacey's head, red dots at right wrist, right elbow, and right shoulder identifying his shots. His implant said, "Time, point three six seconds. That is exceptionally good. However, your accuracy continues marginal with no hits in the central body mass"—the silhouette's torso pulsed red for emphasis. "In a true firefight, you may not be lucky enough to get limb hits if you are so far outside your aiming point. Speed is less critical than accuracy."

Computers have no sense of humor, so Lacey avoided even the edge of a smile when he heard it refer to what it imagined had been his aiming point. He had raped, openly and with deliberation, and had forever lost his capacity for a similar act. He would not make the same boastful error if he ever found it necessary to kill: *that* must look to be an accident.

He was a violent man in a world of arrogance—of Sig Hanse and his Sepos, of the sneering Red Team which had taken him into custody years before, of the myriad counterclerks and bureaucrats taking their frustrations out on the nearest target. Lacey avoided an actual explosion only because he knew his hand had the power of life and death over every one of them individually. If the Psycomp had noticed that murderous streak, it had weighed it against Lacey's depth of control and usefulness—then passed him as acceptable to the State.

Targets continued to flash. He sprayed the edges of five more—on one he hit a swinging medallion three times and got zero credit since, of course, a real medallion would have deflected the needles which grounded themselves only after penetration. Finally his implant announced, "Chauffeur 5 Damien has reported to her car."

"Patch me through to her," Lacey said, slapping a fresh magazine into his gun before he holstered it. He turned to the nearest window. For cleaning purposes the whole two-meter vitril panel pivoted inward.

"Ready."

"Morning, Tamara. I'm in the target range, Level 15. Drop down and pick me up, will you?"

The girl's voice was deepened by the car microphone and Lacey's implant. "No landing stage on fifteen, sir."

"Sure, but the windows open."

"On the way."

Lacey swung the vitril off its catch. The gush of air as the car dropped past it, then rose and steadied, brought a startled protest from the shooter beside Lacey. He ignored the other man, set his left foot on the sill and stepped into the back of the car. The slightest queasiness in the vehicle would have catapulted Lacey thirty meters to the pavement. Tamara kept it rock solid until he was seated, then moved off a few meters to where she did not have to fight the eddies around the building.

"You didn't do that to save yourself a walk," she chided. "Trying to prove something to me?"

"That's right," he agreed. "That I can safely trust you with my life." He leaned forward, grinned up at the scanner, and said, "We're going to the airport, friend Tamara, to arrest a man named William Anton Merritt for multiple counts of murder. He wasn't in it alone, Lord knows, but it'll be simpler for a Psycomp to dig out his accomplices than it would be for me and a scanner."

She moved the car off smoothly without apparent emotion, gaining speed and altitude as she headed west. There were no lane markers in the sky, but cars were few and almost all drivers professionals. On balance it was safer than street traffic had been fifty years before.

"You are good, aren't you?" Tamara said at last in a jerky voice. Lacey made no reply. "Don't you even wonder why a, a *citizen* like Bill Merritt would start a p-plot like this?"

"Wonder?" Lacey repeated. "Not really. He was, is, a very damned able man himself. The killings, the planning for them, proved that. Hanse could and did shunt him out of the service, of course, but Merritt's own contacts must have been nearly as good. As Chief of Operations he could have . . . not seen it, I think, because Hanse's a sharp boy too . . . but felt it when some members of his own organization got together with rich men, men with connections outside the country where arms could be stockpiled and soldiers trained. You could take over this State, I think, with a few men in the right place and not too many more scattered around to look menacing. You could do it because damned few of the rest of them care. Of us care."

"Bill cares. He found—a lot of us who do."

"Sure he did, friend Tamara. And he killed not just eighteen people but likely two or three others standing too close to each of the ones he aimed at, too. I won't arrest him for caring, just for the murders; because it's my job and I'm better at it than he hoped."

She turned toward Lacey at last, her eyes full of tears and fire. "Do you know how many thousand they'd have killed if they took over? How many Hanse *will* kill if he gets away to Argentina this morning? Do you call *that* justice?"

"Justice? What's that?" Lacey demanded. "But they pay me to enforce the law, and yes, that's damned well the law!" He took a deep breath. "Now, mind your flying. If we go down, there'll be a Red Team around Merritt before the echoes of the crash have died. Believe me, he'd rather I take him than those animals in uniform. . . . Believe me, I've been there."

She obeyed but the tears gurgled in her voice. "Don't you think you owe anything to society?" she asked.

"This society?" Lacey repeated with savage incredulity. "The society that made me what *I* am?"

Tamara said nothing more for a minute, concentrating on the thickening traffic as they approached the huge concrete slab of the port.

"We've got a priority clearance," Lacey said. "You can set us down on the terminal building."

"We couldn't get close to Hanse," the girl said, as much to herself as to her companion. "When he flew it was in his own CT-19, and he always carried his own car with him. He didn't trust anyone, anything. We delayed, hoping he would slip up; but we waited too long. And so their plans were so close to ready that if Hanse gets to Parana now, he may be able to bring it all off even with Follard and the others dead."

A heavy cargo aircraft lumbered aloft a hundred and fifty meters from its painted bay on the great field. Three seconds later a private supersonic, incredibly expensive to own or operate, streaked skyward with its wings folding even as it climbed. Short takeoff and landing requirements made full runways a thing of the past, but the congestion and varied speeds near the port still demanded rigid control.

Lacey had noticed the girl start as the supersonic shrieked away. "Merritt's in one like that?" he asked. "Don't get excited, it wasn't his that time. I've put a hold on him, blocked his controls through the port computer. He'll be waiting for us."

Tamara angled for a slot on the crowded roof of the terminal building. A closed car sped up to reach the same parking space, then spun away as Tamara hammered it with the draft of her fans. Lacey, gripping the bulkhead tightly, grinned over at the furious red face visible through the cabin window of the other craft.

Tamara cut the drive and they ghosted to a halt. She looked back at Lacey. He said, a trifle awkwardly, "It'll be ten, twelve hours before they start dragging actual names out of Merritt. Somebody who'd gotten out of the State before then—used Sig Hanse's access code to fake exit privileges to Munich, say—would be gone for good."

The girl stared at him, her eyes an acid blue and her hair springing up like a cobra's hood as she doffed her helmet. "Bill had me assigned driver to whoever got tapped to investigate Follard. He pulled a few strings, nothing major for somebody who has as many friends as Bill Merritt does. There was a chance that by giving him a nudge in the right direction, we could get a CS agent interested in what Hanse was doing. You didn't need the nudge—or care about what you learned without it.

"But I'm not going to use the position Bill put me in to, to save myself."

"It's your life," Lacey said, breaking eye contact as he climbed out of the car. "The Lord knows I'm not the one to tell you what to do with it."

"I'm coming along," Tamara insisted, swinging into the narrow aisle between their car and the next one over. Lacey shrugged and walked toward the stair head.

Hanse too would be somewhere in the port. Lacey had said he did not care about the Sepo conspiracy, and in a way that was true; but the scar on his neck throbbed like molten steel at the thought. He jostled his way down the crowded stairs, Tamara an orange shadow behind him. At the ground floor he followed the directional arrows toward a balding fat man serving one stall of the console marked TRANSPORTATION TO AIRCRAFT. There was a line but the investigator stepped to the front of it with a gruff, "Excuse me."

To the clerk he said, "Priority. I need a car to Slip 318," and he cocked his ring finger. The fat man's display obediently lit red in response to an authenticating signal from the CS net.

"Door 12, then," the clerk said with a nervous shrug.

"But look, buddy, we're short today, there won't be a driver for seven, eight minutes."

"I didn't ask for a driver." Lacey turned, took the twenty long strides to the indicated portal without speaking. Half a dozen ground cars were lined up on the concrete beyond; nearly a hundred would-be passengers stood beside them docilely, waiting to be taken to their flights.

A big man, one of the pair of guards with Hanse the day before, stepped out of the crowd. It rippled away from him like sheep from a wolf in their midst. He had dropped the poncho which had cloaked the weapon along his right thigh, an automatic powergun with a drum magazine and a flask of liquid nitrogen under the barrel for cooling and ejection. "That's far enough, Lacey," he said with a smile. "You must have known we'd check what you were doing yesterday. So. . . ."

The bodyguard swung up the muzzle of his weapon. Lacey drew without hesitation, shot the Sepo twice in the trigger hand. A fist-sized chunk of concrete blew from the field as the Sepo spasmed off a shot, but his paralyzed body was already twisting into the ground.

"Lacey!" the girl screamed. He spun, his gun leading his body around in a glittering arc—too slowly. Tamara was leaping for the second guard, his eye as black as the bore of the powergun it stared over. Lacey heard the sudden grunt of the shots, saw the cyan glare catch Tamara in mid air and use her own exploding fluids to fling her backward with her chest a slush of blood and charred bone. A cloud of ice crystals hung at the Sepo's side and his plastic empties were still spinning in the air when Lacey shot him in the right eye.

The charge that would have stunned elsewhere blasted the optic nerve and ripped down that straight path to the brain. The Sepo arched in a tetanic convulsion that broke his neck and back in three places. The powergun spun into the building, cracking the vitril and ricochetting to the pavement.

Lacey did not look again at the girl, but he had seen her face as the burst slashed across her. Holstering his needle gun, he mounted the driver's seat of a twelve-passenger crawler and threw it into gear. The numbers on the empty slips were hard to read, scorched and abraded by the lift fans, but Lacey had his implant to guide him across the baking concrete. Once a huge CT-19 freighter staggered aloft just after he had passed its bow, but either luck or the watchful Terminal Control preserved Lacey while his quarry, a spike of silver fire, grew in front of him.

"Status on Merritt?" Lacey asked his implant.

"Three minutes ago requested permission to lift, destination Buenos Aires. Placed on safety hold by Terminal Control on orders of the Crime Service net."

"Umm. Status on Sig Hanse?"

"Cleared for Parana in a CT-19 with five crew and seven passengers, one air car declared as cargo. Estimated lift-off is three minutes thirty."

"And it'll have a battalion aboard when it and a thousand others come back," Lacey muttered, but he did not trigger his implant.

Close up, the craft that looked so slender among the cargo haulers was a study in brutal, wasteful power. Its turbines were spinning fast enough to raise a whine but not dust from the concrete. Lacey pulled in close to the port side, in between two of the ducted intakes. As he did so the cockpit canopy three meters above sprang open. The aging black man Lacey had seen only on the scanner before began to climb down the rungs which had extended from the ship's side.

"Citizen Lacey?" Merritt said as he reached the ground. He stretched out his hand, as dry and unyielding as a cypress knee. "Now I understand why Terminal Control froze me for a circuitry check. I don't suppose they were going to isolate the problem quickly, were they?"

"No, not till I gave the word," Lacey agreed disinterestedly.

Merritt shook his head with a faint smile. "Of course, of course. You're a very able man. And I can almost admire your singlemindedness, since after all that's the way I am. Well, shall we go back and meet your team of brain-wreckers?"

Lacey ran a hand along the stress-rippled skin of the aircraft. "What would you have done if Control hadn't held you?" he asked. "Lifted off in a few minutes?"

"Something like that."

"And you'd have laid your throttle wide open wouldn't you? Put it right through the middle of Hanse's CT-19. Wouldn't that be pretty? You and twelve other people falling out of the sky like shaved meat? You know, I don't ever remember meeting anybody who liked to kill as much as you seem to."

Merritt bit his lip. "Citizen Lacey," he said, "I've lived in this democracy 54 years, worked toward its safety for 31. I would be less than a man if I weren't at least willing to die for it; and to keep it and the world out of the hands of Sig Hanse and his sort— yes, I'll kill."

The emotion behind Lacey's smile was not humor. "Must be nice to know what's best for the world," he said. "I've got enough problems deciding what's best for Jed Lacey, and that's the only thing I've tried to worry about. Figured it was mostly me I had to live with."

"No doubt," Merritt said flatly. "Then if you have nothing further to say, shall we get on?"

"Sure," Lacey agreed. He triggered his implant. "Release the hold on William Anton Merritt," he ordered. "Clear him for immediate lift-off." He stepped back to the ground car alone, waving a casual hand back at the older man. "Have a good flight, Citizen Merritt."

Lacey's car was half a kilometer away when he heard Merritt's turbines shriek up to full power. From further across the concrete came the deep thunder and subsonic trembling of a CT-19's beginning effort to stagger skyward. Lacey's implant cut out both sounds when it announced, "Reply to support request, theft from PDT stockpiles."

"Ready."

"Four hundred liters removed from Redcliffe Arsenal, Toronto Subregion, on 4-23-02. Currently believed being transported in reserve fuel tank of private aircraft number—"

Lacey had anticipated the next words, so he was out of his seat and diving toward the concrete when the concrete rose to meet him. Twenty meters above the field, Merritt's aircraft had collided with Hanse's. The supersonic caught the CT-19 abaft the starboard wing, stabbing through the bulbous cargo hauler like a swordsman seeking the heart. The first microsecond of rending metal was lost in the bellow of the engines; then the PDT went off.

All sound ended as an orange fireball devoured the merged aircraft. The blast that followed was like nothing heard since the end of nuclear testing.

Alive but uncaring, stripped by the winds and hammered by the bucking concrete, Lacey lay on the field. He could let the tears come now.

In his mind, back-lighted by the afterimage of the fireball, was the vision of a girl with blue eyes, jet hair, and a smile of love and triumph.

# THE PREDATORS

Above the buildings slid air cars. A single private vehicle as luxurious as any of them shared the street below with the wheeled trucks and buses. The closed rear cabin was empty but the chauffeur, a youth whose uniform matched the landeau's smoke-blue paint, drove with the arrogance of one conducting a prince.

In front of the Coeltrans Building he nudged his wheel to the right, edging up over the curb between a pair of trucks unloading yard goods. Pedestrians leaped to avoid the blunt prow. Smiling, the chauffeur set the brake, cut the alcohol flame to idle under the boiler, and tilted a wing mirror to check his appearance. Shoulder-length black hair framed a face whose complexion was as unnaturally brilliant as the best parchment. His lips were red and well-shaped and cruel.

Satisfied, he slid from the ground car's saddle and entered the building, leaving his vehicle for the cameras to watch. They scanned this street as they did every street, every room, in the State; and at the first sign of someone tampering with the car, a monitoring computer would alert the police.

Within the large, single room, narrow aisles separated booths selling fabric and garments. Even during daylight the inner tables were lighted by glow strips to bring out the colors of their merchandise. Eyes turned toward the chauffeur as he passed, some drawn by his iridescent livery but many by his carriage and frame. The body beneath his tight uniform would have done credit to a *kouros* of ancient Athens. He acknowledged the glances only by hooking the left corner of his mouth into a more pronounced sneer.

At the spidery framework of the elevator in the center of the room he halted. Four slim, chromed vertical rods rose from the floor here all the way to the roof of the building. The chauffeur touched the call plate with his ID bracelet; the radio-cesium key imbedded in its silver threw a switch invisibly and the cage began to whine down from the fifteenth level.

Shop owners in the Coeltrans Building were used to the activity, but there was a stir among their customers. Many of them had never seen a working elevator before. The cost of power to run elevators made them rich men's toys—and rich men had air cars to get them between the top-floor suites of their fellows. Supported by the four thin columns, the cage sank through one-meter circles cut through each level. Little more itself than a floor with a waist-high rail plated to match the verticals, the cage appeared shockingly frail. A more substantial construct would have sometimes blocked the fields of the three scanning cameras covering each floor. No citizen, no matter how rich and powerful, could be granted that potential for secrecy.

The chauffeur stepped aboard and the cage began to rise. He lounged back against the guard rail, whistling as his fingers beat time against the chrome. On each identical level, banks of clerks looked up from their desks as the cage rose past them. The motor in the elevator's floor raised it effortlessly past stairs which were theirs to climb every time they reported to work. The elevator was for Citizen Wilhoit alone—and for this youth.

Only on Level 15 was there a break in the vistas of desks crammed into 60-meter circular floor plans. Here the outside walls were pierced not by windows but rather by translucent panels cast in various pastels. The room was actually brighter than those below it, however, because of the sheets of sunlight-balanced glow strips in its ceiling. Underlings sat in ordinary desks around the level's outer perimeter, but the central twenty meters were held by a jungle of potted plants and a single huge mahogany desk no less impressive for the litter of papers and instruments on its surface.

The cage stopped. The chauffeur continued to whistle, his back to the mahogany desk and the gray-faced man beginning to stand behind it. Then the current surged through the elevator's handrail and snapped the chauffeur into a screaming arc.

Alternating current of over 600 volts tends to fling away those who touch it, saving lives that lower voltages might have taken. DC instead clamps and holds and kills; and to avoid inductance losses, Greater Greensboro and most other cities now ran on direct current. The charge ripping through the chauffeur's body broke his ribs with unrelieved muscle contraction, and the screaming stopped only when there was no more air to be forced through the lifeless throat. Seconds later the flow cut off as suddenly as it had begun, and the charred body slumped to the floor of the cage.

The cameras on Level 15 recorded every visible nuance of the death.

➤    ➤    ➤

Lacey gave the final command to the Crime Service computer. It would send a Red Team after the airport smuggler he had identified following a week of studying the operation from every angle. He swung the scanner helmet up against its counterweight and grinned his wolf's grin of accomplishment. His hand was massaging the old scar on his neck and holding the glow inside him when Billings, the investigator at the desk to his right, got up. "You knocking off too?" Billings asked. He was a blond man with a round face and a quick smile.

Lacey came out of his reverie. He looked at his neighbor, then at the clock across the circular room. 15:40. For the past three nights he had caught cat naps at his desk as leads branched and twined and he wanted thirty hours a day to study scanner images. "Might, yeah," he agreed. There were five hundred desks and investigators on Level 17 of the State Building. Lacey knew and cared as little about Billings as he did about any other of his co-workers.

Billings was straightening the pleats of his collar. "I put in for two hours in the target range," he confided to Lacey's disinterest, "but really I got a date. Lovely girl, lives in the section next to ours. We're going to a time house and buy an hour of privacy. It'll cost a bundle, but it's worth it to keep my wife from learning."

Before Lacey could make his noncommittal reply, the light on Billing's desk blinked orange and the blond man stiffened as information came through his mastoid implant. He swore with frustrated bitterness, punching his left palm with his other hand. "She'll *never* believe this," he said. "They've cancelled my range time and given me an accidental death to check out. An accident!"

"Maybe the computer's a secret puritan," Lacey said, more of a smile on his mouth than in his eyes.

"I always get the leftovers," Billings whined. "You think they'd give me a murder where I could get a little recognition? Hell no! But let some clod touch a hot wire and fry, they drop it in my lap and expect me to work every bleeding hour till I prove it's an accident. And you *can't* prove something didn't happen!" Billings thudded his hands together again. "That tight-assed bitch Sutter's had her thumb on me ever since I offered to give her the time back when I was first on the unit. She won't let the Net give me any decent assignments!"

Billings face suddenly smoothed and he looked at the close-coupled man still listening with bare politeness. "Look, Jed"—Lacey had never called Billings by his first name, did not even remember it—"look, for me this damn thing'll take forever, checking out the number of times each electrician burped for the past year before the Net'll take a negative report from me. But if you took the call, hell, you know how they'll pass just about anything on your say-so. You do five minutes' scan and report 'no crime,' they'll clear it, and we both get the afternoon off."

The younger agent saw and misinterpreted the chill in Lacey's eyes. "Ah, say . . . Marie's got, I mean, she's got friends and . . . I think maybe we could—"

"I'll pass on that," Lacey said very softly. The scar on his neck stood out in relief against the veins pulsing there. He caressed it with his stubby, gentle fingers. "But I'll take the call, yeah. I didn't have much on for the afternoon."

"You're a champ, Jed," Billings said, squeezing Lacey's biceps and then striding quickly toward the stairway. He was toying with his collar ruff again, a beefy man who would always be allotted bottom-priority calls and would never understand why.

Lacey sighed and pulled his scanner helmet back down to cover his head like a fat, black artillery shell. Quirking his left ring finger to activate his implanted link with the Crime Service Net, Lacey said, "You just routed a call to station four-three-seven. Transfer it to me and give me a current scan."

"Accepted," said the computer voice from Lacey's mastoid, and the Net tapped his helmet into the output of one of the cameras on Level 15 of the Coeltrans Building. The screen showed emergency technicians who were laying a body on their medicomp, a dull-finished unit that looked like a coffin on casters. God knew why the men bothered, because the charred corpse was clearly beyond repair by any human means. There would be little enough of the victim to send to the Reclamation Depot after Lacey had cleared it for processing.

The rest of the level was normal enough, eccentrically furnished but in the fashion that executive levels of powerful corporations could be expected to be eccentric. Part of the work force was still at its desks, following routine as though that would deny the ghastly incident in the center of the room. The remainder were divided between those elbowing for a closer look at the body and those forcing toward the staircase, waiting to be passed by the bored Red Team securing the death site. No one sat at the broad mahogany desk which stood like an island in a green sea of carefully-tended plants.

Lacey triggered his implant. "Section six," he called, naming the imaginary sixteenth portion of the scanner's view which showed the guard rail of the elevator. "Twenty magnifications." The image zoomed and Lacey could see that what appeared to be a single gleaming circuit was actually divided by four thin insulators, so that each of the verticals of the shaft was insulated from the others. The victim's carbonized skin lumped two quadrants of the ring. Since the rods had to hold the power cables for the elevator's motor, stripped insulation was the obvious cause of the death. As Billings had said, a five-minute job.

Suppressing a yawn under his helmet, Lacey ordered, "Okay, give me camera two at the time the line shorted."

Obediently the Crime Service computer switched to data stored in the vaults that extended for miles under Greater Atlanta. In Lacey's helmet screen the chauffeur stiffened as the jolt crossed him. A blue nimbus threw his screaming face into high relief. Behind him, rising from the big desk, was a man in conservative clothing with a face as transfigured by horror as that of the victim himself.

"Bloody hell," Lacey whispered. He recognized both men. "Bloody *hell*," he repeated. Then he flicked awake his computer link. "What's the priority on this call?" he demanded.

"Tenth," replied the computer. Its programming did not allow it to add, "Of course."

"Well, better raise it," Lacey said. "You've handed me a murder to clear, and I may need a hell of a lot of help to prove it."

The car was waiting when Lacey swung through the outside door. On his mere statement the Net had rerated the assignment to Priority Two, a comment as to where his stock stood with the computer on the basis of his past performance. The new rating included use of a State vehicle and driver, which Lacey took immediately to the scene of the death. He loved the scanner helmets and did most of his work seated under one; but he could not use them to question witnesses, and he had some questions he needed answered.

Transit time between the pad and the Coeltrans Building was four minutes. Lacey did not waste them, using his implant to get an ID and economic data on the victim and the man behind the mahogany desk. The first was easy. "Terrence Oscar Silvers, age 23; licensed ground vehicle driver employed by the Company for Electrical Transmission for five years, nine months," stated Lacey's mastoid. There was a pause. "Robert Sawney Wilhoit, age 47," the computer voice resumed. It halted. In a different timbre it requested, "Access code, please."

Without surprise or concern, Lacey punched his 8-letter code on the panel set into the back of the driver's seat. Wilhoit's wealth and authority had been obvious from the setting of his office; it would have been unusual if he had not used his power to see that idle thrusts into his personal life should be turned aside. Lacey on a murder call did nothing idly, and he could be as difficult to turn aside as Juggernaut's carriage.

Assured of Lacey's authority, the data bank continued, "President and Chairman of the Board of the Company for Electrical Transmission. Developed and holds patents on three basic processes in DC voltage step-down technology. Extensive holdings in various corporations, primarily in the field of electronic components and design."

Lacey's driver was tapping him on the knee and calling, "Coeltrans Buildings, sir." They were twenty meters above the roof pad of a modern cylindrical structure. One of the vehicles already parked on the roof was a ten-seater with leg shackles and wristlets on several benches: the van that had brought the uniformed police in response to a howl from the computer.

"Fine, set us down," Lacey said. They stuttered to a halt at the stairhead. "Crime Service," he muttered as he brushed past the uniformed man stationed there.

"Hey, why didn't you just turn us loose through the Net?" the patrolman asked. "You didn't have to show up yourself." Lacey ignored him and stepped down the stairs into the greasy stench of the room below.

In the nervous chaos of the fifteenth level was a woman who had not been there when Lacey had scanned it minutes before. She was tall and fat, wearing stained coveralls. She sat on a wheeled toolbox and shouted angrily into a phone clipped to it, "You stupid son of a bitch, there *can't* be a short. We were *touching* the bleeding line thirty seconds before this beggar fried!" Sweat was bright on her forehead and heavy jowls, and her knuckles were white with her grip on the phone.

The electrician's shout had quieted the room so that her partner's voice from the speaker was clear as he replied, "Look, Margie, the meters show the juice came from the emergency generator. Nobody could've gimmicked 'em with us working here, so it *was* a short. And for god's sake, what else could've done it? Bloody lightning?"

"Crime Service," Lacey said to the woman. "I need to ask you some questions."

"Oh, god," she murmured. Her flesh had lost all resiliency and gone gray in the blaze of the glow strips above. "Oh. . . ." Everyone in the room was staring at her and the investigator. "Will they—" she began and choked back her own words. Looking up at Lacey with a sudden fatalistic calm she started over. "Will you put Jim and me under the Psycomp for this? Will you wipe us?"

"You'd better tell me what happened," Lacey said neutrally.

She shrugged and stood, towering over him. The hand phone made a premonitory squawk and she cut it off. "They hired Jim and me—Coeltrans did—hired us to cross-connect the elevator. It—" almost without pausing, she drew a rubber glove onto her right hand and gestured with two fingers—"runs up cog rails in the verticals, these rods. Two of the rails are hot, insulated from the outer surface of the pole but feeding juice through the gears themselves to the motor in the cage floor."

Lacey leaned forward for a better look at the slots in the inner faces of the chrome supports. "Get back from there!" the woman snapped. "I got one deader on my conscience already today!"

Lacey blinked at her without emotion. "Go on," he said.

"We were supposed to set up a current path in the other two rails, too," she said, wiping her face with a sleeve. "Separate service from an emergency generator, a failsafe in case something went wrong with city power. We punched the lines through by section but we kept the circuit shut down except for testing at night after the building closed. There were bubbles in the insulation, so until we got 'em out we couldn't charge the line when anybody was around. In case, in case . . ." She nodded toward the corpse though she refused to look at it again. The technicians were now fitting the body into a pressure-sealed bag to be carried down to the street. "We'd got all the shorts out of it, we thought, but we weren't quite done testing. Guess I left the switch on last night but it seemed safe—we were touching the posts, *touching* them, Jim and me just before this guy . . . went."

"Why run a generator circuit to an elevator?" Lacey asked. He was watching the electrician's face.

"Why does anybody want an elevator at all?" she replied. The fear was gone, replaced by a dawning curiosity. "It was for the boss himself, Wilhoit. You know, he's a regular guy? Last night he—*oh god!*"

All of the fat woman's confidence suddenly disappeared. If she had been gray when Lacey first spoke, she was white now with memory. "He was watching us last night when we ran the tests, moving the cage up and down. Talked to us some—hell, he was the boss, we couldn't tell him he couldn't hang around when we were working. Nice guy. But when we were packing up, he grabbed rails three and four—the new circuit, you see? Took one in each hand and I thought, 'Thank god we've got all the bugs out'. But we hadn't, you see? Just for some reason the line didn't short then, waited till this afternoon and got this stiff instead of, instead of . . ."

"I want you to find that short for me," Lacey said, "you and your partner. He's in the building too?"

"Down in the basement," the woman said with a nod. "We were redding up when the floor manager called and said somebody'd died." Her open face suddenly coalesced into a frown. "Look, you trust *us* to check this out?"

"I don't need a Psycomp to tell if somebody's lying to me," Lacey said. "You stay straight with me, like you've been so far, and you'll come out of it all right."

"All right," she echoed. "All right, then wait thirty seconds and I may have an answer for you." She knelt at the base of an elevator support with a multi-windowed instrument in her hands. Holding it against the pole, she ran a dial across its scale and then used a pair of insulated pliers to bridge the two segments of handrail the victim had been holding when he died. The spark was fat and blue and snapped like a pistol shot.

"One'll get you ten that's it," the electrician said matter of factly. She began to put her tools away. The current had eaten a chip out of the nose of the pliers. "Inside the chrome plate, each rod's filled with

Dorafeen. It's easy stuff to use, you inject it like grease and let it set. It's hard, it's strong, and it's a hell of a good insulator usually. But if you trip a block of Dorafeen with a magnetic field of whatever the block's loading frequency is, you can get it to conduct like so much copper."

She gestured with her chin. "That's where the whole company started—Citizen Wilhoit came up with a process using Dorafeen to chop high-current DC into AC to run through transformers to step it down. Anyhow, we bored the columns for our power lines, then ran a bare aluminum cable through them. No need to insulate since there was a centimeter of Dorafeen all around the wire. Except we never thought that if the right—wrong—frequency magnetic field was generated right alongside it . . . well, you saw what it did to the pliers when I'd primed it with my tester."

"But it's just a temporary conductor?" Lacey asked.

"Sure, depends on the mass and a lot of other things," the woman said with a shrug. "A couple seconds for this block, milliseconds for the wafers they use in power stations. I wouldn't have believed that a microgauss field could trip that whole rod, but . . . that's the only way the accident could've happened. Some coil with just the right number of windings, laid against the column and switched on while the elevator was being used."

Lacey's tongue touched his lips. "I'll call you if I need anything more," he said to the fat woman, dismissing her. Her face smoothed in relief and she began to roll her tool chest toward the stairs. Raising his voice to cut through the whispering, Lacey addressed the whole room: "All right, who's the highest official on this floor right now?" Answering murmurs were too confused to be intelligible, but a hundred faces turned and triangulated on a plump little man, one of those still seated at his desk.

Lacey grinned so that his teeth glinted. His neck scar was tense and stiff and crawled beneath his skin. "Let the rest of 'em go, Corporal," he called to the chief of the uniformed patrol. "You and your boys can blast too. I'll just talk to this citizen a moment about what happened."

The red-capped police stepped aside and began filing up to their car, precipitating a rush of civilians down the single staircase lest the agent change his mind. The seated man watched Lacey approach with the intentness of a rabbit awaiting a black-snake. Like Lacey, he was dressed in gray, but in a muted solid instead of the tiger stripes that blurred the agent's outline. His beard matched his suit in color, a short, smooth arc that seemed a little incongruous beneath the baldly pink skull.

"Good afternoon, Citizen," Lacey said. "Your name and position, please?" He could have gotten the information as quickly through his computer link, but the opening question, the first thrust into his subject's persona, was a needed part of this interrogation.

"I'm Lewis Ashby and I, I assure you that I have far more to do than concern myself with, ah, drivers," the plump man said. His voice was generally steady, his tones rotund—but his eyes would not meet Lacey's.

"You knew Silvers, then?" Lacey prodded gently. "Knew he was a driver?" He and Ashby were about of a height, but the investigator was standing and dominating the clerk physically. He had let his overblouse fall open so that the holstered needle stunner was visible at the level of the civilian's face.

"I didn't say I knew him!" Ashby blurted. "You don't have any right—I don't care who you are, you can't put words in a person's mouth!"

"Did he always use the elevator when he visited Level 15?" Lacey asked, his voice still smooth but his muscles hardening slightly.

"I don't know."

"Umm, well . . . do you know how a Psycomp works, Citizen Ashby?" Ashby's face tilted up at the question, the mouth in a grimace or snarl, the eyes open. He said nothing. Lacey reached down, took a handful of fabric at the other man's throat and guided rather than jerked Ashby erect. "Maybe I'd better tell you, then, because it could be you'll be spending a long time in one yourself. You see, they give you a short-term anesthetic and slip you into a nutrient bath loaded with oxygen. Filling your lungs with it takes the anesthetic, but your body adapts to the system just fine.

"And you lose a little muscle tone, sure, but they won't really atrophy. The techs, though, they've run leads into your brain and as you lie there fed and filtered and breathing without being able to blink, a computer starts playing games in your head. It feeds in signals and sees what your brain does with them. Pretty soon it knows your head better than god himself does. It gets the answers to any questions it's been programmed to ask, and it goes around correcting any things that it's been programmed to correct. So long as it's in there anyway, you see."

Lacey's voice was the husky purring of a cat about to feed. His face was close to Ashby's and he was speaking with great distinctness. The clerk's eyes were bright with panic, and only the touch of Lacey's hand on his garments kept him from bolting. "It's not . . . comfortable," Lacey said, "lying there while a machine turns over every rock in your mind. And sometimes something goes wrong. Sometimes the computer goofs and a fellow comes out normal enough to look at but ready to kill at the slightest provocation, the least little thing that doesn't go his way . . .

"Oh—I forgot to tell you where they sink the leads into your skull, didn't I?" Lacey added. He tossed his head so that his brown-blond hair flew back from his forehead. With his free hand he touched two fingers to the white dimples at the hairline. "They go here. At least they did on me." He dropped Ashby and the softer man sagged into his chair like a scarecrow with half the stuffing gone.

"Now do you want to tell me about the driver?" Lacey asked; and through his sobs, Ashby told him.

Robert Wilhoit was afraid of heights. Not to an incapacitating degree, but enough that when he made it big he had begun to travel by ground vehicle despite the awkwardness of not being able to skim over the commercial traffic. For at least the past year, Silvers had been Wilhoit's driver.

The first time Ashby had seen them together was a day that the clerk had arrived early. Wilhoit had left his car and purred up the elevator while Ashby trudged the fourteen flights of stairs to which his position made him subject: no one but Wilhoit ever used the elevator. Three weeks later, the chauffeur had shared the cage with his employer, his haughty smoke-blue livery pressed tight against Wilhoit in the narrow space; and soon after that, the young man had his own key to the device and frequently rode it alone.

"I've worked for Coeltrans for twenty-three years," Ashby explained. Once started, the year of anger that had built up in the clerk spewed out like pus from a squeezed boil. "That's from the day, the very *day* that Citizen Wilhoit incorporated. Did he ever let me ride his elevator? Did he even speak to me, say, 'You're doing good work, Ashby'? Ha! But this little, *greasy* child. . . ."

Ashby raised his face and cupped hands to Lacey, pleading for the agent to understand something that he could not articulate. "He would ride up the elevator, get off at one floor or another. He didn't have any business in the building, he was just a driver. He talked to the younger clerks and the senior people, the floor managers—yes, me!—couldn't stop him. We were . . . we were afraid."

"Did Citizen Wilhoit ever, ah, threaten anyone for trying to get Silvers out of their work area?" Lacey asked.

The clerk grimaced, unwilling to answer the question but unable to avoid it even in his own mind. "Nobody tried to. We were afraid. The whole thing was . . . wrong. Citizen Wilhoit was ignoring it all, pretending that nothing was going on. Except that when this *person* went up to the Citizen's desk and whispered to him, they would leave together. Again and again. . . ."

Lacey looked over at the slab of oiled mahogany. Most top executives would have placed their desks on whatever part of the outer wall gave them the best view. Because Wilhoit disliked heights, his desk was central. The ceiling lights pooled brightly around the desk and the serpentine rings of foliage about it.

Lacey stepped over to the plants where the Outermost circle of them lapped against the elevator. Festoons of tubing to carry water and nutrients linked the individual pots. He touched a squat plant whose leaves were like narrow fingers streaked with yellow and green. "Really likes plants, hmm? Don't any of them have flowers?"

"They're Citizen Wilhoit's hobby, not mine. If you want to learn about them, you'll have to ask his gardener."

"Even a gardener?" Lacey said mildly. There was a flower, after all; a pink geranium in a pot beside the elevator. Part of what snaked from its foliage was not plastic tubing but wire.

"Of course a gardener," Ashby was saying, but Lacey was no longer listening to him. The agent had unsheathed his hand scanner and was recording every detail of the apparatus connected to the geranium. The room's three integral scanners covered it in the sense that if it had been empty, at least two lenses would have born on every centimeter of surface. In practice, although opaque objects over 80 cm high were strictly controlled, there were blind angles near the floor which only spot checks by human operatives would record. By chance or otherwise, the geranium was in such an angle. Two short loops of wire were clipped to the leaves. At the other end they disappeared into a sealed, fist-sized box tacked to the nearest post of the elevator.

"What's this?" Lacey called back over his shoulder.

Ashby looked startled. He stood and peered over at where the agent knelt. "No, I told you I don't know anything about plants."

"Not the plant, for god's sake, the box!" Lacey snapped. "You know about electronics, don't you?"

"Certainly not. I'm an accountant, not a, a technician."

Lacey's expression went briefly flat and his scar stood out. Then he began to chuckle. He was laughing fully, open-mouthed, as he walked past the cringing clerk and up the stairs to where his car and driver waited.

Level 17 was lighted and busy when Lacey got back to the State Building, though it was technically after quitting time and most of the floors below had emptied. Seventeen belonged to the hunters, and the good ones were lonely people. You couldn't take a companion under a scanner helmet with you. Some investigators worked long hours for the thrill of the chase, some because they tracked criminals by rote and had by now no other way to order their time. Lacey worked like a slave at an oar bench, driven by an overseer no one else could see. No one, at least, besides the Psycomp which had shunted his profile to the attention of Crime Service recruiters at the same time it carved away Lacey's ability ever to rape another woman.

His Unit Chief was waiting for him, seated on Billings' chair with her legs crossed at the knees and a glass of something sparkling in her hand. She set the drink down and smiled as the agent approached.

"Hello, Ruby," Lacey said, sitting on the edge of his own desk. "Slumming or hiding?"

The Crime Service Net was a huge computer complex that directed its agents with more than mechanical skill, but it could not interface them with the world. That job took humans—not hunters themselves, but humans who could understand the terrible loneliness and exhilaration of the hunters, who could cushion them against the realities of housing and economics and sex. Ruby Sutter was one of them, and she was one of the best. Tall for a woman, taller than Lacey's own meter seventy, she looked slim and fragile until one noted the muscles knotting close beneath the skin; then she looked only slim. Her hair was darker than brunette, and though her normal work did not require her to use the scanners, she wore it in the tight ringlets that would be comfortable beneath a helmet.

"Working, Jed—got your example to follow, you know." Sutter's station was on the fourth level, not the seventeenth. "Had a citizen complaint about you, as a matter of fact, and I was asked to take care of the problem. Asked from pretty high up."

Her face was bland. Lacey frowned in genuine

surprise and asked, "Since when do the high-ups care what citizens think, for god's sake?"

"When the citizen looks a good bet to develop a matter transmitter in the next couple years, they manage to get interested."

Lacey slid down into his chair. "Umm. Sure. Wilhoit wasn't around, but he probably had access to scanner inputs from his own building, huh? Not really supposed to, but. . . . And I don't guess he liked what he saw, either." The squat man chuckled. "That's real freedom of information, isn't it? A murderer using a scanner to track the cops?"

Sutter took a sip of her drink. "The Net says it's an accidental death. Ninety-nine plus probability."

"Going to pull me off it, then?"

"Not if you say it's murder."

Lacey felt his muscles loosen. He had not realized until then how tense he had been. "That's good," he said, running a hand across his forehead. "I was going to nail him anyway. Though I guess you knew that already."

"You do your job, Lacey, and leave me to mine," Sutter replied. The smile left her face and she leaned forward, careful not to touch the agent or even threaten to. "But be careful, Jed. You can't push Wilhoit the way you did Ashby. Even with your past record and everything I can do for you, it'll be your ass if you go one step beyond the law with somebody with Wilhoit's clout."

She leaned back and grinned again. "But just between us and the data banks, that was a lovely bluff you ran on Ashby. Pretending the Psycomp had scrambled your brains and you were going to tear him open unless he talked."

"Bluff?" Lacey repeated. "Oh. Well, he was going to talk. He was the kind who would."

Sutter reached out a hand to brush the air inches short of Lacey's arm, a caress in intent but not in execution. Ever since the Psycomp had gotten through with him, physical contact with a woman threw Lacey into vomiting and convulsions. Sutter knew that and knew why, as she knew everything necessary to the well-being of her agents. It did not keep her from caring. "You're not going to lose control of yourself, Jed," she said. "Not over Ashby. Or anybody."

She stood and walked away.

Lacey was humming to himself very softly as he pulled down his scanner helmet and began running data on the victim. Silvers had spent four nondescript years driving Coeltrans delivery trucks before being picked as Wilhoit's personal chauffeur after the suicide of the previous driver. The data bank showed no reluctance to release information on the boy. Unlike the electronics magnate, Silvers was one more out of billions and his file was open to anyone with access to the computer. There was not even need to show cause.

But the life stats were as uninteresting as they were open. So, with a careful precision that combined years of practice with a knack beyond any experience, Lacey began to dig into the scanner records which stored Silvers' whole life.

"Death site minus 30 seconds," he ordered, using his mastoid implant to control the scanner helmet. Silvers' lounging beauty flashed up obediently, one hand on each of two quarter-circlets of railing that would soon be lethal. Lacey flicked the CS Net to attention again. "Tracer request."

"Go ahead," the computer link said.

"Terrence Oscar Silvers. Template as currently on screen."

"Ready." In a microsecond the Net had analyzed Silvers as he appeared moments before death, taking

into account not only externals but details of height
and bone structure subject to change only by trauma
or the most extensive surgery.

"Same camera, same template—scan to death minus
one week," Lacey ordered.

Using the analysis it had made on the victim during
life, the Crime Service computer ran the past week's
input from the Coeltrans scanner Lacey had made his
vantage point. It quickly found and marked congru-
ent subjects. A man could have made the same
check—but only if he had a week to spend. Computer review was labor saving, though in the same
sense that a power drill saves labor—per hole. It does
not mean that a miner at the rock face works less
hard than his grandfather did, only that he cuts out
more ore.

"Two samples," the implant reported.

"Run the latest," said Lacey.

The scene in the scanner was visual proof of the
story Ashby had told. Silvers was arriving in his blue
and smoke livery, a stim stick between his gum and
cheek to diffuse its alkaloids into his bloodstream. His
walk missed being a swagger only by its fluidity. Wilhoit
was aware of him as of nothing else in the room, but
he kept his head bent down and only the tension of
his hand on the desk edge was a communication.

The chauffeur sidled between desks, watching with
bored superiority as clerks tapped figures into the
displays across their desktops. Some stumbled under
his gaze. Once Silvers spoke to an employee, a blond
boy whose bones must have been translucent to give
him so ethereal an air. Lacey switched to another
camera for a view of Silvers' lips, but the words were
a bland question about how long the other had worked
for Coeltrans. The embarrassed clerk only muttered,
"Sir, a week is all," but his eyes followed Silvers until

the driver left, alone, as suddenly and inexplicably as he had come.

Lacey sent his left ring finger the message to curl. The rerouted nerve triggered his implant. "What's Silvers' home address?" he asked.

"Suite 12, Level 3, 184 West Mangum Street."

"Suite" sounded plush, "Level 3" sounded plush—a low walk-up but high enough to be clear of the noise and odors of the inevitable stores on the ground floor—and the street address was in the middle of a very good neighborhood indeed. "Same template, same scan frame, Level 3, 184 West Mangum Street," Lacey directed.

"Five samples."

"Run the latest."

By law and in practice, every room in the State of over five cubic meters was covered by the interlocked fields of three scanning cameras. The law did not regulate minimum size or occupancy for rooms, but the staggering use-tax linked to every required camera guaranteed that space—and the scanners covering it—would be efficiently used. Silvers' rent was indicated by the fact that his apartment level was planned into fifty suites when many middle-class levels would have held five times as many units in the same area. Lacey's helmet showed him a late-evening scene: Silvers entering from the lower staircase and sauntering along a serpentine corridor to his own suite. He was out of livery, wearing instead a cape and jumpsuit cut conservatively but from lustrous material that flowed through a range of colors. Because the scanners worked on infra-red in the darkness, the precise shades were doubtful; the cost of the garment was not.

The corridors and suites were divided by double floor-to-ceiling sheets of vitril, sound-deadening but kept visually transparent by an expensive static cleaning

system. Silvers palmed his lock plate, entered, and
began fixing a meal in the kitchen.

"Who's paying for this?" Lacey asked.

The CS Net cleared its throat with a click, then said,
"All charges are paid through Personnel Accounting,
Coeltrans."

"On whose request?"

"That information is not available."

A written or verbal order, than, not one punched
directly into the corporation's accounts from a high
level. Available to Lacey when he began running scanner images and questioning clerks. He didn't need the
knowledge yet, and it would still be waiting for him
when he did.

Lacey swung away his helmet and rubbed his eyes.
The level was almost empty and the sky beyond the
windows was black. "Late," he thought, then glanced
at the clock hands illuminated over the doorway and
realized that instead it was early—and not all that early.
He did not feel tired, only light and insubstantial and
happy in a way that drugs could never leave him. There
was one more matter he could clear up through the
helmet while it was still dark outside.

"Same template, same scan frame—Level 9, 304
Corcoran Street," Lacey ordered, shrouding himself
with his helmet again.

"One sample."

"Run it."

On the screen flashed a moving image of the anteroom of Hell. In a nation without privacy there can
be few statutory crimes. This is neither altruism nor
liberality, simply economics. Since every human activity
was scanned and the inputs monitored by computers
which would ring alerts on every instance of activity
they were programmed to find unlawful, there had to
be sharp limits to make actual enforcement possible

by a police force of acceptable size. In earlier decades, patrolmen could be writing parking tickets within twenty feet of a mugging or rape in progress. Now no crime was ignored and, without the lubricant of ignorance which made the old system work, the statute book itself had to be streamlined into the realm of possibility by a ruthless paring of minor offenses and victimless crimes.

To the State, no form of consensual sexual activity was a crime. Society, however, had a separate opinion.

When poverty becomes the norm, everything is for sale somewhere; but ascetic religion becomes the only real anodyne for the masses. If present squalor is only God's furnace to purify men for posthumous glory, what matter the lack of food and energy, the endemic diseases and the evidence that all over the world Man was staggering down a slope which he was unlikely to rescale. Purity is not a physical fact but a religious state of mind.

Level 9 was the entrance to the accommodation house, the time house, on the floor above. Clients paid for use of one of the hundreds of canvas-walled cribs, each with a single scanner unit mounted in the ceiling above it. You could not shut out the cameras, but the cameras did not care what—consensually—you did or to whom.

In the helmet screen, on the next to the top level of the sleazy residence building, Terry Silvers stood hipshot as his date, a wizened, balding man in a suit of natural silk, paid the attendant to be allowed to climb to the cribs.

"Cancel," Lacey said. He did not need or want to follow Silvers into the accommodation house.

No law of the State had been broken there. If Society wished to stigmatize homosexuals as brutally as had Victorian England, if riot squads not infrequently were called to put down the spontaneous violence offered by mobs of the upright to uncovered paederasts, it was no business of Lacey's.

No one in an accommodation house is upright.

"Death site minus 30 seconds," Lacey ordered. Silvers' doomed, smiling face appeared with Wilhoit and the rest of the room beyond it. "Tracer request."

"Go ahead."

"Robert Sawney Wilhoit, template as currently on helmet screen."

"Ready."

"Level 9, 304 Corcoran Street. All samples in the past six months."

"Twenty-seven samples."

"Run the latest."

Another night on the screen but the same guard and Silvers with the same haughty expression as he waited. This time Citizen Robert Wilhoit, inventor and executive, was paying for the crib. He had the rigid look of a man whose legs were being amputated without anesthetic. There were other customers coming down the stairs, a middle-aged man and a woman too plainly garbed to be a prostitute. They avoided looking at Wilhoit just as he did them.

No one was upright in an accommodation house.

"Cancel," Lacey repeated and swung the helmet away. Wilhoit had, perhaps, enough power to escape the Mob's censure, but he could not have escaped his own upbringing. A self-made man rather than an aristocrat raised to believe in the propriety of whatever he chose to do, public exposure of his homosexuality would have horrified Wilhoit as surely as it would have the clerks in his office. And he had been willing to kill to keep it . . . not secret, but unproven. The scanner image was evidence of motive for the computer. Lacey had already known it, of course, because he had a sharp memory for faces. He had remembered Wilhoit and the victim from a night some months previous when he had seen them together, leaving the accommodation house as Lacey entered it for his own private needs.

Morning was bright in the windows and the room had begun to fill with returning agents. It remained to learn where Wilhoit was at the moment. Using the scanner helmet once more, Lacey checked the magnate's office and found him seated at his desk speaking into a face-covering hush phone.

Lacey stood. "Ready me a car," he ordered the computer. "I'm going to visit an apartment while its owner's away."

The palm lock set in the clear panel of the suite's door was impossible to pick by conventional means. The flat pouch over Lacey's left hip, balancing his needle stunner, held an electronic pick that was by no means conventional. Itself a terminal to the Crime Service Net, its face was a mesh of microscopic beads that raised, lowered, and changed their conductivity under the direction of the computer. If a pattern was on file, the pick duplicated it instantly, if not, the computer ran a random search certain to open any palm lock within a minute.

It took Lacey a little longer than that to get in, because instead of picking the lock he summoned Wilhoit's live-in house staff to admit him.

There were two of them, both men in their forties. One wore the livery Silvers had died in, a burly, smooth-stepping man, obviously a human watchdog and obviously angry. Lacey had announced his presence by having the CS Net override every sound unit in the suite, ordering the occupants to unlock immediately or face arrest. As the door swung open the guard snarled a quick curse, but he backed off from Lacey's lifted brow and the threat in the eyes beneath it.

The other man was the one Lacey had come to see. He had thin hair and a worn tunic whose loops and pockets held a score of scrupulously clean tools. The light reflected from the myriad plants filling the suite gave the man's pale complexion a greenish cast, and it seemed to fit. He blinked at Lacey with the same mild interest that he might have displayed toward a cafeteria server.

"You're Charles Dornier, Citizen Wilhoit's gardener?" Lacey asked, as an opening rather than because the matter was in doubt.

"Why yes, do you have a delivery for us?" the wispy man responded.

Lacey grinned with something close to humor. "Not exactly," he said. "I'd like to see Citizen Wilhoit's plants, but I'm a Crime Service agent." He turned back to the guard. "You can wait outside in the hall," he said. "And I mean wait. Take three steps away from the door and there'll be a Red Team on you."

Dornier had ignored the words, ignored also the glowering and slammed door with which his companion exited. "It's really a splendid collection," he was saying, "and though I must admit it lacks a certain . . . focus, I suppose, I think the variety makes it far more interesting. Don't you?"

Lacey had already found what interested him. Amid the waist-high rows of foliage were six geraniums with gray boxes like the one in the Coeltrans Building clipped to them. "What're these?" he asked.

Dornier knelt beside Lacey, warming with pride. He traced a circuit with his index finger. "It was my own idea," he said, "but Robert has gotten very deep in it himself and that's—well, he's a very brilliant man, you know, very brilliant. I've attached electrodes to different portions of the same plant to measure the resistance across the current path. That depends on the number of ions in the veins and the volume of fluid—and *that* can depend on outside stimuli, including thoughts the plant's owner directs at it."

"Oh, god have mercy!" Lacey spat. It had been a rough search already and he didn't need a load of silly dreck to fuzz the edges further. "You're telling me that plants *think*?"

"No, I'm not telling you that, Citizen, and you're not listening to what I *am* saying," Dornier snapped back. The gardener's eyes flashed with anger and an affronted dignity that Lacey could appreciate. He suddenly realized that there was a core of ability in Dornier as real as that within him—that there had to be, or Wilhoit would never have hired him in so personal a capacity.

"I'm sorry," Lacey apologized. "Please explain." He squatted, his rump just above the floor and his face close to the geraniums. The blooms were odorless but the leaves themselves had a bitter, unexpected tang.

"I've never heard anyone insist that encephalographs think," Dormer said, not wholly mollified, "just because they register brain waves."

"But not thoughts."

"Well, Psycomps then; though perhaps you'll say they do think?" The gardener shrugged, then continued, "But machinery is Robert's field, not mine. And mind you, I'm not saying that my friends here"—he stroked the furry edge of a leaf with a finger that was stained, calloused, and very gentle—"don't think. It doesn't particularly matter to me at the moment. What does matter is that I can make any of these six raise or lower the resistance of their leaves, just by thinking at them from across the room."

For a moment the suite was so still that the drip

of moisture from the plant-watering conduits was audible. Lacey rested like a mottled gray stone until he asked, "What would happen then?"

"Anything, anything," the gardener said with a trace of sharpness directed at what he saw as a silly question. "What happens when you flip any switch? The lights go on, the door opens, the, the rocket ignites. It's a control you can touch at a distance and through walls, that's what it is. What happens here is that the recorder, that's the box the electrodes hook to, marks the peak."

"Umm. And does a little coil energize when that happens?" Lacey's voice was as soft as the fur on a cat's belly.

"You'd have to ask Robert about that, of course. He built the system for me. For us, now—he's been testing a plant himself at his office for the past several weeks."

Lacey looked up at one of the level's scanning cameras. It stared straight at him and Dornier and recorded their every movement. But not their thoughts: that would have to wait for a further improvement in the machinery. "And anybody can do it?" he asked.

"I think so, at least," said Dornier cheerfully, again tracing a leaf with his fingernail. "Of course, it takes a little preparation, a, a tuning of yourself and the plant. Watering it, talking to it"—he broke off quickly and added in response to a comment that had not been made, "I'm not saying that it understands what you say any more than a chameleon understands that bricks are red and leaves are green. It's just a matter of tuning, that's all."

Lacey stood. "You've been a lot of help," he said, "and I appreciate it. And I really believe you've found something here." He walked to the door, looked out at the guard scowling through the vitril. "I'll tell you, though," he added over his shoulder before palming the latch, "I think you'll have one hell of a hard time convincing anybody else."

"Well, with Robert's backing, you know . . ." Dornier said.

"Yeah, well. Good luck, anyway."

Lacey whistled between his teeth as he walked to the aircar and ordered his driver to take him back to the State Building and wait. Still whistling, he washed his hands in the male lavatory on Level 14, returned to his desk, and made a quick check with the scanner helmet and the Net.

He was back in the air car ten minutes after he had left it, giving the driver a new destination.

Ruby Sutter found Lacey drowsing at his desk in the late afternoon. He awakened at her approach and his smile was a spreading contrast to the grim set of the woman's face. Billings had quickly ducked under his helmet at sight of his superior. Sutter sneered at his back. With a concern she tried to hide, she asked Lacey, "How close to a kill are you, Jed?"

"As close as I can come without putting Wilhoit under a Psycomp. I know why he did it and how; but to prove it, I'd have to get into his mind."

She slashed her hands and turned away. "Then it's over. There's no way to get him under a 'Comp. No way."

"Sure, that's what I thought too."

Sutter cursed, bitterly and at length. She poised her hips on the edge of the desk and looked Lacey in the eyes. "Jed, I'll be very lucky to save your job as it is. I had another talk with . . . well, several officials. They want you off this Wilhoit thing. If there was a chance you could close it, I'd . . . but if you can't. . . ."

Lacey's smile changed as all his muscles tautened. His voice burred, like a saw on hard wood as he said,

"They could come to me directly, these officials. Do they think I might—might take offense at them?"

He laughed suddenly and stood, his laughter genuine—that of a cynic who sees his worst forebodings proven true. "Look," he said, "I know you'd go to the gallows with me, for me, Ruby. That wouldn't do a bit of good. So I *am* going to drop the investigation, mark it as an industrial accident—but I'm going to see Wilhoit one time before I do that."

"I'll come along."

"To hold my hand?" Lacey asked with a grin. "No, you can watch here just as well."

Sutter bit her lower lip. "Look, just let me run down to my desk and I'll be right back."

"Ruby, you wouldn't need a gun for this anyway—and I really don't want you to come. You'd threaten Wilhoit in the wrong way."

"I'm supposed to trust *your* judgment?" she asked, but she bent a smile around the question. She was watching his back as he walked through the door to the landing pad; then she covered her head with his scanner helmet.

As Lacey entered the top level of the Coeltrans Building, eyes all around the room turned toward him like filings aligned by a magnet. The man in the center of the pool of plants was no exception. He stared over the mahogany desk and the litter of charts and tools and components upon it. Paying no attention to the employees, Lacey picked his way through the snaky aisles of plants leading to Wilhoit. The silence was uncanny. Only the hiss of his clothing on the leaves seemed to mar it. "Good afternoon, Citizen Wilhoit," the agent said. "I'm Lacey."

The executive nodded. "You were here this morning, too, while I was in a board meeting. I would have

expected you to check through your—cameras to see
if I was here before you came."

"I did." Lacey poised the fingers of his left hand
on the desk for support. He looked at ease but the
scar on his neck burned like a magnesium flare. "I've
been investigating your murder of Terry Silvers—but
that's not news either, is it?"

Wilhoit picked up a delicate construct of glass and
etched metal. His short, capable fingers turned it over
for his inspection. Without looking away from his hands,
he said, "I didn't kill Terry Silvers. Or anybody."

"But there's evidence, isn't there?" Lacey pressed.
"There's all the records you could ask for that he was
blackmailing you—"

"Citizen," Wilhoit said, now staring in the agent's
face. His voice was no less vibrant for being pitched
too low to pass beyond the circles of plants surrounding
him. "You can prove my—orientation, if you want. And
you can prove that Silvers was using the threat of
exposing it to extort things from me that he would not
have been granted otherwise. He was an animal, yes,
a predator more interested in the fact that he could
ruin a powerful man than in any real benefits the fact
brought him, but yes. . . . What you don't have proof
of, because it doesn't exist, not in any form the Justice computers could accept, is that I killed him. And
so you can't arrest me, and you may as well leave."

"Oh, I can arrest you, all right," chuckled Lacey. "If
you're right, of course, you'd be released as soon as
you had your preliminary hearing at the State Building."

"And you would be fired, perhaps even prosecuted
under the circumstances."

Lacey ignored the comment. "You gave Silvers a
key to the elevator," he said. "You knew how the
support rods were constructed—you're the sort who

would—but I'll bet you checked the working drawings anyway before you ordered the work done on the elevator. That I could prove."

"It wouldn't mean anything." Wilhoit had set his electronic tracery back on his desk.

"Then you rigged the recorder for your geranium experiment," Lacey went on, "so that it had a coil of the right frequency to trip the Dorafeen in the column. You could have used an electronic trigger instead of the plant, but computers understand electronics. Sure, the coil'd do something reasonable as well, move a stylus or the like—but you're used to thinking about multi-use components, aren't you? And then you waited for the right time and . . . conducted your experiment. Quite a job of planning." He looked sidelong at Wilhoit. "What, ah, formula did you use to send the plant off? I think I'd try something like, 'You are life; I am life; we are one in the universe,' since the idea is to blend with the plant."

"You too," Wilhoit said. His breath was hissing as he rose to his feet, his flesh gone sallow and trembling. "Just like Terry, aren't you? The lust for a chance to bring down someone who really can do something important in this wretched world. But you won't do it, either—if your scanners don't show a damned thing, you can't prove a damned thing. Now get out!"

Lacey straightened. His face was a mask. "Robert Sawney Wilhoit," he said, "by virtue of the authority vested in me by the State of North America, I hereby direct you to accompany me in order to be formally charged in connection with the murder of Terrence Oscar Silvers."

Wilhoit slammed the desk with his fist. "You're going to play this farce to the end? I'll be released as soon as your Receiving Unit processes the charges. Do you think that people of the level who *could* override the

computer's decisions are going to *want* to, to destroy
me just so that you could win your game?"

"It's not a game, Citizen," said the agent with a smile
as stark as a naked skull's. "It's my life. Winning, beating
people like you, is about the only thing I've got left
since they put me under the Psycomp. I can't lose. I
can't afford to lose." He took a breath that shuddered
like the wind in a loose-braced sail. "Come up to the
air car."

"No!" Wilhoit shouted. He looked around, saw the
open mouths of his staff gaping at him. "No," he
repeated in a lower voice, "I'll meet you at the State
Building if you must, but I won't ride in an air car.
You'll have to shoot me to get me in one."

"Suit yourself," the agent shrugged as if it did not
matter. "I'm not worried that you'll try to run. Go on
down to your own vehicle, then."

Feet clattered on the stairs from the roof pad—Ruby
Sutter, wearing a high-necked sheath of red and orange
and a death mask in place of a normal expression.
Lacey moved to her swiftly while Wilhoit, still standing, began to poke buttons recessed into his desk and
speak soft commands to the microphones they
activated.

"I was watching you," Sutter said. They were in the
middle of hundreds of clerks, all straining to hear but
afraid to look up at the two intruders. "You know that
Receiving can't hold him. Jed, for god's sake don't throw
yourself away! There's still time—"

"There's no time." Lacey looked back at Wilhoit who,
his conversation with attorney or politician finished, had
shrugged on an outer jacket and stepped to his elevator.
Lacey took from his side pocket an empty plastic bag
with a sealable edge and the glitter of a few drops of
water within. His fingers toyed with it as he concentrated on something else.

Sutter bore his silence briefly, then demanded, "What've you got there?"

"Oh, I washed my hands this morning and saved the water to pour in that geranium," Lacey said, pointing to the recorder-linked plant by the elevator shaft. Wilhoit's head had just sunk below floor level. "It struck me that wash water might be a faster way of getting in tune with a plant than what Wilhoit's gardener was mentioning."

His unit chief blinked in puzzlement. "I don't understand," she said.

"Wilhoit would," said Lacey.

A scream burst from the elevator shaft, cutting through even the roar of a high-voltage arc. It hung over the blank faces of the clerks as smoke and the stench of burned meat began to bubble out of the shaft.

"I can't afford to lose," repeated Lacey.

Sutter looked at his face and shuddered. After a time, the screaming stopped.

# UNDERGROUND

Two sections of floor collapsed and armed figures began to leap upward into the electronics emporium above. Two of the three Commissioners scowled as they watched the projection sphere, though they knew that the scene had actually occurred more than a year before. Lemba, the Chief Commissioner, was fat and black and too experienced to show emotion except as a ploy. He gestured toward the sudden chaos in the sphere. "At the start, no one was killed. Knocked around, threatened if they got in the way of the looters, but—"

A red-capped policeman burst through the outside door, carrying his heavy-duty stunner at high port. The projection brightened as a dazzling crossfire cut the patrolman in half.

Arcadio, the other male Commissioner, swore under his breath. "Powerguns, when we can't get them ourselves."

Lemba nodded.

Except for the Commissioners themselves, the sixty-meter room was empty of its usual crowd. Further, though scanning cameras recorded the events of the room as they did the events of all other rooms in the State, the data of this meeting were restricted to the Security Police alone. Newshawks could appeal the Interdict to the courts, but even if they were successful, the delay of several months would kill news value in a society that lived from day to day.

Chains of pale, ragged looters were shifting equipment down through the gaps in the floor. Others guarded the hundreds of frightened hostages and the outside doors. The raiders were armed with a variety of weapons, including the powerguns which were supposedly only in the hands of the military. A stocky, red-haired woman raised her pistol and fired. One of the scanning cameras exploded into gobbets of burning plastic. The looter turned and blew apart a second camera. The scene in the projection sphere lost much of its precision, but the computer directing the simulacrum still managed to import an illusion of three-dimensionality.

The woman turned to face the remaining scanner. What looked like a bead necklace trembled on her bare bosom. As she leveled her powergun she grinned and extended the middle finger of her left hand. The whole screen spurted cyan, then went transparent.

"At the end of it there were five dead," Lemba said to his colleagues. "The one you saw, and a patrol car that exploded in the air. Red Teams were dispatched automatically, of course, and they weren't equipped to deal with powerguns."

"It isn't just the dead, though," objected Arcadio.

"That's right," agreed Kuhn, whose hair today matched the giraffe-patterned brown-on-blond polygons of her suit. She slapped the data print-out in front of her. "Of the 212 persons inside when the raid began, 27 are missing. Some—most—can be presumed to have been abducted for reasons one can guess. But there were several others, men and women who nobody'd have grabbed for a brothel or ransom. They were just ordinary people who opted to go Underground when they found the way clear. And *that's* the frightening thing."

"Not in comparison to the reason for this particular raid," Lemba replied equably. "Perhaps you thought this incident"—he waved at the vanished projection—"merely underscores the fact that Underground is organized and controlled by persons who are utterly ruthless?"

Arcadio and Kuhn stared at the fat man. Their expressions were compounded of disgust and irritation. "If you've requested an Interdict merely to play games—" Arcadio began.

"What's really frightening," Lemba went on, tapping his own data sheet with a callused index finger, "is that this raid provided all the necessary control components for a fusion powerplant. Coupled with other recent raids and . . . various other sources of information, Central has determined that Underground *has* a fusion unit in operation now. Beneath the City, where it will kill ten or twenty million people when it fails. And it's up to the three of us to decide how to shut that plant down before the disaster."

The hard faces of the subordinate Commissioners went blank. After a moment, Lemba continued, "Since I had a little advance notice of this—"

"Something this critical should have been routed to all of us, immediately!" Kuhn interrupted.

"—I was able to get a possible answer from Central Records. The data bank states that while a full-scale assault would almost certainly fail, an individual infiltrator might be able to eliminate the plant . . . and its personnel. It's probable that we will get only one opportunity, so we need to choose the most effective person for the task. The man the data bank recommends is a Crime Service employee in Southern Region. His name is—"

"Field Agent Jed Lacey?" queried a young man in a crisp yellow uniform. The legend printed on his cap band read, "TAKE PRIDE IN OUR CITY."

Lacey looked up abruptly. His mastoid implant was useless out of Greater Greensboro Subregion. He felt naked without it, his link to all the knowledge in the State. For that matter, Lacey missed the needle stunner which normally rode high on his hip. "Right, I'm Lacey," he said when he had identified the speaker from among the throng filling the airport terminal. "You my driver?"

"Well, I'm your guide, citizen," the City employee said with a false smile. "My name is Theron Barbee. We'll be taking public transit to the Commission offices. We don't approve of the waste of air cars here, you see."

"Right, I see," Lacey said sourly. He nodded toward the sky. Air cars streamed among the buildings like foam on a rocky strand.

"Well, of course that's private sector," the guide said with a sniff as he led Lacey toward the long queue for the buses.

"Sure," agreed Lacey. "Well, if they won't give their people tools to do their jobs right, they needn't be surprised when the jobs get done half-assed. But it's not my City."

The sprawling crowds were an emotional shock to Lacey, though intellectually he had known what to expect and had tried to prepare for it. His suit of red-orange covered him throat to digits in high style. He liked the color, though it was too blatant for him to have worn it while working. Lacey had stopped working the moment he boarded the airliner in Greater Greensboro, answering a summons relayed through his superiors.

But more than the color, Lacey liked the fact that the suit left only his face bare to a woman's touch. For fifteen years, physical contact with a woman was all that it took to crumple Lacey as effectively as a kidney punch could; and in the crowded City, he knew he could not avoid such contact.

When the third bus hissed up to their stop, Barbee called, "Quick now!" and swung aboard without further warning. Lacey followed the yellow-clad man, using his locked fists as a prow to split the would-be passengers who had pushed ahead of him. He ignored the yelps, the elbows chopping at his ribs and the boot-spikes gouging his shin armor. He had tried to ignore the other people, because half of them were women; and if he even let himself think of that for a moment, he would collapse in uncontrollable nausea. Though his suit kept him from actual contact, Lacey's real problem was a psychic one: a repulsion implanted in his mind by a Psycomp after his conviction for rape.

The bus moved off slowly. A dozen people gripped the door jambs with all but their fingers and toes outside the vehicle. "It's an express," the guide shouted to Lacey over the babble. The powerplant itself keened through a hole in its condenser tubing. "It'll take us straight to the City Complex."

Lacey muttered something under his breath.

Actually, they were still a kilometer from the Complex when the bus halted in a traffic jam the like of which Lacey had never imagined. "Well," Barbee said with a bright smile, "I guess we'll just walk from here."

"This happen often?" Lacey asked as he jumped to

the sidewalk. The buildings glowered down at him. They had been too massive to demolish and rebuild at heights which could be served by stairs. Though the cost of power for elevators was almost prohibitive, there were people who would pay it for the privilege of living and working in this giant replica of a termite colony.

"Well, it happens," the guide replied ambiguously. He set off at a rapid pace.

They climbed over and scraped between the vehicles which had mounted the sidewalks in vain attempts to clear the jam. At last Lacey saw what the trouble was. An entire block was covered, building-front to building-front, by a roiling party of more than 5,000 people. They were dressed and undressed in a multiplicity of styles. Banners shaded the gathering with slogans which were meaningless to the Southerner. As he began to thread his way through the celebrants, Lacey realized that they were homosexuals.

The squat field agent bumped a man whose nude body was tattooed in a pair of polychromatic starbursts. The man turned and raised a cup of something amber and alcoholic. "Join us, love," he offered.

"Thanks anyway, friend," Lacey said and moved on by. When he had caught up with Barbee—the local was far more adept at slipping through the dense crowd—Lacey demanded, "Where the hell are your cops?"

The guide looked back with distaste. "You'd better get rid of your provincial sexual attitudes fast," he said with a sniff.

Lacey snorted back. "Look, if they're out of *my* sub-region, I don't care what they do to who with what. I just mean I'd expect your Red Teams to pay some attention to people blocking a street—in the middle of town, in the middle of the bleeding day!"

"Well, they're quiet, they're not hurting anybody,"

the man in yellow said. Then, with some embarrassment, he added, "Besides, the patrols are understrength now. Finances are, well. . . ."

"Sure," Lacey said, glancing over his shoulder at the party. He was visualizing how twenty men could clear the street with a tanker of stun gas and enough trucks to hold the bodies. It wasn't his city, though; and Lacey was far too intelligent to believe the State would be a better place if everyone's instincts were like his. Control was the key . . . but no control was as important as his own self-control.

Barbee stopped finally in front of one of a line of concrete buildings, new enough to be twenty stories high instead of eighty. The windows were opened in more facets than a beetle's eyes. "Here you are," said the guide, "the Tweed Building. You're to report to Captain Max Nootbaar on Level Twenty. He'll have your instructions."

Lacey looked upward. Yellow-painted air cars burred to and from the landing stage on the building's roof. At least somebody on the City payroll had access to transport that couldn't be mired by block parties. "Crime Service headquarters?" the Southerner queried.

"That's right."

"And no elevators, I'd guess."

"Of course not."

Barbee was already walking away, toward a more distant building of the vast Complex. Lacey let out an inarticulate scream and leaped upon the slimmer man, throwing him to the ground. The Southerner brought a flat tube from under his tunic. It snicked out a 5-cm blade when he squeezed. "I'll kill you!" he shouted to the guide. "I'll cut your heart out!" Only someone who had seen Lacey in a killing rage before would have noticed that this time his neck scar did not writhe against flushed skin.

The street was straight and broad; a dozen scanning cameras on it recorded the incipient mayhem. Relays tripped, panels glowed red, and a patrol car slowing to land on the Tweed Building instead plunged down toward Lacey. In contrast, the pedestrian traffic surged outward like a creek against an obstructing rock. The passers-by continued to move as if they were oblivious of the mingled screams of victim and assailant.

Lacey suddenly stood, closing and slipping away his knife. He reached out a hand to help Barbee up. The guide screamed again and tried to crawl away. Fear wedged his body against the seam of building and sidewalk.

The ten-place patrol car slammed to the pavement behind Lacey. "Get 'em up!" a hoarse voice shouted.

Lacey raised his hands and turned with a quizzical expression. The four uniformed policemen had him covered with needle guns and a stun gas projector. "Good morning, sergeant, patrolmen," Lacey said calmly. "I'm Field Agent Jed Lacey from Greater Greensboro. I'm due for an appointment with Captain Nootbaar. My guide here tripped on that crack in the pavement. Must say I'm a little surprised to have a Red Team react to that." He smiled. "I'd have expected Public Works, if anyone."

The sergeant frowned. Barbee saw that Lacey's back was turned. He began running down the sidewalk, first in a crouch and then full-tilt. Lacey glanced at him. "Must be in as much of a hurry as I am," he remarked disinterestedly.

The patrolmen wore puzzled expressions. Their sergeant queried his mastoid implant, then waited for the answer with his hand cocked. When it came, he spat disgustedly and reslung his gas gun. "Yeah, Captain Nootbaar says send him up," he said. "Two bleeding false alarms in one day."

"If you don't mind, I'll ride up with you," Lacey said, lowering his hands as the Red Team locked its weapons back on safe. "I was afraid for a moment I'd have to climb twenty flights of stairs."

"Sure, room we got," the sergeant grunted. "Men, no, but we got room." The driver lifted them vertically, faster than they would have dropped in free-fall. "First the computer crashes us in on a strangling. That turns out to be two kids screwing under a sheet. Then we're held over our shift 'cause the bloody Streets Department sits around with its thumb up its ass instead of fixing the sidewalks. I swear, a bit more of this and they'll have to look for me Underground too."

Captain Nootbaar had been alerted by the sergeant's call. He waved toward the doorway to attract Lacey's attention. The captain's desk was a little larger than most of the hundreds of others crowding the unpartitioned room, and extensions from the desk supported three scanner helmets instead of just one. Lacey made his way to Nootbaar with practiced care; governmental offices were just as crowded in Southern Region as they were here. At a glance, Lacey assessed the captain as sixty, softly massive, and a better cop than this place had any right to hope for.

"Expected you by the stairs," the big man said as they shook hands. He tapped his scanner helmet. "Interesting replay here of how your guide tripped."

Lacey smiled. "I'm an honored guest of the City," he said. "They could find me a car. Besides, it's been a while since you've climbed any stairs yourself, hasn't it?"

Nootbaar looked down ruefully at his gut. "Well, there's a patrol inbound past my block every morning at 0655. Wouldn't be efficient for me to waste energy walking, would it?" His eyes raised and caught Lacey's. "You know, if I'd realized you weren't just some rube the brass was wasting my time with, there'd have been a car at the airport. Sorry."

Lacey smiled more broadly. "Guess if I'd needed your help, I wouldn't have deserved it, hey?" The smile passed. "Though you *can* help me learn what the hell I'm doing here."

Nootbaar shrugged. "Pull down some headgear," he said as he reached for one of the scanner helmets himself. "I'm supposed to give you background," he went on, his voice muffled by the two helmets. "I don't know quite what they want you to do with it; but if they give you a chance to back out, Lacey, don't wait for them to ask twice."

Lacey's helmet formed a dull image in response to Nootbaar's direction. "I'm picking this pretty much at random," the local man explained obscurely to Lacey. They were watching a sub-surface level of an old building converted to residential occupancy. Sparse glow strips provided less light than would suffice for reading. Transparent panels, waist high, marked off narrow aisles and living units scarcely more spacious. "Do you have a district, a tolerated zone, where you are?" Nootbaar asked.

"You mean, no scanners, no police?" Lacey said. "Enter at your own risk?"

"That sort of thing, yeah. A place all the decent folk kind of ignore, unless they need something that's sold there. Violates State statutes as well as local, but let the State try and enforce it if they think it's so damned important."

"I know the theory," the Southerner replied. "There's places I've been that have them. But not Greensboro. Christ, there's nothing you can't buy legally, unless it'll permanently injure somebody else. And if it's just that you don't want the scanners watching—" Lacey paused, his flesh trembling with the memory of his own needs being satisfied under a scanner's glare—"that's tough."

"We got a district here," Nootbaar said. "It's called Underground."

On the helmet screens a figure rose from out of the floor and began scuttling toward the open staircase. "There's one for sure!" the captain exclaimed. He boosted the magnification. First the scanner focused on the wooden grating that had been shifted to give entry to the level. Then Nootbaar switched to close coverage of the figure itself as it scurried up the stairs. "Probably an old heating duct," Nootbaar said, presumably referring to the access hole. Lacey waited with the silent patience of a sniper who moves only enough to start a bullet toward an opponent's heart.

After walking up three levels of stairs, the figure exited to the outside. Street cameras automatically shunted their data to the watching helmets. The subject was a woman in flowing gray coveralls and a hat whose brim flopped over her eyes. She turned into the doorway of a quality clothing emporium. The floor within was leased on a square-meter basis to scores of individual boutiques.

Without warning, the woman scooped up three dresses awaiting alterations on a counter. The boutique manager shouted and leaped atop the counter. The thief ran for the door as the manager collapsed. A "customer" standing in the next booth had stitched him through the chest with a needle stunner before following the woman out the door.

Thief and guard burst back outside. The light-sensitive fabric of the stolen garments blazed like a sodium flare. There was no patrolman in sight. Heedless of the slow traffic, the pair darted to a pedestrian island in the middle of the six lanes. A metal plate there hinged downward. In the instant before it closed again over the fugitives, Lacey caught a glimpse of stone steps and a dozen other faces.

"Old subway entrance," Nootbaar said with dismal satisfaction. "That's all the show. We may as well look at each other for a while."

Lacey swung up his counterweighted helmet. "You've got a Coventry for *thieves* up here?" he said incredulously. "You just ignore them if they make it to ground before you catch them?"

The bigger man sighed. "Maybe there was a choice once," he said, "but the size of it scared people. The subways'd been closed because they were inefficient and the surface streets were enough without private cars. There were water and sewer mains; some of them forgotten, some operating but big enough to hide in anyhow, to splash through . . . almost all the time at least. Cable vaults and steam ducts and sealed-off sub-basements; parking garages and a thousand other things, a maze twenty levels below you.

"You close one off and somebody breaks into it again before the crew's out of sight. Set up a scanning camera and in ten minutes it shows you a man reaching toward it with a crowbar. Send down a Red Team and nobody comes back." Nootbaar looked up. "And it's all so easy to say, 'They want to live like rats, what's that to you or me or the State?'"

"So it's a separate society?" Lacey offered.

"It's a worm in the guts of the City!" Nootbaar snapped back. "It's fences who sell goods at a tenth their surface price; cribs where they hose the girls off because they're too wasted to clean themselves. It's a family living in a section of 36-inch pipe, with no water and no light within a hundred meters. It's slash shops that generally poison their customers even when they don't mean to. And Lacey—" the captain leaned across his narrow desk, his eyes black and burning with furious despair—"it's ten thousand people, or a hundred thousand, or just maybe—and they don't believe me, Lacey, but I've been down there—just maybe a million rotting devils and more every day."

Nootbaar shook himself and leaned back in his chair. "It's called Underground," he repeated.

Lacey traced his neck scar with one stubby finger. "What do they expect me to do?" he asked.

The heavy captain spread his palms. "I don't know," he said. "I don't think anything can be done. We can't cut them off from water or electricity—they tap the distribution lines. We'd have to shut the whole City down. We can't close off the exits from their warrens, because there's at least one opening in every block in the City. If we arrested everybody who came out of Underground, we'd have half the population in the slammer by Sunday morning. It's a cut that's bleeding us day by day, and some day it'll bleed us out; but there's nothing we can do."

"So take the gloves off," Lacey said. The captain's ironic smile grew broader. Lacey ignored it. "Get the State to send help. Hell, get the military in, it'll be a change from the Cordillera Central. Go in with stun gas, back it with powerguns; and when you've cleared a stretch, seal it for good with a long-term toxin like K2 so nobody'll try moving back in fifty years or so. It'll cost something, cost a lot; but it's still cheap at the price."

"You'd have enjoyed talking to Director Wheil," Nootbaar said reminiscently. "He planned it just that way, ten years ago."

Lacey frowned. "Don't tell me you couldn't shoot your way through a bunch of untrained thugs, even if they were tough," he said.

Nootbaar shook his head. "We were making good headway—not cheap, but like you say cheap at the

price—when about a thousand of 'em came outa the
ground and took over Stuyvesant Armory." Nootbaar
paused and sucked his lips in, his eyes focusing on
the close-chewed nails of his left hand. "It wasn't the
powerguns they took, though the fighting down
below'd been hot enough already," he continued.
"And it wasn't just that they got enough explosive
to crater the City Complex like an asteroid hit it.
The real thing was, they got all the K2 we'd stockpiled to close Underground after we'd cleared it.
Used right, there was enough gas in Stuyvesant to
wipe out the whole City; and nobody thought the
people who'd planned the raid couldn't figure out
how to use the goodies they'd taken."

Nootbaar looked at Lacey. "We hadn't figured a
counter-attack, you see. Everybody we could trust with
a gun had been sent Underground. So they recalled
us without waiting for a demonstration; and that was
the end of the only chance this city was going to have
of getting shut of Underground."

Lacey drummed his left middle and index fingers.
"You know pretty much what goes on down there?"

Nootbaar shrugged. "Sure, Intelligence Section runs
people in all the time. For that matter, cops get laid
and get drunk and buy hot goods too. But any time
we've really tried to assassinate the leaders down
there—Bill Allen, Butcher Bob Poole, Black
May . . . especially Black May—the people we send
don't come back. There's lines from here to Underground, and they go a ways up. They've got access to
the scanners for sure."

Lacey massaged his short hair with both hands.
"What's the drill, then? What am I supposed to do?"

"I'm to send you over to the Fernando Wood Building and the Commissioners'll tell you themselves,"
Nootbaar said, rising. He grinned, a transfiguring flash.

"Wouldn't be real surprised if there was a patrol headed that way about now. After all, it's only a hundred meters—unless you have to go down and up twenty flights of stairs in the meantime."

Lacey laughed and shook the heavy captain's hand. Nootbaar sobered and added, "Look, if there's anything I can do for you. . . ."

"You gave me some good advice at the start of this," the Southerner assured him. "I'll go listen to what your Commissioners have to say, but I'll bet I'm going to do just like you said. I'll get my ass back South where it belongs."

Nootbaar frowned. "I'm not telling you anything you don't know," he said, "but remember: all you need to get elected Commissioner is a constituency. You don't need brains or ability, and you sure as death don't need ethics. Don't give them anything they haven't paid you cash for."

Save for a narrow anteroom, the City Commissioners' offices filled the whole top level of the Wood Building. The anteroom had its own trio of scanning cameras, along with four clerks and a dozen uniformed guards who checked all would-be visitors before they were allowed into the Commissioners' sanctum.

Lacey bore the questioning with equanimity and even some interest. He had never met the elected powers of his own subregion. The whole business amused him.

When Lacey passed through the inner doorway, an alarm bell rang. Scores of people, both petitioners and functionaries, were already within the larger room. They got up at once and began to stream outside. Many stared at Lacey as they passed.

Puzzled, the Southerner turned to follow the crowd. From the center of the room, a fat, black man in a pneumochair with synchronized desk called, "No, not you, Citizen Lacey. Come over here."

The door closed. Lacey was in a huge chamber, alone except for the scanners and the three seated persons: the City Commissioners. Off-hand, Lacey did not believe he had ever before shared so large an enclosed space with so few people. Carefully, fighting an impulse to look over his shoulder, he walked into the semicircle of desks.

"I've placed an Interdict on this discussion, Citizen Lacey," the fat man said. The woman to his right glared from under a mass of green hair that matched her dress. The black grinned and corrected himself, saying, "Pardon, I should have explained that *we* placed the Interdict. Commissioner Kuhn—" he nodded right; the woman's glare transferred itself to Lacey— "Commissioner Arcadio—" he nodded left at the man with long, nervous fingers and a nose like an owl's beak—"and I myself am Chief Commissioner Lemba. I mention the Interdict only so you realize how important the matter you are about to learn is considered by ourselves . . . and by the State."

"All right," Lacey said quietly. There was a small secretary's console nearby. He slid it over to him, sitting on the desk rather than the low-slung seat.

Lemba continued, "you've been given the background on Underground. It's an unfortunate situation, especially since there appears to be a misguided minority which thinks it better to live in squalor and anarchy—" his voice swelled—"than as a part of the greatest city this world has ever known!"

"I've never voted in my life, Citizen Lemba," Lacey interjected, hunching a little as he sat. "And I couldn't vote in this region if I wanted to."

Lemba blinked, Arcadio smiled for the first time, and even Kuhn's eyes had briefly less of hatred in them than before. She must have seen his life stats, Lacey thought. Couldn't expect her to like them.

"The problem, citizen," Lemba continued in less rounded tones, "is that some of those who have gone Underground are scientists of international reputation. One of them—" a head formed in a projection sphere over the desk on which Lacey was sitting. The Southerner stood and walked back a few steps to where he had a good view of a balding, white-haired man with a look as sour as Kuhn's—"Dr. Jerry Swoboda, seems to have built a fusion powerplant down there."

The Chief Commissioner took a deep breath, more as a rhetorical device than from any onset of emotion. "I don't have to tell you how dangerous fusion power is. Environmental groups and the State Regulatory Board shut off even research on it two decades ago. And I don't have to tell you how many innocent men, women and children would die horribly in the event such a plant failed beneath the City.

"*Will* die. Unless the plant is shut down and destroyed, and Dr. Swoboda and his associates are—" Lemba looked up at one of the room's scanners, still operating even though its output was restricted—"prevented from building another such death machine. Central Records says you are the best man to carry out this crucial mission."

Lacey filled his cheeks, then puffed the air out glumly. "Do the data banks give any reason why I'd want to carry out your 'mission'?" he asked.

"How about ten million lives, citizen?" Commissioner Kuhn snapped. Her irises had been dyed to match her hair and clothing. "Or don't you care about lives?"

Lacey met her glare. It did not bother him—as Lemba's growing smile did. "Look, it's not something we can argue about," the Southerner said in a reasonable voice. "You want to save them, then you go down and save them. Myself, I can live the rest of *my* life without your City. I've lived the past fifteen years without things that were a lot more impor—"

Lacey's voice died. He turned again to face Lemba. "You son of a bitch," he said to the commissioner in awe. "You knew I wouldn't be able to go down there without being able to touch women. . . ."

"What a Psycomp did, a Psycomp can undo," Lemba agreed in satisfaction. "Your psyche, Citizen Lacey, isn't the sort of thing that everyone would care to own. Still, I thought that in exchange for our unblocking it again, you'd be willing to do the City a little service."

Commissioner Kuhn was standing, her face flushed in ugly contrast to her clothes. "It's bad enough a man like this still walks the earth!" she shouted at Lemba. "Did you *see* what he did to get wet-scrubbed? You're *not* going to turn him loose the way he was before!"

Arcadio interrupted her for the first time. "What happened fifteen years ago doesn't matter," he said. "What's important is what is going to happen right here if we don't act promptly."

"Citizen Kuhn," Lacey said.

She whirled on him, mouth opening to rasp insults; but ungoverned behavior had not brought her to a commissionership. She waited for Lacey to speak.

"I'm not, I won't be, the guy I was before they . . . wet-scrubbed me," the Southerner said. His hands were locked tightly together. "I don't say I'm any better; but I'm not as young. I won't risk my—mind—on another gesture. Unless the gesture is more important than I ever expect anything to be again."

Kuhn looked at Lacey in disgust, then looked back at Lemba. "I won't argue with two votes," she spat. "But if he comes back alive, it's on your consciences.

And it's up to you to explain to the female voters of this City."

Kuhn walked out of the meeting room, letting the door bang to behind her. Lemba beamed at the standing agent and said, "Dr. Kabiliak is waiting on Level 3 with a Psycomp team—I rather suspected you were going to volunteer. We'll prepare everything else you'll need during the three days you're in the tank. We need to hurry on with this, you know." The Chief Commissioner chuckled.

Lacey turned and walked toward the door. He was already planning his insertion into Underground. He had as little feeling as he would have had if someone else were wearing his flesh.

Lacey vaulted the stair railing and dropped the eight feet to the floor of the lowest level. His bent knees absorbed the shock, then thrust him down the dim aisle at a run. Boots clattered on the stairs one level up, growing louder.

Two women were gossiping across the aisle as they would have done over the back fence of earlier ages. They lunged away, calling to their children in high voices. Lacey squirmed through an opening in the floor that had been an 18-inch drain pipe. A few feet down it made a 90° bend. Someone shouted from the stairs and a sheaf of stun needles clicked against the concrete flooring and vitril partitions. Lacey shoved himself forward with an echoing curse, heedless of the nub of ceramic pipe that was gouging his suit and the thigh beneath it.

A pair of needles flicked his boot-sole, minuscule taps like a sparrow's kisses. Then Lacey was through, worming toward a dimness only less black than the tile tube itself. He could have been frozen and dragged back if one of the Red Team in pursuit had simply lowered a needle gun into the drain and fired a burst down its axis; but no one bothered to take that obvious step. Underground was safe, Lacey thought disgustedly; a self-fulfilling prophecy if ever there was one.

When Lacey fell into the sixty-inch pipe under the street, the first thing he noticed was the stench. In part, that was because his eyes had not adjusted to the absence of light. Still, the fetor would have been overpowering under any conditions. Thousands of fans pulled a draft into the tunnels, but tens of thousands of people breathed and sweated and excreted in them.

There were whispers and scrabbling. Lacey tensed for attack from unseen direction. Fingers traced his throat and down his torso. "Come for a good time, honey?" a voice croaked. Other fingers, arthritic and cold, sought Lacey's hand and tried to drag it toward their owner's body. "Crystal'll show you a good time, better'n any a' those—"

Lacey shook himself loose. "I didn't come for that," he said. "I just needed to get away."

He crawled toward the main drain. Part of the evidence for a functioning fusion plant Underground had been the suddenly-increased theft and even purchase of lights and glow strips. Power pilfering had, if anything, decreased at the same time. The blackness here emphasized the enormous volume of tunnels which not even epic banditry could illuminate.

Hunched over, Lacey began to walk toward the diffused light twenty meters away. The pipe, sloping upward to either side, made footing tricky. Hands caught him again.

"No!" Lacey shouted.

There was a blur in front of him, another figure or figures. More groping hands at his belt, his pockets, his groin. Lacey blazed with conscious loathing spawned

by fifteen years of necessary avoidance. His boots and
elbows slashed out. The little knife was in his hand,
its blade already smeared with dried blood. The hands
dropped away. Cracked voices lifted in a chorus of
ecstatic pain.

The light came through a gap hacked without
finesse into a subway line. The tracks had been
reclaimed for their metal after the system was shut
down, leaving an echoing waste of concrete and
ballast. Now the axis of the great hollow was lumped
with cribs and shanties of every style and construction. At intervals of twenty meters or so, glow strips
were spiked to the tunnel ceiling. Their light would
have been called inadequate even in the cheapest
tenements above ground, but here it formed luxurious pools.

Lacey paused to get his bearings. He tucked away
his knife. A grizzled woman was leaning the back of
her chair against the tunnel wall beside the opening.
She dropped the chair legs to the ground and whistled
toward a seated trio fifty meters away. Near them a
flight of steps led upward to a subway entrance. The
three men rose and began walking toward Lacey and
the woman. Weapons trembled in their hands.

Lacey glanced at them, then took a step toward a
near-by canvas shanty. Four patrons were drinking from
mugs and arguing with the blocky bartender. The
woman behind Lacey tapped him on the shoulder. In
the dim light she had seemed to be carrying a short
bamboo cane. It was in fact a length of steel reinforcing
rod.

"Where you going, buddy?" she demanded.

Lacey's tongue touched his lips. "Look, I got in a
little trouble—" he shrugged one shoulder in the direction he had come—"topside. Thought I'd—"

"Says he's a mole, sure enough, Mooch," the woman

cackled to the leader of the approaching trio. "He thinks he is." Then, "Watch him, he's got a knife."

"Does he?" said Mooch. He was taller than Lacey and his broad shoulders supported arms so long his hands dangled near his knees. Mooch's bare torso sagged over his belt. Despite the fat, the muscles were there as well, and the many scars suggested how they had been used. "Funny, I got one too." He caressed the hilt of a long bread knife thrust bare between his belt and waist-band. Slung across Mooch's back was a gunpowder weapon whose magazine protruded over his right shoulder.

"Let's see your knife, boy," the burly man ordered flatly. The two men with him tensed. Lacey heard a whisper of metal as the woman moved behind him.

The Southerner's tongue touched his lips again. Very carefully, he brought the little weapon from its concealed pocket and handed it to Mooch. The bigger man turned the hilt over as he inspected it, looking for the mechanism. His thumb and forefinger accidentally squeezed together on opposite sides near one end. The blade shot out and nicked his palm. Mooch cursed, swapped ends of the knife, and snapped the blade off with a sideways flick of his thumb. He let the pieces clatter to the ground. A drop of his blood splashed on them.

"Cute," the leader said. More to the others than to Lacey, he added, "Bill's coming, I buzzed soon as Angel here whistled . . . but I don't guess he'll mind if we see what this mole's got on him."

"Bet you thought you could just come Undergound and nobody'd think twice, hey?" said one of Mooch's henchmen, a twisted black in a caftan.

Lacey felt himself edging backward even though he knew the woman was there with the steel rod. "Christ,

there's a million people come down here each week,"
he stammered.

The black laughed and spun the chain in his hands
as if it were a short jump rope. "Sure, but you wanna
stay, you wanna be a mole. And we got word to watch
out for moles for a while. Well, you may stay at that."

"Turn your pockets out," Mooch said.

Lacey obeyed without protest. He handed the burly
man his stylus and his wallet with $32 and a Class IV
bank card. Mooch frowned. "Where's the rest?"

"Look, I didn't mean for this to happen," Lacey
whined. "I didn't make any plans."

"Strip," Mooch ordered. His right hand was flexing
on the hilt of the bread knife.

Again Lacey obeyed, folding his jacket and laying
it on his neatly-arranged boots. Mooch snatched it up.
He squeezed it into a tight ball to see if anything
crinkled or poked within. Nothing did. He dropped
the sheer fabric to the ballast and stepped on it.

Lacey swallowed but said nothing. He took off his
trousers. The fresh scrape was a scarlet pennon on his
thigh. He wore no underclothing. Mooch took the
trousers from him, wadded them, and dropped them
on the jacket. Then he punched the Southerner in the
stomach.

Lacey kept his feet for the first few blows. He
knew that however punishing the big hands might
seem, the boots would be worse once he was down.
His bare buttocks touched the concrete wall. The next
side-thrown fist slammed him to the ground.

In his scanner helmet, Lacey had seen every form
of mayhem humans could inflict on one another. Years
before he had been beaten himself by the experts of
the Red Team that had arrested him for rape. He kept
his fists pressed against his eyes and his knees high up
to protect his groin. It wasn't enough, but it was all

there was to do. The pain lessened after a boot drove his head back against the concrete. Then all Lacey's nerves seemed to be coated in honey.

"Here comes Bill," the woman said.

The boots stopped pounding. "Took him long enough," Mooch grumbled.

The guard's chair was where Lacey had marked it as he went down. He reached for it, rolling to his feet in a motion that seemed too smooth for the red pain it brought him.

"Mooch!" one of the guards cried.

Lacey swung the chair horizontally, not in a downward arc that could have been avoided. Mooch had time to turn his head toward Lacey's fury. A corner of the chairseat caught him in the ribs, just below his slung weapon. Mooch yelped as the air was smashed out of his lungs. The impact lifted the leader's feet from the roadbed. He flew forward, stopping only when his skull slammed the wooden frame of the nearest shanty. The structure sagged while its shouting owner tried to brace it with his hands.

Faces turned from either end of the tunnel, interest spreading like ripples in a long pool.

Lacey's body was white except where blood marked it. The scar on his neck was molten steel. He backed against the wall, waggling the chair. "Who's next?" he wheezed. "Which a' you bleeders is next?"

The chair legs wavered like a forest of spears in the face of the black with the chain. He stepped back, then stared into Lacey's eyes. He took another step backwards.

"Okay, buddy, you made your point," said a new voice. The speaker was also black and a head taller than anyone else in sight. He wore a powergun in an Army-issue holster. It was as much a badge of authority as it was a weapon, an authority underlined by his score of armed followers. "Now, put the chair down or I'll blow you in half."

Lacey lowered his makeshift weapon. He leaned on it, breathing hard.

"Bill," said one of Mooch's subordinates, "he—"

"Shut up," ordered Bill, and one of his own men lowered a shotgun in response to the tone. "Next time Mooch works somebody over before I get there, I'll do worse to him myself."

As if in answer, the fallen thug vomited a mass of bright orange blood. His back arched, the shattered ribs clicking together like knitting needles. The next instant, Mooch went limp and still.

The black chieftain scratched at the butt of his pistol. "I'm Bill Allen," he said, "and you're in my territory. Who are you, and what do you think you're doing here?"

Lacey swallowed. The pain he had suppressed for a chance at revenge was returning. "I'm Jed Lacey," he said, "From Southern Region . . . Greater Greensboro. I . . . am on the street, a bloody queer . . . with his *prick* out, and he touched me, *touched* me . . . I don't know how people can *live* with slime like—" He looked up, blinking the glaze from his eyes. Bill Allen was frowning. "I cut the bastard," Lacey said. "Every way but loose. So I had to run, and I ran here."

"What did he have with him?" Allen asked at random.

The female guard nodded twice to herself and said, "His clothes. And a little knife. And his wallet and a stylus. Mooch searched the clothes and that was all."

"Then put your clothes on, buddy," Allen said to Lacey. To the woman he ordered, "Bring me the rest of his gear."

Lacey limped to his clothing. As the Southerner shrugged on the jacket, his hands tangled with the sleeves, Allen drew the pistol. "Now freeze right there, sucker, until you tell me how a stranger knew that pipe would lead to Underground."

Lacey held as still as a poised mantis. "Because I'm a cop," he said. "Because I was being briefed to lead a hundred men from my subregion down here next month. Us, and maybe fifty other subregions, and the Army; *and* every goddam cop in this city. Because they're planning to shut this place down for good and all."

No one within hearing made a sound. Allen's hand tensed on his gunbutt, then relaxed.

In the same wooden voice with which he had made the announcement, Lacey said, "Now can I put my pants on, citizen?"

"Put your pants on," Allen agreed. He knuckled his forehead with his gun hand. To no one in particular, he added, "We'll take this one to see Black May, he can talk to her . . . and god help him if he lies."

They moved fast through the hollow layers beneath the City. The number of people in the dim tunnels was amazing. Even more surprising was the constant traffic up and down passageways to the upper world. Underground was no less a part of the City than intestines were parts of the body that housed them. Say rather, an intestinal cancer.

At first Lacey thought there was no pretence of sanitation; then the Southerner noticed a gang of persons chained in pairs at the ankles. They were shovelling manure into a cart which two of them pushed along the aisles beside the cribs. The chains made them awkward, but they could not dash up one of the outlets to the surface. They appeared to be unsupervised.

"What're they?" Lacey asked Allen as they squeezed by the wagon.

"Umm?" the big man grunted. "Committee slaves. Those're mine, though I guess May thinks she's the Committee all by herself. They don't carry a full honeywagon down to the Basement, they don't get fed."

"Basement?"

"Where they grow the plants and crap," Allen said. "You know." He looked more sharply at Lacey. "Or if you don't, you don't need to. So shut it off."

Because there were so many entrances to Underground, there had been neither need nor effort to group its pleasures by type or quality. To get from one parlor house to another, a squeamish customer could walk a block on the surface and thus avoid entering a warren of slash shops and dollar cribs.

One huge establishment, The Boxcars, completely blocked a tunnel intersection with walls of transparent sheeting. Girls paraded nude behind the wall when they were not working customers. Passage through the armed guards at either end of the house required purchase of a drink at the bar filling the lowest of the three levels, or a trick with one of the girls. The drinks were slash distilled from anything that would ferment. For additional kick, it was mixed with stolen industrial alcohols of which methanol was one of the least harmful. The whores were cheaper than the slash and, on the average, probably a greater risk to the user's health.

The guards nodded obsequiously when the recognized Bill Allen. "Any calls?" the big chieftain asked.

"Noonan put some messages on your desk," the guard captain said, nodding toward an opaque door at the end of the bar. "Nothing that won't keep."

Allen grunted and lead the way through the far door. Lacey noted that two of the party had dropped off in The Boxcars instead of continuing on with their leader.

The organization Underground was beyond anything
Lacey could have imagined without seeing it, but the
discipline appeared to be something short of a military ideal.

They had walked over two kilometers. There had
been at least a single guard at each direct outlet to the
surface. Despite the darkness and the maze of passageways, Lacey was sure he could find his way back. It
was an ability demanded by his years of service beneath
a scanner helmet, tracking subjects by rapid leaps from
camera to camera and keeping his orientation at all
times.

Allen's entourage turned from a subway spur into
a dry 8-foot main of some sort and then to a new
opening burned through concrete and bedrock by the
most modern mining equipment. Just inside the cutting was another band of guards lounging in a pathetic
mixture of squalor and finery. There were more of
them even than accompanied Allen—and they were
better armed. Over half the men and women carried
powerguns. The remainder had gunpowder weapons of
one type or another, in addition to an arsenal of edged
or blunt instruments. A small brazier warmed the fetid
air. To Lacey's surprise, a telephone was glued to the
rock wall. Shadows of microwire ran both inside and
out in the direction from which Allen had led them.

"Got somebody to show to May," Allen announced.

The guards were rising, pocketing their dice and
drawing weapons more for display than out of apparent need. Their leader was pale as boiled rice and
missing his left arm from the elbow. "Got the hit man
that's s'posed to be coming?" he asked.

Allen shrugged nonchalantly. "Maybe so, maybe not.
We stripped him clean."

The guard chief shrugged in turn. "He goes down
in chains anyway," he said. "You know the rules." He

pointed his powergun at Lacey's midriff. "Get over there by the fire," he ordered, "so we can fit you for some new jewelry."

Lacey obeyed as humbly as he had Mooch. His mind was on something else. Nootbaar had warned him that Underground had a pipeline into the City administration, but Lacey had not expected confirmation so quickly or so off-hand. Not that he was a hit man, exactly. . . .

As directed, he rested his feet one at a time on a stool. A scabby dwarf tried hinged leg irons for size above his ankles. When a pair fit, another guard held the halves together while the smith fitted a hot rivet to the hole. He peened the ends over against a piece of subway rail. The shackles were locked to both legs with half a meter of chain between them. Lacey could shuffle, but he could not run or even walk normally.

And if the Underground's source of information were good enough, Lacey would not even be able to shuffle for long.

"Zack, Slicer," Allen ordered as soon as the second cuff was riveted home. A pair of husky cut-throats lifted Lacey by his shoulders and ankles. They carried him toward a steep flight of stairs. Allen's party had entered toward the middle of a multi-level parking garage. The two porters, followed by their chief and the rest of his entourage, descended the stone steps at a deliberate pace. As he passed doorways, the Southerner caught glimpses of barracks and equipment filling the large open areas. Each level was guarded by a separate contingent, bored-looking but armed to the teeth.

On the fourth level down, the lowest, no one looked bored. Lacey was momentarily startled that none of the crew of hard-faced guards meeting them carried powerguns. Despite the lack of that symbol, they were clearly an elite group. Lacey took in the pallets standing in floor-to-ceiling blocks. He grunted in disbelief. At least half the level was stacked with gray military containers of high explosive and bright orange tanks of toxic gas. A powergun bolt here would rock the whole city like an earthquake. The Southerner could suddenly appreciate Nootbaar's concern for how Underground could respond to an all-out attack.

In the midst of the aisles of lethal material was a throne room. A dais and a massive arm-chair, both draped with cloth-of-gold, shimmered under a solid sheet of glow strips. On the throne sat the queen— black and perhaps fifty years old, with no hair on the left side of her head. On one arm of her throne lolled a white man less than half her age. He was dressed in tights and a cloak of rich purple.

"May," said Bill Allen in a subdued voice, "I brought a cop who says he's on the run. Says topside's getting ready to shoot their way down here the way they tried before."

The white youth giggled. Black May did not, but she thumbed toward the stacks of Amatex and K2. She said, "They weren't crazy ten years ago, what happened to them since?" She stared at Lacey, her eyes disconcertingly sharp. "Okay, what's *your* story?" she demanded.

"They seconded me from Greater Greensboro," Lacey began. In a few terse sentences he repeated the partial lie he had told Mooch and Bill Allen: they planned attack, the chance contact with a homosexual in the crowded streets; the knifing and escape down one of the routes his command was to have used for the attack. The story was as real as Lacey's foresight and utter ruthlessness could make it.

"Wank, check this out," Black May ordered. The man at an ordinary secretarial console beside the dais began speaking into his telephone. Radio would be useless for contact within the maze of tunnels. While ground-conduction equipment would have worked, it could not have doubled as a link to the normal communications of the City proper. It was obvious that such links were important to the governance of Underground. Lacey fleetingly wondered whether the Commissioners had any real insight into their counterparts Underground, or whether topside intelligence sources stopped with estimates of bars, whores, and weapons.

"All of a sudden they don't care if everybody on the street at rush hour turns black and dies?" May asked rhetorically. She gestured again at the gas and high explosive ranked about her. The boy laid a proprietary hand on her shoulder, but she shrugged it off impatiently. He drew back with a moue.

Lacey tongued his lips. "They've got an insider," he said. "I never heard the name but I saw him. He's supposed to take you out—and all this—before it drops in the pot."

There was a sudden silence in the big room, marred only by the whisper of the telephone. Black May leaned forward, frozen.

"An old guy, about a meter seventy," Lacey went on. "White hair in a fringe behind his ears. But mostly bald, you know? Very thin, with a nose that's twice as long and half as thick as it ought to be."

"Swoboda!" somebody hissed behind Lacey. May's hand slashed him to silence as she thought.

Wank, bent over the telephone, missed the byplay. "Colosimo checked it on the scanners, May," he said. "Says it's just like the fellow says, a fag turns around and bumps him and this guy cuts the shit out of him. Blade wasn't very long, but it wasn't no fake. The crash crew had to collapse a lung, and if the flit pulls through, he'll do it on one less kidney than God meant him to have. It was real."

The news deepened the tense silence.

Lacey met Black May's eyes for a moment, then blinked. "Look," he said, "I got to take a crap."

The woman chuckled. "Well, don't look at me, sweetie," she said. "You'll have to ease it yourself."

The tension broke in general laughter. Lacey flushed and said, "Look, I mean . . . where?"

Black May waved her hand. "Take your choice," she said. "The honeywagon'll get to it sooner or later."

As if embarrassed, Lacey moved off into the shadow of a stack of explosives. A suspicious thug—courtier was too pretentious a word—peered around the corner a moment later, but she disappeared when she saw the Southerner was squatting with his pants down.

A thirty-gram ball of C-9 plastic explosive had been concealed in Lacey's rectum. He molded it quickly into the seam between the floor and a container of Amatex. Its detonator pellet lay against the stone flooring. If all went well, Lacey would be able to retrieve the charge and place it as intended, at the controls of the fusion plant. If not, it was where it would do some good as soon as somebody sent the right ground-conduction signal. Nature had left Lacey no choice but to remove the tiny bomb from its hiding place soon.

Lacey shuffled back into Black May's presence. The queen broke off in the middle of an order to the lanky red-head captaining her guard. "You!" she snapped, pointing a finger as blunt as a pistol's barrel at the Southerner, "How'd you come to see this traitor?"

Lacey shrugged. "A captain, Nootbaar, was briefing me three weeks ago Thursday when they first brought me up from Greensboro," Lacey lied. He had ordered a computer scan of the data banks to cull out any appearance of Swoboda on the surface during the past year. As the Southerner had expected, the physicist had come topside a score of times. The

most recent instance had been three weeks previous;
Swoboda had talked to a former faculty colleague in
the latter's living area. If the City hierarchy had been
alert, they could have arrested Swoboda then without difficulty—but that would have raised questions
as to why the physicist was wanted. Besides, the
search would have tied up great chunks of computer
time in a subregion in which availability was already
far below requirements.

For now, all that mattered was that Swoboda could
have been doing just what Lacey described. "This bald
geezer walked through the room on his way up to
twenty. Nootbaar pointed to him and said he was going
to zap the big bosses and their goodies just before we
dropped in on them."

"Wank?" Black May queried.

The secretary spread his hands. "No way to tell,
May; a precinct helmet won't get us into the City
Central scanners. Colosimo can follow Swoboda himself, maybe, if he keeps it to short segments and don't
get the oversight program in the data bank interested.
But Swoboda was topside that day—I met him as he
went out and told him to get a tan for me, why didn't
he."

"That son of a bitch!" the half-bald woman snarled.
"And I trusted him. Bill!"

"May?"

"You and a few of your crew come on with me to
the Basement. If this turns out to be straight, Swoboda's
gonna get it where the chicken got the axe." May
glanced at Lacey. "You come too," she ordered. "And
somebody bring extra chains."

Half a dozen of Allen's cut-throats accompanied their
leader in the vanguard. May's personal guards jostled
after them. Lacey was thrust into the midst of May's

entourage, shuffling quickly to avoid the possibility of a knife jabbed with more enthusiasm than care. They moved down an aisle between gray canisters. Lacey's chains clinked discordantly, like the background to a Vietnamese opera. The Southerner pressed his palms together, as close to a prayer as he had made in twenty-nine years.

At the end of the aisle was a steel door, massive and obviously of recent installation. It reminded Lacey of a vault door or of a pressure lock, rather than any lesser type of portal. Allen swung it open; the four locking dogs had not been turned. There was a hint of suction as the door opened out from a meter-by-two-meter slot cut deep in the living rock beyond. Allen and the others began to enter, stepping carefully over the steel sill. It was pitch dark within.

"Keep your hand on one wall," Black May suggested. "There's bends."

"Bends" was not the word for the right angles that broke the narrow tunnel every few meters. Lacey bumped and cursed. "What the hell is this?" he demanded.

May chuckled behind him. "Anybody who came Underground looking for me was gonna have the devil's own time at this end, especially with all the tunnels full a' K2, hey?" she explained cheerfully. Then her mood changed and she snarled. "Unless some bastard thought he'd cut me off on the outside of this!"

There was another heavy door at the far end. It also pivoted outward from the tunnel. In the pause before Bill Allen shoved it open, Lacey felt an edge of claustrophobia. Then there was light in the tunnel, more light than Lacey had seen since he came Underground. Blinking, Lacey stumbled with the pack of killers out into muggy brightness.

There was a squad of the same ilk guarding the

inner door. They nodded respectfully to Allen and his men, then shuffled to their feet when they saw Black May was present as well. "Swoboda and the rest a' the needleheads here?" May asked the squad leader, a stocky redhead. She wore a necklace of what appeared to be dried fingers against her bared breasts.

"Unless they left before our shift started, May," the guard said. She grinned. "Hey, want us along?" she asked, touching the long sheath knife at her belt.

"Just don't let anybody out without I tell you, Minkie," Black May replied grimly. "Maybe nothing's wrong, maybe it is. . . ."

The huge cavern through which they began to stride was incredible to Lacey. Rank after rank of algae tanks marched in all directions. Though stone pillars studded the greenery, there were no walls as far as Lacey could see down any of the aisles they crossed. The roof, three meters above the floor, was bright with daylight-balanced glow strips. "Where the hell did you find *this* place?" Lacey asked in open amazement.

"Find?" May sneered. "Built, sonny, excavated it and sold the rock topside to the outfit filling ocean to build Treasure Isle. Honest business!" she added with a guffaw. "Bought the strips, too; there wasn't any place in the City where we could liberate as much as we needed. No problem, money we got. Only thing we needed then was the power to run them, and I guess we twisted that tail all right too." But the Queen of Underground scowled, and Lacey knew that her mind was on the man who had built her that powerplant.

There were men and women tending the algae tanks. They were as different from the crew surrounding Lacey as rabbits are from weasels, and they eyed the scarred cut-throats with rodent-like concern. May's henchmen, for their part, appeared as ill at ease in the lush surroundings as they were out of place. This orderly Eden had been created for technicians, not blood-letters, and both sides knew it.

"If we depend on topside, they own us," Black May said, as much to herself as to Lacey. "Down here, now, we got synthizers and enough algae to work from to feed the whole City. We got power, a well four hundred meters down for fresh water, and a pair of ducts into the East River to dump waste heat. If we got to, there's the power and the tools here to punch a line out to the ocean. There's a thousand techs to work it, and I got ten thousand guns I can put topside without emptying the bars." May knuckled Lacey's shoulder to make sure she had his attention as she concluded, "They were too late up there, sonny. I got a base. I own the City. I just haven't gone up to tell 'em—yet."

They had finally reached the far side of the artificial cavern. Apartments of opaque sheeting were built against the stone. There was a neatness and order to these dwellings which was missing from what passed for human habitation elsewhere Underground—or topside, for that matter. Some of the buildings appeared to be shops and offices as well.

"Where's your power come from?" Lacey asked idly.

Black May looked at him. "It's here in the Basement," she said. "Don't worry about it, sonny."

A group of nervous techs was drifting out of the nearest building. A few of them carried tools in feigned nonchalance, hammers and hand cultivators. Against May's crew, they were as harmless as dolphins facing killer whales.

"I need to talk to Doc Swoboda," May boomed jovially. The listeners stirred, frowning.

"He's not—" a young black woman began. She broke off when a man stepped out into the bright light. He was old, balding, and knife-nosed.

Lacey pointed at him. "That's the one," he said. "That's the informer."

All but one pair of eyes followed Lacey's gesture. The exception was a squat thug with curling black hair so thick on his arms that it made his pallid skin seem swarthy. His fellows had called him Horn. The girl who had spoken saw where the cut-throat's gaze was focused. Her mahogany skin flushed deeper and she crossed her arms over her breasts, bare in the clean warmth.

"I don't understand," Jerry Swoboda was saying, drumming both forefingers nervously on his sternum. "Is something wrong, May?"

"Hard telling, Doc," the queen said, arms akimbo, "but I need to take you back for a while to see. Put the irons on him, Boxie."

"No!" the black girl shouted. As she leaped forward, Bill Allen blew her head apart with a bolt from his powergun. At the shot, a thug with a sub-machine gun sprayed a burst into the stone floor and his own feet. The lead splashed and howled. The clot of technicians flew apart screaming. The gunman toppled in silence, too stunned for a moment to feel pain.

"For Chris' *sake!*" Black May stormed. A chip of jacket metal had cut her cheek so that it drooled a fat line of blood down to her jawbone. "Get them chains on and let's get outa here."

There was no question as to where the powerplant was located. A great conduit lined across the rock ceiling. Lacey had seen its exit into Underground proper through its own opening above the air-lock door. Wire tendrils from it fed the thousands of glow strips, and the roots of the conduit were somewhere in or beyond the apartment from which Swoboda had appeared. When the time came, Lacey would have no difficulty in locating his target.

His non-human target. Swoboda's eyes had the glassy stare of a fear-drugged martyr. Two women wearing knives were fastening his shackles. They used small padlocks through the holes in lieu of rivets. The physicist was given twice the length of chain that hobbled Lacey; no one was concerned about what the old man could do with a moment's inattention and a sudden leap.

At Black May's order, her entourage turned back the way they had come—with one exception. Lacey had already noticed Horn and what he was doing. Now Bill Allen noticed also and shouted, "Hey!"

There was no response. The chief's face hardened. He took two steps and kicked his subordinate in the buttocks. Horn leaped up from the tech's corpse. His eyes for the instant were as blank as Swoboda's had become. "You stupid bastard!" Allen shouted. "Save that for later!"

"Aw, Bill," the hairy man muttered. He fell into line shamefacedly behind Lacey.

The returning party's pace was faster than it had been as they entered the uncomfortable caverns. Enthusiasm at leaving made up for the need to carry Swoboda and the wounded gunman. Lacey had learned to throw his own chain forward with short, quick steps. He kept up with the others without being goaded. Rather to his surprise, the Southerner found that his mind was no longer on how best to accomplish his real mission. All the way back to the throne room, he was considering how to kill Horn and Bill Allen.

Black May sat down on her gold-draped chair and stared at the chained men. Her boy stopped pouting and began to massage the bare side of her scalp. Lacey tried to look nonchalant. If May didn't order his release now, he was in trouble.

"Bill," she said, "I want them where they're out a'

the way." The bald side of her head was faceted by scar tissue. "Keep 'em where you've got prisoners for ransom—or do you have any now?"

"Naw, two got paid off and the woman's working The Boxcars right now."

"Good. Keep this pair there and keep a guard on 'em. That one for starters—" she pointed a finger at Horn; she hadn't forgotten either. "I'm going to get 38th Precinct to run Doc here's movements for the last few times he was topside. It'll maybe take a couple of days, 'cause it'll have to go in as routine street-sweeps; but if our fink's right, it'll be hard lines for the Doc."

Lacey grinned broadly. It made him look cruel and confident, both of them qualities Black May would appreciate. Besides, it genuinely amused the Southerner that he would soon be unmasked by the very data banks he had served for fifteen years.

As he shuffled toward the steps beside Allen, Lacey suggested, "If you cut these damned chains now, it'll save you having to lug me up these stairs."

The big chieftain snorted. "Sure. I watch you lay out Mooch and I'm supposed to take your chains off when May says not to. Besides, it ain't *my* back you'll ride on. Horn, Ledder—get this bastard up the steps. If you drop him, I'll kick your butts all the way to the bottom myself."

The trip back through the tunnels gave Lacey a charleyhorse in each thigh. Since that came on top of the beating he had taken from Mooch, Lacey was dizzy with pain by the time they stopped. According to his reckoning, they were in a branch tunnel near The Boxcars. Allen unlocked what had probably been an equipment closet. The door was sheet metal and not particularly substantial. Some of the customers in nearby booths watched what was going on. The shills and bartenders did not: they knew Bill Allen, and they knew that his business was none of theirs.

The rock on the other side of the small closet had been cut away recently. Allen shone a hand light within. The new opening gave into what seemed to be a blocked-off elevator well. The area was choked with trash, but in the middle of it stood a massive eyebolt, its base sunk deep into the concrete floor. "Home, simps," Allen said with a chuckle. "Till May gives the word."

A pair of his subordinates had appeared from the direction of The Boxcars, carrying shackles and a glowing brazier. Wank must have summoned them by phone. Allen nodded to the pair and said, "Lock this pair by the wrists, Becky. You can give 'em three meters to be comfortable; but don't knock the leg irons off, hey?"

The smith and her helper riveted a manacle to Lacey's right wrist with a few expert blows, using the eyebolt as an anvil. Then they ran the attached length of chain through the eye itself and manacled the other end to Swoboda.

"Horn," Allen said grimly, "you sit right there at the doorway. Anybody tried to get in or out, you cut 'em apart with your toy there. I'll have a meal sent down in a couple hours. And you do *any* goddam thing but what you're told to, I make a belt of your hide and give the rest of you to May. Understood?"

Horn grunted sullenly. As his colleagues strode off toward drinks and ease, he glared at the prisoners. "You pull any goddam thing," he snarled in unconscious mimickry, "and I cut you apart." He fingered the hilt of the fighting knife in his belt. Then, with his back to the doorframe, he began to throw a pair of dice morosely.

"Why did you lie about me?" Dr. Swoboda asked in a low voice.

Lacey started, but the words were calm and not the prelude to an attack. He could just make out the physicist's form in the light that filtered through the open door. He did not reply.

"You can't just be a boaster who thought he'd denounce somebody important," Swoboda went on. "I don't think anyone in Underground but May herself really thinks that what I've done *is* important." He paused. "Oh," he said, "of course—anyone Underground. But by now the State had probably decided the blackout eight months ago was caused by the load from me starting up a fusion powerplant."

"You've built a fusion plant?" Lacey said, snorting as if incredulous.

"Of course," Swoboda repeated, and it was an instant before Lacey realized that the words were in answer to his question. "It would have been the one hope for the world itself, but that was impossible. Still, there's a self-sufficient colony in the, in the Basement now. Perhaps that will be able to continue, whatever happens to me."

"One hope for this whole island to be blown to slag," Lacey gibed. He brushed a spot cleared of varied garbage and sat down on the floor. "Go on," he said, "you wouldn't have built a fusion plant down here with all those people living over it. Why, I hear it wouldn't even be possible to shut one down safely if it *was* to blow up."

"Nonsense!" the physicist snapped with more spirit than he had shown since being taken into custody. "All that it takes to shut down the plant is to open the fuel feed and chill the reaction. Two turns on a petcock! And the rest of you're saying is *just* as absurd. People have always wanted to live fifty years in the past, and that was all right . . . but it isn't all right any more, it's suicide! Yesterday's fears are going to *kill* us, kill *all* human civilization."

"Such as it is," Lacey chuckled. He felt a sudden added coldness when he realized that he was no longer merely leading his quarry on, that he was actually becoming involved in the discussion.

"That's the point, you know," Swoboda said, returning to the emotionless delivery with which he had begun the discussion. "I couldn't convince the authorities that what I was offering would be safe. They wouldn't even let me experiment in an unpopulated area. They were afraid the newshawks would watch the scanners. They'd report that the laws were being flouted—and they're *stupid* laws!—and that a 'bomb of unguessable destructiveness' was being built; and every person who'd had anything to do with approving my project would be voted out or fired. Myself, I'd go under a Psycomp to have my brain cleaned. But *whatever* the risk—without power for growth, what will this City be in ten years? What will the world itself be like in fifty? What kind of death would be worse?"

Lacey shrugged. "You're talking to the wrong guy," he said.

The physicist sighed. "No doubt, no doubt; but there isn't anyone else to talk to, is there?" He glanced toward Horn, who looked up from his dice to glower back. "No human being, at any rate."

Swoboda started to clear a place on the floor, but he was too nervous to sit. He began walking and turning, a pace in either direction so as not to foul the chain. "I felt like this three years ago," he said, "when I finally realized that I was never going to be allowed to build even a pilot model. The energy source that could save civilization, and it could never be built because the world saw too much and understood too little. That's when Leah Geilblum visited me." The physicist looked at Lacey. The Southerner's eyes had adapted to the dark well enough to catch a sheen of remembered hope in the older man's expression.

"I knew her by reputation, of course," Swoboda continued, "as she knew me. As an anthropologist, she saw even more clearly than I the horror, the irreversible horror, into which the world was slipping; and she saw the hope that my power source could provide.

"Black May had already recruited several biologists, planning her 'base'. It wasn't hard for her, you know. The more intelligent someone is, the more clear the need for a, a bolthole, becomes. And word of mouth moves swiftly in the academic community. Leah—she died only last month—she was 83 and it wasn't at all for herself that the concern lay—she convinced me to try to work with Black May, now that Underground had a single, intelligent leader. And Leah was right. It just seems that that wasn't enough."

There was an interruption from the doorway. Horn scooped up his dice and stood, trying to embrace the lithe woman who carried three meal packets and a canteen. "Rickie, hey, how about a trick, hey?" the guard rasped. "Look, I can pay—"

The woman dropped her burden without ceremony and elbowed Horn in the stomach. "Think I haven't heard, creep? Keep the hell away from me!"

"Look, just a feel, then, Rickie," Horn begged, crouching in desire and extending his hands. Rickie reached behind her back, then extended her right fist wrapped in barbed-wire claws.

"I'll feel the heart right outa your chest, I will!"

Horn's mouth pursed and his hands dropped to his knife. Booth personnel were beginning to view the disruption blackly, and a few customers seemed to be drifting toward other parts of the tunnels. The woman swiped at Horn's eyes. "You try that," she hissed, "and

I'll feed it to your asshole. And if I don't, cutie, what d'ye suppose Bill and May'll do?"

Horn cursed and turned and slammed his fist into the open door. It boomed thunderously. The woman walked back the way she had come. Horn saw the food containers and kicked all three of them violently into the closet. One of them sailed through the opening to the elevator shaft. Lacey ducked. The ruptured plastic spewed juices. Its integral heating element stank with only the empty container to absorb its energy.

Lacey smiled. It was as well for Swoboda's peace of mind that the dim light kept him from seeing the hunter's face clearly. Lacey tugged his companion silently toward the eyebolt so that the old man's hand rested on the metal. All the slack in the chain was on Lacey's side of the bolt.

"Hey Horn," he called to the guard, sitting again in the doorway. "There's rats in here."

"Hope they chew your eyes out!"

"No, I mean they're screwing in the corner," Lacey said. "Shine your light so's we can get a better look at 'em, will you?"

Horn bounced to his feet and raised the flashlight Bill Allen had left with him. Then he paused and shifted the light to his left hand. He drew his knife and gestured with it. "Get smart and I'll spread you all over the room," he said.

Lacey nodded and stepped back. Out of the bright disk of the flashlight, he thumbed a chunk of potato into the pile of trash in the far corner. The litter rustled.

Horn stepped through the opening to the shaft. His knife pointed up at Lacey's throat, but his eyes were on the quivering circle of light. "Where—" he began.

Lacey flipped a loop of chain over the guard's head and jerked him backward. Swoboda squealed. Horn could not shout with the chain crushing his throat, but he slashed out with his knife. Lacey threw himself aside, tugging frenziedly at the chain. His body knocked the physicist down.

Horn tried to rise. He cut wildly to the side; his wrist struck the eyebolt. A cry wheezed past the chain and the knife sailed loose in the darkness. Horn's hand twisted toward the blackjack in his hip pocket, but his fingers would not close.

Lacey moved nearer. The manacle on his right wrist gave him an unbreakable grip on the chain. He planted both feet on the other side of the loop, pinning it to the floor. Then he pulled upward with his whole body. Horn thrashed furiously. Blood flecked his chin and the hairs on his chest. The motions became instinctual, like those of a fish on the sand. He gave a final, backing-arching convulsion and lay still.

Lacey tossed the loop of chain free and collapsed beside the body. His gasping breaths came like sobs. "Get me the knife," he whispered to his companion.

"But we're still chained," Swoboda protested.

"Get me the bloody knife!"

Using the light, the physicist located the weapon. Diffidently, he set it beside Lacey's hand. The Southerner picked it up. The knife was of the finest craftsmanship. Its blade was 7 mm across the flats. Both the edge and the false edge had the yellow sheen which indicated they had been treated to triple density after grinding.

"Hold your shackle against the bolt and keep the light on the rivet," Lacey directed. He slipped Horn's blackjack from his pocket and stood.

Swoboda caught at his lower lip with his teeth. Lacey positioned the manacle as he wanted it. He set the knife edge against the peened end of the rivet, then struck the back of the blade sharply with the sap. The 3-mm rivet sheared.

"Why, that's incredible!" Swoboda blurted.

"Nothing incredible," Lacey said sourly. "Just a hell of a thing to do to a good knife." He pried at the manacle carefully, using the false edge and trying not to cut the physicist's wrist. There was already bleeding from the damage the shackle had inflicted during the struggle with Horn.

The iron popped apart. "Now you get mine," Lacey said, handing the tools to Swoboda.

It took repeated blows by the older man before the second rivet parted, but even so it was only the matter of a minute. Lacey struck off their leg irons. He paused, staring into the physicist's eyes. "Can you get back to your Basement and dog the doors shut?" he asked.

Swoboda thought calmly, then nodded. "Probably. It isn't necessary to pass through the throne room, and the guards at the entrance door should have changed shift by now. They're used to me entering and leaving, so that shouldn't cause any comment unless I chance upon someone who saw my . . . arrest."

The older man rubbed his forehead. "As for dogging the inside door, the guards will probably believe me if I say it's necessary for a few days because we're, oh, raising the humidity briefly to enhance growth."

Lacey nodded. "I'll give you half an hour," he said. "That's all; and if it's not enough, that's too bad. Now get moving."

"Why?" Swoboda asked unexpectedly.

"Why the hell do you care?" the hunter blazed. He flung the knife away from him. It clanged and sparked on the concrete. "Mostly I do what I'm told. It doesn't make any difference, you see? *I* know we're all going down the tubes, I'm not blind. So it's easier." Lacey took a deep breath, fingering his scar. "Only maybe this time it makes a difference. To somebody. Now just get out of here."

Swoboda touched Lacey's hand, then squeezed it. As he turned, the hunter called after him, "You'll have to handle the guards inside yourself, afterwards. But I can't do it all."

No one shouted when the physicist slipped out into the tunnels. People Underground minded their own business; and besides, the thin old man was of small interest, even to the whores.

Lacey waited briefly, then strolled out to a bar. It had more pretensions than the blind pigs around it and there was a twenty-four-hour clock on its back wall. Horn had had some money in his pockets. Lacey used part of it to buy a beer. The liquid was thin and bland—and therefore safe from being loaded with knock-out drops.

Lacey smiled as the bartender eyed him. Actually, there was nothing unusual about the Southerner's appearance compared to that of many others Underground. It was just unusual that someone as battered as Lacey was would have enough money left for a drink.

Lacey nursed the beer for the half hour he had promised Swoboda. He ignored the prostitutes who approached him. If the bartender felt he was not drinking fast enough, he had better sense than to push the matter with the scarred man in red.

When the time came, Lacey up-ended his glass and strode out of the stew. As he neared The Boxcars, the hunter began to jog and then run. His face grew wild and he shoved people out of his way. The guards at the entrance to the brothel braced to stop him. Lacey thrust the remainder of Horn's money out with both hands. "Bill Allen," he wheezed. "I gotta talk to Bill!"

The guard chief frowned, then thumbed inside. "He's in his office," she said. "If he sees you or not's his business."

Lacey pushed through the cordon of naked women who tried to entice him and strip his empty pockets. He flung open the door to Allen's office before a house man could stop him. "Bill, I gotta see you!" he said, slamming the door.

"What the bleedin' hell!" the black chieftain snarled. He was alone in the room, punching buttons on a computer console with one hand while the other held a sandwich. An open floor safe protruded 200 mm from the rock beside him. He banged the heavy lid closed with his foot. "How did you get loose?"

"Bill, Black May's going to kill all of us," Lacey whined. The enclosed privacy of the office was disconcerting to him. "She's going to take her buddy-buddies into the Basement and *gas* us, gas all Underground to keep the topsiders from finding where she's hid!"

Allen was frowning, but he set down his sandwich. Before the chieftain spoke, Lacey blurted, "Look, Bill, I'm afraid your guards'd grab me 'f I tried to go topside alone. You need to get out too—you can take me! Bill, you ever seen what K2 *does* to a guy?"

"Balls," Allen said flatly. "Let's see what May says about this." He began to punch out a phone code, keeping a corner of his eye on Lacey.

The Southerners' face tightened into intersecting planes of despair. "Bill," he pleaded, "Take me topside and I'll give you a gadget you wouldn't believe."

Allen paused, his finger above the last digit of the code. "Talk," he said.

Lacey licked his lips. "Well," he said, "You got the stylus Mooch took off me?"

Allen nodded, his forehead wrinkling. He slid open a drawer in the console and pulled the ivory-colored instrument from the varied truck within.

"It's not just a stylus," the hunter said truthfully. "They learned a trick from Tesla—its a laser that'll cut forever if you just hold the base against a good ground. The wall behind you'd do. You press the button on the side and it shoots forever."

Allen stared eye to eye at the smaller man. "You're lying," he said. With the beginning of a smile, the leader touched the back of the stylus against the wall and pressed the button. The tip was centered on Lacey's breast.

The ground conduction signal shivered into the rock. Nothing visible occurred in the room.

Lacey relaxed. He smiled like a shark feeding. Bill Allen blinked in surprise, not at the failure of the "weapon," but at the hunter's reaction to his attempted murder. "This far away, there's maybe a ten-second delay," Lacey said. He dropped flat on the floor beside the safe.

"What—" Allen began. He groped for the powergun in his belt. The shock wave from the explosion in Black May's quarters reached him before he could draw. The wave front drove the mahogany bar at an angle before it, pulping all of Allen's body between his neck and his diaphragm.

Lacey did not really expect to live through the blast. It drove down the hundreds of kilometers of tunnels like a multi-crowned piston, shattering whatever stood in its way. The Boxcars and everything in it were gone, driven meters or kilometers down the tunnel in a tangle of plastic and splinters and blood; everything but Lacey and the safe that shielded him.

There was no sound, but Lacey found he could see after the ground stopped quivering like a harpooned manta. A hundred meters of tunnel roof had been lifted by the blast. It collapsed when it fell back, close enough to Lacey that his feet touched the concrete morraine when he tried to straighten from the ball into which instinct had curled him.

The air was choking, but with dust and not K2—
yet. The rebounding shock waves of the blast would
suck the stockpiled gas into every cranny of the tunnel
system soon, but at least the lethal cargo had not
ridden the initial wave front. Even with the safe to
turn it, the blast had pounded Lacey like a rain of
fine lead shot. He rose slowly, sucking air through the
hard fabric of his sleeve. Once the ground beside him
came into focus, he saw a dropped powergun. Lacey
picked it up and began to stagger toward an
unblocked staircase.

Those who knew Jed Lacey best thought he was
merciless. They were wrong. He used his weapon
repeatedly before he climbed to the street. That was
the only mercy desired or available to the hideously
mangled forms who mewled at him in agony.

The guards at the anteroom of Level 20 were
nervous and confused, like everyone else in the City.
The lower levels of some buildings had burst upward,
killing thousands. Long sections of traffic-laden streets
had collapsed, adding their loads to the death tolls.
K2 was denser than air, but the swirling currents
raised by the explosion had blown tendrils of the gas
to the surface in many places. Where the odorless
hemotoxin touched, skin blackened and flesh swelled
until it sloughed. Red Teams wearing atmosphere suits
were patrolling streets that were otherwise deserted
by the living.

Lacey pushed through the shouting clot of
newshawks. He was gaunt and cold. His suit had been
shredded into the garb of a jester mocking the Plague.
No one who looked at Lacey stayed in his way.

The door from the Commission Room slid open
to pass a uniformed captain in full riot harness.
"Max!" Lacey croaked. His fingers brushed the heavy

man's wrist to keep him from leveling the slung needle gun.

"Where the hell did you come from, Lacey?" Nootbaar grunted. The guards stood tense and featureless behind their faceplates.

Lacey grinned horribly. "That's right, Max," he said. "Now I need to see the brass—" he thumbed toward the closed door—"bad. I know what happened."

Nootbaar bit a knuckle. "Okay," he said, and he held the door open for Lacey.

Commission staff and uniformed police made the room itself seem alive with their motion. Lacey slipped among them, headed for the three desks in the middle. A projection sphere was relaying the horror of a dwelling unit where three levels had sunk into a pool of K2.

Characteristically, it was Lemba who first noticed Lacey's approach. He spoke silently to his implant. A klaxon hooted and the projection sphere pulsed red for attention. The Chief Commissioner's voice boomed from ceiling speakers, "Clear the room! Clear the room!"

"What the—" Commissioner Kuhn began, but she too saw the ragged figure and understood. "Did he—"

"Silence!" Lemba growled. "Until the room's cleared." The woman glared but accepted the logic of secrecy. Her gown was a frothy ball of red. It was much the same shade that Lacey's suit had once been.

The door closed behind the last pair of armed guards.

"I've done what you wanted," Lacey lied. But he had done what the world needed instead, protected one seed of civilization against the day when it could sprout . . . "Now give me a pardon for what I did for you. Then you'll never have to see me again."

"Nothing was said about a pardon," Arcadio muttered over tented fingers.

"I did what you wanted!" Lacey repeated. He did not raise his voice, but his eyes were balefires licking the bones of each Commissioner. "Give me a pardon and no one will ever know about it. Even you won't have to learn."

"The explosion, the gas . . . ," Commissioner Kuhn whispered. "All these people dead in the streets—"

"They died!" Lacey snarled. "It was cheap at the price, do you see? You've got your city back now, because the scum below blew themselves apart. The ones down there were tougher than you and smarter than you worms'll ever be—but they're dead. Don't clear the K2, just seal all the openings. You're safe forever now—from Underground. You're safe from the dead."

"We aren't going to turn that loose, are we?" Kuhn asked slowly. There was nothing rhetorical in her question.

"The alternative is to try to keep it caged," Lemba noted. He shrugged toward Arcadio. "I doubt that would be a profitable undertaking. And we have a great deal else to concern ourselves with at the moment."

"All those dead," Kuhn said. "And we directed . . ."

The Chief Commissioner coughed. Neither of the others spoke. "Citizen Lacey," Lemba said, "by virtue of the powers civil and criminal vested in me by the Charter of this City, and with the concurrence of my co-commissioners—" he looked at each of them. Arcadio nodded minusculy; Kuhn did not, her cheeks as bright as her garments, but she did not gainsay Lemba—"I do hereby pardon you for all crimes, actual or alleged, which you may have committed within this subregion to the present date."

Lacey nodded. "That pardon's the only thing I'll take with me from this City, then," he said, "besides my mind." He slipped the powergun from beneath his tunic and laid it on the smooth floor. His toes sent it spinning toward the frozen Commissioners. At the door, Lacey called over his shoulder, "Careful of that. There's still one up the spout and two more behind it."

The door closed behind him.

The six-year-old was blind with tears as she ran into his legs. Lacey lifted her one-handed. "Can I help?" he asked.

"The street fell!" she blubbered. "I can't go home because the street fell!"

"Umm. What building?" By now the gas would have seeped back into Underground, but a windrow of blackening bodies kept the thoroughfare empty. The dead did not touch Lacey any more. Only the living mattered.

"Three-oh-three-oh forty-ninth street level ten," the child parroted, her arms locking about Lacey's neck.

"Sure, Level 10, no problem," the Southerner said. He glanced around to get his bearings. "Your parents'll be looking for you, so we better get you home, hey?"

Humming to himself and the girl, Lacey skirted a wrecked truck still lapped with burning alcohol. Lacey was alive, maybe for the first time in fifteen years. It was going to take work, but he thought he liked being a human being again.

▶ END

# THE MANY WORLDS OF DAVID DRAKE

## THE RCN SERIES
With the Lightnings
Lt. Leary, Commanding
The Far Side of the Stars
The Way to Glory
Some Golden Harbor

## HAMMER'S SLAMMERS
The Tank Lords
Caught in the Crossfire
The Butcher's Bill
The Sharp End
Paying the Piper

## INDEPENDENT NOVELS AND COLLECTIONS
The Reaches Trilogy
Seas of Venus
Foreign Legions, edited by David Drake
Ranks of Bronze
Cross the Stars
The Dragon Lord
Birds of Prey
Northworld Trilogy
Redliners
Starliner

All the Way to the Gallows
Grimmer Than Hell

**Other Times Than Peace**
**The Undesired Princess and The Enchanted Bunny** (with L. Sprague de Camp)
**Lest Darkness Fall and To Bring the Light** (with L. Sprague de Camp)
**Killer** (with Karl Edward Wagner)

**THE GENERAL SERIES**
**Warlord** with S.M. Stirling (omnibus)
**Conqueror** with S.M. Stirling (omnibus)
**The Reformer** with S.M. Stirling
**The Tyrant** with Eric Flint

**THE BELISARIUS SERIES
WITH ERIC FLINT**
**An Oblique Approach**
**In the Heart of Darkness**
**Destiny's Shield**
**Fortune's Stroke**
**The Tide of Victory**
**The Dance of Time**

**EDITED BY DAVID DRAKE**
**Armageddon** (with Billie Sue Mosiman)
**The World Turned Upside Down**
(with Jim Baen & Eric Flint)

# BOLO: The Future of War

What is a Bolo? The symbol of brute force, intransigent defiance, and adamantine will. But on a deeper level, the Bolo is the Lancelot of the future, the perfect knight, *sans peur et sans reproche*. With plated armor, a laser canon, an electronic brain, and wheels.

**The Compleat Bolo** by Keith Laumer     0-671-69879-6 • $6.99
Two complete volumes by Keith Laumer. "Without a doubt, Laumer's best work."
      —Anne McCaffrey

### BOLO NOVELS AND COLLECTIONS BY OTHER HANDS

Novels by William H. Keith, Jr.:
**Bolo Rising**     0-671-57779-4 • $6.99
**Bolo Strike**     (HC) 0-671-31835-7 • $19.00

**The Road to Damascus** by John Ringo & Linda Evans
       (HC) 0-7434-7187-3 • $25.00
       (PB) 0-7434-9916-6 • $7.99
**Bolo!** by David Weber     (HC) 0-7434-9872-0 • $25.00
       (PB) 1-4165-2062-7 • $7.99

**Old Soldiers** by David Weber     (HC)1-4165-0898-8 • $26.00

### BOLOS COLLECTION, EDITED BY BILL FAWCETT:

**Bolos: The Honor of the Regiment**     0-671-72184-4 • $5.99
With stories by David Drake, Mercedes Lackey & Larry Dixon, Mike Resnick & Barry Malzberg, and others

**Bolos II: The Unconquerable**     0-671-87629-5 • $5.99
With stories by S.M. Stirling, William R. Forstchen, Christopher Stasheff, and others

**Bolos IV: Last Stand**     0-671-87760-7 • $5.99
With stories by David Weber, S.M. Stirling, Steve Perry & John DeCamp, and others

**Bolos V: The Old Guard**     0-671-31957-4 • $6.99
With stories by J. Stephen York & Dean Smith, Wm. H. Keith, Jr., and others.

Available in bookstores everywhere.
Or order online at our secure, easy to use website:
www.baen.com

# A new Blackcollar novel by
# TIMOTHY ZAHN

The legendary Blackcollar warriors were the only hope of a conquered Earth—if they still existed. Military SF by a *New York Times* bestselling author.

## Blackcollar
## Includes *The Blackcollar* and *Blackcollar: The Backlash Mission*.
### 1-4165-0912-7 • $25.00

## Blackcollar: The Judas Solution
### 1-4165-2065-1 • $25.00

## And don't miss:
## The Cobra Trilogy
### Trade pb • 1-4165-2067-8 • $14.00